GERALD JAY

THE PARIS DIRECTIVE

Gerald Jay is a nom de plume. He lives in New York City and is at work on a second Mazarelle novel.

gerald-jay.blogspot.com

THE PARIS DIRECTIVE

GERALD JAY

THE PARIS DIRECTIVE

A NOVEL

Anchor Books
A Division of Random House, Inc.
New York

The Library of Congress has cataloged the Doubleday edition as follows:
Jay, Gerald.
The Paris directive / Gerald Jay.—1st ed.
p. cm.
1. Police—France—Fiction. 2. Assassins—Fiction. 3. Murder—Investigation—Fiction. 4. Americans—France—Fiction. 5. Dordogne (France)—Fiction.
I. Title.
PS3610.A95P 2012
813'.6—dc23
2011030689

Anchor ISBN: 978-0-307-94749-9

www.anchorbooks.com

For Nancy

"And even those doomed to be the next night's victims
 are full of plans . . ."

—Volker Schlöndorff, *Circle of Deceit*

CONTENTS

PART ONE

1

BERLIN

May 1999

Reiner checked his watch as he waited by the elevator. Within the next sixty seconds, the elegant Frau Dr. Sachs, her chic shoulder-length hair dyed the color of a concert grand, would leave her penthouse apartment for her office at number 18 on the fashionable Friedrichstrasse. Dr. Sachs was a creature of habit. That always made things easier.

The hallway had a thick, ice-blue carpet and smelled of fresh paint. Reiner liked these new Potsdamer Platz buildings, where a penthouse apartment cost a small fortune. With the doctor's specialty of blackmail, he supposed, she could afford it. He himself didn't mind helping people with problems when the price was right. The distinguished Hanoverian judge Gerhard Tempelmann had confided that he was in desperate need of help. Tempelmann's whole world was about to come crashing down.

The judge explained that three weeks ago he had driven to Berlin to accept an honorary degree from Humboldt, the university of Marx, Engels, and the brilliant Einstein. That night on the way back to his hotel after celebrating with old friends, he got lost driving the dark, narrow streets sandwiched between the university and the river. Confused and slightly tipsy, he failed to see the bicycle rider. In his rearview mirror, her mangled, lifeless body lay smeared across the road. He was quite certain that the young woman was dead. There was nothing he could do to help her. But Dr. Sachs, out walking her poodle, Schatzy, near the banks of the Spree, had witnessed the accident and seen his car racing away across the bridge.

When the first letter arrived in his mailbox postmarked Berlin, it asked for ten thousand marks. The judge knew there would be others. One careless second and everything good and meaningful in his life seemed about to be destroyed. "If there's anything you could do," he begged Reiner. There would be no questions, he promised, and money was no object. The next day the judge had fifty thousand marks ready for Reiner. It was a pleasure to work for such a man.

As the penthouse door opened, Reiner hit the elevator button and the light popped on. He ran his hand over his long blond hair, straightened his silk Hermès tie. In a case like this it was always important to make a good first impression.

Dr. Sachs was dressed all in black leather. Even the expensive Italian briefcase she carried was black leather, probably bought in the west on the Ku-Damm at the sleek Mandarina Duck, the shop featuring specially treated calf leather, waterproof and scratch resistant. Utterly impervious to dangers of all sorts.

"*Guten Morgen,*" he said brightly.

"*Morgen,*" snapped Sachs. She had a busy day ahead of her. She banged the elevator button. "What's keeping it?" She looked up at him and decided that she liked the young man's tie, the directness of his gaze. He had the most compelling blue eyes she'd ever seen. He was worth a smile.

"Here we are," said Reiner, as the door began to slide open. He motioned for her to go first, but Dr. Sachs hardly needed any prompting. She stepped forward and only at the last second saw the empty elevator shaft yawning at her feet. Frantic, she clawed the air and somehow managed to pull herself back.

"*Scheisse!*" she cried, struggling to catch her breath. "I almost fell in."

A palm to the small of her back sent Sachs screaming down the shaft, her shrieks trailing after her like a torn parachute.

2

ÉLYSÉE PALACE, PARIS

The great hall with its brilliant rows of crystal chandeliers, its gilded columns, its magnificent Gobelins tapestries and crimson drapes was empty. The reception for the African ambassadors wasn't scheduled to begin for another hour. At the far end of the room, the French doors were flung open onto a garden laid out in tiered, semicircular rows, gradually ascending to a small pool with a fountain. Though still early for roses, the ordered arrangement of the plants usually did wonders for the president. Not this time.

Chirac angrily slammed down the receiver, nearly knocking the telephone off his desk. "The Chinese . . . they've just canceled their participation in the EU trade talks."

The foreign minister, who had been conferring with the president when his telephone rang, asked, "Will you be making a statement?"

"I suppose I'll have to."

Chirac had feared something like this might happen as soon as he'd heard about the bombing of China's embassy in Belgrade. The other day at his impromptu airport news conference in Helsinki, he'd called the bombing "unfortunate. A tragic blunder." Hadn't he, along with Clinton, Schröder, and the other NATO leaders, apologized? Yes, of course, of course he could understand the violent Chinese reaction, but what the hell did they want? Accidents happen.

Standing by the window of his sumptuous office in the palace, he gazed down at the sunlight dancing in the fountain and the gardener in blue overalls. He was reminded fleetingly of a painting by Monet at the Musée d'Orsay that he liked—the deep emerald shadows, the shimmering evanescent light. A luminous, peaceful moment in the Parc Monceau snatched from the general mess and imprecision of things. He thought of how much he'd counted on the enormous Chinese market to bolster the lagging French economy. No wonder he was losing his hair. What lousy timing!

The president knew that the Chinese would eventually come around—Jiang Zemin needed to be accepted by the World Trade Organization for his own survival—but could he himself wait that long without having his own plans unravel? He tried to reevaluate his position, approach the situation as coolly as if it were no more than a theoretical problem.

"If only there were some way to change their minds . . ." Chirac leaned toward the window and tapped impatiently on the glass. Some way, he mused, to make Jiang realize that not all of us were as dumb as the Americans—their CIA incapable of simply opening a 1999 Belgrade telephone book and seeing that they had targeted the Chinese embassy and not a damn Yugoslav arms factory. No doubt all intelligence services had their share of blockheads, even his own. Mitterrand hadn't needed the *Rainbow Warrior* fiasco to realize he'd placed his trust in bunglers, fools, but it was a risk he had to take. Without those nuclear tests, France would have no M4 submarine missiles or tactical neutron bombs.

Though hardly a Socialist, Chirac too had his doubts about the Direction Générale de la Sécurité Extérieure. What his intelligence service needed were fewer thugs and ex-cops, and more *énarques*— bright, young, well-educated professionals, experts who could think subtly, creatively. Burdened with mediocrities, how could he hope to deal with crises like these?

"If only . . ." he began. He ran his hand over his thinning hair the way he often did when faced with a particularly thorny problem. "If only there were some way—unofficially, of course—that we could discreetly let our Chinese friends know just how much we regretted what happened. Show them that we still could be helpful."

The foreign minister, eager to be of help, pushed his chair closer.

Later, when he returned to the Quai d'Orsay, he reported the incident to his deputy, Simone Nortier. She had an idea for him.

3

HOTEL ADLON, BERLIN

His appointment was for 11:45 a.m. The arrangements made the usual way—a message with a name and a number to call. The difference this time was the luxurious meeting place and the French name. Reiner fancied himself an independent contractor. He felt no need to advertise, for there were always clients in want of his services: good people being blackmailed, wealthy couples facing excruciating divorces, successful businessmen desperate to dissolve a partnership, eager legatees with no patience.

The cautious Reiner checked with his French sources to confirm the legitimacy of the new client. The more he learned, the more intrigued he became with Émile Pellerin. This might be the sort of meeting worth his time and perhaps, he thought, even a good deal more.

The majestic Hotel Adlon, which survived all the violence of World War II without a scratch, burned down soon after the fighting ended. Once Berlin's most famous meeting place—situated no more than a block away from the Reichstag, the Brandenburg Gate, and the Nazi chancellery—it had played host to Hitler, Mussolini, and both Theodore and Franklin Delano Roosevelt.

The new Adlon, recently rebuilt on the same site, seemed quite elegant to Klaus Reiner as he strolled past its gleaming shopwindows showcasing Parisian silk scarves, Italian shoes, and fine antique jewelry. He stopped briefly to admire the sturdy German handbags and wallets. To Reiner, it seemed overnight that his world had changed, but actually it had been almost ten years now since the Wall collapsed and reunification began. Yet the East German supermarkets with their well-stocked shelves, not to mention the Porsches and BMWs daily crisscrossing Alexanderplatz, still amazed him. Everything was available now in the new Germany. If you had the money.

In the hotel lobby, he glanced around at the giant vases filled with flowers. Without bothering to stop for information at the crowded front desk, he went directly to the elevators. His appointment was on the fifth floor.

As the elevator door began to close, a striking young woman joined him. She was wearing black stockings and a stylish black satin dress—Berlin high fashion; her raven hair cut severely in bangs, her irresistible perfume filling the elevator. As self-absorbed as a mannequin. She too had an appointment. On the third floor, he stepped aside to let the lady out, and her seductive smile was a totally unexpected reward, reminding him of Hanna Schygulla, one of his favorite actresses. Reiner wondered what she charged for a quick afternoon romp. But business before pleasure.

In front of the gilt-framed oval mirror on the fifth floor, he stopped to straighten his ascot, brush off the lapel of his custom-tailored double-breasted blazer. Swiftly locating the staircases and making sure no one was loitering in the hallway, he followed the sign to 501 at the end of the corridor. Reiner hesitated at the door. There was more than one voice coming from within but, even though his French was excellent (almost as good as his Russian and Arabic), it was impossible to make out what they were saying. He glanced at his watch and knocked. The conversation inside stopped abruptly. After a short wait, the door opened.

"Ah, monsieur. Right on time. *Entrez, entrez.*"

Émile Pellerin—the smaller of the two men—had the sharp, comic face of a Pierrot, but his pale eyes were calm, watchful. He introduced his associate, Blond, a burly fellow with a balding scalp and long strands of thinning gray hair combed across it. Reiner took his proffered hand and felt the blunt, powerful fingers of a meat cutter.

The large suite they occupied overlooked Unter den Linden. Reiner estimated that for this super deluxe double they were probably shelling out a bundle. He knew before he came that money would not be a deal breaker.

"A nice hotel," Reiner said, glancing around the room.

Pellerin smiled at his smartly turned out visitor, a solid athletic six-footer who was somewhat younger and better looking—in a blond German sort of way—than he had expected. He invited him to sit down, have some coffee.

Reiner shook his head. "I don't drink coffee. How can I help you?"

Pellerin approved of his visitor's businesslike manner and reported that monsieur came highly recommended. What they required was a man with his special talents. Above all, his discretion, ingenuity, and ability to remove someone so quietly that the sole question raised by the family and friends was where to send the flowers. The accident would have to occur before the end of the month and arouse no suspicion. Most important of all, it had to be terminal. Was he interested in the job?

"That depends."

"On what?"

"Who it is and where I have to go."

Pellerin glanced at his associate. Hubert Blond shrugged in annoyance, climbed heavily out of his chair, and lumbered into the bedroom, returning with a large manila envelope. He thrust it at Reiner, who noted that he seemed to be sweating. Reiner examined the enclosed papers with care and looked up. "A nice part of your country, I'm told."

"Especially at this season of the year," Émile said, with a touch of nostalgia. "You'll have a wonderful time. The duck confit. The cabécou. And the truffles are always amazing. Then there's the delectable way they do rabbit with Armagnac, vin rouge, cream, and the rich pruneaux d'Agen. I envy you."

A real bullshit artist! Reiner thought. He charged people like that extra for insulting his intelligence. Whatever he was getting into, it wasn't going to be a vacation. He knew a snow job when he heard one.

Reiner went over to the serving cart, which held a gleaming silver coffee urn. Taking a sugar cube from the tray, he unwrapped it, jotted down some numbers on the inside of the wrapper, and casually handed it to Pellerin. A bit of theater—it was in his genes—never hurt in these situations. Especially when there were as many zeroes as he decided to add on the spur of the moment.

Reiner had learned from his foreign informants that Pellerin and Blond were French agents. It was clear that they needed an outsider—a pro with no police record, no ties to the victim, and, above all, someone who wasn't French. Despite what Pellerin had neglected to tell him, Reiner assumed it was a political job. He didn't like that. Nor was he crazy about working in a foreign country, where you didn't know all the pieces in the game. Besides, he didn't trust these two. All of which went into his bill. What they wanted was risky from start to finish but, like good sex, it would have its moments.

"My price." His voice had no more edge than a butter knife. "The money to be paid in American dollars to the Swiss bank at that numbered account I've noted. Two equal installments. One before, the rest upon completion. Agreed?"

Pellerin was amused by the flat, take-it-or-leave-it way the German did business and even more by his cautious cloak-and-dagger manner. But then he remembered that almost every room in the old Adlon had been wired by American agents, scores of tiny electronic ears listening in the walls. It was as if Reiner, though seemingly too young to have lived through it, felt that World War II was still going on. But Pellerin ceased to be amused when he saw how much money the German wanted. Dumbstruck, he nodded.

"A pleasure," said Reiner, closing the deal with a stiff handshake.

After their guest had left—carrying with him a Paris phone number to be called as soon as he'd taken care of the matter—Émile turned with a worried look to his friend.

"What do you think of Herr Reiner?"

"He dresses well."

"He can afford to on what he charges. He may be an *Ossi*, but he behaves like a capitalist."

Blond sneered. "I'll say . . ."

"Okay—but I think he's the right man for the job. Time to call the Quai d'Orsay. We can let Simone know we've made all the arrangements. Keep her up to speed."

"And the price?"

"What the hell! If he's as good as they say he is, he's worth every centime to our friends. We'll know soon enough."

4

L'ERMITAGE, TAZIAC

li Sedak was putting up another section of drywall, hammering away, when someone tapped him on the shoulder. Startled, he whirled around. A big gray-haired guy in blazing red pajamas. He seemed pissed about the noise. It was the new renter of L'Ermitage who had arrived with his wife late last evening. Ali had awakened them. Too damn bad! It was almost eight o'clock! Who isn't up by then except moneybags and pimps? Ali told him that he was doing work for the owner—turning the old barn into a guesthouse. "It's a big job for one man," he said. "Unless I get started early, I'll still be working here by *La Toussaint*."

Ben Reece didn't care if it took him till Kwanzaa. All he was asking Ali to do was start a little later in the morning and work a little later at night. Ben could feel the blood rush to his face as he raised his voice, trying to make this guy understand his French, though he was sure that he did. Their plane trip from New York had been stinko, and even in first class he couldn't sleep. Let alone here last night on his bed's thin, miserable mattress. It was worse than an exercise mat. Who needs a large eighteenth-century hilltop country house with a tower, a private swimming pool, and twelve exquisite woodland acres in the Dordogne if nobody can sleep? He and his friends were paying a helluva lot of money for this French vacation, goddamn it! So not until ten, he said. Okay?

Ali said nothing. He simply threw down his hammer in disgust, grabbed his T-shirt, and left.

Judy, looking out of their bedroom window in the main house, had been anxiously watching for her husband's return. She knew

Ben's temper. Then she saw the surly expression on the young man's face as he came out the barn door. Naked from the waist up, he was well built—compact but not very tall. He had a blue bandanna tied around his forehead and looked like an Arab with his dark skin, his black Persian-lamb hair. She watched as he went quickly to the beat-up white VW parked behind their new rented Peugeot and got in. But where was her husband? "Ben?" she cried, her fear mounting. "Ben!"

The call from Montreal was Schuyler, Ben's old roommate and friend from Dartmouth days. He and Ann Marie had been delayed. Business, of course. They'd be flying out to Paris on the Concorde and then down to the Dordogne. Be there that evening. He couldn't wait. Love to them both.

Going into town was Judy's idea. She was thinking of making a dinner for the Phillipses by way of welcoming them. Taziac was already bustling when they drove into the quaint, partially restored medieval village. The outdoor market was in back of the Gothic church. Judy, who loved to cook, decided on the thick white asparagus and a roast chicken for dinner. There would be a mushroom stuffing using the local cèpes, described in her Périgord cookbook as fungi royalty with an earthy smell that hinted at the woods where they grew. For the wines, Ben chose some good bottles of Sancerre and Médoc, and a straw-yellow Rosette from the vineyards of nearby Monbazillac, home of the great dessert wines.

As he picked up the bottles, Judy asked, "Can you manage all that?"

Ben had noticed lately his wife's growing concern about his drinking. Preferring to avoid a hassle, he said, "What about bread?"

In search of a bakery, they walked by the old castle that was now the Taziac town hall. Posted outside were public bulletins. The one at the top was from the Ministère de l'Intérieur announcing that La Police Judiciaire wanted the Corsican guy in the picture. Presumed to be "très dangereux et armé." And warning that he was not to be approached under any circumstances.

Ben said, "Good advice. Leave it to the pros. He looks like one tough cookie to me."

"It's only the haircut, dear. You wouldn't look so good either if your barber used a machete."

Her husband was not amused. "The man's a murderer," he pointed out.

Judy thought he had nice eyes.

Up the gravel road, there was a small *boulangerie-pâtisserie* surrounded by baskets of fuchsias, pansies, and pinks in a half-timbered English Tudor–style town house. As they opened the glass door, the sweet aroma was overwhelming. In front were a couple of small unoccupied tables, on one an empty coffee cup and a plate with a leftover piece of pastry. Nobody was behind the counter. Judy was contemplating a glorious caramelized tarte tatin when she heard what sounded like the explosive flushing of a toilet from somewhere deep inside the house. Suddenly out came a bear of a man with a great drooping mustache and eyebrows to match. Zipping up his fly, he seemed almost as surprised as they were.

Judy quickly asked for a pain de campagne and a baguette.

The big guy glanced around the shop, then, nodding, he took down the loaves and wrapped them up.

Ben hoped there was a sign in the bathroom reminding employees to wash their hands.

"*Et ça aussi,*" Judy said, indicating the last tarte tatin in the display case, which he promptly took out and slipped into a box. He was tying it up, his big hands doing a surprisingly elegant job with a green ribbon, when the front door opened and Gabrielle, a pretty teenage girl, came rushing in. Straightening her apron and her blond ponytail, she said, "Oh—Monsieur Mazarelle . . ." She appeared flustered to see him serving the customers. She apologized for taking so long to deliver the bread and, winking at him as she snatched the pie out of his hands, asked Judy if she wanted anything else.

A smart kid, Paul Mazarelle thought. He was fond of Gaby but hoped she wasn't too smart-ass for her own good, always *dans la lune*, caught up with boys and dreams the same way her mother had been. He scoffed up the last little piece of his luscious tartelette myrtille, pulled on his jacket, took out his pipe. "*Au revoir, chérie,*" Mazarelle called. Exchanging an amused smile with the customers, he trudged past them out the door. He'd already noted the expensive sunglasses, the gray hair and sportif clothes, the accent—Americans, of course.

Ben watched him go. An odd walk with a little hitch in it. He may no longer be in playing shape, Ben thought, but he's still got the size of a rugby player and a granite jaw to match.

Judy asked the young girl if that was her boss, and she had to laugh the way young people do at silliness. Her aunt, Madame Charpentier, owned the shop and was upstairs in bed with *le rhumatisme*. That was Monsieur Mazarelle, she explained, the famous police inspector from Bergerac who lives here in town. He comes in almost every day for breakfast since his wife died. Everyone knows the inspector, she told them. *Il est très gentil.*

On the way out of the store, Judy whispered, "In Taziac *everyone* knows the inspector."

"He's hard to miss."

5

FRANKFURT

Kring in Frankfurt had just what Reiner wanted. He was a good businessman, had proven dependable in the past, and knew how to keep his mouth shut. Reiner telephoned and made an appointment to see him the next morning.

Reiner's small cramped apartment in the old East Berlin working-class district of Prenzlauer Berg was drafty regardless of the season but especially just before sunrise. Even so, he preferred living inconspicuously in this neighborhood, with its hippies, artists, and outcasts, while working in Berlin. He knew the area well and no one bothered him.

He moved around a lot in his business, and having a few different places to operate from made life easier.

Rolling over on his bed, Reiner waited a few minutes before throwing off the covers. In the austere bathroom—his bare feet accustomed to the cold cement floor—he removed a small can from a paper bag, shook it well, and sprayed its contents carefully over his hair, turning it from blond to anthracite black. As long as he didn't wash the black out and refreshed the temporary color from time to time, his hair would pass muster. He rummaged through the few neatly hung suits and jackets in his closet for something to put on. Hurrying because he was running a little late. Any time he went out of town, if only for a day, he made certain to leave the apartment immaculate. In his business you couldn't be too careful. An hour later when he left for the airport, he was wearing paint-stained jeans, an old weathered leather jacket, and a red Bayern München cap—its concave peak pulled low on his forehead.

The flight from Berlin to Frankfurt was little more than an hour, and when he arrived at Kring's place of business, it was not yet 9 a.m. The store looked closed, but the flashing red lightbulbs spelled out HOME SEXY (OPEN 24-7). Inside were long tables full of adult videocassettes and a couple of gray-faced early-bird browsers bent over them. They paid no attention to the new customer. Walking to the doorway at the back of the store, Reiner ignored the *Eintritt verboten* sign and brushed aside the curtains.

Kring, a fat man in a wrinkled gray vest, turned from the closed-circuit screen where he had been watching him. *"Ach! Bitte, mein Herr."* He pointed to the chair next to his. "Good to see you again."

"So, you have something for me, Herr Kring?"

Holding his back, Kring, a chronic sufferer, slowly got up. He smelled of licorice, cough drops, and menthol. "A minute."

When he returned from the back room, Kring emptied the envelope he was carrying and produced a French passport, *carte d'identité,* and driver's license. They had belonged to Pierre Barmeyer, a thirty-seven-year-old French schoolteacher from Strasbourg. Reiner closely studied the three documents and the attached photos under the desk lamp. An interesting choice, he thought. He'd gotten so used to the name Klaus Reiner that he'd almost forgotten his real name. But he was nothing if not adaptable. Barmeyer was near the same age as he was, grew up in an Alsatian city on the border of Germany—which would help to explain the faint accent in his French—and even bore a slight resemblance to him.

Kring saw it too. "He could be your brother."

"Alive or dead?"

Kring hesitated.

"I told you that I wanted the owner dead."

"He could be, I think he may be. But I'm not sure. His papers were 'found' in a hotel room in Gstaad."

Dead was always better as far as Reiner was concerned. Less chance of his papers having been reported stolen to the authorities.

"How much?" he asked.

A smile flickered at the corners of Kring's cracked, puffy lips. Replacing the three documents in the envelope, he handed them to his visitor. "For you, *mein Herr,* seven hundred marks."

Reiner wasn't pleased. "I could get high-quality fakes for less."

"*Ja*, but not like these. The same signature on each one and each of them still valid for another year or more. A matching set and, as you see, the real thing in mint condition." But Reiner refused to budge.

"Okay, okay." Kring's hands fell helplessly to his sides in defeat. "Let's not argue over pfennigs. *Ich gebe auf!* Have it your way. Five twenty-five for the lot."

Though mildly amused, Reiner knew that he wasn't likely to do better elsewhere, and he didn't have time to shop around. He handed the money to Kring with a warning. "No one must know of my visit. Understood?"

"*Jawohl, mein Herr! Natürlich.* You have my word, as always."

"If not," Reiner tucked the envelope under his arm, "I'll have your eyeballs for breakfast."

The photographs, of course, would have to be replaced. In the taxi on his way across town, Reiner eyed the steel and glass boxes they passed, struck once again by how boring this banking and industrial center seemed every time he visited. A gray city on a humid gray day. The one building that he liked was the new Commerzbank headquarters, the tallest building in Europe, thrusting high above the old cathedral spire, its soaring tower the spirit of the new Germany. Anything was possible nowadays to ambitious young men and women with exciting dreams.

Scheffler Photographie was on a quiet, winding back street opposite a mustard-colored three-story stucco apartment house. The sign in the window promised photographs for all occasions—births, weddings, anniversaries—and passport pictures while you wait. Reiner, announced by a tinny bell, entered the shop. On the wall behind the counter were large photographs of smiling bridal couples and an apple-cheeked young girl with blond braids, her hands clasped in prayer.

From the studio inside, a worried-looking Turk with a stubby black beard appeared and greeted him. His eyes—big, dark, expressive—were those of a silent film actor.

"Where's Scheffler?"

"Herr Scheffler has retired. He lives in Brazil now. Can I be of help?"

"It still says Scheffler outside."

"The name Scheffler is well-known in this neighborhood. My customers don't like change."

"And who are you?"

"Kara. Akin Kara. I'm the new owner. What sort of work are you looking for, *mein Herr*?"

Reiner hesitated, sized him up. Kara might be okay, but could the Turk keep his mouth shut? "I need some official photographs. Scheffler did special things for me. Do you handle custom jobs?"

Kara understood perfectly. Assuring him that he did, he invited the customer inside to his private office. Kara's studio was little more than a metal chair for the sitter, a white curtain for backdrop, a few tripods with cameras, and an umbrella light. In the corner, a small wooden table and chairs—his office.

"*Bitte*," said Kara. Reiner sat down and emptied his envelope on the table. The photographer examined each document with the care of a jeweler. Then taking out a package of Wests, he offered one to Reiner, who wasn't interested, and lit up.

"Well?" Reiner asked impatiently.

"The expiration dates are all different, which is good, but that means two of the three pictures will require retouching for a slightly different look."

"Exactly."

"No problem. All together you'll need three three-and-a-half-by-four-and-a-half-centimeter black-and-white photos. Full face. Let's get started. I have an appointment in half an hour." The photographer went over and turned on his lights. "First we'll take some with the jacket on and then without. Take off your hat, *bitte*."

The picture taking lasted about twenty minutes. Kara used an old Hasselblad rather than a Polaroid, explaining that he preferred the Swedish camera for special quality work. He chain-smoked nervously throughout the photo session. Though he asked the sitter if he was from Frankfurt, and one or two other questions to pass the time as he adjusted his camera and lighting, Reiner ignored him. He was a little too inquisitive for his own good. Once Kara was interrupted by the telephone. When he came back, he seemed even more upset than he had been. Perhaps it was the fixed, unsmiling expression of his customer that was rattling him.

"How long will it take to develop them?" Reiner asked, after he'd finished.

"Not long." Kara showed him the darkroom, which was right behind the studio. When he opened the door, the smell of vinegar was strong.

"What's that?"

"Fixative. Acetic acid. It's used in the developing process."

"Be careful with that cigarette."

"Oh no." The photographer laughed. "It's only a weak ten-percent solution."

"I don't like the smell. I'll wait outside."

"Look," Kara explained, afraid that his strange customer was going to be difficult. "This will take some time. It's not only the developing and printing that has to be done. On two of the pictures I've got to touch up your chin with stubble and, most difficult of all, reproduce the official stamps that must be placed in the corners. That means I'm going to need at least an hour after closing to finish the work. When you come back at six, knock hard on the front door in case I'm in the back. Rest assured, everything will be ready for you."

Reiner stared at him and saw a flicker of fear in Kara's eyes. "Don't fail me. And remember . . . not a word about this to anyone or I can guarantee this will not be the happiest day of your life. By the way, how much do I owe you?"

"Not now, *bitte*. We'll talk about that when you return and see how well you like my work."

Reiner didn't trust a man who hesitated to name his price. The fact that the Turk had his picture only complicated matters. He was worried that his visit to Herr Kara might end badly if he wasn't prepared to take measures, should measures be necessary. Later in the main reading room of the municipal library, Reiner found exactly the information that he was looking for. At 6 p.m., he was back pounding on the photographer's door despite the sign in the window that said CLOSED.

Fumbling with the lock, Kara let him in. He appeared flustered but announced that everything was in order for Herr Barmeyer. Motioning for him to follow, he led the way into the darkroom. This time Reiner said nothing about the smell.

On the light box, which Kara switched on, the three documents were displayed like rare books. Reiner examined the passport picture first because it was the most important and most difficult to insert. Kara, puffing nervously on his cigarette, stood at his side and watched. It was excellent work, good enough to get by even a more than casual scrutiny. Then the other two photographs. The unshaven cheeks and scruffiness made him look like an artist. Reiner liked that.

Kara said, "I thought you'd be satisfied." It was then that he told him how much it would cost.

Reiner glared at him. "Scheffler never charged me that much." Picking up his three documents, Reiner put them away in his pocket.

The photographer, his voice shaking, quickly explained that it was a more difficult job than he'd anticipated, that it had taken longer, that he had to cancel his last appointment in order to finish it on time.

"Now, if you please, the negatives."

"*Ja, ja!*" From the drawer under the counter, Kara quickly produced the negatives and, avoiding Herr Barmeyer's eyes, handed them to him.

Reiner counted nine and his face twitched with annoyance. "*All* of them! There were ten photographs taken."

Surprised that he noticed, Kara had a ready answer for him. "I keep a negative on file to make copies in case you need more. It's merely a convenience for my customers. Here . . . here, take it back. Do you think I'm a blackmailer?"

It had always seemed to Reiner that you could tell a great deal about people by their attitude toward money. Kring, for example, enjoyed the game. There was some humor in his buying and selling, but a deal was a deal to him. Kring was reliable; you got what you paid for. Herr Kara, on the other hand, reminded him of people he'd known in the East. Sullen, mingy. If they couldn't get a hand in your pocket, they'd steal your shoelaces. Whatever they could squeeze out of you. Though the Turk was an artist, he was a sneak thief at heart. Such men, Reiner knew, were dangerous.

He took out his wallet and on top of the light box counted out what he owed him. Kara watched with a look of amazement. Dazzled by the bills, never expecting that he would get all that he'd asked for. As Kara reached for the money, his pleased expression morphed in an instant to a puzzled, wide-eyed, voiceless shriek of alarm.

From behind, Reiner had delivered a crushing blow to the base of his neck, a blow powerful enough to snap Kara's spine in two. The Turk pitched forward, hit the counter, and sank down to the floor in sections like a marionette. Reiner, wasting no time, collected his money and returned it to his wallet. He glanced down at the body just to make sure that the photographer was dead. His movements after that were calm, quick, purposeful, as if they had all been planned in advance.

From the inside pocket of his jacket, he removed the bottle of glacial acetic acid he had purchased, unscrewed the cap, and poured three-quarters of the pure acid into the weak solution in the fixative tray, producing a combustible mixture. He pulled out his handkerchief, covered his nose. The vinegar smell was overpowering in the windowless room. Searching the floor for the burning cigarette, he found it next to Kara's foot. Reiner had warned him about smoking. Emptying what was left in the bottle over the body, he tossed the lit cigarette into the tray. Before long the darkroom was engulfed in roiling black smoke and crackling flames. The heat was intense. In seconds, Reiner was through the front of the shop and out the door, slamming it closed behind him. It felt good to breathe again.

6

DORDOGNE RIVER, BERGERAC

azarelle had volunteered to drive the convict Émile Fouché to the prison in Périgueux. Actually, Rivet, his boss, had asked him to do it, and he thought why not. A nice day for a drive. What else did he have to do that was more important? He owed Fouché a small favor after bagging him for the bank job at the Société Générale in nearby Marmande. It had been no great trick tracking him down, given how amateurishly Fouché had handled things. His fingerprints everywhere. Plus in his excitement, he'd left behind his carefully written note to the teller. A wonder he'd had enough brains to wear a long peaked hat and dark glasses. In all fairness, Fouché was new at the game, a virgin, innocent rather than stupid. But that only came out at the trial.

Fouché was married and the couple had one very sick kid, a retard. Monster bills, of course. Though he'd had a good job with Hewlett-Packard—the American computer company in Grenoble— he'd been pink-slipped months earlier along with several hundred others as soon as the economy began to tank. Last hired, first fired. The family lost their house and Fouché, according to his attorney, fell into a subterranean depression. He was currently unemployed, the three of them now living with his mother-in-law in Bergerac. It wasn't the sort of story that inevitably led to cleaning out banks and the *maison d'arrêt* in Périgueux, but in the inspector's experience it helped.

Mazarelle realized that in doing his job he'd helped too. The kind of case he hated. He couldn't remember ever feeling so down while working in homicide in Paris. All the way to Périgueux, Fouché barely spoke a word, his face as long as an ironing board. The inspector wondered if his condition was contagious. It could ruin his own sunny disposition. Sure, Mazarelle had been bored lately, but he might end up at the end of a rope if he hung around this guy long enough.

"*Bonne chance*," he told Fouché, when he took off his cuffs and handed him over to the guards. The prisoner said nothing until just before going inside. "The bank bastards," he muttered. "They repoed everything—our car, our house. My wife warned me. She said that's what happens when you work for foreigners."

All the way back to Bergerac, Mazarelle thought about his options. He could return to Paris and, if he could still get it, his old job in homicide, or remain on the force here or take early retirement. Or he could even try something new. He needed more time to think things over.

He wasn't happy, despite the unusually warm, gorgeous weather. It was much too nice to be indoors, and a little exercise wouldn't hurt either. Besides, it was too late to return to the commissariat, and anyhow he hadn't had lunch. Where better to go on a day like this than the river?

He picked up a baguette, some Emmental, a paper cone of picholine olives, a bottle of Stella Artois, and rented a rowboat. There were people with babies on the grass and some noisy, laughing, loud-mouthed teenies kicking a ball around. Playing hooky just like him. Rowing out into the middle of the river where it was quiet, Mazarelle pulled up his oars, took off his shirt. On his large upper right arm a tattooed heart with the initials AVO on the ribbon across it. Martine, when he first met his wife, had asked if that was an old girlfriend. "In a way," he told her. "It's Latin. *Amor vincit omnia.*" As for the Glock 9-millimeter bullet holes—an entry wound near the front of his left shoulder and a somewhat larger exit wound higher up on his back that she thought resembled ugly knots in the bark of a tree—they were the real thing.

The sun felt great on his body, soothed his mind. And with any luck, maybe the first tan of the season. He stuck his hand into the water and his fingers went numb. No wonder no one was swimming. Actually there *was* someone—a woman he hadn't noticed gliding smoothly through the water like a crocodile with only the top of her head sticking out. Removing a shoelace, Mazarelle tied one end of his lace around the oarlock, the other around the neck of his beer bottle and dropped it into the river. The bread, cheese, and olives were delicious, and when he pulled up his Stella Artois it was refreshingly chilled. A perfect picnic.

Stretching out, he closed his eyes and felt himself drift away. Thinking of Émile Fouché stuck in the can for the next few years and feeling sorry for the poor chump. A victim of globalization and the celebrated Inspector Mazarelle.

It's only when I'm having a good day in the flics that I'm feeling okay, not bad, thought Mazarelle. Maybe I did someone some good in this life. Makes me feel I paid my dues. If it's a mediocre day, I'm no great Mazarelle fan. And if it's a black day like today—the kind where you wake up in a half daze and your life in the flics marches past you like a circus freak show and you say, "My god, is that what I've done with my life? You mean it was *all* shit?" I've been a policeman now for two decades and more and that's a *long* time. How much crap can I take? I should have left for Paris by now.

Mazarelle opened one eye to see what all the noise was about. Some guy jumping up and down on the shore, frantically waving his arms and pointing at the river, crying for help at the top of his lungs. Mazarelle scanned the surface of the water. A city block away, he spotted the swimmer's head thrashing about. In trouble. Grabbing his oars, he rowed swiftly toward her, so fast his oars in their rusty locks screamed in agony as the boat knifed through the river. For a good swimmer like that it had to be a cramp, and as he raced up to her he could see that it was. No reason to dive into the frigid water. He didn't need to be a hero and freeze his balls off. All he had to do was get her out alive. Mazarelle extended the blade of his oar to the thrashing swimmer and she lunged for it. He grabbed her hands—two ice cubes—and in one powerful move yanked her into the boat. A nice-looking young woman, with a raspberry face. He wrapped his shirt around her shaking shoulders.

"You okay?"

She nodded her head, trying to catch her breath, and he rowed quickly toward shore. It was then Mazarelle heard the commotion behind him and turned to see what was going on. The guy who'd been yelling, "My wife! My wife!" had leaped into the water and sunk like a stone. Two of the teenies jumped in to rescue him.

"What is it?" she asked.

"Your husband. He was trying to save you."

"But he doesn't know how to swim."

By the time Mazarelle had arrived on shore with the woman, the boys had fished out her husband and were standing around the motionless blue-lipped body as if he were already dead. His wife rushed to him but collapsed at his side, exhausted. Mazarelle, fortunately, was trained for emergencies. Once in Paris on the Métro he'd even helped a pregnant woman deliver her baby. *Libération,* reporting the story, called him the "Swiss Army knife of detectives."

Coolly the inspector ticked off what had to be done. First, he ran to his car and put in a call to the local hospital for an ambulance. Then, returning to the sobbing woman's husband, he tilted his head back. Good, he was still breathing. Mazarelle dropped to his knees for CPR and began to pump him out, the river gushing from the man's mouth, his nose. The miserable sinker coughed, his chest heaving, the air rushing back into his lungs, the pink to his cheeks.

"My wife . . ." he mumbled.

"She's here," Mazarelle reassured him. "She's fine. Next time don't be a hero."

When the ambulance arrived and he'd helped the driver load them into the back, Mazarelle shook his head. What a jerk. But at least he'd tried. How could he have lived with himself if he hadn't tried? Poor bastard. The sad truth is he would have lost either way. Mazarelle had learned that what really drives you crazy is when you know it's hopeless, and there's nothing you can do.

7

CAFÉ VALON, TAZIAC

Not far from the main square in Taziac is the rue Blanche, a short, narrow, side street that rarely sees tourists and dead-ends in a scrap metal shop. On the right-hand side, with its blue neon sign in the window, is the Café Valon.

Two old friends sat drinking at the end of the bar nearest the door. They'd been there all afternoon, their eyes glazed and watery. At the other end was Mickey Valon, who owned the place, talking to Thérèse, who used to work for him on and off before she had her baby. Thérèse wasn't bad looking, if you liked the big-boned type, but a little worn around the edges. Her husband, Ali, was bent over the pool table in back, playing a game by himself and dreaming of a killing. He had the soul of a hustler.

Except for Thérèse, all the other customers were men, and at that hour there weren't too many of them. The café was filled with cigarette smoke and the heavy aroma of steaming meat coming from the kitchen. Suddenly the big dog curled at Thérèse's feet jumped up and ran to the door, its friendly tail flailing the air. Mickey glanced across at the unshaven, long-haired hippie in the torn leather jacket who had just come in and told his mutt to stop bothering the customer. "Come here, you big dope! Come here, Javert."

The dog stuck around just long enough to be petted by the stranger and then bolted, darting behind the bar. Mickey asked the stranger what he'd like to drink. Reiner ordered a glass of *rouge*. As he waited, he glanced around the café and noticed the guy in back playing pool by himself. When his wine arrived, he paid, took a sip off the top, and carried his glass to the rear. Standing by the pool table and drinking, Reiner silently watched the stick work of the guy with the blue bandanna tied around his head. The only sound the sharp clicking of the balls.

Ali seemed to pay no attention to the stranger, letting the hook sink in good and deep before he looked up, a cigarette dangling from his lips. He asked the stranger if he wanted a game.

"*Pourquoi pas?*" said Reiner, and snatched a cue from the rack.

The Arab watched him and liked the casual way he did it. With none of the life-and-death attentiveness of an ace duelist selecting a pistol or a blade. It boded well. He held out his hand and introduced himself as Ali.

"Pierre," the stranger said. "Pierre Barmeyer."

From the bar, Thérèse anxiously tried to see what was going on in the back. They quickly settled on the stakes—a hundred points at twenty francs a game. Ali racked up the fifteen balls as if he'd been doing it all his life. They lagged and Reiner won the break, but when he hit his cue ball, it wedged itself harmlessly into the pack. Taking his turn, Ali not only managed to dig it out but pocketed a couple of balls in the process. He followed that with a string of three more before calling the 5-ball, which hung tantalizingly on the lip of the side pocket.

Chalking his cue tip, Reiner dropped in number 5. His cue ball followed. "*Merde!*" he muttered under his breath. From that low point, things disintegrated, and in time Ali put him out of his misery.

Reiner pulled out a twenty-franc note and tossed it on the table. Whisking it away, Ali invited him to another game.

"*D'accord,*" he said eagerly.

As they played, Thérèse came back and looked at Reiner. He fixed her with his steady gaze, his narrowed dark-blue eyes taking all of her in—the short skirt, the long legs, the tight dress that had been washed once too often and now barely covered her backside—until she began to feel uncomfortable and turned away. Leaning over the table, Ali was sizing up his next shot when she whispered something in his ear. "Fuck off," he told her.

"A fine-looking woman," Reiner said, watching her walk back to the bar. The Arab said nothing. "Your wife?" Ali shook his head. It was none of the guy's business one way or the other.

Reiner mentioned that he was looking for work and inquired if Ali knew of anything. Ali asked what he did. Reiner called himself a jack-of-all-trades. Painter, stonemason, electrical work, home repairs, anything that put a jingle in his jeans. Ali said that he was working at a place out of town called L'Ermitage, but he already had a helper. There was nothing for him there. In the past, however, he'd done odd jobs for the English who owned the house on the adjoining property. You can try there, he told him. But they probably wouldn't be arriving till the end of next month.

Thérèse, without glancing at Ali, stormed by the table and he stared after her. She was on her way to the crapper to squat on the Turk and then fix up her face in the scrap of mirror nailed to the wall. Though he hated to let loose of this pigeon, Ali knew it was time to go.

"Let's play another game." Reiner said that he wanted a chance to win back his money. "I feel lucky."

"Another time. I've got to go."

"Come on," he coaxed. "You don't have to go yet. What's your hurry?"

Ali was sorely tempted. He felt Barmeyer was challenging him and wondered where this *savate* got his balls after losing two in a row by lopsided margins. The games had been strictly no contest, and Ali had the forty francs in his pocket to prove it. When Thérèse came back, Ali grabbed her by the arm to remind her who was boss. She waved to Mickey on their way to the door. The two old guys at the bar said good-bye to her. No one said anything to Ali.

No sooner were they outside in the street than she asked, "How much did you lose this time?"

"What makes you so sure I lost?"

"You always lose. And we barely have enough to get by as it is."

"Shut up!" He smacked her hard across the face, turning her cheek scarlet. "Quit nagging me."

Back inside the Valon, Reiner racked up the balls as if he'd been doing it all his life. The more he saw of the Arab, the less he liked him, and since he'd begun watching Ali he'd seen a lot. He didn't like the way he pushed his girlfriend around any more than the way he took his forty francs. But the money was an investment that would pay off.

Brushing his blackened hair out of his eyes, and glancing up front to make sure no one was looking back, Reiner leaned over the pool table and sent the cue ball smashing into the pack. It exploded, a multicolored starburst of balls that shot like radar-guided missiles into the pockets.

The little green Renault passed the sign that said L'Ermitage and continued until it turned off onto the unmarked dirt road that cut back and forth as it climbed the hill. The house was a three-story white stucco with a cupola atop a low-pitched red tile roof. It looked like the right place to him. The grass hadn't been cut in a long time, the shutters closed tight.

Reiner parked the car behind the house so that it couldn't be seen from the road. He went in through the back door. It had a simple spring lock that any fool could open. Ah, the English, he thought, they were so trusting. After a quick examination of the house from top to bottom, he found that it was just as the Arab had said. Empty. Except for the musty smell, a perfect place to hole up for the next few days while making final arrangements. And at forty francs, quite a bargain!

In addition to its privacy and location, the premises had other assets that he felt might come in handy. There were, for instance, a couple of bikes parked in the hallway. And on a hook behind the kitchen door, a good pair of Zeiss binoculars. Bird watchers, natu-rally. The English love their birds. Then there was a small TV that might work, and a gun case hanging on the living room wall. Locked, of course, but child's play for Reiner. He snapped it open with a kitchen knife. There were two guns inside that were probably used for sport and vermin control.

He pulled out the rifle and looked it over. A 6.5-millimeter. Mannlicher-Carcano, the same type of gun that blew the top off Jack Kennedy's head. Reiner checked the bolt action. It was super smooth, slipping in and out like a hypodermic. Very nice! He had to laugh at the reputation the Carcano had of being so poorly made that the only thing it might kill was the shooter. Garbage! It was good enough to do the American president at eighty-eight yards with a four-power scope. But he couldn't find any cartridges, which made it less than useless to him. He wasn't about to go shopping for a box of 6.5s anywhere in the area. The double-barreled shotgun, on the other hand, had two twelve-gauge number one shotshells in it, which experience had taught him could do more damage than either double-zero or triple-zero shot. A powerful instrument at close range, though crude and not to his taste. Wiping both guns off carefully, Reiner replaced them in the case. He had another plan for the unlucky tourist.

Ben felt as if his head were exploding. He opened his eyes. In the dim light coming in under the door, he could see that Judy wasn't there. He crawled out of bed, dragged himself into the bathroom, put his head under the faucet. The cold water helped. They had been going out to dinner every night since their friends arrived and lately he'd been drinking a lot. What the hell, he thought, it's a vacation.

Showered, dressed, and with a few aspirins under his belt, he was feeling almost human when Judy opened the door a crack. Her face—tan and smiling—glowed in the morning light.

"Ah, I see you're finally up, sleepyhead. How are you feeling?"

"Tolerable. Why?"

"You were snoring like a foghorn."

Picking up his wallet from the top of the night table where he had tossed it the night before, he glanced inside, wondering if he'd remembered to put away his Visa.

"What's the matter, Ben?"

"Did you take any money from me?"

"No, why?"

"All my five-hundred-franc notes are gone."

"You sure?"

"Of course I'm sure."

"How many did you have?"

"Five." Although his smaller French bills were still there, he remembered quite clearly the five five-hundreds.

"You probably spent them last night at the restaurant."

"Don't be silly. I used my Visa card." He showed her the receipt in his wallet. Flipping through his credit cards, he ticked off each one carefully, and then turned to her in astonishment. "It's not here."

The previous evening the four of them had driven down to Villeneuve-sur-Lot to have dinner at the Toque Blanche, a terrific hilltop restaurant with a magnificent view of the countryside. When he called to ask if they had found his Visa, the woman who owned the place remembered "*les quatre américains,*" but no card had been left behind. Judy wondered if perhaps it might have fallen out of Ben's wallet and suggested that he look in their car.

He rummaged through every part of the Peugeot, scouring the interior and growing more and more frustrated, his annoyance heightened by the nonstop hammering in the barn. It suddenly occurred to him that Ali was the only stranger around. That was it. The Arab had taken his money and credit card.

"That's ridiculous, Ben. He's been in there working since he got here. Besides, you've been sleeping all morning. How would you know?"

"Were you over there watching him?"

"Come on . . ." A troubled Judy gave her husband's arm an affectionate squeeze. "Cut it out, Ben."

"Well maybe it wasn't him. But somebody sure as hell ripped me off."

Though Judy tried to talk him out of making a big deal of it—certain that he'd spent the money and that his lost Visa card would eventually turn up—her husband was adamant about going to the police. Judy decided to go along, keep an eye on him.

In Taziac, the *gendarmerie nationale* was located on the edge of the village, a one-story stucco building surrounded by a chain-link fence. Parked inside the fence was a blue van marked Gendarmerie. The door in the fence was padlocked.

"I told you nobody would be here on Sunday," said Judy, considerably relieved. "Now let's go home."

"Not on your life."

Throwing the car in gear, Ben hit the gas, and his rear wheels kicked up a shower of gravel as he sped north. It was only about twenty minutes to Bergerac. Ben hoped that the bruiser from the bakery, the famous Inspector Mazarelle, worked weekends.

8

COMMISSARIAT DE POLICE, BERGERAC

ergerac was a city of twenty-six thousand. That Sunday nearly every one of them seemed to be out on the road. Inching its way up the rue Neuve d'Argenson, Ben and Judy's car crawled along bumper to bumper, past the square, past the *mairie.* "Here it is!" Judy shouted, when they reached the boulevard Chanzy. "Make a right."

The two-story-high vertical sign on the side of the stone and stucco building announced Hôtel de Police. Ben pulled into the fenced courtyard and parked around back beside the lone car. There were iron bars on the first-floor windows. The tricolor hung limply over the front door. Peering through the glass, Ben saw someone inside and tried the door. It was open.

In the small waiting room, the empty chairs hugged the wall like a police lineup. A young female officer in a blue uniform sat behind the high counter, her frizzy- and short-haired head bent over her desk. Ben waited for her to look up. On the wall behind her, a framed message bearing the city's coat of arms asked visitors to "Support Our Police." Ben was willing in principle but quickly ran out of patience. Clearing his throat by way of introduction, he said, "Inspector Mazarelle, *s'il vous plaît.*"

The suspicious cop looked him over as if he were a ticking duffel bag dropped on her doorstep. She asked if he had an appointment. Ben figured Mazarelle was there and explained why he'd come. Picking up the receiver, she spoke briefly in a low, tight-lipped voice. Was she trying to protect him from strangers? Hanging up, she announced he'd be down shortly. Ben glanced smugly at Judy, pleased with himself for coming. Twenty minutes later he wasn't so sure.

Mazarelle—his collar open, his shirtsleeves rolled to the elbows exposing cable-thick forearms—had been working at his computer when the telephone rang. It was Lucille with some American tourists who had been robbed. Though in no rush to go downstairs, he didn't mind the interruption. He was getting bored doing paperwork. Nobody wanted to be in the commissariat on Sundays, but since Martine's death at the end of last year, one day was very much like the next for him.

He thought of how different it had been in Paris. Not always good by a long shot, but Paris was Mazarelle's city. Born and bred from its sounds, its smells, he had a career there, a job that meant something. It was the one place in the world in which Mazo, as his pals called him, felt most alive, most in tune with his flesh, and every day was a new throw of the dice. Never knowing what the next mail would bring, the next phone call, the next knock on the door. And everything, no matter how insignificant, seemed to add up.

But when her doctor found cancer and said *"C'est grave,"* Martine told Paul that she was going back to Taziac, the village where she'd grown up, to die. She never asked him to leave Paris, leave the work that he loved at the heart of France in the Police Judiciaire. She never asked him to transfer to the boonies. He knew that it made no difference to her one way or the other, though she said it did.

The truth was, it came as no surprise to him that a creature so young and lovely could be so hard. Marrying her, he knew from the start what he was getting into but not how bad at times it could feel. He gazed at Martine's picture on his desk, taken only a few years ago in the Tuileries. How could he have been so lucky? A beautiful young woman half his age and brimming over with life caught brushing back her long windswept blond hair while smiling mischievously at the photographer (a complete stranger as far as Mazarelle knew).

There had always been bits and pieces of his wife's life that he knew nothing of, and it was just as well. He told himself: ask no questions and she'll tell you no lies. If she disappeared for a few days, that was her business. Not that these absences of hers didn't hurt. They had had their share of battles, nasty knockdown fights marked with bloody scratches, black-and-blue bruises, her clothes trashed on the floor, his precious jazz records broken. Even so, he hadn't given up all hope of her fidelity, but he'd come to realize he was clinging to a frayed rope. No matter. He was always glad to have her back whenever she came.

From the top drawer of his desk Mazarelle pulled out a plastic pouch labeled Philosophe. It was his favorite, a mixture of tobaccos that included some orientals, a whisper of perique, and latakia from Syria. They gave the blend its dark, meditative aroma. One of the few luxuries he still took pleasure in. Specially ordered from Paris. The English tobacconist who sold it was located in a gallery just off the Palais Royal. As Mazarelle lit his pipe, the tobacco flaring up with a ruby glow, he recalled Monsieur Small's soigné shop with its woodcuts, its polished mahogany display cases, its wonderful odor. Merely to enter it—even after a day of being mired hip deep in the crap of society—made him feel somehow improved, judicious, a soupçon more civilized.

A loud, bloodcurdling cry jolted him. It seemed to be coming from downstairs. At first he thought it was the noisy drunken bastard they had brought in last night and tossed into a jail cell to sleep it off. Hearing shouts outside, he went to the window. On the field behind the commissariat one of the players was down on the grass, writhing in pain. Probably kicked in the balls on a high, sliding tackle. And all the ref did was hold up a yellow warning card. The handful of screaming fans wanted his head.

There was usually a game there on Sundays, and Mazarelle had forgotten all about it. As he had Lucille's call. He seemed to be forgetting more and more lately. The names of old movie stars, restaurants he was once fond of in Paris, even some friends from the past with whom he'd played rugby. All gone, lost because of alcohol and age, he supposed, along with his alleged good looks and a few brain cells. No big deal. As long as it didn't affect his appetite. He shrugged, par for the course. Satisfied to see Asterix zipping over the Saharan dunes to save his computer screen, he went to find out what Lucille had waiting for him.

The inspector recognized the couple from the *boulangerie* at once. Perhaps he wasn't ready for the scrap heap quite yet. He even remembered the tarte tatin they had bought and asked madame how they enjoyed it. Mazarelle was genuinely interested in people, curious about what made them tick. But it wasn't always easy for him to soften his tone from that of the trained interrogator.

Moving heavily up the stairs ahead of them, he led the way to his office, where Ben told him of the missing money and credit card, insisting that the inspector do something.

Mazarelle recognized the type. A born upper-middle-class pampered darling, used to making demands and getting his own way. Confirmed by the elaborate style of his signature, Benjamin Reece, on his American passport. Mazarelle listened to his talkative visitor, noting that he spoke French reasonably well, wore an expensive gold watch, an unusual gold wedding band that matched his wife's, and smelled strongly of alcohol. The inspector considered the latter a vote in his favor, but even he ordinarily didn't start drinking this early in the day. On the other hand, he reminded himself, Reece *was* on vacation.

Mazarelle was curious why Monsieur Reece suspected the owner's handyman, Ali Sedak. Ben admitted that he had no proof. Merely a hunch. He didn't trust the man. Sedak came and went at odd hours and walked into their house—to use the phone, ask a dumb question—whenever he wanted. He always had some excuse.

Mazarelle asked, "Anyone else living on the premises?"

"Only our friends from Montreal—Schuyler and Ann Marie Phillips. They arrived here the day after we did."

The inspector appeared interested. "Who are they?"

"The Phillipses?"

"How long have you known them?"

Ben and Judy looked at each other. She laughed and said, "Schuyler is one of my husband's oldest friends. They were roommates at Dartmouth. You're not suggesting—?"

Ben, unable to restrain himself, broke in and asked, "Have you ever heard of the Canadian multinational corporation Tornade,

Inspector? Makers of jet planes, high-speed trains. The owners of Tornade Financial Services."

"Go on."

"Sky Phillips is the CEO of their entire worldwide operation. He doesn't need my Visa card. As I told you, Inspector, Ali Sedak is your man."

Though Judy didn't object to letting her husband have his little bête noire, she was confident the inspector wasn't about to believe such nonsense without evidence. He was no fool. She wondered if the pretty young woman in the framed picture was his dead wife. He had decked the photo out like an impromptu shrine with a sprig of deep yellow forsythia in an Orangina bottle. How thoughtful! She might have been his daughter she was so young looking. Judy wondered why some girls marry men old enough to be their fathers. Or grandfathers in the case of Saul Bellow and Pablo Casals. She had to admit the inspector was certainly a good listener, which any woman yearns for in a man.

After hearing Monsieur Reece out, Mazarelle leaned back in his chair and lit his pipe. Sparks flew into the air and smoke wreathed his face. Crime, as they no doubt realized, was not unknown in Bergerac. A major contributing factor was that, except in the smaller surrounding villages, people no longer knew their neighbors the way they once did. And families nowadays fell apart like wet tissue paper.

He sighed, a ghostly stream of smoke rushing out of his mouth. With the stem of his pipe, the inspector gestured toward the local map on the wall. Pinned to it were dozens of tiny green, yellow, and red paper flags. Each one, he pointed out wearily, represented an *unsolved* crime. Fortunately, all relatively minor. There were no black flags because there had been no murders, the last one a *crime passionel* three years ago—long before he arrived—in which the killer was never in doubt. If only they weren't so badly understaffed and underfinanced. Unfortunately, that was the way it was here in the Dordogne. Judy felt genuinely sorry for him. Maybe it was those sad, sympathetic brown eyes of his and the droopy mustache. He seemed to need more help than they did.

In any case, he explained, it would be difficult to track down their lost money. The Visa, if stolen, was quite another matter. Though he promised nothing, he said he'd do what he could. Getting up, he asked if Monsieur Reece had notified the company about his missing credit card. Feeling stupid, Ben admitted that he hadn't. Mazarelle studied him for a few seconds without a shred of enthusiasm and suggested that whether his Visa was lost or stolen, he thought that would probably be a good idea. *"N'est-ce pas?"*

Downstairs at the door, the inspector shook hands with each of them. Should anything develop, he said he'd be in touch. Ben was afraid the inspector was a dead end.

Back in his office, Mazarelle picked up the pad on his desk and glanced at the notes he'd taken. Though he wasn't sure about the exact location of L'Ermitage—the hilltop house outside of Taziac where they were staying—he knew the road below them that bordered the Chambouvard farm and the nearby gravel pit. He wondered why the Reeces hadn't gone to the gendarmerie in Taziac to file their report rather than to the commissariat. It seemed that even tourists knew the difference between the *police nationale* and the tin soldiers in the village. Outside his window the shouts grew louder as the game heated up.

While waiting impatiently for the Reeces to come out, Reiner sat scrunched up in his little Renault and watched the game. The midfielder ran breathlessly down the field and sent a diagonal pass ahead to the racing striker who had broken free of the defense. He kicked at the ball wildly, and it trickled into the net past the lunging goalie. The fans went wild. Waving off the goal, the ref declared him offside. The small crowd of idiots roared at the poor man, but Reiner saw he was right.

Reiner loved what Pelé called the "beautiful game." But it was torture watching this one, even with only half an eye. All they did was kick the ball as hard as they could and run after it like panting dogs. "It's the ball that needs to run, you *narren*," he muttered, "not the player." Each side huffing and puffing as if it couldn't wait to give up possession to the other. No plan, no discipline, no control. The qualities that made the great Matthäus such a joy to watch. Not only did the crack German playmaker know exactly what had to be done on the field, but he had the skill and power to do it.

Reiner had recently read the amazing story about Murdoch, the Australian press czar, bidding one billion dollars for Britain's Manchester United. He dreamed that one day he himself might have enough money to buy a club. A *Bundesliga* championship team of his own! He had to laugh at those *Ossis* still clinging to their Trabis and the good old DDR days of Stasi, shortages, watchtowers, and barbed wire. Idiots! Weak-minded sentimental fools suffering from *Ostalgie* and longing for a workers' paradise.

Someone was coming. Reiner slumped down in his seat and waited to see who it was. The two of them came marching around to the back of the commissariat and walked toward the Peugeot. Reiner checked his watch. He'd been staking out their car for almost an hour now. They were arguing about something, but they had started out that way when they left L'Ermitage. The comings and goings of everyone in that house were important to him the closer he came to the end of the month. He was surprised by where they had gone, curious to know what it was about. The one thing he did know was that it had nothing to do with him.

9

L'ERMITAGE, TAZIAC

einer went to call Zurich the next day. A public telephone was at the intersection not far from the house where he was holed up. On one corner a small, tile-roofed, rust-stained factory, its metal shutters closed. Diagonally across the way, a Total gas station. At the side of the road, a glass telephone booth that stood out in the midst of farmland like a solitary hitchhiker.

Reiner leaned his bicycle against the empty telephone booth. With the door closed, it was warm inside. The afternoon sun beat on the glass, where a wasp shrugged its paper-thin, pale yellow wings. Reiner turned his back to the glare and dialed the long number. As he waited for someone to pick up the phone, he recalled drizzly Zurich and the comforting solidity of the gray bank building with its thick granite walls, its marble floors. He'd been most impressed by the contrast between the noisy bustle on the bank's main floor and the mortuary hush and kid-glove deference that greeted him upstairs. Finally someone answered.

Reiner asked for Monsieur Spada in Numbered Accounts. Identifying himself to Spada's satisfaction, he told him precisely what he wanted. In less than five minutes, the accommodating bank officer was back on the line with the information.

Reiner smiled. He liked doing business with reliable people. But in any event, he never made a move until at least half the amount agreed upon was deposited in his account. It was one of five that he'd tucked away in different corners of the world. He thought of the money in them as *Schlafmünzen*, his sleeping coins. Though his bank in Monte Carlo would have been more convenient for this job,

Reiner, fearing the proximity and control of France, had decided not to use it. If the French ever got lucky and discovered that account, they could squeeze Monte Carlo for information about him that they'd have a hard time getting from the tight-lipped Swiss.

He hung up the receiver. *"Sehr gut."* With a lightning motion, his palm came down on the wasp, smashing it against the glass. "Tomorrow then," he told himself.

Reiner had a good idea why the two retired French intelligence agents wanted him for the job rather than doing it themselves. He wasn't so stupid that he allowed flattery to turn his head. Pellerin and his beefy boyfriend were clearly keeping their distance, intent on insulating themselves from him and from what very soon was about to happen. If pressured, they'd cut him adrift without a second thought. He was well prepared for that. Wiping the delicate silky wings off his hand, he picked up his bicycle. It was then he noticed the rear tire.

Reiner walked the bike over to the gas station. *"Avez-vous une pompe?"* he asked the old guy in the office. Without looking up from his newspaper, he pointed to the hose hanging outside on the wall and told him to help himself. The tire seemed to hold the air he put in okay. Reiner crouched down, spit on his index finger, and wet the rear valve, looking for a leak. As he watched the slow bubble form, a gray Mercedes roared into the station and pulled up to the gas pump. The car's twelve-star EEC license plate had a D on it, but when the couple got out Reiner could tell that only the middle-aged driver was German. From Munich, he guessed by the accent. The curvy young blonde looked to him like a Natasha. While the attendant filled the tank, they went inside to use the toilet.

The newly filled tire, despite its leak, would do to ride back on. It wasn't that far, and he'd neither the time nor desire to fix it. Reiner thanked the guy for his air and, as he climbed on his bike, admired the sleek German car. The attendant nodded. But expensive, he said, pointing to the gasoline pump, where the dials for liters and francs crazily raced each other higher and higher. The big, pricey car guzzled gas the way his son put away wine. That's why he never showed up for work here on time. *"Salaud,"* he complained.

The old fool understood nothing about German engineering and the S500. Although it had a powerful 5.0 liter engine, Mercedes-Benz had developed an automatic cylinder shut-off system that reduced fuel consumption by 7 percent. As soon as the V-8 engine dropped into part-load operation, its electronic management system would deactivate cylinders 2 and 3 on the right bank and 5 and 8 on the left, effectively reducing the fuel consumption. A beautifully made machine, the S500. Reiner knew all about Mercedes-Benz cars. Could take them apart blindfolded. He'd have no need for a flashlight tonight, he thought as he pedaled merrily away on his slowly leaking tire.

The Phillipses had gone to bed late. But the restless Ann Marie couldn't sleep and, despite plans to visit Sarlat with Judy the following day for sightseeing and shopping, she stayed up reading Wilkie Collins's *The Moonstone,* a novel she'd found downstairs in the bookcase. Along with the English policeman, she too had been wondering what the three Indian jugglers seen in the neighborhood had to do with the disappearance of Miss Verinder's enormous diamond, when she heard them scratching at the window, trying to break into the house. Opening her eyes wide, Ann Marie sat bolt upright. The sound had awakened her. Thankfully, the small bedside lamp was still on. She swiveled her head from side to side as she tried to pin down what it was—weird, frantic scraping sounds that resembled bony skeletal fingers clawing their way out of a sealed vault. She looked up. The noise seemed to be coming from directly overhead.

"Woodchucks," said a sleepy Schuyler awakened by the commotion. He remembered the ferocity of the digging under the cabin they once rented in the Laurentians. "But what are they doing up there?"

"Bats."

"Well . . . maybe." He pulled up his blanket and turned over. "Could you please shut off the light, dear?"

"*Taisez-vous!*" Ann Marie shouted at the razor-toothed nocturnal revelers, but the racket continued. Picking up her book from the floor, she hurled it at the ceiling—all at once, silence.

"That's better." Rather pleased with herself, she crawled back into bed, switched off the light, and, burying her head under the blanket, was soon fast asleep.

But that night there would be no rest for Schuyler. Unable to get back to sleep, he climbed out of bed. It was warm in the room, but at a little after three, he'd no wish to go downstairs. He carefully unlocked the French doors and slipped out into the pleasantly cool air on the balcony. Glancing up, he scanned the canopy of stars. The moonlight silvered the treetops, the thin ribbon of road, and the fields beyond. The silence was magical. Schuyler was astonished at how long it had been since he last thought about anything that had to do with his work and wondered why he was doing so now. Guilt, he supposed, smiling. These days in Taziac with Ann Marie and Ben and Judy had been a wonderful change. He was thinking what a good time they were all having when he heard something moving on the dirt road below.

Though he couldn't see through the trees, he imagined from the sound that it was a large animal. He'd seen deer in the fields while driving. Or perhaps one of the neighbor's cows had wandered away from the herd. The footsteps, though not loud, grew increasingly clear in the stillness. They sounded almost human the closer they came to the house. He searched the shadows, straining his eyes.

The shape that emerged into the pale moonlight was unquestionably human. Schuyler pulled back from the balcony railing lest he be seen. He'd no idea who it was. No one he recognized. The dark figure moved furtively up the hill to the top and, just before disappearing behind the house, turned.

The moonlight flashed on something in the figure's hand. Schuyler shifted his weight and felt a sudden sharp pain in his right thigh. Only a cramp, he guessed, but it was almost as if he'd been hit by a bullet. Damnit, he thought, annoyed with himself for not yelling at the poacher. Hunting was forbidden anywhere in France at night.

Of course, he might have been wrong about the gun, but it had looked like a rifle barrel to him. The poacher was probably after rabbits or some nocturnal feeder. Rabbits were all over the neighborhood. Schuyler had nothing against hunting and wasn't a bad shot himself, but people with guns trespassing about at night gave him the creeps.

The next morning at breakfast Ann Marie was full of their previous evening's adventure with the bats in the tower. She explained to Judy and Ben, who had a nasty hangover, how they had finally gotten to sleep after being shaken out of bed by the weird noises of the bats.

"Owls," Ben corrected irritably.

Ann Marie didn't think so.

Judy noted her husband's badly bloodshot eyes and, intent on keeping the peace, recounted what Monsieur Chambouvard, the farmer across the road, had told them about the famous owls of Taziac.

Ann Marie looked at Schuyler. They both had to admit they could be wrong. Under the circumstances, Schuyler said nothing about the phantom poacher he'd seen. In the muted dove-gray morning light, he seemed as gossamer as dreamland.

The weatherman predicted rain and clouds for that day, and the map on the small television screen showed ominous black thunderheads and flashing bolts of lightning hovering over Périgueux, Bergerac, Agen, and Cahors. No rain yet, thought Reiner, glancing out the kitchen window, but a thunderstorm sounded promising. The ideal weather for an accident. He stirred the pot on the stove and lowered the flame.

The guy being interviewed was Dr. Claude Roehn of the Institut Pasteur. He seemed to know all about bovine spongiform encephalopathy and a new form of Creutzfeldt-Jakob disease transmitted to humans from infected cows. Roehn said it caused spongy holes in the brain and was invariably fatal. The next person to appear was a young farmer from Fougères who had been accused of selling his herd and concealing the fact that one of his animals may have died of BSE. He claimed he knew nothing about mad cows. He was no scientist. He insisted that the loss of his entire herd would have put him out of business.

The woman interviewing the farmer felt no sympathy for him.

Reiner, on the other hand, recognized a soul brother. True, the guy was a selfish son of a bitch, but it was either that or the poorhouse. Enlightened self-interest. Wasn't that what capitalism was all about? People had to survive somehow. Speaking of which . . . perhaps it was time for him to cut back on steak and other red meat. In pursuit of better health, he'd already eliminated such favorites from his diet as coffee, eggs, butter, heavy cream, and sauerkraut. Turning the burner off before the milk boiled, Reiner poured his cocoa into a mug, shut off the TV, and went upstairs.

The window in the upstairs hallway was the only one in the house that had an unobstructed view of the property next door. He sipped his cocoa and contemplated the red tile roof of L'Ermitage, less than fifty meters away. Putting down his mug, he picked up the Zeiss binoculars from the table and trained them on the back of the house. He had seen the blue Peugeot leave earlier that morning with the two women. So far so good. With any luck they'd be gone all day. The other two cars—Ali's VW and the Phillipses' big, wine red Mercedes—were exactly where they'd been when last he looked. It was merely a matter of patience now. Even though he knew how the drama would end, it was always exciting to watch a live performance. As usual, the hard part was waiting for the curtain to rise.

First came the drizzle and then the wind. Next the low, rumbling thunder, hinting at the drenching downpour to follow. The trees shook and the sky darkened. He could barely make out Ali as he ran to his VW and jumped in. Reiner quickly adjusted the binoculars and watched the little white car disappear down the road. Though he wasn't counting on the Arab going home for lunch, as he occasionally did, it was high on Reiner's wish list. The fewer spectators the better.

Not long afterward, the threatening sky opened and a deluge cascaded down. Reiner pulled on his rain parka. He was about to leave for the Total station to call L'Ermitage to report Madame Phillips's accident to her husband, when he thought he heard a car door slam. He ran back to the window. The Mercedes was revving up. Phillips hadn't moved his car since he arrived. Reiner couldn't believe it. Most of his victims went to their deaths, kicking and screaming, but this Phillips couldn't wait to lay his head on the block. Reiner snatched up the binoculars. It was impossible to see through the car's tinted windows. As the Mercedes, gathering speed, splashed through the mud, and plunged down the hill, Reiner watched with a fixed intensity to see that everything worked smoothly, confident that it would. The streaking car suddenly was swallowed up behind the green hillside, dense with ferns and trees. If the Mercedes hit a linden or fir head-on at that speed, his job was done.

Reiner would have much preferred a simple fall onto a hard surface from a height of at least twenty-two meters. The police barely noticed such accidents. All that was needed was a rooftop, a balcony, an elevator shaft, an open window. But this was the country. Fortunately for Reiner, it was a German car.

The Mercedes was still going when he caught sight of it again. Speeding out of control and racing faster and faster like a toboggan down a chute. It had occurred to him that the car might get all the way down to the bottom of the hill without slamming into anything, but it seemed very unlikely. And the faster it went, the better. He could hear the horn blowing frantically as if the panic-stricken driver were pressing it with all his might. Moving his binoculars a little to the right, Reiner saw the oncoming gravel truck on the road below. There was so little traffic past their house that, despite the quarry, this sort of coincidental stroke of luck had seemed one in a million.

The truck driver slammed on his brakes. The timing of the collision would be so perfect there'd be no one left to tell the tale. Reiner held his breath as the eighteen-wheeler skidded on the rain-slick tarmac and began to jackknife, sending up an ear-piercing, jagged shriek as the Mercedes, horn still blaring, hurtled across the road in front of the truck and flew into the wheat field on the other side. Barreling into one huge wheel of hay after another, it knocked them down like tenpins until the slowing car flipped over on its side and came quietly to rest, the two upended tires spinning like roulette wheels.

The trucker jumped out of his cab and raced into the muddy field. He ran to the car and, climbing on top, pulled open the door to see if anybody was still alive. The face of the man behind the wheel was chalky white.

"*Ça va?*" called the trucker.

His hands shaking, the driver fumbled with his seat belt, trying unsuccessfully to unbuckle it. The trucker reached in to help him. Rattled and confused, Ben babbled that he didn't know, that he'd no idea what the hell had happened. Maybe he did something wrong. It wasn't his car, he said. He had borrowed his friend's to go buy some Scotch. All he knew was the brakes didn't work.

Struggling to free him, the trucker was amazed the damn fool was still alive. Lucky for him the car was built like a bulldozer. Even so, this guy must have been born under a lucky star. Strange, he thought, that an expensive car like this had no air bags. With the trucker's help, Ben crawled out with barely a scratch and stood up shakily, the rain pouring down on his head. It felt wonderful.

Reiner, who'd been at the window watching everything, slammed down his binoculars in disgust. He loathed surprises. Picking up his cocoa, he saw he'd nothing left and let out a furious howl. "*Verdammte Scheisse!*" he shouted, hurling the mug with all his might against the wall, where it shattered.

10

CAFÉ LE RICHE, BERGERAC

Mazarelle, when the call came two days later, wasn't expecting it, though he was not without hope. He'd notified banks throughout the region of the stolen credit card, and it had turned up right under his nose in Bergerac. The way things often do in police work. Goyard, the bank manager at the local BNP branch on the rue Neuve d'Argenson, reported that he had Monsieur Reece's missing Visa in his hand. The inspector said, "I'll be right over."

Before entering the bank, Mazarelle followed the arrow around to the side of the building where the ATM was located. He peered through the locked glass door and was pleased to see a surveillance camera high on the wall.

Goyard rose from his desk to shake the inspector's hand when he came in, clearly impressed by how quickly he'd arrived. Mazarelle took the proffered Visa card by the edges as if it were one of his cherished Fats Waller records and examined it, then, carefully turning it over, studied Benjamin Reece's signature. The extravagant swirling loops of the American's capital letters fit the man he'd met to a T.

In reply to the inspector's question, Goyard said that their ATM had seized the card late the previous evening when someone had tried several times and failed to enter the correct PIN. Mazarelle placed the plastic card into a cellophane envelope he'd brought. Then he asked the manager to drop by the commissariat that afternoon for fingerprinting. The banker turned pale. "A formality," Mazarelle explained. "Merely a way to eliminate your prints from any others on the card."

Before leaving, he mentioned the surveillance camera. Goyard said, "Yes, yes, of course you can have any pictures. Take the tape." If it contained what he needed, Mazarelle would call it a good day's work.

On the Place Gambetta in Bergerac the sidewalk tables in front of the Café le Riche were crowded with couples drinking. PMU—short for Pari Mutuel Urbain, the French state-controlled sports betting system—on the green front door promised the excitement of live thoroughbred racing from Paris. Inside the smoke-filled café, the long communal tables were occupied largely by sullen dark-skinned men who looked Spanish or North African. They spoke softly among themselves, shifted their weight uneasily on the creaky wooden chairs, their dark eyes always returning to the raised television screens on the side walls as they waited for the next race.

Ali sat talking intently to his round-faced, unshaven, ponytailed pal Rabo, who had enough gaudy rings on his fingers to be a pimp. Suddenly Ali wheeled around. "What do you say, Grandma?" he asked the elderly woman seated behind them, scanning a racing form. "Who do you pick in the fifth?"

The old lady took her glasses off and stared at him. Tied to a cord around her neck, the glasses hung down on her large, matronly bosom.

"Métronome. At five to one, it's a steal."

"That's good enough for me."

He had seen her and her dyke friend—the tight little gray-haired package in dungarees standing over by the bar who, with the sleeves of her blue work shirt rolled to the elbows, resembled Popeye the sailor—clean up on the last three races, while all his stiffs ran out of the money. Ali hurried up to place a bet on Métronome before it was too late.

The PMU booth was painted a bright, hopeful green. The middle-aged woman inside wore a jockey hat in an identical shade of green. She handled all the bets and, for the lucky few, the instant payoffs afterward. Métronome was number 7.

Ali sensed a good omen. Didn't Al Borak race through the seven heavens of the Koran? Feeling like a winner, he upped his bet to two hundred and put down the third of his five-hundred-franc notes. The good news was he still had two left. Back at the table, Ali waved his ticket at the old girl in appreciation. Lifting the glass of cognac her friend had just brought her, she toasted their success.

From the start it was a tight race. The ten horses jockeying for position, the speedster Bernadette taking the early lead. Ali, along with almost everyone else in the café, had his eyes nailed to the screens. At the halfway pole, Bernadette was still out front but pressed by a trio of horses coming up out of the pack. Spotting number 7 among them, Ali silently urged on the big black mount. By the three-quarter mark, Bernadette, fading fast, had run out of steam, and Métronome, with Chez Nous and Séducteur hot on his heels, had vaulted into the lead. The track announcer's voice throbbed with excitement as number 2, a pale gray with legs flying, suddenly came up on the outside, and side by side the quadriga thundered down the stretch. As their mounts reached for the finish line, the riders beat away on them like tom-toms and Ali, battling the other jocks, pounded the table.

Eldorado was first, Métronome second, and Chez Nous third.

"Eldorado," Rabo groaned. He wondered aloud if the winning horse was owned by Johnny Hallyday and named after his big hit. Offering Ali his condolences, Rabo told him he had something to cheer him up outside in his car.

Ali, muttering as he tore his ticket in two, was about to leave when he noticed Popeye coming back from the payout counter with a fistful of francs. He stared, incredulous, as she split the money with her girlfriend.

"You told me Métronome," he fumed at the old bitch, a scowl like a dueling scar marking his face.

"Sure. Didn't you bet him to place?"

"Putain!" Snatching up her racing form, he was shredding it into bits and pieces when Popeye, cursing the *bicot*, launched herself at his head. Ali, neatly sidestepping her flailing fists, knocked her to the floor. The woman behind the counter came running out with a club in her hand. Rabo grabbed his friend and pulled him away. It was time to go. He'd no wish to wait for the flics to show up.

11

L'ERMITAGE, TAZIAC

The morning sun turned the lawn, still damp from the night's rain, into a molten lake that stretched from the cool green shadows of the bushes below the high terrace wall all the way down the hill. It was going to be a steamy summer day. Up above on the terrace, the four friends sat outside, leisurely finishing breakfast, chatting and enjoying their buttery brioches and coffee. Somewhere in the distance a dog was barking. Then they heard the car coming up the hill. Although Ali hadn't yet arrived for work—unpredictable, as usual—it didn't sound like his old VW.

Next door, Reiner heard the laboring engine too. He didn't need binoculars to see the police markings on the car's hood and trunk, the blue light on its roof. He supposed it had something to do with the accident. Eager to find out what the cops knew, he made his way over to the neighboring property under cover of the trees. It was dangerous, of course, but a calculated risk never troubled Reiner. Darting across the open dirt road, he slipped soundlessly into the shadows between the terrace wall and the bushes, and, placing himself directly beneath where they were sitting, he waited, still as a lizard.

Mazarelle had had no trouble finding the L'Ermitage turnoff. As he approached the house, he marveled at how many attractive châteaux were tucked discreetly away in the hills outside Taziac, houses that even the locals knew little about. One like this, he estimated, probably cost more to rent for a month than he could make renting out his little place in town for a year. Should he decide to go back to

Paris, which he'd been thinking a lot about lately, he'd probably do better to sell it outright, take whatever he could get, and forget the past. Close the book on all those months of pain and remember just the good times. Taziac had nothing more to offer him now.

Judy Reece invited the inspector to join them out on the terrace for coffee and introduced him to their friends. Though she had told them about him, she recounted the amusing way they'd first met Inspector Mazarelle behind the counter in the *boulangerie*. Schuyler thought the sad-eyed, burly man with the hairy horseshoe under his nose looked exactly the way a French detective should. So did Schuyler's Canadian wife. Given the inspector's large, open face, Ann Marie believed that the serious downward curve of his mustache gave him the gravitas his police role demanded.

Judy, who found Mazarelle attractive and in need of care, felt that he could be a poet. A big one, to be sure, with a limp. Perhaps like Jacob, he too had wrestled with some terrible power and walked away from their fearful encounter forever changed. To Ben, he seemed heavy, country slow, and terminally incompetent. But Ben had to reconsider when the inspector announced that he'd come to return his missing Visa.

"That's fabulous! You mean you've cracked the case already?"

"*Doucement,* Monsieur Reece. Not so fast. We have the card but not the thief." He asked Ben to drop by his office as soon as possible for fingerprinting. But Mazarelle had to admit he wasn't too hopeful about identifying the thief from fingerprints. Most of the latent ones they found on the plastic card were either smudged, distorted, or fragmentary. Also complicating his life, though he spared him this, was that lately there had been so many court challenges by defense lawyers of false-positive identifications, it was getting harder to convict with fingerprints alone. What he did say was that he had something he wanted to show them.

The three photos were thirteen-by-eighteen-centimeter blowups of pictures taken by the bank's surveillance camera. Unfortunately all three were dark and grainy, the images not very sharp and lacking in contrast. Mazarelle apologized for their poor quality. The videotape hadn't been changed in a long time. Nevertheless, he hoped that the face of the man using Monsieur Reece's Visa at the ATM might be one they recognized. Despite his doubts, the inspector cleared a space on the table and laid the pictures down like three aces.

Ben nodded his head. "It's him! It's Ali. I told you he stole it." Though he'd no idea who the woman with him was, Ben had no doubt about Ali. Mazarelle turned to Ben's wife. Judy bent over the photos, studying them closely. "I suppose it's possible . . ." she allowed, but she was far from certain. As for Schuyler and Ann Marie, they didn't think it was Ali any more now than when Ben had first voiced his suspicions.

Judy asked the inspector if he'd ever seen Ali. He shook his head. It wasn't true, but if he said yes, he'd have to answer her next question. Mickey had pointed Ali out to him at the Café Valon, and Mazarelle thought that perhaps the reason he didn't recognize him now was because the pictures were so lousy.

"It's *him*! It's him," Ben insisted, angrily tapping the photos with his index finger. The same nasty confrontational glare he'd seen in Matisse's *Seated Riffian* in the Barnes Collection. A fierce, haughty, selfish North African rebel restrained by no laws. And as Ben knew, Ali also had a rotten temper. "That's the handyman, all right," he shouted.

Mazarelle urged him not to excite himself. Thanked them all for their help. Gathering up the photographs, he cautioned them to say nothing to Ali about his visit. He hoped that aside from this little unpleasantness, they were all enjoying their vacation in Taziac.

"Yes and no," Schuyler hedged. He recounted his friend's recent hair-raising automobile accident so vividly that he might have been in the car. A miracle that Ben wasn't killed.

Mazarelle turned to Monsieur Reece, expecting to get more of the story. But Ben simply shrugged and dismissed the incident as a crazy accident. He hadn't wanted to mention it at all, especially after filing a complaint about the loss of his money and credit card. Ben had no wish to appear a complete fool.

Schuyler described how the brakes on the rented Mercedes had failed and the air bags hadn't inflated. The car rental agency in Bordeaux was so glad not to be slapped with a serious lawsuit that it had provided a brand-new Mercedes free of charge.

Out of curiosity, Mazarelle asked Reece, "Were *you* the one who rented the Mercedes, monsieur?"

"No, I did," Sky said, grinning at his friend. "They might have been less generous had I told them who was actually driving when the car went out of control."

Reiner, his shirt soaked from pressing against the cold damp wall, had heard enough. Dashing back across the road, he disappeared into the empty house. It had been worth the risk. A new plan had taken shape in his mind as magically as if it had been there all along, boxed and gift wrapped, waiting for the right occasion. It was daring and would need a little time, which he disliked. And it lacked the anonymous casualness of chance. But it was breathtakingly neat and came ready to use with all the parts inside.

On the twenty-fourth of June, Ali didn't arrive at L'Ermitage until late in the afternoon. He untied the wooden planks from the top of his white VW and carried them into the barn. For a man his size, he was unusually strong. Schuyler was inside, bent over the handyman's large metal toolbox and rummaging through it. Ali dropped the planks on the floor, sending up a cloud of dust, and asked what the hell he was looking for. Schuyler needed a Phillips-head screwdriver for the kitchen cabinet hinges. Ali knew just where it was, which was amazing given the clutter of tools, rolls of tape, drill bits, blades, and assorted boxes of nails, washers, and screws. Much to the vacationing executive's amusement, Ali insisted that when he had finished with it he put it back exactly where he had found it.

After several weeks of sightseeing, Sky had had enough. Lately, he'd been helping Ali renovate the barn. He loved sanding down the new doors, windows, and cabinets, the smell of sawdust. And perhaps most pleasurable of all for him was losing all sense of time. It was a quality common to many of the things he enjoyed most, like flying, sailing, cross-country skiing, and, of course, making deals. Especially big ones. Like the billion-dollar deal that had delayed his departure.

As for the handyman, Ali didn't mind free volunteer labor as long as Phillips didn't get in the way and minded his own business. This one seemed to know what he was doing. Ali had completed putting down the new floor and Schuyler was going over it with a rented electric sander when Ann Marie came up behind him.

"It's really coming along," she said approvingly. Schuyler smiled and was about to give her a kiss when he noticed that she was already dressed for dinner.

"What time is it?"

"A little after eight. Our reservation at Chez Doucette is for nine. Aren't you coming, dear?"

He didn't feel like quitting just yet, and he wasn't particularly starved. "If I get hungry, I'll find something later in the refrigerator."

"You okay?" she asked, more concerned than annoyed. Her husband loved to eat and definitely liked Chez Doucette, the best restaurant in town, and its owner.

"I'm fine."

Even though Ali was busy at the other end of the room, Ann Marie could tell that his ears were tuned to every word they said. It gave her a very uncomfortable feeling. She wondered how much English he really knew. "You sure, Sky?"

"Tell Ben and Judy I'm sorry."

"Suit yourself."

It was a quarter to ten when Ali, complaining that he'd done enough work for one day, abruptly packed up and left.

"À demain," called Schuyler.

Tired and hungry himself, after a while Schuyler too thought he'd knock off. That day they had put in the new windows and the hardwood floor was ready to be stained. As his wife said, the place was shaping up. The funny thing was that, despite the pleasure he took in the work, he'd never have thought of doing anything so relaxing at home. For one thing, he'd no time for it. And for another—wiping the sawdust off his scraped, dirty hands—that's what money was for, and they had plenty of that.

Schuyler flipped off the lights. He was about to close the barn door and go see what was in the refrigerator when he heard footsteps. At first he thought it was Ali returning. But Ali's VW was gone—as was Ben's Peugeot—and the only car parked under the ash-gray outdoor lights was his new Mercedes. He peered into the darkness, trying to make out who it was.

From the shadows emerged someone Schuyler had never seen before. Tall, long-haired, he moved like a hunter—stealthily, on the balls of his feet—as he approached the lit kitchen window of the house. Schuyler didn't like his looks at all. Nor the gun he was toting or the furtive way he peeked through the panes, scanning the room. This guy was trouble.

Motionless and dumbstruck, Schuyler watched as the intruder glided over to the door and went into the house as if he'd been there before. With his gun and large rubber boots, he could be the poacher Schuyler had seen the other night. Perhaps the same uninvited guest who had ripped off his friend's money and credit card and was coming back for more.

Schuyler was certain that it wasn't Ali who had stolen Ben's Visa. He put his hand in his pocket and felt the comforting bulge of his wallet. Though Ann Marie had probably left some expensive earrings and bracelets in their room, everything was insured. He wasn't worried about that. He longed wistfully for his car keys or his cell phone, which were nestled among his silk handkerchiefs in the top drawer of the bureau. Some official tough guy like Inspector Mazarelle would be awfully good to see about now. Schuyler wondered what the creep was doing in there. Why was he taking so long? Could he have already left by way of the back door or the terrace?

When the intruder finally came out, he looked across at the barn. Schuyler's heart sank. Even before the guy started toward the barn door, Schuyler had begun feeling his way into the darkness of an interior whose layout was by now familiar to him. Although there was no other way out of the barn, he knew of a perfect hiding place. It was in the rear storage area where they kept old boxes, barrels, cartons, and trunks. And as Ali one day had shown him, it also contained a secret room that once, long ago, had been a granary. Laughing, Ali had suggested that maybe during the war when the Vichy cops came looking for Jews, the owner hid them in there. It was even less funny to Schuyler now than when he first heard it.

Outlined in the doorway, the stranger stood for a moment framed by the ghostly light behind him, his face lost in the shadows as he entered the barn. Either he couldn't find the light switch or had no desire to turn it on. As fast as Schuyler could go, he groped his way to the back of the barn where the air was damp and musty. Moving quickly, as much with his hands as his feet, he felt along the wall until he came to a pile of suitcases stacked atop a huge wicker basket and, grabbing the handle with both hands, pulled the basket slowly toward him so as not to knock over the loose tower of luggage. Nothing fell as the large basket, which was bolted to the wall, inched forward, pulling with it a section of the wall behind. The wood scraping on the stone floor squealed like the steel wheels of an elevated train rounding a curve.

Shit, he thought, that's all I needed. Without a moment's pause, Schuyler hurled himself into the utter blackness and pulled the wall closed behind him with a second high-pitched, agonizing sound. It wasn't until he'd shoved the thick wooden bar into place on the back of the door that he felt momentarily safe.

Then came the stealthy approaching footsteps. Followed by the noise of barrels being shoved lightly aside as if some powerful stalking animal were hunting for its frozen prey. Who was this guy, Schuyler asked himself, and why me? What the hell did he have against me? What was he doing now? There wasn't a sound. Straining to catch the slightest hint of movement, Schuyler, barely breathing, pressed his ear against the back of the door.

From the other side of the wall, a low voice called softly, "Come out, come out, wherever you are." There was a sudden hammering on the wall, furious blows as if someone was trying to punch a hole through it to get at him.

Was the man crazy? The thought was as frightening as the surreal situation in which Schuyler found himself. How do you charm a madman? His chest pounding, he reached into his back pocket searching for a weapon, something with which to defend himself, and impaled his palm on a steel point. Though bleeding, he was so cheered to find Ali's screwdriver that he hardly felt the wound. It wasn't an ice pick, but it was better than nothing.

He longed to hear Ben's car with the three of them returning from dinner. They had been gone a long time. Instead what he heard was the banging of the suitcases being violently tossed aside, one after the other, and the wicker basket on the floor squeaking and rattling as the lid was opened and tugged at savagely. Then dead silence. It was as if his pursuer had momentarily lost the scent. Schuyler gripped the handle of the screwdriver so hard that the pain in his hand was excruciating, but he barely noticed as he waited for the door to move.

12

CHAMBOUVARD FARM, TAZIAC

Georgette Chambouvard awoke with a headache after a bad night of dreams. She'd been tossing and turning for hours, and in the morning when her father came to wake her, she dimly remembered snapping at him and hearing the door slam, the house shake. Her dinner had not gone down well. She'd told her mother when she went up to bed that she thought it might be the mussels. And today was Friday. She knew she had to get up early to go to work.

She squinted dubiously at the day. Behind her on the wall, the great Bernard Hinault, with a smile big as his heart, rolled jubilantly across the finish line, both hands raised high above his head. It was the 1980 World Championship in Sallanches. "Le Blaireau," known by cycling fans the world over as the badger for never letting go of his prey, had won again. The other poster showed the irresistible Jean-Paul Belmondo in bed with a lit cigarette in his mouth, a gold chain around his neck, and Jean Seberg in his arms.

Georgette glanced at the clock. She'd skip breakfast—wasn't hungry anyhow—and make herself coffee at work. As Georgette got on her bicycle, a small black dog came racing toward her—tail wagging and galloping at a crazy angle—her bark a shriek as she fell down and picked herself up again. The scraggly chickens ran for their lives.

"*Tais-toi*, Mimi." The dog gave a whimpering cry as if she'd been kicked in the face, and dragged herself away. Mimi was blind.

Georgette raced away. The sunflower-fresh morning air filling her lungs helped her head, and she felt much better pedaling past her father's fields as she tore along the road to L'Ermitage. There wasn't a car to be seen, and she sprinted all the way to the turnoff, where she quickly slowed down and shifted gears. No problem for her Peugeot PX-10, which had eighteen speeds and Mafac "competition" hubs and brakes. Georgette was a triathlete and once had Olympic dreams before she was kicked off the national team. But that was bad luck and ancient history. She attacked the steep dirt road that led to the house as if it were an alpine stage of the Tour de France, her muscular legs churning up the hill like pistons. Though breathing hard, she had scarcely more fat on her thighs than the steel frame of her bike and had barely broken a sweat by the time she got to the top. Not bad, she thought, pleased with herself.

Propping up her bike with its trademark *arc-en-ciel* rings against the house next to the other Peugeot's rampant lion, Georgette wondered where Ali was. She didn't see his Beetle. Glancing up at the house, she noticed that the white shutters were still closed. They must have gotten home late again last night. She'd like to have a vacation like that. Nothing to do but eat, sleep, and screw around, instead of wiping up other people's slop. She cleaned for them twice a week and made extra for doing the laundry. The pay was good, the work wasn't much, and they were nice people. As jobs go, she wasn't complaining. But one of these days . . . she told herself. She was looking forward to getting paid today and buying a new dress.

Georgette went up to the door and was surprised to find it locked. They had never before bothered to lock the door or she would have asked for a key. Irritated, she marched around the house to the back door, and luckily it was open. She pushed up her sleeves and in her usual no-nonsense fashion got down to work at once, opening the shutters in the living room and airing out the cigar smoke. They had been drinking. On the dining room table were four glasses and a bottle of wine that was almost empty. Taking the tray from the oak sideboard, she cleaned up the table and emptied the ashtray on top of the scraps of food left over on the plate, which she piled along with the silverware, bottle, and wineglasses onto the tray. It struck her as odd that only one of them had had anything to eat. With foreigners you never knew what to expect, but maybe that's what she liked the most about them.

Lifting the heavy metal tray, Georgette carried it into the kitchen where, without warning, she felt dizzy and all the strength seemed to drain out of her arms, her hands. The tray slipped from her fingers, clanging and splintering glass as it struck the bloody tile floor. She couldn't believe what she was seeing. Blood streaked and splattered on the windows, the walls, the ceiling, and pooled around the bound and twisted body on the floor. His eyes wide open, Monsieur Reece stared sightlessly at the blood on the ceiling, his head tipped back as if straining to see it and his gaping throat ripped from ear to ear. Where were the others? His wife? His friends? How could they have slept through such butchery?

Georgette tried to scream, but the air caught in her throat; trapped there the choked spasmodic moans she made came in guttural waves. Unable to breathe, she felt herself shaking uncontrollably. The thought of staying in that nightmare house another second was unbearable. She had to get out of there and find help. Call the police. Leaping on her bike, Georgette fled down the hill, pedaling frantically faster and faster, her whirling feet a blur.

PART TWO

13

PLACE MESTRAILLAT, TAZIAC

After listening to the evening news on France 2, Mazarelle turned off the TV as if he were slamming a door. The reporters had nothing new beyond what had already been disclosed. The first serious case to come along here since he arrived, practically right on his doorstep, and they give it to the local gendarmes. He supposed that was only fair under the circumstances. First come, first served. Still and all, it was a pain in the ass. He had to get out of this place. While Martine was still alive he had a reason for being in Taziac, but not now.

Everything about this trim, stone house reminded him of her. Small wonder. It was Martine's house, and her family's before that. A jewel beautifully renovated about fifty years ago on the Place Mestraillat, a lovely, quiet corner of the village. He pushed the lace curtain aside and gazed out at the dark, empty, windblown street. The three Callery pear trees surrounding the old stone pump shimmered in the starlight.

Mazarelle went over and sank down into his large, red, overstuffed armchair. It seemed as grossly out of place here as he now felt. They had brought the chair from Paris along with their other furniture. No sooner had he sat down than Martine's cat showed up. Climbing onto his lap, Michou snuggled against his belly and made herself at home. He envied her.

For the past three days all he could think about was L'Ermitage. The TV newscasts and newspapers were full of it. A grisly business. Three of the four foreign visitors staying there had been found bound and gagged in different rooms in the house, their throats cut, and no sign of Monsieur Phillips anywhere. According to the Taziac gendarmes, he seemed to be the leading suspect. Mazarelle wondered what evidence they had.

Even though he'd notified them immediately of Monsieur Reece's stolen Visa card and missing money and that Reece had identified the person at the ATM in Bergerac as the L'Ermitage handyman, there was no mention of Ali Sedak. But it was still early days. They were bound to latch on to him sooner or later. Though not directly involved in the investigation, the inspector supposed it was his personal contact with the victims that quickened his pulse and ironically made him feel a little less dead himself.

From the shelf holding his large record collection, Mazarelle selected one of his Columbia Jazz Masterpieces. The Benny Goodman Sextet, featuring for the first time Charlie Christian. The year 1939, with France and Europe on the eve of disaster. As soon as he sat down, Michou was back on his lap to listen. Michou loved jazz. And the incomparable Benny was playing "Memories of You," his clarinet floating each liquid note so effortlessly, so wistfully that even a dumb, self-absorbed cat could appreciate it. And following Benny came Hampton with his luminous vibraphone and Christian, the young genius of the electric guitar, to weave their spell.

Michou stretched herself luxuriously as Mazarelle, lost in thought, rubbed her belly. She was a lovely animal to look at—a rich satiny gray with big pointy ears and a mincing feminine walk—but she came at a cost. The back of his chair was as clawed and shredded as the one in Proust's cork-lined bedroom that they had seen in the Musée Carnavalet in Paris. Then there was his allergy. His sneezes arriving not in single bursts but whole fusillades. And having felt the preludial itch, Mazarelle in anticipation was reaching for his handkerchief when the telephone rang.

It was Rivet, and completely unexpected. Mazarelle shut off the record player. The only time his boss had ever called him at home before was to offer condolences when Martine died. Though they were hardly friends and Rivet was inclined to be an ambitious pompous ass, the youthful commissaire was always *correct*. They got along. Rivet had approved his transfer from Paris despite Mazarelle's reputation as a hotshot. The commissaire didn't mind having another experienced man on the force as long as he was clear about who was in charge. Familiar with the petty fiefdoms of police bureaucracy, Mazarelle, busy with his sick wife, had stayed out of Rivet's way.

Mazarelle placed his hand over the phone until he finished sneezing and, wiping his nose, snuffled a hello.

"What was *that*?"

"Sorry."

"You sound like you're coming down with a cold."

"No, only my damn allergy."

"Oh yes. You should take care of that. Anyhow, I just got a call from Périgueux. The procureur isn't satisfied with the people in charge of investigating the Taziac murders. He said the ministry in Paris recommended you, if you were available. He'd like you to take over the investigation immediately. Does that appeal to you?"

"If not, I should be a hardware salesman."

"I thought so. I told him I had no objections. He'll be expecting your phone call early tomorrow morning. Okay?"

"I'll be happy to do what I can, naturally."

"Don't forget. He said *early*."

"Right."

Putting down the phone, Mazarelle sprang up from his chair lightly, as if free of the accumulated deadweight of pain, loss, and boredom that had clung to him since Martine's funeral. He felt a new surge of excitement, a half-forgotten sense that all wasn't over for him. Perhaps there was something to look forward to after all—the pleasure of tracking down whoever was responsible for these three savage murders and the satisfaction of bringing him, or them, to justice. There was something else too. L'Ermitage, he reminded himself, was the sort of high-visibility case that might resurrect a fading career. The sort of case that with any luck could soon return him to Paris. But in order to conduct a major crime investigation, he'd need as much help in the way of resources as he could get from the procureur. He'd know soon enough.

Mazarelle considered his pipe rack on the shelf, a xylophone of shapely pipes and subtle woods, and plucked out his long-stemmed meerschaum. Curved like a saxophone with a large, deep *écume de mer* bowl. He tamped down the tobacco and joyfully lit up, wondering who it was in the Ministère de l'Intérieur who still remembered his name.

Up the next morning at the crack of dawn, Mazarelle waited until a decent hour before placing his call. Phillipe d'Aumont was the procureur of Périgueux, the d'Aumonts a well-respected family in the region. Though he'd never met the man, Mazarelle was aware that Phillipe's father had been an eminent judge and supposed the son was also well connected.

The procureur said he had been expecting his call, actually sounded pleased to receive it. Not only did he know who Mazarelle was but he was delighted to discover that Mazarelle was now working not far away in Bergerac. And close to the scene of the crime. It was reassuring, he said, to have a man of his skills, his reputation taking over the inquiry into these ghastly Taziac murders. D'Aumont promised him his complete support.

Whether it was the man's easy charm or merely his innate noblesse oblige, Mazarelle distrusted him from the start. And his skepticism was justified when the procureur's "complete support" proved vague on the numbers. Pressed by Mazarelle, d'Aumont finally committed himself to a task force of twenty judiciary police and technicians. But then removing his velvet glove, d'Aumont made it very clear that in exchange he wanted results.

"This job gets top priority. You'll have to drop everything else you're doing."

"Yes, of course."

"I want action, Inspector. Paris wants action. Remember that four foreign nationals are involved in this ugly business. The press will be after us like mad dogs. Local politicians are already complaining about how this will kill their tourist season. It's like a plague. And especially bad now when unemployment is breaking our backs. Oh yes," he added, "one thing more. Make absolutely certain you keep me informed of your progress. Don't fail me, Mazarelle."

Recognizing the peevish tone, Mazarelle liked d'Aumont a little better. From top to bottom in major cases, everybody always had a gripe. But pressure was something the inspector had learned to live with in high-profile homicide cases over the years—the biofeedback of experience—and he handled it well.

Mazarelle's next call that morning was to Duboit. Bernard Duboit was a young cop the older man liked and trusted. Though not terribly ambitious or always dependable, he was actually a pretty good cop, well liked by his friends at the commissariat who called him "Doobie," and someone whose loyalty in a pinch could be counted on, a quality that Mazarelle prized. Besides, there was something else. Bernard and his wife, Babette, had gone to Taziac high school with Martine, and when she returned from Paris—years later and seriously ill—they couldn't do enough for her. In a difficult situation they'd been very kind, unlike some of her old friends, and Mazarelle was grateful.

He knew that Bernard, who now lived in Bergerac, would probably still be at home at this early hour because he was usually late to work and always with some lame excuse: an argument with his wife, his youngest kid sick with a stomachache, the older one with an earache, or he himself wasn't feeling so top-notch. This time it was the toilet. It had backed up and shit was floating all over the bathroom floor.

"Call a plumber," the inspector advised. "Right now I want you to go to the gendarmerie in Taziac and ask Captain Béchoux for his report. I expect to have it on my desk when I get to the office. Understood?"

"What sort of report?"

"Don't be a jerk, Bernard. We're taking over the investigation of the L'Ermitage murders from the gendarmes. The procureur has instructed Captain Béchoux to prepare an account of what they've done so far. Get it for me."

"That sounds great. But why can't *you* go and get it? You're right there in Taziac."

Mazarelle sighed. Though he'd a good heart, young Duboit had some authority issues that needed tending to. There was this curious father-son element that had crept into their relationship. Maybe it was partially his own fault because he'd never had a son. Or a daughter either, for that matter.

"Just do it, Bernard. Do it for me. Okay?" He'd no desire to rub salt in Béchoux's wounds by personally showing up to take the defeated captain's sword. Duboit was still whining like a teenager forbidden to use the family car when Mazarelle hung up.

14

COMMISSARIAT DE POLICE, BERGERAC

While waiting in his office for Béchoux's report, Mazarelle spent the time setting up his special task force, a small handpicked team of cops who were at home with homicide and whom he knew he could rely on, especially Roger Vignon from Bordeaux and Jérôme Bandu from Périgueux. Vignon was a solid detail man, expert on computers and a whiz at electronic research and surveillance. Bandu was a rock. He had a reputation for great courage and the medals to prove it. With barrel-chested Bandu, what you saw was what you got. His face had two expressions: tough and tougher. A guy like that might come in handy in a case as violent as this one. For DNA and most other lab work the inspector planned to use La Police Technique et Scientifique at Toulouse, one of the five regional police technical and scientific facilities in France. It had been a good morning's work, he thought. Now where the hell was the report?

When Duboit finally ambled in just before noon, Mazarelle's face was not a welcome mat. "He was busy," Duboit was quick to explain. "Then their copy machine got jammed. I had to wait."

"So did I. Give me that."

Mazarelle dove into Béchoux's report with an eagerness that impressed the young cop. He hadn't seen the inspector so interested in anything other than his sick wife since he first came to work there.

The report said:

At 8:12 on the morning of the 25th, Gendarme Bruno Leduc received a 17 emergency police call from Georgette Chambouvard, who works part-time as a cleaning woman at L'Ermitage, a house located on the road from the quarry near the intersection with D14, not far from the village. She reported finding the dead body of one of her employers, Monsieur Reece—a vacationing American—on the floor in the kitchen. She said he had been murdered.

Gendarmes Leduc and Sigala responded. Inside the house, they discovered the body of a fully clothed man in his fifties on the kitchen floor. His hands were tied behind his back with blue plastic tape. His throat was cut and he had what looked to be multiple stab wounds in his chest. There was a great deal of blood all over the kitchen. They reported finding a wine bottle, ashes, scraps of food, and pieces of broken glass on the floor.

At first, there seemed to be no one else in the house. But when they entered the nearby bedroom, they came upon another body in a pool of blood on one of the twin beds. This time it was a middle-aged woman. She was bound—hands and feet—and gagged with the same sort of blue tape, and her throat had been cut many times. Both her legs were sliced just below the calves. She was wearing a white cotton dress and did not seem to have been sexually attacked. Except for the victim, the room appeared normal.

Nothing in the rest of the house seemed out of the ordinary until they went upstairs and found a third body in the tower. Another well-dressed middle-aged woman also bound and gagged with blue tape, her throat slit open several times and her calves slashed in exactly the same way.

The gendarmes examined the suitcases in the house, which they found in their rooms (the Reeces' suitcases downstairs, the Phillipses' in the tower) and identified their owners as Benjamin and Judith Reece from New York and Schuyler and Ann Marie Phillips from Montreal. They were also able to acquire the three victims' passports. The passport of Monsieur Phillips appears to be missing, but it should be noted that they did find the return plane tickets for all four.

As to the murder weapon or weapons—a bloody knife of

some sort—none was discovered, although the house and grounds were searched carefully.

The crime scene has been frozen and experts from the Institut de Recherche Criminelle de la Gendarmerie Nationale have gone over it. I have included their photographs herein. Other results will be made available to you as received. The victims' suitcases, passports, plane tickets, papers, and medications have been collected and placed under seal. The cadavers, as property of the case, have been removed and sent to Bergerac for autopsies and identification.

Based upon the following:

1. the ferocity of the three murders,

2. the fact that nothing appears to be stolen (note Monsieur Reece's obviously expensive wristwatch and the gold rings of the two women in the photographs),

3. the sudden disappearance of Monsieur Phillips,

4. Phillips's use of the antidepressant fluoxetine, along with a number of other prescribed drugs, and

5. my interview of Georgette Chambouvard . . .

I strongly suspect that this is a crime of the heart. The work of a jealous husband and a sick mind. We have sent out a missing person's alert for Monsieur Schuyler Phillips on *le réseau Rubis.* When we find Phillips, I believe we will have our murderer.

Except for Béchoux's signature—with its elaborate Spanish *rúbricas*—Mazarelle found the report unimpressive, long on romantic speculation and hot air, otherwise bare-bones. Not even a mention of Ali Sedak, despite the fact that he too seemed to have disappeared.

Turning to the photographs in the envelope, the inspector laid them out on his desk. The faces contorted in pain, the bound, bloodied bodies twisted like roots. Awful. How could anyone human have done this? Transformed breathing flesh into bloody knots. The ferocity of these killings was as gruesome as anything Mazarelle had ever seen in Paris. It gave him once again that weird mix of excitement, fear, revulsion, and overwhelming anger—the addictive cocktail of feelings that comes from murder.

He wondered how Phillips alone, one man with only a knife, could have controlled three adults. It was possible, he supposed. He'd seen psychos with incredible strength, ordinary-looking people possessed by demons who could hold off a half-dozen officers trying to subdue them. If it were Phillips by himself, he must have gone through the house with the fury of a cyclone. No, on second thought, more like a human neutron bomb that destroys life but leaves property untouched. In any event, it seemed unlikely to Mazarelle that the captain was right, but he'd know more once they'd tracked Phillips down.

15

L'ERMITAGE, TAZIAC

As their car groaned up the hill to L'Ermitage, Duboit reassured the inspector once again that he'd replaced the gendarmes guarding the crime scene with two of their own men. Mazarelle feared it was by no means a sure thing. But as they got out of the car, he was pleased to see Thibaud and Lambert. Maybe Bernard was growing up. The two of them sitting in front of the side door goofing off. Better there, at least, than inside tracking through all the rooms and tampering with the evidence. The house was wreathed festively in yellow police tape marking it as a crime scene. Ducking under the tape and approaching the door, Mazarelle nodded at the two men.

"Anything new?"

They shook their heads. Lambert held the door open for him. As Mazarelle pulled on his latex gloves, he asked Bernard, "And yours?"

Duboit fumbled in his pockets as if he expected to find them. Then he looked at Mazarelle sheepishly.

"You're lucky you didn't forget your shorts," griped the inspector. Reaching into his pocket, he produced another pair of latex gloves. "Here, take these. Come on."

The hallway with its barometer on the wall, antique piano, immaculate tessellated black-and-white tile floor, and vase of dazzling sunflowers was an interior decorator's notion of country living. Just the way Mazarelle remembered it. Nothing seemed to have been touched.

Preoccupied, he wasn't even aware of the smell at first. Then it seemed inescapable to him. Though Béchoux's report said all the bodies had been removed from the house for autopsy, the queasy, sickeningly sweet odor of death still hung in the air as if oozing out of the walls. An early warning system that set Mazarelle's stomach churning. Not for the first time he thought how odd it was that he'd chosen to make his living doing something that involved a smell that so repelled him. In a way perhaps this made him a little better at what he did. For eons past, an aversion to the putrid odor of rotting flesh had helped the human species survive. Mazarelle hoped it would continue working as well for him.

"Let's look at the kitchen." The inspector led the way inside.

"*Merde!*" muttered a stunned Duboit. He stood in the doorway beside his boss, his latex-gloved hands out of sight behind his back. He could feel them shaking. Even with Reece's body removed, the spattered, congealed blood clung to the walls and windows like death itself. With the windows shut, the close, fetid smell made it difficult to breathe.

Mazarelle stuffed his hands deep into his pockets and tried to crawl in after them. He wondered if he was getting too old for this job but shook off the idea, concentrating on the chalk outline of the dead body, the telltale patterns of the victim's blood. He thought of early pictures of martyred saints with their throats cut or beheaded, the blood pouring freely out of the wounds, spurting high in the air. The focus on their sacrifice. Not here.

He imagined the bound Monsieur Reece, propped up against the sink before the fatal blow. The blood splattered on the kitchen walls in a medium-high-velocity spray pattern had been thrown there by the killer's knife. Mazarelle sensed the frenzy of an obsessive ego reveling in the act. It seemed to him much too personal and violent a crime to be motivated by greed or politics, unless of course the man he was after was simply mad.

Mazarelle wondered if it was no accident that Reece was driving his friend's Mercedes when it crashed. The only accident may have been that he'd survived. "It was a miracle Ben wasn't killed," Phillips had told him. "A miracle." Wasn't that what he called it? In any event, Reece hadn't escaped this time. Perhaps, as Béchoux said, love and jealousy were at the heart of this case after all. How French, he thought glumly.

"Look there!" Duboit pointed to the set of knives hanging on the bloodstained wall. "Over there. One of them is missing."

Mazarelle hadn't noticed the empty holder. "You're right, Bernard. Good work. It could be what we're looking for. Now let's see if we can find it."

Béchoux's techies had been all over the room, leaving behind their trail of white powder. He told Bernard to check with Captain Béchoux about fingerprints.

As the inspector opened the cabinets under the sink, he was annoyed to discover a half-filled garbage bag that had obviously been overlooked. Picking gingerly through the coffee grounds, apple cores, and remnants of coq au vin, he removed the crumpled papers and flattened them out. One was a bill from Chez Doucette for 1,047 francs. Dated June 24, it was for three menus and one coq au vin, three Badoit, two bottles of Nuits-Saint-Georges, three crêpes, and a lemon tart. It looked as if on the night of the murders they had all dined at Doucette's and one of them had brought home leftovers. Either that or . . .

"What's that?" Bernard gazed at him expectantly.

"The time they left Chez Doucette—ten fifty-one p.m."

Not surprisingly, the uniforms had missed a thing or two. Mazarelle told Bernard to check the room thoroughly, see what else he could find. Meanwhile, he said, he was going out to look over the terrace before they went through the rest of the house. He didn't say that what he really wanted was some fresh air. He had an urgent need to clean out his head, put a pipe in his mouth, get the dizzying smell of death out of his nose.

Lighting up—his wooden match flaring in the summer breeze despite his cupped hands—he remembered the last time he was out here with the four of them. Clearly they were people of wealth able to afford foreign travel and rent luxury cars, houses of distinction. How civilized it had all seemed, how comfortable they were with one another despite their disagreement about the ATM pictures. He'd detected no underlying friction between any of them. But Mazarelle knew well that unlike Maigret, Poirot, or the other literary detectives, observation had never been his strength. Perhaps that was the difference between fiction and the real world. Most often, he found his intuition much more reliable. Martine had once told him that in some ways he was more like a woman than she was. It was a compliment, she said, and may have meant it. Martine, however, had a wicked sense of humor that on occasion truly surprised him.

Lost in thought, Mazarelle wasn't prepared for the scream, a sudden, loud, jagged cry that hit his ear like a chain saw. Up on the roof, a huge black crow flapped down on the red tiles and snapped its wings closed like an umbrella. High above in the seamless blue sky, a broad, cottony contrail lazily drifted apart, the plane that made it nowhere to be seen. It was a disappearing act worthy of Phillips. On the other hand, the inspector wondered, why did he leave his car and plane ticket behind? Patience, Mazarelle, patience, he cautioned. All in good time.

It was after he'd gone through the rest of the house with Bernard that the inspector began to consider the possibility of theft more strongly. The bedrooms had not been turned upside down by any means, but it was clear that someone had been through the drawers looking for something. Of course it might have been the gendarmes, but even they wouldn't have been so sloppy. Mazarelle, who didn't like to carry his cell phone, asked Bernard for his.

"My mobile? Sure, boss, you want it?"

He dialed Dr. Langlais, the forensic pathologist in Bergerac, who handled autopsies for the police. When Langlais got on the phone, the inspector told him what he wanted. Langlais didn't recall, but he said he'd check Reece's pockets. It took a while until he finally came back.

"No," he said. "Keys but no wallet. Anything else?"

"The murder weapon. How would you describe it?"

"I think there were two."

"Huh—?"

"One maybe a large double-edge hunting knife—very long. The other smaller, sharper, and pointed like a dagger."

"And the time of death?"

"All three died about the same time. Based upon the temperature and rigor of the bodies when I examined them the following day, I'd say they probably died some time before midnight of the twenty-fourth. But I can do better than that for you after I've run the potassium tests on their eyes. I've got a lot more work to do."

The inspector paused. "Anything unusual about the bodies?"

"The violence." The doctor's answer came back with the speed of a blistering net volley return. "I've never seen anything like it. Whoever killed them was right-handed and incredibly strong. A killer in complete command of his weapons. In each case, he cut through the carotid arteries and the trachea in a single blow. The murdered man's throat was torn open so deeply that his head was nearly severed from his body. The chest wounds delivered so powerfully that four of his ribs were fractured. But that wasn't enough for this killer. There were twenty-three stab wounds in the male victim alone. A few no deeper than pinpricks. He seemed to want to torture his victims first, as if he relished inflicting pain on them. Or perhaps he was after information and didn't want to kill them immediately."

"What about the women?"

"They weren't raped, if that's what you mean."

"What about their legs? The cuts?"

"Their Achilles tendons were sliced in two. They couldn't run away even if they wanted to."

"Their feet were taped together," the inspector reminded him.

Langlais didn't like being corrected. "I've got to go," he said, and hung up.

If it was information that the murderer wanted, what information was he after? The missing wallet of Monsieur Reece pointed Mazarelle in a familiar direction. Phillips wasn't the only one who had disappeared since the murders.

"Where are we going now, boss?" Bernard asked.

"I'm going to see Georgette Chambouvard. As for you, my friend, you're going to stay right here and go over every inch of this place inside and out until you find me a couple of murder weapons. I'll be back."

On the way out, he told Thibaud and Lambert to be on the lookout for Ali Sedak, the handyman. "If he shows up, keep him here. I'll be back soon."

Madame Chambouvard announced that Georgette would be down in a little while. Her daughter hadn't been feeling well ever since she discovered the dead body. And madame herself hadn't slept a wink. Who would believe such a horrible thing could happen in Taziac?

"And such nice people. Do you know yet who killed them, Inspector?"

"Not yet."

She asked if he cared for a cup of coffee and led the way into the dining room. It was small, spartan, and subfusc with a dark wooden chest for dishes and a heavy wooden table and chairs. The one picture on the wall was a framed sepia-colored marriage photograph—the bearded groom seated stiff as cardboard, his bride standing beside him. From the sunlit adjoining kitchen with its white walls wafted the delicious aroma of peaches stewing on the stove. Mazarelle had often seen madame in the village. As for her daughter, he didn't actually know her but had heard stories. A promising triathlete who had been dumped from competition for taking andros and EPOs as freely as vitamins.

Georgette, when she came down, was as tall as her mother. She had lines under her eyes, her face was drawn. She shook the inspector's hand and huskily complained that she had already told the police all she knew. Mazarelle noted the deep voice; her thin, muscular arms; the acne on her cheeks. At least she hadn't yet lost her hair to the steroids or, worse yet, gotten cancer. He felt sorry for the intense young woman, hoped that she wasn't still taking the little blue pills in pursuit of her dream.

Mazarelle said he'd only a few more questions, but before he could ask the first she began talking nonstop—describing how she had found the house locked up when she arrived, the shutters closed, and thought that everyone was still asleep. How she'd gone in through the back door and started to work, cleaning up the dining room table where the four of them had been drinking, and how it wasn't until she went into the kitchen and found Monsieur Reece on the floor, trussed up like a turkey, his blood-smeared face staring up at her with one ear hanging down by a thread, that she'd raced to get help.

The inspector, who had heard the outside door slam and the heavy footsteps approaching, turned to see Chambouvard in the doorway. He made a lot of noise for a man his size. Working in the field, the farmer had spotted the police car turning into his driveway and hurried back to the house. He'd had enough of the gendarmes hassling his daughter, first about drugs and now this. They were nosy, pushy, and always ended up costing him time or money or both.

"What now?" he demanded.

"It's okay, Papa. Only a few questions."

"Why don't you go find the murderer and leave us alone?"

The inspector rubbed his mustache and shook his head like a man with few options. "I can do this one of two ways. Either here or at the commissariat in Bergerac. Which would you prefer, mademoiselle?"

"Okay, okay." Her father knew when he was beaten. "Get on with it."

Mazarelle wanted to know whether Ali was working that morning at L'Ermitage when Georgette arrived. She said she didn't see him, and as for the day before, she had no idea because she wasn't there. He came and went as he pleased.

Chambouvard interrupted. "I know when he left. I was on my tractor working late that night in the fields and saw his car leave about ten or ten thirty."

"Could it have been a little later?"

"Maybe. I don't wear a watch and I don't punch a clock. But one thing I know for sure is that old white bug he drives."

Mazarelle turned to Georgette and asked if there were any hunting knives at L'Ermitage. She folded her arms defensively and told him no knives, no guns. The only knives were the ones in the kitchen.

"How did the two couples get along?"

"If you mean was anything going on between them the answer is yes. I'd say so. Monsieur Reece and Madame Schuyler loved the sun. They were always up at the pool together, sunning themselves."

The inspector's bushy right eyebrow rose like a circumflex.

"So what?"

"*Naked.*"

The way she said it clearly indicated that she didn't care to say any more on the subject or need to—especially while her father was watching her like the pope. Interesting, Mazarelle thought, but hardly decisive. He chalked it up to a romantic young woman and an overheated imagination thunderous with heavy breathing. The last question he asked before leaving was whether Georgette happened to notice if any of the four visitors owned a cell phone.

"Monsieur Schuyler. His wife complained about it all the time."

16

CHEZ DOUCETTE, TAZIAC

The restaurant's parking lot was almost empty when Mazarelle pulled in. The last two lunchtime customers were just leaving, one man holding the other by the arm and talking nonstop as they stood in the sun out front beside the small stone fountain. The inspector had picked a good time to speak to Doucette. He found him in the back room with his wife, rubbing his eyes. Looking up, Doucette quickly put his glasses back on and, seeing who it was, took the inspector's hand. He asked how he was and poured him a glass of wine. His wife nodded a silent greeting.

Though Sandrine Doucette had nothing against the policeman, she'd never cared for his wife. They had gone to high school together and Sandrine thought Martine was a snob. Too good for Sandrine and her friends and Taziac. And wild too. It didn't surprise her at all that as soon as Martine got knocked up, she'd dropped out of school and left for Paris to get an abortion. She had always talked about living in Paris. What Sandrine didn't expect was that one day she'd marry a cop and come back.

Mazarelle took the bill out of his pocket and asked Doucette if he recalled the four foreigners. Of course he remembered them. They were good customers who'd come several times since they arrived in Taziac. Lovely people. He called their deaths a tragedy and an awful thing for the village. The frightening news all over the newspapers, the TV. He'd heard that reservations had already been canceled at the Fleuri, which was the only hotel in town. Though Chez Doucette was a popular restaurant, he was sure business would suffer if the killer wasn't caught soon.

"Any new developments, Inspector?"

Mazarelle shook his head and pointed to the time on the bill. "Was that when the four of them left?"

"Three."

The inspector looked at him.

"They had a reservation for four, but only three of them came. Madame Phillips said that her husband wasn't feeling well. That's why she took home some dinner for him."

"I see. And the time?"

"Yes, around eleven. That would be about right."

"Did you notice anything unusual about them that night?"

"No, they all seemed to be having a good time. There was some discussion about who was going to drive home because Monsieur Reece had ordered a second bottle of wine, but there was nothing unusual about that."

Mazarelle recalled thinking when Reece came to his office that if he kept up the drinking, by the time his vacation was over his liver would look like a lace tea bag. But the way things turned out, Reece had nothing to worry about from alcohol. Go figure.

Sandrine said, "I think he gave his wife the car keys before leaving."

"How did the two men get along?"

Madame deferred to her husband.

"Fine. They were friends," he said, and shrugged. "Oh, once or twice they had their little arguments, but that happens with friends. And frankly it's hard for me to imagine anyone being angry with Phillips very long. Even the night his friend got into a loud fight with the young people at the next table, Monsieur Phillips was able to smooth things over. I can't believe he's responsible for this."

"We'll know more when we find him. What were they fighting about?"

The restaurant owner shrugged. "The usual. The noise they were making."

"Who were these young people? Did you know them?"

"Never saw them before in my life."

Returning to the house of the dead, Mazarelle noted the long black-velvet shadows cast by the trees on the front lawn of L'Ermitage and glanced at his watch. He hoped that the techies from Toulouse had shown up by now.

"Come and gone," Lambert replied, standing at the door. "They filled up their little bags with goodies and went home. The dogs you ordered from Civil Protection are still here. Thibaud went to get us some coffee."

"Where's Bernard?"

"With the dogs."

Mazarelle glanced at the shutters and recalled what Georgette had said about finding them closed and the door locked. The murderer had taken pains to make it seem as if no one was inside. Giving him more time to get away before the bodies were discovered. The cars of his victims couldn't be seen from the road. What he didn't count on, or perhaps forgot, was that Georgette would arrive early the next morning. Mazarelle would have felt much more comfortable if they'd recovered Phillips's passport along with the others.

He heard the barking before he saw the dogs. Two large German shepherds bounded out of the woods, each straining against the leash of its handler. Bernard brought up the rear, trotting behind them and puffing hard to keep up, his face red and sweaty with his effort. A young man like that, Mazarelle thought. He sounds like an old Soviet tractor. He needs more exercise. He should be in better shape.

"Any luck?"

Bernard, wiping his face, caught his breath. "The dogs found some blood on the trail and ran down to the lake. They raced around but were stumped. We all thought Phillips was hiding there. Now they're excited again."

The dogs were barking loudly at the back of the house and pawing the narrow, crooked door. One of the handlers tried the doorknob. It was locked. Then they both tried. Seeing the inspector, they asked for permission to use force.

Bernard said, "That must be the prune room, boss."

The inspector scowled at him.

"I found a note tacked up on the kitchen wall with a list of the local market days. Underneath someone had written that the prune room was kept locked at all times and no one was to go in."

"Why the hell didn't you tell me that before?"

"You just got here."

Mazarelle limped over and, rearing back with his good right leg, kicked the door in. It was dark inside, but he could see there was nobody there.

"Well, well! What have we here?"

The walls were covered with shelves filled with unlabeled, dusty, brown liter bottles. Mazarelle opened one and took a sniff, then a swallow. He wiped off his mustache. Eau-de-vie de prunes, home-made and excellent. "Have some," he said, handing the bottle around and then, putting back what was left, closed the door.

The inspector soon tired of watching the handlers with their dogs. He asked Bernard to show him the trail of blood. As they walked into the woods, Mazarelle told him that only the three victims had been at Doucette's the night of the murders. According to Phillips's wife, he wasn't feeling well.

"I don't think so," Bernard objected. He guessed that it was more likely the two men had had a fight. Phillips was angry. His wife was carrying on with his friend. He didn't go with them because he didn't want to go.

"Doucette did mention something about arguments."

"You see!"

The inspector was amused. Bernard, despite being a solid family man, was still a young stud at heart. Like Georgette, Duboit also thought that Reece and his friend's wife were lovers. As for himself, Mazarelle saw too many anomalies in the triple homicide to believe this was a *crime passionnel*.

"You and Béchoux," he said.

"What?"

"He thinks Phillips was the murderer too."

Bernard winced. He knew what his boss thought of the gendarmes.

"I could still be right, you know."

Mazarelle had a hunch that whether Phillips killed the others or not, he'd be dead when they found him. Pointing to the dark brown stain on one of the worn wooden planks covering what appeared to be a well, Mazarelle asked if the dogs had stopped here. Bernard nodded. "We looked into the well but didn't see anything, so no one went down."

Mazarelle blew out his cheeks in disgust. "Go get me a long heavy rope and a flashlight. Hurry!" he shouted, as he began pulling away the planks. Their job would be that much harder the later it got.

When he uncovered the well, Mazarelle couldn't tell if it was dry. He knelt down on the ground and peered in, trying to see the bottom, but it was lost in shadows. There was a trickling noise coming from deep inside as if the heart of the earth had a leaky valve. He tossed in a rock and heard a splash. Water—but not much from the sound of it. When Bernard came back he didn't have a rope at all.

"Where did you get *that*?"

"Up by the pool." He dumped the heavy coil of green hose on the ground, glad to be rid of it. "I couldn't find a rope."

Mazarelle shook his head. Quickly he managed to tie one end around the trunk of a nearby tree. "Where's the flashlight?"

Duboit was taking it out of his jacket pocket when his boss stopped him. "Keep it. You'll need it down there." He tied the other end of the hose around Bernard's waist, hoping it would hold. "I double knotted it, but don't let go till you're down."

"Me?" It was a touching cry, somewhere between a whine and a bleat.

"Come on, Bernard. We don't have all day. Move your ass."

"Why can't *you* do it?"

"Because I weigh more than one hundred twenty kilos. I'd pull you in after me."

"You're stronger than I am."

"Now you're getting the idea." Mazarelle picked up the hose and braced himself to lower the young cop. "Please, Bernard. Don't try my patience. Just go."

Clutching the hose with both hands, the white-knuckled Duboit stepped into the well and Mazarelle, hand over hand, slowly lowered him down.

"Not so fast!"

As the coil unwound, Mazarelle feared the hose wasn't going to be long enough. It was then he felt Bernard touch bottom.

"It's wet down here."

The beam of Bernard's flashlight darted over the surface. Mazarelle followed it, trying to help in the search, when he heard him cry out, "There's something here . . ."

"Tell me."

"Hold on— It's a knife."

"Aha!"

"A large one."

"Don't touch it! Use the gloves. Put on the gloves first."

"Okay."

"Is there another knife, a smaller one, nearby?"

"No. Come on, boss, get me out of here. I'm freezing my ass off."

Taking pity on his young assistant, the inspector hauled him up with his prize. But it wasn't a knife at all. To Mazarelle, who had done his military service after the war, it looked more like an old World War II bayonet. A strange murder weapon—if that's what it was—in 1999. What seemed promising to him, in fact really cheered him up, was that it must have landed at the bottom on a mound of mud, and, despite having been down there for at least several days, the bloodstains on the blade were still visible.

Thibaud returned from the village with a couple of cans of beer but had to leave at once for Toulouse. The inspector's instructions to the PTS lab were to run fingerprint and DNA tests on the bayonet as soon as possible. Taking a sip of Thibaud's beer, Mazarelle handed the rest to Duboit, who was talking to Lambert. He glanced toward the barn, where the dogs' barking had turned leather-lunged and insistent. They had found something.

The three of them hurried inside the barn, where, in the storage room at the back, the dogs excitedly scratched and sniffed at a large wicker basket. No sooner did their handlers throw open the lid than the dogs—their tails whipping back and forth—were up on their hind legs peering into the basket. It was empty. Without a hint of disappointment or a backward glance, they scampered away.

The inspector started to leave and stopped.

"What's the matter?" Bernard asked.

Mazarelle, with an effort, got down on his knees. He ran his fingers over the curved scrape marks etched into the stone floor. Breathing heavily, he straightened up and examined the wall behind the wicker basket. Although the door was practically seamless, the outline of it—even in the dim light—was visible if you knew where to look. And the door, he shrewdly realized, was why the basket was bolted to the wall behind. Mazarelle pulled on the handle, but the basket didn't budge.

"Let me help."

Mazarelle and Bernard each took an end and tugged at it hard, but they were out of synch. The basket quivered and creaked noisily. The wall to which it was attached appeared solid and unyielding. Although Bernard was eager to try again, Mazarelle brushed him aside. He wrapped his big hands around the handle, planted his legs, and yanked with all his might, falling back as the basket tore away from the wall.

"*Salaud!*" Picking himself up with Bernard's help, he brushed off his clothes and eyed the basket disagreeably. The inspector was certain that the dogs had been on the right track. What they were looking for had to be right behind the basket. But who expects a sealed room with no windows in a barn?

"Give me your flashlight," he told Bernard, and sent him out to the car to see if there was a floodlight in the trunk.

With the aid of Bernard's small flashlight, Mazarelle went over every inch of the wall. He tapped sharply on the surface with his fingertips like a doctor checking his patient's lungs. It sounded hollow—a hollow chamber. Could Phillips still be hiding inside? If there was no other way, Mazarelle was fully prepared to have his men tear down the entire wall.

"Nothing in the trunk," Bernard announced. "Should I go back to the commissariat and get—"

"Never mind. Come on. There must be another way in."

Going outside and around to the rear of the barn, Mazarelle

found what he was after. Bernard had said that in Taziac old barns like this one sometimes had granaries, and sure enough there was an outside chute.

"See. I told you."

"So you did."

The young cop saw the look on his boss's face. "Okay, okay, I'm going." He pulled open the chute and peered in. "Do you think I can fit in there?"

Behind him, Mazarelle drew back. The familiar sickeningly sweet stench that poured out was overpowering. "Like a prick between a *putain*'s legs."

"Very funny."

"Here, take this." The inspector returned his flashlight. "Now hurry. Hurry!"

Putting his head and shoulders into the chute, Bernard inched his way along, crawling through and climbing down. He turned on his flashlight, curious to see what was inside. The place stank like an abattoir. Awful!

"Well?" demanded his boss from outside.

"It stinks in here!"

"I noticed. Hold your nose. Anything else?"

Bernard moved his light beam slowly around the room.

"Well? Well?"

"There's something here."

"Okay, okay. What is it?"

Duboit hadn't spotted the body at first because it was sprawled facedown in a corner. Shouting to his boss, he told him what he'd found and reported that the entrance was bolted from within. Duboit lifted the wooden bar. After much effort, he managed to push open the door. Mazarelle was already there, puffing on his pipe and, wreathed in a cloud of smoke, impatiently waiting to get in.

The light flooding through the open door washed over the blood-splattered floor. Viewed from the back, the motionless figure stretched out on the floor and wearing sandals, chinos, and a blue polo shirt might have been napping. The inspector, holding the man's rigid arm, turned the body over to see who it was. There was no doubt he was dead.

"Jesus!" The whites of Bernard's eyes gleamed.

The corpse's head resembled a swollen pomegranate from which crows had pecked out the crimson berries and eaten one whole side.

"Where's his face?" Bernard asked.

"Blown away, I'm afraid. A shotgun will do that. And whoever killed him popped off both barrels at point-blank range. He wanted to make damn sure he did the job."

"You mean you don't think Phillips killed the others and then committed suicide?"

"Don't be dumb, Bernard. If it was suicide, where's the gun? What happened to the cartridges?"

"But the door was barred from the inside. How did the killer get out?"

"Same way you got in—through the chute."

Duboit wasn't satisfied. "It doesn't make any sense. If the killer had a shotgun, why didn't he use it on the other people he murdered?"

"I don't know. Perhaps," Mazarelle suggested, "there were two murderers."

"You think?"

He shrugged. In any event, he'd been right about Phillips. Mazarelle knew that when they found him Phillips would be dead. "Come on. Let's get out of here before I lose my appetite."

"No, wait a minute." Bernard had an idea. "Maybe this isn't Phillips at all."

"It's him. Didn't you see the logo on his shirt? 'Gray Rocks. Mont-Tremblant.' As we know, Monsieur Phillips is from Montreal. And furthermore . . ." The inspector reached into Phillips's right-hand pocket. He tried the left one. Then his two back pockets. When he straightened up, he seemed genuinely disappointed not to have found his wallet, his passport. Nothing was easy in this case.

17

CENTRE HOSPITALIER DE BERGERAC

The main hospital in Bergerac was not far from the commissariat, and before work the next day Mazarelle dropped in to see Dr. Langlais. A small man and, despite having slept only a few hours the previous night, ramrod straight. They greeted each other warmly, Langlais's hand almost lost in the bearish paw of his visitor. Langlais had good news for the inspector, who had mentioned fluoxetine when the body was brought in. Fortunately, as the doctor explained, fluoxetine has a long half-life.

"Which makes a very hard job, of course, somewhat easier." The body had tested positive for the antidepressant. "I think you may have your missing Phillips."

"Aha." Clearly pleased, Mazarelle thanked him for laboring through the night. But before he let the doctor get on with his work, he had one more question.

"Was Phillips murdered before or after the others?"

"Hard to tell. Given the condition of the body, he probably was killed on the twenty-fourth too, the same evening as the others. As for the time, the three of them died shortly after dinner. Based on my tests of their eyes, however, not before ten thirty p.m."

Close enough. Mazarelle knew it had to be after 10:51 p.m. but held his tongue. He didn't think the doctor would care for a second opinion.

"As for Monsieur Phillips," he went on, "my guess is he was murdered before that. In fact, based on the contents of his stomach, I'd say that he didn't have any dinner at all."

Which to Mazarelle meant that, despite appearances, the food

Madame Phillips brought back that night from Chez Doucette was never touched by her husband.

"You sure of that?"

Langlais glanced at him in annoyance, but before he could say what he thought, there was a knock at the door. The doctor went to answer it and, obviously impressed, added a dash of sugar to his voice. His visitor had come to see the bodies of the victims. Langlais asked if she knew Inspector Mazarelle.

"Only by reputation."

He introduced them. Though Mazarelle had had little to do with Christine Leclerc, he certainly knew who she was. A well-dressed, middle-aged woman, her intelligent eyes peered at the world from behind large, round glasses. She was wearing a cerulean Chanel—straight shoulders and indigo buttons down the front—her long black hair pulled back into a tight chignon. *Madame le juge* was more chic than most of her colleagues. Her wealthy family owned a shipping company in Bordeaux. He'd heard that she was serious, tough-minded, and had a girlfriend who taught in town at the Conservatoire de Musique. She was also, she told him, the newly appointed investigating magistrate in the L'Ermitage murder case, having just been assigned by the procureur. She too wanted to be kept fully informed of developments.

"Yes, of course."

"How is the investigation going?"

A cop's natural mistrust of a *juge d'instruction* made him hesitate. Folding his arms defensively, the inspector drew himself up. "Still early days. But we're making some progress," he confidently assured her. No reason to go overboard. "We have a weapon PTS is testing that may prove of some importance. Now you really must excuse me, madame. I have to get back to my men. Dr. Langlais will fill you in on the latest news." Taking leave of the owl-eyed Madame Leclerc, he promised her, "I'll be in touch."

When Mazarelle turned into the driveway of the commissariat, the courtyard was crowded with newspaper reporters and TV cameramen from Canal Plus and France 2. It felt like old times to the inspector. Driving around to the rear, he went in the back way. But before he could get into his own office and phone downstairs to his task force to find out what was going on, Rivet caught sight of him. Calling Mazarelle into his office, he told him to sit down and slammed the door shut. His blue dress-uniform jacket, hanging on the back of the door and worn only on ceremonial occasions, flapped angrily. Rivet was not a happy young man. He marched to the window and pointed down at the noisy crowd of reporters.

"What's that all about?"

"Damned if I know. I just got here."

"They seem to think there's been a new development in your case. Is that true?"

"Well, yes, as a matter of fact." Mazarelle told him about discovering Phillips's body. It wasn't the first time that reporters seemed to know almost as much as he did about a case. He couldn't understand how they'd found out so quickly.

"I don't care how they found out. Get rid of them. They're turning this place into a circus. And, oh yes . . ." A sour look crossed the commissaire's angry face. "That sign you put up downstairs on the door of the meeting room I gave you."

"The sign? You mean Mazarelle's Murder Squad?"

Rivet squirmed at the sound of it. "Couldn't you tone that down a little?"

"It is what it is. It's not a book club, sir." Mazarelle felt himself losing it.

"Damn it! You know what I mean, Inspector. Change it."

Mazarelle wondered if Rivet was already regretting having helped set him up here in the homicide business. Odd, he thought, glancing at the large photograph of Chirac on the wall behind his boss. It was curious how much the young commissaire—with his hands clasped behind his back and that same pained look and tight-lipped smile—resembled the president of the republic. Was Rivet grooming himself for higher office?

Downstairs there were more than a dozen reporters from all over France milling about in the courtyard. Everything from *La Dépêche du Midi* and *Nice-Matin* to *Le Monde*. Mazarelle waved to Jacques Gaudin, who worked for the local edition of *Sud Ouest*. He also recognized Hervé Stein, an old acquaintance from Paris, who covered crime stories for *L'Express*. Unlike Gaudin, Stein had the prosperous look and self-importance of someone who wrote for a major national publication.

Mazarelle was about to reach into his jacket for his pipe when he remembered something an old girlfriend had once told him. She'd seen a picture of him in a newspaper and laughed because he looked more like some dotty old professor, she said, than a hotshot cop.

The inspector thrust his hands in his pockets and exchanged nods with Stein. Despite what his critics once said about him at his old commissariat in Paris—that he was dying to be a celebrity, a TV star, a cop who would do for crime what Bernard Pivot had done for books—Mazarelle genuinely liked reporters and they seemed to like him. Maybe that was because he didn't bullshit them. He said what he could and knew when to keep his mouth shut. This time they wanted to know if he'd found another body, and he acknowledged that he had. After that, the questions came thick and fast.

Calm as ever in front of their cameras, he waited for them to finish before cherry-picking the ones he'd answer. "It was the dogs," he began. "The way they ran into the barn and pawed at this large wicker basket. It turned out to be empty, but I knew they were on to something. Not long after that, we found the body."

This last victim, Mazarelle explained, had been tentatively identified as Schuyler Phillips, the fifty-nine-year-old American husband of one of the murdered women. Phillips was the CEO of the Canadian corporation Tornade. Unlike the three others who were murdered in different rooms of the main house at L'Ermitage, the fourth victim was discovered in the nearby barn. Phillips was sprawled out dead on the floor inside a hidden, windowless chamber behind a barred door, the entry to which was concealed by a wicker basket.

"Hold on!" Stein interrupted. "You mean the door was barricaded from the inside?"

"Correct. Now if I may continue . . ."

Earlier investigations, he pointed out—that is before he was asked to take over the case by the procureur of Périgueux—had speculated that the missing Phillips, perhaps for personal reasons, might have been responsible for the other three deaths. It was obvious now that the industrialist had not committed suicide but had been killed with great savagery. In Mazarelle's opinion, Phillips at the time of his murder was attempting to hide from his attacker, a ruthless killer using a shotgun at very close range.

Yet the puzzling question remained: How did the killer get into this barricaded secret room where Phillips sought refuge? The inspector guessed that he must have known that years ago it had been a granary. Once he'd located the outside opening of the old chute, the rest was simple. He entered and left without a trace, leaving behind nothing but a corpse. Although this wasn't exactly true, there was no reason for Mazarelle to tell them everything.

As of now, the inspector acknowledged that these four murders were unquestionably the most brutal and mysterious crimes to have occurred in this peaceful region since the war. But regardless of whether the murderer was a deranged random predator or this was a revenge killing by a person out of their past or simply a crime of greed, he promised that the outstanding special task force he'd assembled would track him down.

"Above all," he concluded, "I urge the public to remain calm. There is *absolutely* no cause for general alarm."

As Mazarelle hurried back to his office, he wished he could be sure of that. His phone was ringing when he got upstairs.

"Mazarelle," he said, a little out of breath.

It was Roger Vignon with more news about Schuyler Phillips that he'd dug up on his computer. "Did you know his reputation for being ruthless with business rivals?"

"Where did that come from?"

"I found a profile of him in the Canadian magazine *Maclean's* that claimed he was a sweetheart socially but a monster to do business with."

"Yeah? Which one of his friends said *that*?"

"Phillips's second-in-command, a guy by the name of Jean-Paul Dargelier. He was pretty open about what happened. Boasted that his boss took Duncan Cross, the big shot American billionaire, to the cleaners. Muscled him out of a large investment he held in production subsidiaries of Tornade. And Cross was only one of several competitors who couldn't stand Phillips's guts."

"What are you suggesting?"

"Maybe one of them hated him enough to hire someone to tear up his ticket."

"What about the other three?"

"Oh yeah . . . Right, I'm working on that."

"Fine. Meanwhile, do me a favor and get me the phone company records for L'Ermitage. I want to know all the calls that were made to and from there since they arrived. But *especially* the night of the murders."

18

CALPE, SPAIN

outh of Valencia, near the little Spanish former fishing village of Calpe, there is a spit of land that runs into the sea and ends in a huge thousand-foot-high exclamation point known as the Rock of Ifach. It can be seen for miles up and down the Costa Blanca but dominates the view from the luxurious sunbaked houses opposite, high up on the hills. Unlike the other residences, traditional Mediterranean-style buildings in stucco with tile roofs, Max Kämpe's modern villa in the Mies van der Rohe mode made no compromises with its setting—three enormous slabs of concrete and glass resting on top of one another with terraces jutting out in different directions, all of it enclosed by a high wall. The sort of place that promised privacy and, along with the panoramic views of crystal blue sea and mountains, a less stressful way of life.

Reiner had almost forgotten how laid-back it was here and how good Pilar's cooking was. The simple lunch of fish and rice, a local favorite, had been delicious. Naked, he stretched out on the deck chair under a tall date palm by the pool and poured himself a coppery-amber glass of Carlos I, the best brandy Spain had to offer. Raising the fragrant snifter to his lips, he took a sip. "Hmmmm, liquid gold. *Wunderbar!*" It was good to be back free and uncluttered, but best of all to be out of France.

Of all his personas, Max Kämpe was Reiner's favorite. He enjoyed Kämpe's style, his villa, his cars, but they were hardly a weakness. Simply another safe house, another setting, another mask to put on for a few days or weeks while doing business before moving on. He also enjoyed the three-hour Spanish lunches but, as he'd discovered not long after he bought the house, more as a concept than a fact. For the truth was that though it always took him a while to unwind when he arrived, he soon became annoyed by the waste of time. Perhaps that was why he never stayed here very long.

Reiner had been in Spain three days now and still couldn't relax. But the Spanish sun helped, soaking into his bones and his hair, which was now washed back to its original blond. The sun felt as if it were purifying him, burning all that he'd been through out of his flesh, his mind. And his headaches, thankfully, seemed to have gone. But not the black dreams. What had started out as a simple enough job that should have ended with a run-of-the-mill car crash—not so different from others he'd done—had gone wrong and turned into a sloppy bloodbath.

How could that have happened when everything seemed to be falling into place for him the night he returned to L'Ermitage? All of them gone except Phillips. It was a perfect setup. But when he searched the house, Phillips wasn't there, or in the barn either, it seemed at first. Then he found him. The two twelve-gauge number one shells in the shotgun were all Reiner had to work with, but that was all he needed. And it didn't take long. He was on his way out when the three friends unexpectedly came back. He'd been too busy inside the barn to hear their car arrive. Call it bad luck all around. It wasn't that he was unprepared for emergencies or too rigid or lacked the imagination to improvise if need be, but the unexpected always made Reiner nervous, angry. The bastards! They could have easily ruined everything for him. Reiner slipped back inside the barn before anyone saw him and found what he wanted in the Arab's toolbox. As they got out of the car, he stood there, blocking their way. The look on their faces was priceless. Herding the three of them into the house at gunpoint, he told them to shut the fuck up and walk, almost as if he himself believed that his shotgun was loaded.

What followed still remained jumbled in his mind. Maybe because killing with a blade at close range was as trackless and alien to him as the Arctic. Which explained, he supposed, why he could barely recall exactly what came next. Except for his growing sense of exhilaration, fear, disgust, and fury as he went from one to the next in a frenzy of blood and muffled cries. Controlling events had always been central to everything Reiner was and did, and here in an instant he'd broken free of the gravity of habit. Free of the limits he'd known all his life. Excited beyond his wildest imagination, he felt amazingly liberated, as if falling headlong through space in a mindless rage for the next blow, the next sound.

"Another bottle, Senor Kämpe?"

He looked up. It was Pilar, her eyes fixed appreciatively on his bare genitals as if they were being exhibited at the Prado. Reiner couldn't care less. If she wanted to look, let her gaze to her heart's content. She needed a little sex in her life, poor woman. *Aber*, he thought, *Vorsicht Kunst*. Drive her out of her mind.

He wondered if at that hour he could reach Spada in Zurich. He told Pilar to bring him his red phone, but her mind was elsewhere.

"*En seguida!*" he snapped, and she scurried away.

Reiner's housekeeper had little education, but she wasn't stupid and ordinarily did what she was told. Exactly what he wanted. A single woman in her forties with a birthmark that covered one whole side of her face like a purple ink blot. He thought it a plus when hiring her—assuming that she was a quiet spinster—but as he learned, her disfigurement didn't stop Pilar from having admirers. Rodrigo was the sleazebag who nearly cost Pilar her job. The three-car garage on the property held Max Kämpe's black BMW; his red Ferrari; and, his personal preference, the Bentley Azure. One day, her beloved Rodrigo took the Bentley out for a joyride, and when he was stopped for driving under the influence, he of course didn't have the registration. The *policía* called the house and told Pilar what had happened.

Reiner, who was away at the time, would probably never have heard of the incident if Rodrigo had been alone in the car instead of with another woman. When he did hear, Reiner was livid. He warned her never again to bring her drunken lovers into his house. He said if he found another Rodrigo there, he'd cut off his nuts and kick her out on her ass. The well-paid Pilar had no intention of losing a good job. After that, he had no more trouble with her. That is, except for the budgies.

It happened one perfumed night when the air was filled with guitars and the scent of Valencia orange blossoms. Restless and hungry, he'd gotten out of bed and gone down to the kitchen for something to eat. It was then he heard them, the honeyed voices. They were coming from Pilar's room.

"*Mi bella. Mi amor. Eres tan caliente, querida. Haz el amor conmigo, mi corazón.*"

Enraged, Reiner burst through her door like a battering ram. The two of them stared at each other in dumb amazement. The room was full of caged birds. The uncaged yellow-and-gray one in bed with her, who had been doing all the yapping, flew up to the light fixture on the ceiling crying, "Pilar! Pilar, *mi amor!*" As Pilar attempted to coax it down, the bird cooed, "*Bésame, guapa.*" Reiner told the housekeeper to get her gabby friend back in his cage pronto and shut him up, or he would. Storming out of the room, he slammed the door behind him. Better birds than boyfriends, he thought, and never mentioned her roommates again.

Pilar returned with the red phone and he snatched it out of her hands, dialed Zurich, and waited for the bank to connect him to Numbered Accounts. Reiner recognized the bank officer's velvety tones immediately. "Ah, Monsieur Spada." He gave the manager the number of his account and asked him to check on the latest deposit. Spada was not gone very long.

"You're sure of that?"

"Oh yes. Quite sure."

Reiner felt the muscles at the base of his neck throb. They were tight as clamps. As soon as he'd left Taziac—his job finished—he'd called the phone number in Paris that Pellerin gave him with the news. Blond said he'd tell him. But that was three days ago, and the rest of his money still hadn't been deposited. He loathed any delays in payments, any changes or irregularities in agreed-upon financial arrangements. Reiner jumped up and hurried into his bedroom where he slipped into his tennis whites, grabbed his racquet, wallet, keys, his expensive aviator shades. Calls like the one he had to make required a public phone, and Benidorm was only a short ride away.

The Bentley, with its top down and whisper-smooth 6.75-liter V-8 engine, was a joy to drive and could hit over 230 kph if there were any decent roads in the area to drive on. He took a deep breath. The smell of the magnolia-white leather seats, the lamb's-wool rugs, the walnut trim, everything about his Bentley soothed. So did the CD he was playing, the debut album of Oliver Schmid's German sextet Lacrimas Profundere, an amusing heavy-metal band full of gothic groans and heart-tugging weltschmerz. It took the edge off how rankled he felt. He couldn't bear an unreliable client.

Entering Benidorm, Reiner pulled up in front of the Gran Hotel Delfin, which faced the beach, and got out. The door of the Bentley closed with the satisfying solidity of a bank vault. From the house phone on the front desk, he notified Senor Rincón that he'd be out on the court in fifteen minutes. The Delfin's tennis pro was always available for a fast set with Senor Kämpe, followed by a bracing single-malt whiskey chaser in the bar. Just off the lobby, Reiner went to the public phone booth and placed his racquet on the floor. Dialing the number in Paris, he waited for what seemed to him a long time before Pellerin picked up the receiver.

"Ah, so you're there. Good. I wouldn't want to have missed you a second time. Did Blond tell you I called?"

"Yes, of course."

"Well?"

"Well what?"

"Don't jerk me around. I took care of your business. Now it's your turn. Where's the rest of my money?"

There was a long pause.

"I don't like the early reports," Pellerin broke out. "We asked for one soloist, not a whole damn quartet. Jesus, what were you thinking of?"

"Nothing to get exercised about. It was necessary to make a few last-minute improvisations. You wanted terminal, and that's what you got. But don't worry. There'll be no extra charge."

"Fine. But we also wanted restraint, discretion, no questions asked, and instead Taziac has already turned into a horror show—an international incident. What's wrong with you? Didn't you understand what we expected?"

"Calm down. You have nothing to worry about."

"You can't be serious. The story is all over the newspapers, the radio, the TV."

"Mere blips on the radar screen. That will all be gone in a few days when they arrest the murderer."

"What?" Pellerin sounded startled. "What's that supposed to mean?"

"Don't strain your mind. Trust me. You'll see," Reiner assured him. "I told you a few days."

Pellerin found the German's telephone voice as chilling as the accounts he'd read of the gruesome murders. Hard to reconcile with the handsome young man he'd met in Berlin. Of course he'd known there was a sinister side to Reiner. But this man was all sinister. Pellerin hated to have him in his ear.

"I hope you're right, monsieur. Okay, a few days. We'll expect a call from you then. And," Pellerin added, "that's when you'll get your final installment." There was a dead silence at the other end of the line that he didn't care for at all. He wondered if his caller was still there.

When he spoke again, Reiner's voice was ice. "If I don't get my money, I'll do better than give you a call." He hoped the Frenchy understood this as a threat, because it was.

19

THE OLD MILL, TAZIAC

On the south edge of Taziac a tiny stream trickled past an old stone water mill surrounded by dust-covered vines. There were few in town who could remember when it was still working. The baby out front slept soundly in the sun despite the large green flies buzzing around its carriage. Even the noise of the police car driving up failed to awaken it. Thérèse, who had been hanging the baby's wash on the line in back, dried her hands and came hurrying out, eager to see who it was. When she saw the two cops her expression changed.

Mazarelle announced that they were looking for Ali Sedak. "Is this where he lives?"

Thérèse nodded and tried to keep calm. Out of the corner of her eye, she saw Ali's face peering from the window.

"Is he here?"

"What do you want?"

Following her glance, the inspector abruptly turned his head and spotted Ali ducking out of sight.

"There he is," said Duboit.

"What do you want with him?" she shouted.

Mazarelle took her gently by the elbow and led her toward the door. "Let's go inside."

As the policemen entered the stone house, Ali, who was fully dressed and stretched out on top of the unmade bed, propped himself up on a pillow and demanded, "Who are you?"

"Police," said Mazarelle.

"That doesn't give you the right to barge into my home. Get out!"

"Are you Ali Sedak?"

"What do you want?"

"Shut up and answer the inspector's question."

To the young cop, Ali, who hadn't shaved in several days, had the look of a religious fanatic, a terrorist. Duboit didn't like anything about this messy setup—the cocky little Arab stretched out on his backside, his French wife (or more likely *poule*), their half-breed bastard, and the place reeking of couscous and merguez and pot. It smelled to him like a Maghreban whorehouse.

Mazarelle held out his hand. "Your papers, *s'il vous plaît*." He glanced at the plastic card Ali gave him and, returning it, asked what he did for a living.

"I'm in the construction business."

Duboit snorted derisively. "Handyman."

"And where are you working now?" the inspector asked.

"At the villa L'Ermitage, not far from the gravel quarry."

"You mean where the recent murders occurred?"

"What murders?" Ali looked both confused and indignant. "I know nothing about any murders."

"You're joking," Duboit sneered. "Do you think we're idiots?"

Mazarelle gave him a squelching look and, clamming up, Bernard folded his arms angrily. The inspector turned back to Ali.

"On the evening of the twenty-fourth, four foreigners who were living at the villa were murdered."

"Oh, really. You don't say?" Ali sounded not especially interested. "I know nothing about it."

"Were you working there that night?"

Outside the house, the baby began to howl. "Will you shut him up?" Ali told Thérèse.

She ran out the door and returned with the momentarily quieted baby in her arms, though the cute, olive-skinned, dark-eyed child soon began to fuss again, screaming as if in pain.

"Something wrong with him?" Mazarelle asked her.

Ali jumped out of bed and in one fluid movement was at Thérèse's side. "Here," he held out his hands. "Give him to me."

No sooner was the infant cradled in his father's arms than he stopped crying, started to suck his fingers, and went back to sleep. Mazarelle was struck by how much the two of them resembled each other. He liked sleeping babies. Awake all they did was bawl and shit.

"Well," he said, "were you there that night?"

"I don't remember. I work when I want to and leave when I want to."

"Why didn't you go to work the next day?"

"My back—I hurt my back. I could barely move. I've been in bed ever since."

"You're better now, I see."

Ali avoided the inspector's eyes. It was plain that his little game was up.

"Okay. So I knew about the murders," he admitted. "So what? I didn't say so because I didn't want to get involved. Thérèse told me what happened. Didn't you?" he said to her.

The look that passed between them was an electric current draining the color from her face. "Yes," she told the inspector, "a terrible thing." She had heard about the murders on the radio.

Mazarelle said to Ali, "Your white VW was seen leaving L'Ermitage very late on the night of the crime. What time was it?"

"Maybe around ten thirty or eleven. It was late, but there was a job to finish. Phillips liked to help me with the guesthouse I'm building. We were putting down a new floor."

"Where were his friends?"

"They went to eat somewhere. I left before they came back."

"You're *sure* about that?"

"Sure I'm sure. I know nothing about any of these murders. *Nothing*," he insisted, his voice rising and the cords popping out in his neck.

"And where did you go when you left?"

"I went home. Where do you think I went? I got back here about twenty minutes later and went right to bed. My back was killing me. Didn't I, Thérèse?"

"That's right. He came home and went straight to bed."

Mazarelle took out one of the surveillance photos that the bank manager of the BNP in Bergerac had given him and asked if she recognized the face of the man. Ali watched Thérèse anxiously as she studied the picture, her fingers trembling. She shook her head as if she didn't trust her voice.

"And you?"

Ali glanced at the photo and quickly handed it back. No one he knew.

"All right, thanks." Mazarelle looked for Bernard and spotted him near the rear door. "Let's go."

"Look what I found."

Pulling out a handkerchief, his boss took the rifle from him. Mazarelle thought Bernard had found a shotgun by the excited tone of his voice, but it was a pump-action .22.

"Is this yours?" he asked Ali.

Thérèse said, "It belonged to my father."

Mazarelle promised to return the gun when he was through with it. "By the way," he asked Ali, "you don't own a bayonet, do you?"

"A bayonet! No, why?"

"Just wondering. Sorry to bother you. Nice earrings," the inspector complimented Thérèse, as he walked past her on the way out. Silver teardrops with an intricate engraved design. "New?" he asked.

Thérèse, her cheeks glowing like burning embers, nodded. "A present," she said softly.

"Nice."

Duboit could no more hide his emotions than a lion could mute its roar. He was seething. He couldn't understand why they weren't bringing in the son of a bitch for questioning. As soon as his boss put the rifle into the trunk and got in the car, Duboit said, "You don't honestly believe that he wasn't there when the three of them came back from the restaurant, do you? They probably discovered him with Phillips's dead body or going through the house searching for loot, and it cost them their lives."

Mazarelle started the car and put it in gear. "It's possible."

"Then why the hell aren't we taking him in?"

"Jesus, Bernard, take it easy! There's work to be done first before we can do that. You get so excited, you'll end up bald as a hubcap before you're thirty."

"That's not funny." Sensitive about his hairline, Duboit stared out the car window and sulked.

Mazarelle barely noticed. He was busy going over in his mind what had just happened with those two. Sedak was lying as fast as he could, and his woman was frightened enough to swear to anything. But why? he wondered. As to the pump-action .22, there was a possibility that, even if it didn't kill anybody, it was at the scene of the crime, held by an accomplice. As soon as they got back to Bergerac, he wanted it gone over for prints, for whether or not it had recently been fired, and checked for ownership.

The inspector pulled into the parking lot in front of the small cream-colored stucco building with the mansard roof. The Crédit Agricole was the only bank in Taziac.

"Why are we stopping here?"

"I want the tape from the surveillance camera for the ATM over there." He indicated the machine to the left of the front door. It was the only ATM in town and the closest one to where Sedak lived. Though he'd have to have been a fool, it was possible. "Tell Desforges, the manager, it's for me. I'll pick you up later at Madame Charpentier's for some coffee and cake. I've got an errand to run."

Duboit made a face and unlocked the door. Before getting out, he asked, "Do you think he stole those earrings?"

His boss shrugged. "Who knows? Maybe. We'll see."

"What about the gold chain?"

"What chain?"

"The gold one he was wearing under his shirt."

Though annoyed with himself for missing it, Mazarelle gave no indication as he elbowed his young friend out the door. "Don't worry, Bernard. We'll bring him in."

On the road out of town—not far from the gendarmerie and a few kilometers beyond it—was the small Taziac cemetery. They'd passed it on their way to the old water mill. Mazarelle had felt a little guilty about not stopping. It was a while since he'd paid Martine a visit.

The cemetery, a bleak patch of earth even on a bright, sky blue day like this one, was surrounded by a dreary six-foot cinder block wall, gray and dirt streaked. Parking next to the pickup truck in front, Mazarelle opened the squeaking rusty metal gate and headed toward the cypress tree in the center, his lame foot dragging through the gravel. Down the row to the right of the mournful solitary cypress, Martine's mother and father were buried near the far wall beneath a stone sandbox filled with gravel. Close beside them was the grave of her sister, a dutiful wife and daughter even in death. The grave of Mazarelle's wife, the black sheep of the family, was at the far end of the line.

Martine had never told him—or anyone for that matter—that she had a daughter who lived in Taziac with her elderly friend Louise. That was why she'd chosen to come back here to die. But Mazarelle wasn't a detective for nothing. Besides, the reason didn't make any difference. He loved Martine and that was enough. If she didn't want to say anything about Gabrielle, that was her affair. The past was the past and the hell with it. Another dysfunctional family just like his own.

One day Mazarelle's father, Guy, a serious boozer and womanizer, had walked out of their house to go to work and never came back. An actor—a large, handsome man before all his drinking and whoring caught up with him—Guy was a peacock who fancied himself a star but was really only a bit player. A good voice though, a big resonant stage voice that reminded one critic of the American performer Paul Robeson. He made a career out of that review, dining out on his part as the Fire Chief in Ionesco's *Bald Soprano*.

An impossible snob, Guy regarded his son Paul's choice of career as a flic an embarrassment. And his choice of a bride—a young woman from the provinces who worked in Paris as an *esthéticienne* at some *institut de beauté*—seemed so shameful to the old boy that though he swore to be at their wedding, he never showed. No surprise Mazarelle had little love of families.

Glancing down at his wife's grave, Mazarelle didn't know why he even bothered to come. This stark, gray, dreary place represented everything that Martine hated in life and, except perhaps for a few scraps of her genetic code, had nothing to do with her. He wished he'd brought some flowers. Maybe he'd come by in a few months on Toussaint and bring her some carnations. Martine loved carnations. When they first met, she also loved to hear him talk about his work, but that was a long time ago. After their marriage, his shoptalk seemed to bore her.

Nevertheless, he thought that if she were alive, she'd be glad to see him. Might even think he was looking well. Much better than the last few times he'd been there. Would probably have asked if that meant he'd found himself a new girlfriend, her teasing, adorable laughter the wind rustling through the giant cypress. He tamped down his tobacco and lit up, the smoke billowing over his head. Though he'd no flowers for Martine, Mazarelle did have some news. I've got a new case that I'm working on, he told her. A multiple murder case. She'd have guessed that was it. There was hardly anything that cheered him up as much as murder.

And why not? Mazarelle thought. Normal human relationships—even without violence—tended to be emotionally complicated, vexed, and painful, whereas homicide, while not always easy to solve, was relatively simple to diagram. There was a murderer and a murderee. He loved the moral clarity of it. But most of all the satisfaction of tidying up the mess at the end and making the world a little better for the survivors. Even Martine might have been interested in this new case. Mazarelle drew on his pipe and the smoke streamed from his lips and sailed away. The best he could say was that though he didn't have any idea who did it, he thought he knew who didn't do it. But he wasn't even sure of that. Hell, it was only the beginning. He smiled to himself at the idea and it cheered him up. A real ballbuster, he thought.

20

DISTRICT ATTORNEY'S OFFICE, NEW YORK CITY

Molly Reece sat at her desk, crossing and uncrossing her long shapely legs as she went over the list of questions she planned to ask at the deposition. It was a case that raised her temperature even higher than most she handled. A fourteen-year-old kid in a junior high school's bilingual education program had been raped by her math teacher. Afraid to tell her parents, she nearly died after an illegal abortion. Fortunately she had told her best friend when it happened or there'd be no case. The defendant was now asking to have a translator at the trial because his English was weak. Molly had no objections. Who says every rapist has to speak English like Orson Welles? Besides, in court a translator would probably work to her advantage with the jury. What really ticked her off, though, was that his lousy English had been good enough to get him a job teaching in the New York City public school system. Surreal, she thought. Like *Alice in Wonderland*.

When the telephone rang, Molly assumed that it was the math teacher's lawyer from the public defender's office, calling her back. The voice was low, edgy, and identified the caller as Dwight Bennett. Though busy, Molly figured thirty seconds and guardedly heard him out. He asked if this was Molly Reece.

"How can I help you?"

"The daughter of Benjamin and Judith Reece of Manhattan?"

"Yes . . ."

"Are they currently vacationing in France?"

"All right, what's this all about?"

Dwight explained that he was calling from the American embassy in Paris. He was sorry, but he had some bad news. There had been an accident in Taziac.

Molly, who was about to hang up, hesitated. He knew where they were. This wasn't some nut caught up in the New York County Court system getting an ADA on the phone and trying to push her buttons.

"What are you talking about? What sort of accident?"

"A very bad one, I'm afraid. I'm truly sorry to have to be the one to tell you, Ms. Reece . . ." He paused. "Your parents are dead."

"Dead? My parents *dead*. What? What?" She tried to catch her breath. "Oh no . . . You can't . . ." Her voice cracked, her eyes tearing up. "Both of them?"

"I'm sorry. Yes, both of them."

Her mom and dad dead. Molly couldn't wrap her mind around the idea. She had just seen them off at JFK. They were so excited. All they could talk about was their French vacation. Putting the phone down on her desk, she closed her eyes. Then taking a deep breath, she picked up the receiver again.

"Ms. Reece," he said. "Are you still there, Ms. Reece?"

"I'm here."

"I know how awful this must be for you. If I can be of help in any way—"

"Tell me, how did it happen? Were they driving?"

"No, they weren't driving. They were murdered."

It was a whipsaw, first their deaths and then this. Murdered! It was beyond belief. How? Who? Though she'd had some experience with murder and the grieving families left in its wake, it certainly hadn't prepared her for these deaths. Molly—a crushing weight on her chest—felt herself growing angrier and angrier.

And even much later, sitting in a 747 at thirty-five thousand feet and watching the eye-popping dawn come up, warming the clouds from gray to rust to salmon pink above the Normandy cliffs, Molly still felt that oppressive weight. She wanted answers and intended to demand that her caller, Dwight Bennett, provide them. It was as if she thought he was the French investigating magistrate rather than some lowly U.S. State Department official based in Paris. But Bennett had offered to help and that's where Molly planned to start.

Kevin had known at once something was wrong by the sound of her voice. She'd caught him on the way out of their apartment in the Village going uptown to rehearsal. The news shocked him. He was fond of Ben and Judy, laughingly called them the "odd couple." Molly knew what he meant. As far as her bohemian boyfriend was concerned, she was so different from either of them that she might have been deposited on their Upper East Side doorstep in a basket.

Though Kevin thought of himself as being good in an emergency, he was less good at recognizing when he was confronting one. Molly, on the other hand, was focused and well organized even in the worst of times. She told Kevin that her boss would be arranging for postponements of her cases. She'd already bought her plane ticket from Air France. She was leaving for Paris that evening. Molly knew the city well, having spent her junior year at Barnard studying at the Sorbonne. Besides, she was only planning to stay overnight at the Hotel Lenox Saint-Germain and then fly down to the Dordogne the next morning. As soon as she knew where she'd be staying there, she promised to call.

Kevin volunteered to go with her. The independent Molly made it easy for him. Calling his offer sweet, she said she preferred to do this alone. There was, however, one thing that she did want him to do.

Never having met Sean Campbell, Kevin knew that he'd have to tell Ben's partner the news of his murder face-to-face. He would have much rather done it on the phone. Kevin had been up to the Reece-Campbell Gallery with Molly only once or twice, their last visit for a show he really enjoyed. Any actor would. The work of the young Austrian artist Egon Schiele was full of self-conscious poses, expressive gestures, brutal sex, torment, lyricism, loneliness, and death. All that and only twenty-eight when he himself died. Despite the amusing Klee drawings that Kevin passed as he walked through the uptown Madison Avenue gallery, death was very much on his mind.

The young woman behind the desk finally glanced up. Good-looking, he thought, surprised to see how duded up she was. Not the careless, plain-Jane look of the women who worked in the downtown SoHo and Chelsea art galleries. Kevin explained that he was a friend of Molly Reece's. He'd a message from her for Mr. Campbell. Mona, the gallery assistant, said she was sorry but both Mr. Campbell and Mr. Reece were away on vacation.

Kevin, who knew how to lower his voice without losing his best lines, leaned across the desk and said, "This is important."

"He's out of the country. But he'll be back in a few weeks. Can't it wait?"

"No, it can't wait. I wouldn't be here if it could wait."

Maybe it *was* important, Mona decided, recalling that perhaps she had seen him in the gallery with Molly. "Mr. Campbell is in France. He's traveling at the moment. I have no idea where, but I do expect him to call. I'd be glad to relay a message for you."

Kevin supposed that would be okay with Molly and told her what it was, watching her black-rimmed eyes dilate in disbelief, her face pale. Mona promised to make sure her boss got it. Kevin thought it a little odd that Campbell was in France too and that Molly didn't know anything about it. He'd probably heard the news of Ben's murder already.

Taking a slip of paper from her desk drawer as soon as he'd left, Mona went into the office, closed the door behind her, and sat down at Ben's desk. She dialed 011, then 33 for France, 1 for Paris, and then the rest of the number Sean had written. She could hardly wait to tell him the awful news, fairly bursting with tragedy. "Hello, Sean, Sean . . ."

21

THE AMERICAN EMBASSY, PARIS

The Lenox was a small, quaint hotel that Molly had stayed at on her first trip to Paris. It was just a few blocks from the Seine and, across the river, a short walk to the Place de la Concorde and the American embassy.

Molly, aware that it was harder traveling east than west because of the loss of time, had read somewhere that drinking lots of water helped to prevent jet lag. It seemed to have done the trick. She was so wired, so adrenalized that she wasn't even tired. But if she stopped for a minute, she was afraid that bad things might happen. Things she didn't want to think about. After washing up and putting on her black linen suit, which was chic, short, tailored, and which, according to the mirror in her room, had come out of her suitcase better than she had any reason to expect, Molly left for the embassy. It was still early morning in Paris, the streets washed clean of dog shit, the river jeweled and sparkling in the sun. It almost made her feel guilty just for being there.

In the park along the avenue Gabriel, Molly paused by a giant sequoia to read the placard that said it was the embassy's gift to Paris. She gazed across at the gleaming, four-story, white stone structure with its American flag flying from the balcony above the main entrance. It was surrounded by a high metal spear-tipped fence, and the French police had set up portable steel barriers in front. The embassy looked as if it were under siege. Molly wondered if it had anything to do with the political fallout from the recent NATO bombing of the Chinese embassy in Belgrade.

She went up to the gendarme with the machine gun slung over

his shoulder standing by the barrier and inquired how to get in. He smiled when he saw who had asked. Her French was excellent. It was her easy, open, confident American manner that gave her away. Tipping his kepi, he indicated the small temporary wooden gatehouse to his right. Inside, they asked what she wanted and weren't satisfied until one of them had called Dwight Bennett's office for authorization. The other examined the contents of her shoulder bag.

At the embassy door, she was immediately stopped by a guard in civilian clothes with a crew cut—obviously an American, probably an ex-Marine. All he seemed to be missing was an earphone and a pair of Ray-Bans. He asked for her pass. Looked at it and then at her with Secret Service eyes, the coldest that she'd ever seen, his mouth locked down like a prison.

"Second floor," he mumbled in a sullen voice, pointing to the stairs, and watched her go up. Molly wasn't accustomed to security this tight. What were they afraid of?

On the second floor, she was directed to the Economics Department. Molly thought it odd that Dwight Bennett worked in Economics but assumed they were short on space and he was doubling up with somebody. "He'll be with you shortly," his secretary said.

Ken McCarty had stopped by Bennett's office to drop off some information for him and return a photograph of several people coming out of the Hotel Adlon in Berlin. Bennett had circled two of them in red. McCarty told him that it had helped. Bennett took the five by eight from the stiff old pro with a smile. Though ticked off that he hadn't brought it back sooner, Bennett knew how to get on with people, especially anyone who might be of use to him. As for the rest, he dealt with them like second-class mail—the way he treated new case officers. McCarty was useful.

Ken McCarty did black bag operations for them and had just come back from Brussels. He was an expert in special intelligence. He had been doing SI in Europe for a long time and as early as 1974 had been active in Vienna. It was McCarty who first learned via electronic pickup that OPEC was about to lift their yearlong oil embargo against the United States. He had the calm focus of those who work clandestinely and well under pressure. Communications intercepts were his specialty. He was particularly skillful at handling phone and computer taps and the secret monitoring of conversations both indoors and out.

"I checked. Nothing wrong with the bugs, Dwight," McCarty assured him. "They're the best. Each no bigger than a microchip and because each one draws its power from the telephone, it requires no battery. They can last forever. Not only are we able to cover calls with them but whatever else is said in the room as well. You'll see from my report. Your two friends must be away now. Maybe they're still in Berlin. Okay?" he asked, not wishing to leave on a sour note. He'd been around long enough to know that Dwight Elgar Bennett wasn't anyone you wanted to make unhappy.

"Okay."

McCarty put out his hand. "I'll keep you posted."

"Do that."

Molly watched the man with the photo ID around his neck come out of Bennett's office. He was in his late fifties. Big, broad-shouldered, with spiky iron-gray hair, rimless glasses, and, she guessed, less humor than a slide rule. No wonder they call economics "the gray science," she thought.

When Dwight Bennett's secretary told her she could go in, Molly wasn't sure whether she was more surprised by the size of his comfortable office or by Bennett himself. Though he might have been in his mid-forties, he looked like early thirties to her. Only the conservative, three-button, banker's-blue striped suit made him seem older. His trim, lanky build suggested he'd be more at home on a tennis court in shorts. Bennett wore a white shirt; a muted red paisley tie; and thin black-wire-rimmed glasses that looked good on him, heightening the fineness of his patrician features. He probably looked good without them too, she thought. As for what he thought about her, it was obvious.

Bennett couldn't have been kinder, more considerate. He was so sorry to have been the bearer of such ghastly news. Too sorry, perhaps, for a complete stranger. There was something about him that she didn't quite believe or, more to the point, trust. Like some oleaginous blind dates she could remember. If he really wanted to be sympathetic, compassionate, consoling, Molly felt he was overdoing it. Her question when it came was so direct, so blunt, that it cut through his spongy sentimentality like a meat cleaver.

"Do they know yet who killed them?"

Bennett heard the steel in her voice. This was not just another pretty face. "No . . . not yet. I've been told they may have some suspects, but nobody's been arrested. Look," he asked, "have you had any breakfast?"

Molly shook her head.

"How would you like to go out with me and get something to eat?"

"I'm not hungry."

"How about some coffee? You look as if you could use some coffee. And I could use some myself."

Molly hesitated. "I don't—"

"Oh, come on." Grabbing his jacket and taking his attractive visitor by the arm, Bennett marched her out of the office, telling his startled secretary, "Hold the fort, Barney. If London calls, take a message and say I'll get back to them. See you in an hour."

Maybe yes and maybe no. Elizabeth Barnes wasn't about to hold her breath. For the first two years that she worked for him, Dwight Bennett had been as dependable as GMT, but since his divorce anything was possible. His ex-wife was now back in the States. Barnes had liked Claudia. Though their divorce had been a messy one, it certainly hadn't killed her boss's interest in women. But what Dwight really needed, she felt, was someone he could depend on. If she wasn't almost old enough to be his mother, Elizabeth might have applied for the job.

On their way downstairs, Bennett promised Molly the best coffee in Paris. "And it happens to be right next door," he said, as they swept past the security guard at the door who had given Molly a hard time.

"Morning, sir," the guard shouted after him, practically saluting. Who was this Bennett anyhow? she wondered. Molly was sure that he was no junior accountant.

Nearby was the five-star Hôtel de Crillon. The uniformed doorman smiled deferentially as he ushered them in. Bennett led the way. Molly wasn't ready for the glittering chandeliers and the operatic scale of the lobby or her heels noisily clicking on the marble floor. She wondered where he was going. It turned out to be the Crillon's bar, a cozy room with a red carpet, red armchairs, a grand piano, and a large vase of orange and rust-colored chrysanthemums. Sitting down at one of the low tables in the empty room, Molly glanced at the bottles of Marie Brizard, Bacardi, Bushmills, and Johnnie Walker displayed like paintings on the mirrored wall behind the bar and, turning, gave Bennett a squint-eyed, unamused stare.

He laughed. "Trust me."

Though Molly didn't know it at the time, "trust me" would prove to be one of his favorite expressions. She was in no mood for this. Molly glanced out the window at the embassy across the street and wondered why she'd even bothered to come with him.

The young waiter in the red-and-gold-striped tie greeted Monsieur Bennett warmly. He had good news, he said. They'd found the gold earring that his friend had lost the night before. There was also his American Express receipt that he'd left behind. The waiter put them both down on the table. Molly had never seen such a hefty bar bill. It must have been quite a party. So that's what happens to our tax dollars, she thought. Coffee wasn't all he drank here. But when the silver pots of coffee and hot croissants did appear, they were as good as advertised.

"How did you get my name?"

Bennett explained that when any American citizen died in France it was customary for the French authorities to notify the embassy. "And, of course, in a murder case—" He decided there was no comfortable way to finish that sentence. "So when the procureur's office in Périgueux called us, I contacted Washington and they did a search for family information—beginning at the passport office—and after a few days I had your telephone number. Nothing to it really. It just takes a little time."

"How come you've got *this* job?"

By now he was used to her direct ways and deflected the question by gazing into her large gray-green eyes and saying, "It's not so bad."

Molly was not about to be put off by charm. "I mean you are in economics, aren't you?"

"We take turns. Somebody's got to do it. Besides, something like this doesn't happen very often . . . fortunately."

"Do many Americans die here every year?"

"Maybe about a hundred or so."

"*That* many?"

"Not so many, not really. Especially when you consider that as of three years ago, according to U.S. Department of Commerce figures, we had thirty-four billion dollars invested in France, and each year roughly two million Americans come here to do business or as tourists."

His mention of the Department of Commerce made her eyelids flutter and feel heavier than wool. She assumed it was just the delayed effect of the awful news and long trip. The coffee, at least, helped.

Bennett asked about her parents. Molly wondered if talking about them would make her feel any better. Fill in the gaping hole in her life that she feared nothing would ever heal. She told him her father visited Paris almost every year on art business. His New York gallery was known by collectors all over the world. But this visit was strictly vacation. They were staying in the French countryside with their old friends, and her mom had arranged everything. She was so proud of herself. Molly could hardly keep her voice steady as she spoke.

Bennett's eyes never left her face. He listened hard but didn't say anything at first. There was something on his mind.

"Did their friends the Phillipses have any children?"

"No, I don't think so. Haven't you been able to contact any of the family?"

Bennett admitted that he hadn't. The Bergerac police were expecting someone from Phillips's company in Canada to help them identify the bodies. He asked Molly if she'd ever met them.

"Just him. Once, a long time ago at my dad's twenty-fifth college reunion. Dad and Schuyler were roommates at Dartmouth."

"You may be able to help with him too."

"Help who?"

"The police."

In any event, Bennett felt sure that he'd be able to help her with the French authorities when she went to identify her parents. He volunteered to go down with Molly the next day on the TGV—the high-speed train—to Bordeaux and from there they'd rent a car and drive to Taziac. He'd made all the arrangements. Told her to expect a call that afternoon to let her know what time he'd pick her up tomorrow.

"That is," he paused, "if it's okay by you?"

Molly didn't like being manipulated. Though she was the sort of woman for whom men did favors, Molly—a New Yorker born and bred—would ordinarily have been more on guard than she was. But she suspected that his generosity had something to do with her boss, the legendary Manhattan District Attorney Bob Morgenthau. He had friends everywhere and her dad happened to be one of them. She wondered if the DA had called someone he knew in Washington at the State Department. They couldn't possibly do this for every American with a death in the family who arrived on their doorstep.

"Sure. Okay."

"Good." He seemed genuinely relieved. "Oh by the way, where are you staying?"

22

POLICE INTERROGATION ROOM, BERGERAC

andu listened impassively to Duboit complaining about the cost of antibiotics for one of his kids who had something wrong with his ear. A good sort, Doobie, but he talked too much for Bandu's taste. They were waiting for Mazarelle to get off the phone and tell them why he wanted to see them.

"*Au revoir, monsieur, et merci.*" Mazarelle, with a tiny enigmatic smile, hung up the receiver. The procureur was apparently solidly behind him. D'Aumont's enthusiasm had a mildly unsettling effect on the inspector, who found it, at the very least, premature.

"Okay, now." He turned to the two waiting men. "I want Ali Sedak. Bring him in for questioning."

"Finally!" Duboit lifted his eyes heavenward. "With *his* record I don't know why they let him into the country in the first place."

"Somebody slipped up," Mazarelle said. "That's always how it happens. Overworked and underpaid and sloppy." The clever Vignon had managed to track down Sedak's *liste des infractions* from Algeria. Even as a teenager, the young Arab had already accumulated an impressive collection of crimes, including breaking and entering, robbery, resisting arrest, and drugs.

"But that," Mazarelle said pointedly to Bernard, "doesn't make him a murderer. At least not yet. And apparently he's been a relatively good boy for the last ten or so years that he's been here. That is, if you don't count two suspended sentences for a barroom brawl and drug possession."

"What about the domestic violence charge against him that was dropped?"

Mazarelle nodded approvingly. "Very good, Bernard. I see you've done your homework. Okay, bring him in."

When Lucille called to tell the inspector they had arrived and were waiting for him downstairs, there was something in her voice that made him uneasy. What now? he wondered, picking up the folder from his desk and tucking it under his arm. Mazarelle saw what it was the minute he entered the interrogation room and an irate Ali Sedak glared up at him. His left eye was a fiery red and swollen half closed. It would be shut tight and black-and-blue by tomorrow. Mazarelle hated to think what the press would do with that.

"You see? Look! Look what they did to me."

"Button up, asshole," Duboit whispered.

The inspector turned to the two cops standing behind Sedak with their arms folded and waited for an explanation. Duboit averted his eyes sheepishly, tried hard not to smile.

"An accident," Bandu called it. "Monsieur was on the way out of his house and ran into the front door. It happens."

Mazarelle stared hard at the joker to remind him that this was no time for stupid gags that might fuck up their investigation. If Sedak made a stink to the media, the investigating magistrate could make Mazarelle's life difficult. He'd found Madame Leclerc an even tougher cookie to deal with than d'Aumont. But he'd taken the precaution of notifying both of them of his intentions regarding Ali Sedak, and they agreed there was no need to have a lawyer present during questioning because no charges had yet been filed against him.

"Why am I here anyhow?" Sedak shouted. "I told you everything already. I know nothing about these murders. You're hassling me just because of my name."

"Calm down," soothed the inspector. "Relax, monsieur. Do you smoke? Give him a cig."

Bandu took out a package of Gauloises and tossed one onto the table.

Mazarelle pushed the dented tin pie plate that they used for an ashtray in front of Sedak and lit his cigarette. Sedak inhaled voraciously. Taking out his pipe, Mazarelle lit up too, some glowing flakes of tobacco spilling out onto the floor as he torched the bowl.

"There we are . . ." He dropped his lit match into the tin plate. "That's better, isn't it?"

"You've got nothing on me. Not a thing."

"We need your help, monsieur. So . . ." He nodded to Bernard, who switched on the tape recorder. A tiny red light went on. "*Allons*, let's begin."

The inspector reminded Ali that he said he worked late the night of the crime, and though he left L'Ermitage about 10 p.m., Monsieur and Madame Reece and their friend Madame Phillips had not yet returned from dining.

"It was earlier. I told you nine thirty."

"Sorry. Left about nine thirty p.m. and said that—except for the killer—he was probably the last one to see Monsieur Phillips alive. And by nine fifty or so he was back home and fast asleep. Is that right, monsieur?"

"My woman said so, didn't she?"

"She did. But later that night did you happen to wake up and go out for a walk, a breath of fresh air?"

"How could I? My back was killing me. I couldn't move."

Ali flicked the ash off his cigarette, feigning indifference, as the inspector removed a photograph from his folder and passed it across the table. It was fairly sharp for a print from a surveillance camera, but Taziac's Crédit Agricole was a new bank. The picture also recorded the date and time it was taken, which was 1:24 a.m. of the twenty-fifth—the morning following the night of the murders. Though the man at the ATM had his face partly averted, he was wearing a blue bandana around his head very much like the one Ali wore. He angrily pushed the photo away.

"What are you trying to pull on me?"

"I see you noticed the resemblance too. I have something else you might be interested in." The inspector drew an ATM receipt from his folder and showed it to him. The time and date stamped on it were the same as the photo. The amount withdrawn was two thousand francs.

"I know nothing about MasterCards," Ali insisted. "I don't even own one."

"Yes, of course, this one belonged to Monsieur Reece. And whoever took the money from the machine knew his PIN and was in such a hurry that he forgot to remove the receipt."

"Maybe Reece was tired and wanted to get home. Maybe he had to take a piss."

"Stop being such a smart-ass," Duboit warned him.

Mazarelle gave Bernard a narrow, sidelong look and he shut up. "By one twenty-four a.m. Monsieur Reece was dead." Reclaiming the receipt, he tucked it away and said casually, "You might be interested to know that only last week he'd reported his Visa card missing. We found it at a BNP in Bergerac, where someone had been trying to use it. Monsieur Reece thought you were the one who had stolen it."

"The big *zozo*. He didn't like me. I could tell."

The inspector tapped his fingers impatiently on the table. "Did you steal it?"

"Crap!"

"And what about his MasterCard? Did you steal that too?"

"What do you take me for? I'm not a thief."

Ali Sedak watched with a worried look as the inspector hunted among his papers. Every time he reached into his folder, it had turned out bad for Ali. It was like being at the dentist.

"*Voilà.*" Mazarelle held up Sedak's *liste des infractions* for him to see and pointed to number 3. "Apparently you are. That's the one year inside they gave you for robbery in Biskra."

Ali thought he'd left all that behind in Algeria. He should have known better. "That was a long time ago."

"He's a goddamn liar," Duboit flared up again. "Why bother questioning him? You can't believe a word they say."

Oppressed, Mazarelle flipped off the tape recorder and warned the young cop that he wanted no more interruptions. "Understood, Duboit? No more."

He turned the tape recorder back on, apologized for his brief coughing fit, and announced that he was continuing with his questioning of Ali Sedak. Leaning forward as if in confidence, the inspector told him that they'd just received a lab report on a bloodstained bayonet found on the grounds of L'Ermitage. The DNA matched that of three of the victims.

"So what?"

"Your blood is on it too."

"How do you know it's mine?"

"It's yours," the inspector assured him. Thanks to Bernard, the PTS lab in Toulouse was able to make the match and identify the murder weapon. Bernard had pocketed the roach from the reefer Sedak had been smoking before they arrived to question him. The inspector thought that someday, if he ever grew up, Doobie might actually be a good cop.

"It could be mine," Ali Sedak conceded. "Maybe I cut myself accidentally. I use it for opening paint cans. The killer must have stolen the bayonet from my toolbox in the barn."

Mazarelle smiled amiably as if satisfied with his explanation but then seemed perplexed. "I thought you told me that you didn't own a bayonet."

"I never said that. Are you trying to trick me?"

Duboit's face reddened like a tuba player, but he held his tongue.

"And . . . oh yes," the inspector continued. "Your fingerprints . . . They were found on the blue tape three of the victims were bound with. How do you explain that?"

Ali took a last drag on what was left of his cigarette and tossed it smoking into the tin pan. "It was probably mine."

Duboit muttered under his breath. "Of course it was yours, you dumb *salaud*."

Ali glowered at the two cops behind him and his breathing was shallow and quick. He had the look of a trapped animal.

"Don't you see?" he appealed to the inspector. "Whoever went into my toolbox for the bayonet must have also taken my tape. Somebody's trying to frame me."

The inspector puffed on his pipe as he thought it over and nodded his heavy head.

"Yes, yes, of course that's possible. But there is this evidence, you see. And enough coincidences and causes for concern with your story that I'm afraid we're going to have to hold you here in *garde à vue* until we sort all this out. You understand."

Getting up, he whispered something to Bandu, who indicated that he would, and lifted the startled Ali to his feet in a single motion that was closer to a weight lifter's snatch than a clean and jerk.

"What—what are you doing? This is a mistake. I'm innocent."

Mazarelle followed them to the rear of the commissariat, where the four *garde à vue* cells were located. The two with steel doors and narrow slots to peer through resembled medieval helmets; the two with Plexiglas doors were for those who had to be under constant surveillance. As Bernard emptied the prisoner's pockets, taking his money and keys, and Bandu removed Ali's belt, shoelaces, blue bandana, and gold chain, the inspector told Ali that sometimes even very observant people failed to mention everything they've seen or heard at a crime scene. He wanted Ali to think over very carefully what had happened the night of the L'Ermitage murders and try to recall if there was anything at all he'd forgotten to tell him.

"Otherwise . . ." Mazarelle warned him, "who knows? You yourself could end up gathering dust in one of the cages they've got for wiseasses at the Maison d'Arrêt in Périgueux. And before long your kid will be calling some other creep Daddy. As for you, you'll be Uncle Visiting Day."

"What are they doing with my money, my stuff?" Ali demanded. "I want a lawyer."

"By and by." Mazarelle told his men to finish processing the prisoner, and that he'd be right back.

"All right," Bandu ordered Ali, "off with the clothes."

He gazed in confusion at the two cops, all his cockiness apparently drained out of him.

"Come on, come on. With your record you know the drill. You're no virgin when it comes to body searches. Don't make me ask you twice."

Slowly Ali took off his shirt, dropped his pants, and stood there, tan to the waist, white from the waist down. Bending over, he waited, naked and shrunken in the middle of the floor.

"That's better." Bandu gave him a passing grade. "Now let's see you spread those cheeks wide and crack a smile."

Duboit bristled when Sedak grinned. No matter how rattled, the Arab was still very much a wise guy. "Not that end, you smart-ass. *This* one." He kicked Ali in the butt and he went sprawling. When he crawled onto his knees, he spotted the inspector hurrying back.

"The bastards, they're trying to humiliate me."

"Get up and get dressed and shut your mouth." Taking Bernard aside, Mazarelle handed him the *garde à vue* logbook and instructed him that when entering Sedak's name he should note that it was a suicide watch.

"What about the handcuffs?" Bandu asked.

"I told you what the investigating magistrate wanted. She said whatever it takes to get to the bottom of these murders. Put the cuffs on and leave them on."

Madame le juge had been calling the inspector almost every day, making sure she hadn't missed any new developments. Keeping his nose to the grindstone because the procureur or somebody else upstairs was constantly in her ear. Mazarelle called it his trickle-down theory of criminology. He knew that even the procureur wasn't immune to being pissed on, and, of course, he himself had more than once felt the heavens open from above. Mazarelle, as ordered, would make it as tough on the *pégriot* as he legally could. See what a little pressure could do to help his memory.

"But I stop at torture, Bandu. Clear?"

"Clear, chief." Bandu nodded, then yanked Sedak's hands behind his back and slapped on the cuffs. Opening the Plexiglas door of one of the cells, Bandu threw him in. Sedak, losing his balance and one of his unlaced shoes in the process, fell hard against the cinder block wall.

"But I'm innocent!" he screamed.

For all the inspector knew, Sedak could be innocent, but Mazarelle was dealing with four savage murders and he was certain that the Arab was holding out on him.

23

THE MORGUE, BERGERAC

They left for Bordeaux from the Gare Montparnasse at 6:50 a.m. No sooner were Molly and Dwight Bennett settled side by side than the doors closed and the high-speed train, sleek as a snake, glided away from the station. It flew down the tracks. Molly felt amazingly cushioned, insulated, and glad to have Bennett beside her as the landscape rocketed by outside. This was the breathtaking way her world had been moving ever since she'd gotten his shocking news. Molly wondered if anything would ever be the same again.

She asked about his life in Paris and how he liked living there.

"Very much. But it's pricey."

The economist, she thought. A mind like a cash register. "Where in the city do you live?"

Bennett described his apartment on the rue de l'Odéon with a sigh. "A good location but it's small and, of course, overpriced." Molly's lips parted in a paper-thin smile.

By 10:24 a.m. their train was already pulling into Bordeaux's Gare Saint-Jean and, after renting a car, they were off to Bergerac. On the way, he mentioned that yesterday he'd called the commissaire de police in Bergerac to inform him they were coming and learned that the inspector in charge of the case might be someone he once knew in Paris.

"If it's the same Mazarelle, he's a first-rate investigator with a solid reputation. Not a bad guy either."

When later Bennett met Commissaire Rivet for the first time, they got along as if they were old friends. Molly noted that both men had clearly mastered the social skills for advancement in a government bureaucracy. And as to her painful loss, the commissaire couldn't have been more considerate. He promised to leave no stone unturned in finding who was responsible for the death of her parents and described the detective he'd placed in charge of the manhunt as *"subtil et tenace"*—in fact, one of his best.

Having been alerted by Rivet that they were coming, Mazarelle could hardly claim ignorance when they found him at his desk with his shoes off, his feet up—a hole in the toe of one of his socks—munching on a cold croque monsieur. He'd simply forgotten. It had been a busy morning for the inspector. He'd been questioning Ali Sedak, who appeared to be seriously shaken by the constant light burning in the cinder block shoebox into which they had squeezed him as well as by not being able to sleep or wash or scratch his itching nose because of the handcuffs. But he was still holding out on them. Nevertheless, Mazarelle thought it only a matter of time before he cracked.

The inspector quickly wolfed down what was left of his grilled cheese; wiped off his fingers; and, getting to his feet, shook hands with Bennett, whom he remembered very well from the American embassy in Paris. He turned to Bennett's radiantly redheaded companion and Bennett introduced them.

The striking beauty of the tall young American woman with the steady gaze was not lost on the inspector. "Mademoiselle Reece . . ." Taking her hand, he glanced at her sympathetically and said, "I'm truly sorry."

Molly thanked him. It was hard for her not to be struck by the size of his hands, the softness of his sad brown eyes peering out from under his bushy eyebrows. She tried not to smile or stare at the crumbs littering his mustache, his shoeless feet. He seemed more like someone's favorite uncle—a teddy bear—than any of the cops she knew.

Bennett could tell that Mazarelle was genuinely touched by her loss. The inspector, he recalled, had always had a soft spot for women. Apparently, quite a ladies' man. There had been all sorts of stories he'd heard about him: that one of his girlfriends had committed suicide when they split up, that his wife was a knockout—much younger than he was with an active social life—and that his marriage was in serious trouble. Bennett wondered if Mazarelle was still married and how he'd ended up here in the sticks.

Mazarelle announced that the medical examiner had been notified that they were coming. Then he looked at Molly and appeared to have second thoughts. "I'm afraid it's not very pretty over there. You understand, mademoiselle: it's a morgue, not a funeral home. The sights and smells can be difficult at times even for trained professionals like me. Are you sure you want to go ahead with this? You don't have to. We have photographs," he revealed, and was pleased to see that pictures seemed to appeal to her. "Yes, that's it. We could do it with photographs, *n'est-ce pas?*"

Molly shook her head firmly. "I didn't come all the way here to see pictures. Let's go."

In the hospital morgue, which smelled oppressively of chemicals, Dr. Langlais had taken the two bodies out for viewing. They'd been placed on tables behind a faded green curtain. He cautioned Molly not to disturb the sheets that covered them up to their chins. Then without ceremony, he drew back the curtain, and there side by side under the cold fluorescent light lay her parents as motionless as if their heads—her father's swathed in a towel—were chiseled in stone on top of a sepulchre. The last time she'd seen them alive was when they were preboarding their plane at JFK. Then she'd watched the wing and taillights twinkling festively as the plane took off and was sucked up into the darkening sky. The vacation from hell, she thought.

Molly stepped closer, terribly moved by her father's stillness, his scruffy cheeks, his five-o'clock shadow. Her dad, who prided himself on his immaculate grooming—always freshly shaved, even on weekends. She asked herself, When does the hair finally stop growing, when does the body notify the follicles that it's all over? The one present she'd ever given him that he actually loved was the gold soap bowl and badger brush from Jagger's in England.

She wondered if her mother was wearing the silver necklace that Molly had bought her for her last birthday. Her very last. Her mom, who had sworn that she'd never take it off. Whenever they got together, she'd worn it, even at the airport when they were saying their final good-byes. The sudden realization that she was an orphan now was a cold chill that pierced her heart. Leaning forward toward her mother, Molly reached for the sheet and drew it down.

"No, no!" called Dr. Langlais.

Molly jerked back, turning away from her mother's slashed neck and, as her eyes darted about the room looking for a safe place to rest, she uttered a cry so heartfelt, her voice cracked into a dozen pieces. Perhaps it was the pungent smell of formaldehyde in the air mixed with the aroma of pine-scented disinfectant that made her feel so dizzy, so nauseous.

Mazarelle, who hadn't taken his eyes off the spunky young woman since the viewing of the bodies began, saw the color drain from her face and, with a move surprisingly nimble for a man his size, caught her just as her knees began to buckle. The young woman felt like a healthy armful. Carrying Molly out into the hall, he sat her down and told the others to get her some water.

He stroked Molly's hands, rubbed the back of her lovely neck. Mazarelle wondered what another woman would be like after so many years—a different smell, a different shampoo, a different sweat—but there was only one smell in his nose now.

"Ça va?" he asked, taking the glass of water from Langlais and holding it to Molly's lips. As she sipped, the pink seeped back into her cheeks.

"Better?"

Molly nodded.

"Good. Have some more."

"Sorry," she apologized. "Yes . . . it's them."

She got up, hating the fuss she'd caused. "I just wasn't expecting . . ."

"Naturally, of course."

Male condescension infuriated Molly. But how could a human being have done such a thing? She couldn't believe that anyone could have been so cruel, so depraved, so consumed by evil to pitilessly chop away at her mother as if she were firewood, a good woman who'd never harmed a soul. Such monsters were beyond help, incapable of redemption. Though she'd always hated the idea of capital punishment, perhaps she was wrong. The world would be better off without them.

Molly asked, "Does France still have the death penalty?"

"*La guillotine?*" The inspector rolled his eyes. "Not since 1981. Ancient history. I was happy to see it go. I'd much prefer to put such animals away in cages for life. However, in a case like this," he sympathized, "I can understand how you feel."

The families of victims were always the hardest for the inspector to deal with. He was relieved that she hadn't pulled the sheet off her father too and seen the gruesome way he'd been carved up. The cruelty was incomprehensible. Mazarelle made a silent vow to get the son of a bitch, remove that cancer from society. He'd already come to the bleak conclusion that the murderer in trying to learn Monsieur Reece's PIN had turned him into a flesh and blood cutting board. The man, whoever he was, had a diabolical sense of humor. A sadistic bastard, for sure, even possibly a madman. What an odd coincidence, he thought, reminded of Simenon's *The Madman of Bergerac*. Algeria played a role in those murders also. He was mildly amused, and not for the first time, to find life mirroring art.

"Where are you going?" he called out, trying to stop her from returning to the viewing room, but Molly was determined.

"I'm fine," she insisted. Approaching her mother's body, she asked the doctor if she might see her left hand. Langlais carefully lifted the sheet and held up Judy Reece's rigid fingers. Molly noticed the black-and-blue bruises around her mother's wrist. If they upset her, she gave no indication.

"Where's her wedding band?" she icily demanded of the medical examiner. "Did they take that too? Is that what they were after?"

"*Doucement*, mademoiselle. We have it, I'm sure."

"And my dad's?"

Dr. Langlais did not like being questioned in such a tone about trivialities. He assured the overwrought young woman that her father's keys, his ring, his watch, and all of the jewelry her parents were wearing was safely put aside for her. He promised to return everything before she left. As Mazarelle had concluded already, the killer had not been after jewelry.

Bennett asked the doctor, "Could we see the body you think is

Schuyler Phillips? Mademoiselle Reece may be able to help with the identification."

Langlais looked as if he didn't understand him or, perhaps closer to the point, didn't want to. "That won't be necessary."

Molly didn't know what to think. She glanced at the inspector.

"You don't want to see it. Besides there's hardly anything left of his face to identify."

"I don't need his face."

What could you do with a young woman like that? Expecting that in the end he'd have to scrape her up off the floor with a teaspoon, Mazarelle shrugged and turned to the doctor. "As you like," he said, with a careless wave of his hand.

When the body was brought out, it was shrouded from head to toe like a mummy. They all watched expectantly as Molly approached. "Just show me his legs," she said. Dr. Langlais pulled back the sheet to reveal the dead man's muscular, ivory-colored limbs.

"There!" She pointed to the long, lightning-bolt scar just under his right kneecap, a legendary wound from the blade of a hurtling Harvard skater. Just as Odysseus could always be identified by the scar on his thigh from the tusks of a great boar, Schuyler—according to her dad—had his telltale hockey scar. "It's him," she said, biting her lip to keep back the tears. Everyone in her family loved Schuyler.

After quickly agreeing to show Molly and Bennett the house where the murders had occurred in order to get rid of them, Mazarelle ran into the bathroom, feeling a major allergy attack coming on. Leaning over the sink, he spit out one of the two cloves that he'd stuffed into his nostrils. As the other clove shot out of his nose, he began to sneeze violently. The aromatic dried buds had made bearable what had promised to be a difficult task for him. A little trick of the trade he often used in Paris. As he blew his nose and washed up, the inspector wondered why an attaché from the American embassy had come down here together with the young woman. Most unusual. Perhaps these people were even more important than he imagined. Mazarelle wondered if he could have been right years ago about the clean-cut, callow-looking American. He'd always suspected Bennett was the CIA station chief in Paris.

24

THE CRIME SCENE

Molly had made up her mind to stay overnight near the crime scene. She wanted to be close to the house where her mom and dad and their friends had been vacationing.

Bennett claimed there was only one tiny hotel in Taziac. "No bigger than a broom closet, according to my secretary."

"Sounds cozy."

"It probably doesn't even have any rooms available."

"Let's go see."

Though Barney following his instructions had made reservations for them in Bergerac at the Gambetta, the best hotel in town, Bennett didn't want to argue. He'd more bad news to tell her as it was.

Driving south on the way to Taziac, he tried to amuse Molly. Told her a story he once heard of Mazarelle waiting for his wife in some noisy Left Bank café and, being stood up, he got so rip-roaring drunk that he finally reported her a missing person. The tinkly, seductive sound of Molly's laughter was gentle as wind chimes.

"If you don't mind," he said, "I'd like to ask you something."

"That depends on what it is."

"Are you Jewish?"

She stared at him. "Yes, I'm Jewish. Why?"

"Orthodox?"

Molly reached up and grabbed a hank of her flaming red hair. "Does this look like a wig?"

"No, no." Bennett laughed uncomfortably. "Not at all."

"What's this all about?"

He explained that the inspector had told him that all four of the victims had already been autopsied. There had been no time to get her approval about her parents. He hoped that she understood. It was standard French police procedure in a murder case like this.

Molly sadly shook her head.

"I once had a problem about an autopsy with an Orthodox Jewish family. I didn't know it was against their belief."

"No, I don't mind." She regarded nothing about her mom and dad as orthodox. "Anything that will help catch the monster who did this."

There was something else he feared she wasn't going to like.

"I know you were hoping to return to the States tomorrow with the bodies of your parents, but the inspector says he's still not finished with them. I think he wants Dr. Langlais to run some more tests."

"How much longer does he need?"

"I'm not sure. He's in charge, and there was nothing more I could do. I'm sorry, I tried."

Molly was obviously upset.

"Please don't worry. I'll take care of everything here. As soon as the bodies are released, I'll ship them home to you in New York immediately. I promise."

Molly sank down in her seat and her silence was worse than anything she might have said to him. It was about as unpleasant a job as he'd expected.

The Hôtel Fleuri, on the main square in Taziac opposite the church, was not much larger than Bennett had suggested, but it did have an available room.

"*Une chambre très bonne et tranquille,*" said the worried-looking man behind the desk.

"We'll need *two* rooms," Bennett said.

"Of course. You're Americans!" He loved Americans. He handed Bennett a registration card and suggested he fill it out at his convenience.

"Where's mine?"

"No, no, mademoiselle. You needn't trouble yourself. One card is more than enough." As for the price, it was a bargain. The *petit déjeuner* cost a little extra but, he assured them, was well worth it. Business must be awful, she thought, wondering if the other five rooms in the hotel were empty.

He introduced himself as Louis Favier, the owner. A short, thick, round-jawed man with a hairy mole on his chin, a ludicrous beauty mark that for some reason he didn't mind calling attention to with his stubby fingers. Favier thought they should know he often watched American films on the TV. "Did you ever see *Morocco?*" he asked them, kissing his puckered fingertips. *"Pandora's Box?"* He loved the young Cooper, Louise Brooks, the great Brando.

Molly, too tired for Favier's movie stars and ready to lie down, asked for her key.

Later that afternoon, with directions from Monsieur Favier, who seemed surprised when he heard where they wanted to go, they drove to L'Ermitage. The cop at the top of the hill said that Inspector Mazarelle hadn't arrived yet, but they could wait for him as long as they didn't get out of their car. After that, he watched them like an air controller eyeing wayward blips on his radar screen. It was a half hour more before the inspector and Duboit finally showed up.

Mazarelle had regretted agreeing to meet Mademoiselle Reece here as soon as he'd done so. Though he felt like an idiot, he hated to say no to such a sad and lovely young woman. He guided them around the grounds—strolling past the swimming pool to the well, where, he told them, one of the murder weapons had been found. Then on to the barn, where Phillips's body was discovered hidden in a secret room, victim of a double-barreled shotgun.

Bennett asked, "Can we see the room?"

"I'll show you," Duboit gallantly offered the attractive young woman.

Naturally, thought his boss as he watched them go.

Duboit led the way to the rear of the barn. At the half-open door, he explained that it had been barred from the inside and how the murderer must have gotten in and out. He knew better than to enter the room to demonstrate how it was actually done. In any event, the yellow police tape all over the door made entry out of the question.

Mazarelle brought his visitors across to the house. Escorting them around the outside of the building, he described the layout of the rooms and the bodies—exactly what had happened and where—but when Molly asked to go in he apologized.

"I'm sorry, mademoiselle, but that's impossible."

"Ms. Reece is in law enforcement," Bennett informed him. "She's an assistant district attorney in New York City."

"The crime scene is closed." Mazarelle was in no bargaining mood. He didn't give a damn about Bennett and assumed that if Ms. Reece was in law enforcement, she'd understand. Besides, he'd no desire to show her the kitchen where her father was murdered—his dried blood still covering the ceiling, windows, and walls like gruesome wallpaper, the kind that could kill you if you weren't dead already.

Molly, ticked off with him, didn't understand at all. Punishing her because she had almost fainted. Typical, she thought. She hated the way some men try to overprotect women. It was, after all, nothing more than a power play, just another way of keeping us in our place. *Kinder, Küche, und Kirche.* Eyeballing the inspector, Molly asked where his investigation stood as of right now, and her tone suggested that she would not be put off.

"Yes . . . yes, of course. Well, we're coming along. I can tell you that." The inspector took out his pipe and lit up.

"Perhaps I didn't make myself clear. What I want to know is how close are you to breaking the case?"

"We have an interesting suspect, if that's what you mean." Mazarelle told her about Ali Sedak, the man they were holding as a material witness, whose fingerprints were found on one of the murder weapons as well as on the tape with which all the victims in the house were bound. Sedak, according to the inspector, was somehow involved in all the murders, even if he didn't actually commit them all. "Or," he added, with a puckish gleam in his eye, "any of them, for that matter."

At the moment, Molly had no patience for paradox. "Who is he?"

"Sedak?" Duboit knew all about him. "A tough little sidi. Works here at L'Ermitage, doing odd jobs on the property. He's a *beur,* lives with a French woman and a baby who looks a little like him. Dark skin, dark hair, dark eyes. Mixing up those Arab genes of his with ours. It's disgusting."

"Shut up, Bernard! They're married."

"He's still a *beur.*"

"So what? He speaks French as well as you or I do."

Molly asked, "What's a *beur*?"

"You know," Duboit told her, "the same as Jews and Gypsies. What can you expect from people like that?"

Mazarelle didn't have to see Mademoiselle Reece's face to sense that she was unhappy. He told Bernard to go back to the car, to wait for him there. He'd be along shortly.

When he'd left, Molly asked, "Where did you get *him*?"

The inspector shrugged helplessly. "What can you do? Even in the police we have a few who confuse fascism with law and order. But Bernard isn't really so bad. He's a provincial. And the Front National's racist, anti-Semitic ideas are not unknown in this part of the country. I'm sorry to say that only a few kilometers away in Villereal we have our own local Jean-Marie Le Pen in René Arnaud."

Dwight Bennett knew all about Arnaud. "He's almost as bad."

Mazarelle sighed and turned to Molly, who was still seething. "I can tell you this, mademoiselle. Your father's credit cards and money were almost certainly stolen by Ali Sedak. Furthermore, he's admitted being the last one to have seen Monsieur Phillips alive. And it's very possible these crimes were all drug related. Sedak is a known user. He has a record of violence and being a pusher as well. We think he may have been working together with a local dealer they call Rabo."

"Rabo?" He sounded like a Vegas gangster to Molly. "Is he an American?"

"French," snapped Mazarelle. "His real name is Rabineau." Was there something he said that amused her? "And that's where we are," he said, abruptly concluding the matter. Mazarelle promised that when she returned home to New York he'd keep her informed of any major developments in the case. "Now I really must go."

As he limped away, Molly felt depressed by what she'd heard.

Though she basically liked the inspector, she wasn't exactly thrilled with his progress. Or with his "interesting" suspect. Or by that bigoted creep Duboit. Faced with cops like that, Ali Sedak might be as innocent as Jesus and still end up on the cross.

A number of reporters, having heard that the daughter of two of the murdered Americans had arrived in Bergerac, were waiting for Molly at the commissariat when Inspector Mazarelle drove into the courtyard. But only Jacques Gaudin, who wrote for the local edition of *Sud Ouest,* had tracked her down at the Hôtel Fleuri in Taziac.

Sitting in the hotel's small lobby, Gaudin was killing time with an old copy of *Paris Match* when he heard Favier calling to him in a whisper from behind the desk. The woman who came in was tall and had red hair. A very classy dame with great cheekbones. Tossing aside his magazine, he hurried to the door and introduced himself. Bennett quickly stepped between them, insisting that Mademoiselle Reece had had a very exhausting day and was not giving any interviews.

"That's okay," she said. "I don't mind a few questions. What do you want to know?"

She was as nice as she looked. Was he falling in love again?

"Do you think the man the police are holding, Ali Sedak, killed your parents?"

"No, I don't."

Gaudin coolly scribbled down her reply on his graph-paper-ruled notepad, but he was almost as surprised as her friend was by the strength of her conviction.

"May I ask why not?"

"And certainly not alone. I don't believe any one man by himself could have killed all four of them. Schuyler Phillips was a great athlete and my father was a big man in pretty good shape for his age. Not to mention my mother, who was not someone who scared easily. And even if Schuyler was already dead in the barn and there were only the three of them still alive in the house, this one guy with a knife was unlikely to be able to tie up all three and then murder them in different rooms."

"I understand your father, Monsieur Reece, was an important figure in the New York art world. Did he have any enemies?"

"None that I'm aware of. People who knew my father had the highest respect for him. On the other hand, I can't imagine anyone who owns an art gallery in New York who doesn't have a few enemies."

Molly said nothing about Sean. As for that, she'd always supposed their relationship was like any marriage, with its ups and downs. They were successful partners, after all, and had been for years. But what if Sean felt that he was going to be turned in to the police by her dad for dealing in stolen art, felt that it was the end of his career and there was only one way to save himself from doing time? Could Sean have hired someone to murder him? But why kill all four of them? Only a maniac would do something like that.

"That's enough questions," Bennett said, seeing how tired she looked. He took her arm. "Come on, Molly."

"Just one more, mademoiselle. How long are you planning to remain here?"

"As long as it takes. I'm not going home until I find out who murdered my parents and their friends. They deserve that. Not to be forgotten. Besides, I'm an assistant district attorney in New York City. I may be able to assist your police in their investigation. I'll help in any way I can."

On their way upstairs, Bennett said, "You're not serious about that, are you?"

"About what?"

"Not going back with me to Paris tomorrow."

"Look," she said, and stopped at the landing. "We both know how the process works. As long as I stay here nobody is going to forget about what happened. And certainly not the police. I'd hate to see them get away with convicting some poor schnook they don't like just because he's an Arab. Why shouldn't I stay?"

"Well, for one thing, if you're right about Sedak not being the killer, then the real murderer may still be around here. You could be in danger."

"Don't be silly. Why would anyone want to kill me?"

"Maybe for the same reason he killed your parents and their friends."

"Let's drop this subject, okay? I'm tired."

Though she'd told him that she wasn't interested in dinner, Molly was glad later when Dwight knocked on her door. The restaurant Favier recommended was Chez Doucette. She didn't care for the corny rustic decor, but the food was good and the wine even better. And Dwight was good company. He knew all sorts of amusing stories and could tell them well. A terrific mimic, he had more voices than Canal Street. By the end of the evening Molly thought she'd finally mellowed out. She even agreed to think over going back to Paris with him in the morning, which he kept encouraging her to do.

Later in her room, the sweet smell of the rain brought tears to her eyes. She couldn't stop sobbing. After a while, she settled down and crawled into bed, listening to the rain lightly tapping on the window, and fell asleep. Around three, she got up to go to the bathroom and returned to bed, feeling as if she were the only one still awake in all Taziac. A grieving orphan cut off from even her memories of old, shared, familial joys. The church bell's clanging stroke falling on the night faded away and left nothing but loneliness. Picking up her Walkman from the night table, Molly put on her headphones and played with the dial. Getting waves of static, then Radio One coming in crystal-clear from Cork.

"That was Erroll Garner and 'Misssty,' for *yooouu*," the deejay told her in a deep, alcohol-soaked baritone, before promising gale-force winds over the Irish Sea. "So lay on a fire," he suggested, "and cooozy up with a blanket to Ella singin' 'Baby It's Coooolld Outside.'"

A little after 4:00 a.m. and unable to get back to sleep, she picked up the phone. It was still only 10 p.m. in New York. She told herself that she didn't really expect Kevin to be home yet, but she knew how rotten she'd feel if he wasn't.

"Lo . . ." His voice sounded as if it had been tucked in bed for the night.

"Kev! Hi, sweetie. Did I wake you?"

"Molly! Where are you? I was getting worried. I've been trying to reach you. Did you see your folks?"

"Oh, Kevin, it was awful."

"I bet."

"The worst."

"I could kick myself. I should have been there with you."

"But you couldn't. You have the new play. I understand. How're the rehearsals going?"

"Geoffrey is all nerves. It's a small stage. He keeps changing the blocking, which is a drag. Other than that, not bad. What time is it there anyhow?"

"Four fifteen."

"A.m.! What the hell are you doing up at that hour?"

"I couldn't sleep."

Lifting the receiver closer to his mouth, Kevin whispered, "I wish you were here, Molly. Miss you, honey. When are you coming back?"

"Don't know yet."

"Seems as if you've been gone ages already. Come home, Molly."

He didn't want her to stay any more than Bennett did. "You too?"

"Me too what?"

"Did you get a chance to speak to Sean and tell him what happened?"

"That's what I wanted to tell you. I tried, but he wasn't around. The gallery assistant promised to pass on the message to him when he called in. Did you know that he's in France?"

"Sean's in France? Where?"

"She didn't know exactly. Which reminds me, where are you?"

"The Hôtel Fleuri in Taziac."

Molly gave Kevin the number pasted on the phone and before hanging up promised to call as soon as she knew what she was going to do. She really couldn't decide. I'll sleep on it, she thought.

A few hours later, when Bennett knocked on Molly's door, he was glad to see that she was dressed and waiting for him.

"Ready to go?"

"I'm not going."

"Let's talk over breakfast."

Downstairs Bennett could tell it was hopeless to try to change her mind and gave up. Instead, he ordered a chocolat and dropped in three cubes of sugar. Poor thing, she thought. He seemed to be feeling deprived. Over the *petit déjeuner* he asked if she'd like him to drive her to the Hertz in Bordeaux, where she could get her own car.

Later in Bordeaux, he took out an embassy card from his wallet and wrote down his home phone number.

"I can be reached at either of these numbers. If there's anything you need, Molly . . ."

She thanked him and gave him a French send-off on both cheeks.

"And above all," he warned her, "don't go playing detective. Remember, you're in France now. That's Mazarelle's job. Be careful, Molly."

25

MAZARELLE'S OFFICE

Though Molly didn't know what to make of the news that Sean was in France, she thought it important to tell the inspector right away. She also told him about her father's falling-out with his partner over his dealings in stolen art. Molly couldn't believe Sean murdered her father and mother, let alone their friends. That in some way he might be at the bottom of what happened, however, she accepted as a distinct possibility.

Mazarelle received her information with more than routine interest, his eyes fixed on Molly, streams of smoke shooting up from the bowl of his pipe. He was open to following up any outside lead that seemed promising. Recalling the accident in Schuyler Phillips's rented Mercedes, he wondered if her father had been the intended victim after all. He asked how long Sean Campbell had been in the country, which she didn't know, and then took down a description of him, the address and phone number in Manhattan of the Reece-Campbell Gallery. Mazarelle assured her that if Campbell was in France, he'd find him.

They stood up and shook hands. She was almost as tall as he was. No ring on her left hand except a small one with an oval peridot birthstone that matched her green eyes. Independent, intelligent. A Leo, if he believed in such nonsense. He supposed that back home in the States she had a lover. More than one, probably. She's good material for love, he thought. He liked the easy way she moved, the way she lit up a room when she walked in, her courage. To have both her parents chopped up like hamburger and, rather than go home and grieve, to be so strong, so determined to get justice . . . Yes, a remarkable young woman. He'd seen the interview with her in the morning issue of *Sud Ouest*. Underneath all that beauty she was tough as a tank, and she didn't miss much. As long as she stayed out of trouble, Mazarelle didn't mind in the least having Mademoiselle Reece in the neighborhood for a while longer.

26

BENIDORM, SPAIN

The weathered kiosk near the beach in Benidorm—open only summers—sold newspapers from all over Europe and lottery tickets for anyone feeling lucky. Reiner gathered up copies of the *International Herald Tribune, Le Monde, La Dépêche,* and *Las Provincias* from Valencia. Three of the four carried stories about Ali Sedak: "Handyman Named Prime Suspect in Taziac Murders." He'd been taken into custody by Inspector Paul Mazarelle, head of the police special task force investigating the crime.

That was all Reiner needed. With the papers under his arm, he blew into the lobby of the Gran Hotel Delfin and hurried to the phone booth, pulling the door closed behind him. Now the Frenchies would pay, or he'd close their account permanently. Either way, Reiner knew it'd be his last call to this Paris number.

He recognized the voice that came on instantly. Pellerin wanted to know where he was.

"Did you see the papers?"

"Who hasn't?"

"It's all over. Now you've got what you asked for, and they have their murderer. Time to pay up."

"That's not what I ordered."

Reiner didn't care for his peevish, constipated tone. "As I told you, I had to make some adjustments."

"Don't worry. You'll get your money."

"Today."

"That's impossible."

"How long does it take to make an electronic transfer of funds? A few seconds?"

"The banks are already closed for the weekend. It's too late. Besides, we have some unfinished business to discuss with you."

Reiner didn't like the sound of that at all. "Unfinished business?"

"I'll meet you halfway. Bourges. The Hôtel de Bourbon. It's convenient, right near the railway station. How's Sunday for lunch?"

The Frenchman seemed to assume that he was still in the Dordogne. "What about the money?"

"Don't worry. You'll get it. Then we're on for lunch. Good. They have a splendid restaurant, the Abbaye Saint-Ambroix, with the best foie gras anywhere. One's mouth fairly drips."

Pellerin, the gourmand. As usual, the French flaunting their stomachs like jewel boxes. Reiner had no pretensions about food; he kept his machine running smoothly even if it meant yogurt and nuts. Though by no means eager to return to France so soon, and fully aware that this might be a trap, Reiner was willing to meet him halfway. Especially for the money.

"*D'accord,*" he said, and proposed one small change in their plan. They'd meet in the cathedral rather than the hotel. He preferred a large public place and Saint-Étienne at the top of the hill was one of the largest Gothic cathedrals in France.

"But it's huge. There's no privacy."

If Pellerin assumed that its size eliminated the church as a choice, he was wrong. As far as Reiner was concerned, it was just right. He promised he'd be in the Jacques Coeur chapel of the cathedral at noon and, before Pellerin could say anything, hung up.

On his way to the front door of the hotel, Reiner breezed past the manager, who greeted him warmly. "No tennis today, Senor Kämpe?" the manager asked.

27

ENCOUNTER AT THE OLD MILL

Reluctantly, Favier gave Molly directions. He seemed to disapprove of Thérèse as much as Duboit hated her Arab husband. Were they all racists around here? Molly wondered. In any event, it was none of the hotel manager's business where she went or why. Anything she could do to aid the inspector with his investigation, she was eager to do. And the wife of Ali Sedak seemed a good place to start.

It was a short, pleasant drive, showy crape myrtle trees lining the road, their leaves shimmering gloriously in the sunlight. The old stone water mill she was looking for struck her as charming rather than what Favier called *délabré*, and, as she drove up and parked next to the dusty white VW, the butterflies fluttering across the shallow stream added to the quiet, picturesque scene.

When Thérèse came to the door, she stood there with her blouse open, nursing her baby, and sized up her visitor. Molly introduced herself, asked if she had a few minutes to talk. The name at first meant nothing to the young mother until Molly explained who she was. Thérèse's eyes shifted about uncomfortably as if she couldn't make up her mind.

She finally nodded and went back inside with the baby.

Molly reached into her shoulder bag, switched on her tape recorder, and followed her into the house. Sitting down opposite her at the table, she admired the mother's cute, black-eyed child in his blue blanket. "*Quel beau bébé!*" Molly gushed, by way of warming her up, and asked his name, how old he was. She congratulated Thérèse on her baby's beautiful disposition.

Sometimes, Thérèse told her. She asked for the diaper on the back of the chair next to Molly. Tossing it onto her shoulder, she placed the infant on top and patted him on the back. Her uncombed hair, which covered the side of her face, parted as she straightened up and Molly noticed the large purple bruise on her cheek. Her husband had left her a going-away present. In Molly's job she'd seen too many women who had been turned into human punching bags by the creeps they loved. With a temper like that, maybe he *was* the murderer.

Thérèse wanted her to know she was sorry about Molly's parents and their friends, but Ali was innocent. Completely innocent. He didn't even know about the murders until she told him. And at the commissariat in Bergerac, they'd refused to let her see him, talk to him. She couldn't even give him a comb, a toothbrush, anything. Thérèse had no idea how long he was going to be kept there or what to do next. They had hardly any money. She couldn't afford a lawyer. Her eyes reddened, and with a corner of the diaper she wiped away the tears.

Molly, despite her carefully cultivated professional caution, was touched and she sympathized, but didn't know how far she could trust Thérèse. Molly asked about the events of the night of the murders and Thérèse told her what she'd told the police. Ali came home late that night—around 9:30 or 10:00—with a bad back. He had a couple of beers, ate hardly anything, and went right to bed.

It wasn't until later, when Molly asked if anything else had happened that night, that Thérèse remembered the telephone calls. Two of them maybe twenty-five minutes apart. The first about 1:00 a.m. She'd been sound asleep, and when the phone rang it was like an electric finger touching her heart. Each time she picked up the receiver no one was there. Some breathing, that was all. No, she'd no idea who it was or whether it was important. But Ali had heard nothing, never budged, and, going back to sleep, she forgot.

There was a vulnerability about Thérèse that Molly liked. They talked softly while the baby slept, and time slowly slipped away until they were interrupted by the sound of distant motors growing louder. The sleek machines roared up into the front yard amid swirling dust, and the riders, revving their thunderous engines, shut them off. Friends, Molly supposed. Time for her to go. Thanking Thérèse for her help, she opened the door.

Three motorcycles. Two Yamahas and a Scout. The three riders in black boots, faded jeans, helmets. The big, bearded one had a bull neck with a chain draped around it from which hung an Iron Cross. The two in black T-shirts were thin, wiry, and had tattoos all over their skinny arms. They might have been twins. All three helmets were stamped SHARK, as colorful as fireworks with flashy streaks of white, green, red, and yellow. France loved her athletic clubs, she thought, bicycle clubs, football clubs, sailing clubs. They were members of a motorcycle club—a bit oddball perhaps, like the Stanford marching band. What troubled her was that they didn't take off their helmets, and because of the tinted visors she couldn't see their faces.

Molly looked again. What at first glance had seemed amusing wasn't funny at all. These guys were grief. And if Ali Sedak wasn't there, they'd settle for the Arab son of a bitch's French squeeze or anyone else on the premises.

Without actually running, street-smart Molly began to walk quickly to her rented car, fumbling for the car keys in her shoulder bag. The three of them shouted after her, calling her a *melon* lover and telling her to slow down, not so fast. They wanted to know if she still had something left between her legs for a Frenchman. Molly pulled the car door open and was about to jump in when she felt herself being grabbed from behind. It was one of the thin ones. His bony fingers clamped around her waist, he yanked her away from the door. Wheeling around, Molly raked his neck with her car keys and he began to bleed. His *copains* howled. As for him, he seemed surprised, then smacked her across the side of the head, slammed her against the car.

Thérèse screamed as she stood in the doorway clutching her howling baby. *"Casse-toi, vous fils de merde!"*

The three of them turned. "Look who's there. The bitch herself." They began walking toward her. "And that must be her boyfriend's bastard. Willya look at that kisser on him? How can a kid with a mug like that be French? And living off us too on welfare. It's disgusting!"

Before they could grab her, Thérèse slammed the door and bolted it closed. The bearded bruiser pounded on the wooden door. Its frame shivered. Hinges groaned. He picked up a rusty lead pipe and joined his buddies, who were smashing the headlights of Ali's white VW. Hovering over the front trunk, he beat on it viciously, as if Ali were trapped inside.

Molly snatched up her fallen keys, threw herself into her car, and locked all the doors. Though the engine started up almost instantly, it seemed to take forever. The three bikers suddenly looked up, and Molly, wide-eyed and scared out of her wits, shoved the car into gear. Slamming the gas pedal to the floor, she held it there as she raced down the road, her eyes constantly checking the rearview mirror. Once after rounding a bend, she glanced back over her shoulder and thought she saw them coming after her, pitiless as Nevsky's knights, their helmets glittering in the sun.

As soon as she was safely back in her hotel room, Molly dialed Mazarelle. The inspector was glad to hear from her. That is, until she told him where she'd been.

PART THREE

28

DARGELIER'S IOU

The Emerald City. Ringed by water and bathed in light, Montreal glowed green as the Boeing 747 broke through the clouds at eighteen thousand feet and descended for a landing at Dorval International Airport. With only carry-on baggage, Pellerin and Blond breezed through customs and were soon checked into the InterContinental, near the Vieux-Port and not far from the world headquarters of Tornade. Booked for a quickie overnight stay. Their first step after getting the job had been Berlin and the accident artist. Now came step two—Montreal and the multinational's new broom. It was time to collect on Dargelier's IOU.

The front of the Tornade building was a skyscraping wall of tinted glass surmounted by a massive green letter *T*. Security wanted to know who they were. Pellerin showed him a copy of the e-mail they'd received in Paris with the time of their appointment. After checking his clipboard, the guard labeled them each Guest, and in they went. Blond asked the woman behind the information desk what the green circles were on the huge map of the world covering the lobby wall. Malachite, she explained, marking the dozen cities in which Tornade had plants. The company, a diversified giant with more than sixty thousand employees worldwide, was organized into four divisions: aerospace, trains, ships, and finance.

Pellerin asked, "And Jean-Paul Dargelier?"

She said, "Our new CEO. You'll find him on the thirty-third floor, the top of the Tornade."

The new CEO was waiting for them in his office. On a bright day like this one, the windows—even through tinted glass—were filled with crystal blue skies and a glittering view of the St. Lawrence River. There were Oriental rugs on the floor, soft leather chairs, a wide-winged diptych computer monitor, but no clocks. The place reeked of power. At forty-five, Tornade's new CEO was the youngest in the history of the company.

Dargelier, as he came out from behind his heavy mahogany desk to welcome them, might have been a bit of a letdown if they hadn't met him a few years earlier at the Paris air show. He was in his early forties then and already in charge of Tornade's aerospace division—the third largest builder of civilian aircraft in the world after Boeing and Airbus. Clearly a young man on the make, his brilliant career rising like a rocket.

On the short side, Dargelier had a quiet manner and a thin, dark, ferret face that by six o'clock would probably require a razor before he took it out for cocktails. Not too impressive, if you failed to see the steel beneath his saturnine exterior. Pellerin was not one to make that mistake. He could even feel the ambition in Dargelier's handshake.

"Congratulations," Pellerin said. "We knew when we last met you in Paris that it was just a matter of time."

Dargelier sighed. "But how could you know? Schuyler was still such a relatively young man."

Blond corrected him. "*You're* a young man."

"I mean out of the blue like that. Totally unexpected. His death was quite a shock to everyone here."

"I'm sure," Pellerin said coolly, anxious to get down to business. "The good news is that even the darkest clouds often bring the needed rain." He glanced about the room, admiring the CEO's large corner office with its spectacular view. "This is all yours now. Didn't you tell us it was time for a Canadian to take over the reins of Tornade?"

"Did I say that? I suppose I did. Though that was probably only the gin in my martini talking. But even then there were people here who thought so. In any case, Schuyler left behind a full plate of projects for his successor. First of all, there's our unmanned aerial surveillance vehicles being made for the Canadian military, then there's the new ultra-long-range corporate jet to compete in the U.S. market with Gulfstream, and add to that our latest high-speed train for Chad—a country without any railroads and few passable roads of any kind."

Pellerin knew all about the African project. "But what Chad does have," he pointed out, "is loads of natron for manufacturing glass, ceramics, soap, and paper. And what you didn't mention is that the French-owned Chad Development Corporation is willing to pay a great deal of money to transport it out of that unhappy, impoverished, landlocked nation to the African coast for export."

Dargelier's eyes opened wide. "You know your Chad, monsieur."

"Not really, but I have visited their corporate headquarters in Paris."

The new CEO's glance went from Pellerin to Blond. "Are you both still working for the French government?"

Blond hesitated.

"You might say so," Pellerin informed him, chuckling, "but in a different capacity. We're now independent contractors. In fact, that's in part what brought us here. You may be in a position to do us a little favor." He paused to let his words sink in. "After all, you do owe us one, you know?"

Though puzzled by his visitor's remark, Dargelier looked interested. "What sort of favor?"

Pellerin mentioned a recent article he'd read in *Le Monde*. It was about the first delivery to Tornade of a new NATO trainer from Zalltech Aerospace in Houston.

"Yes, that's right! The T-9AX." Dargelier's enthusiasm for their acquisition was obvious. "Tornade will be handling instruction in the plane's advanced technology. It was the last major deal Schuyler made for us—and what a deal! The advantages for NATO countries are clear. It gives them a quality, cost-effective pilot training program with highly advanced avionics, such as its cockpit electronic display system for navigation, radar, satellite, and anticollision data. And *all* without the need for these NATO countries to purchase the training planes themselves. It's a win-win agreement. The one major hurdle was that this was the first transfer of U.S. military technology to the private sector of a foreign country. Naturally Washington was anxious about it falling into the hands of unfriendly nations. But what helped seal the deal for us, of course, was that Schuyler was an American."

Pellerin inquired, "How many of the planes did you receive?"

"In the first shipment? Ten," Dargelier replied.

"Good. Then you won't be likely to miss one."

"What do you mean?"

Pellerin quietly explained, "We'd like you to include one of the new NATO trainers in your next shipment of high-speed railroad parts to Chad. It will have to be packed in the same sort of large wooden crates and addressed exactly like the others to the Société de Chemin de Fer du Tchad. Can you handle it?"

Dargelier's smile was the sort you might give a child. "That's ridiculous. Why would I want to throw away an expensive plane like that?"

"Because you owe us that little favor we mentioned."

"Do I?" Dargelier was still smiling.

"I thought you understood. There's a tape of our conversation in Paris."

His smile fell like a trapdoor. "What tape? What are you talking about?"

"Surely you weren't so *éméché* you've forgotten telling us that the one person who stood in your path at Tornade was Schuyler Phillips, and that the only way he'd go is if he were pushed."

"But I never said *murdered.* I only meant—"

"Whatever you thought you said—or meant to say—the French investigators of the Taziac deaths might find it more than a little interesting, *n'est-ce pas*? But of course, you do us this favor and that tape disappears."

"I still don't understand. What are they going to do in Chad with a NATO trainer?"

"No problem. It's not going to stay there very long. It'll be going elsewhere. And we'll take care of that."

"I see." Dargelier's voice faltered, his face darkened as if he'd slipped behind a cloud. "That might very well be a problem."

"What are you getting at?" Blond demanded.

"It's very simple. If that plane ends up where it shouldn't be and Washington gets wind of a possible violation of the U.S. Arms Export Control Act, our agreement with the United States would probably be finished."

Pellerin said, "Who says they'll find out? If push comes to shove, all you know is it went astray. You're free and clear."

"Free as a bird," chorused his friend.

"With no ugly rumors about the death of Phillips to ruin a glassy-smooth succession. Think of it, another win-win agreement and this time of your own making."

Dargelier sank back in his chair and considered the possibilities. "Let me think about it."

"Of course." Pellerin got up to leave.

"But not too long," Blond advised.

Stopping at the office door as if he'd left something behind, Pellerin wheeled around.

"Think it over. When you've run the numbers, you'll soon see that all this will cost you are a few dollars for the loss of one plane rather than millions for the entire contract. We'll call for your answer tomorrow morning from the airport."

29

MAZARELLE'S SQUAD

andu walked over to the barred ground-floor window with his mug. *"C'est dégueulasse."* As he tossed out what was left of his coffee, it splashed against one of the black iron bars.

"Merde!" Wiping off his damp hand, his shirtsleeve, he muttered, "Tepid piss." No one in the task force really liked the watery coffee made by their machine, but their chief didn't seem to mind. He supposed it was something to wet Mazarelle's whistle and keep his eyelids propped open when working late into the night.

Bandu and the others were waiting for him in their small downstairs meeting room—the temporary office the commissaire had given them—at the rear of the building. They'd brought in their own computers and programs, file cabinets, telephones, and infamous coffeemaker. The two windows overlooked the rear parking lot, which was almost always crowded these days. A frequent source of bitching among Rivet's officers because so many of the cars belonged to Mazarelle's men. That morning, shoehorned into the noisy, smoky room, they were expecting their *patron* any minute.

Rivet had stopped Mazarelle outside the meeting room to complain about the parking situation when he noticed the new sign on the door: Mazarelle's Squad. From the exasperated expression on the commissaire's face, the inspector knew that he shouldn't ask but did anyway. "All right, what's wrong with this one?"

Rivet blew out his cheeks in disgust. "It's as bad as the first. Maybe worse. Much too much like the gendarmes. Too military. That's not us. We're not a 'troop,' or a 'platoon,' or a 'squadron.' We're the police. So why not something less official sounding and"— his expression softened as if bathed in a rose light—"more like Mazarelle's 'team'? Or 'band'? Or 'bunch'? That sort of thing. Isn't that better?"

"Hmmm," Mazarelle pondered. With a major murder case on his hands, how come he had to put up with crap like this? The young commissaire sounded like a fool, which he certainly wasn't. So why, Mazarelle asked himself, is he all of a sudden busting my balls? He figured all it meant was that the former homicide hotshot from Paris was getting too much media attention, and it was driving Rivet crazy. "Let me think about it."

The men jammed into the meeting room fell silent as the inspector's bulk filled the doorway. Limping across to the coffeemaker, he poured himself a full cup, took a sip of the dreadful stuff, and, deadpan, put it down. Mazarelle reminded his men that they couldn't hold Ali Sedak in *garde à vue* too much longer without bringing charges. Tacked on the wall behind him were a half-dozen grisly photos of the crime scene and its victims. The four bodies were either slashed or buckshot riddled in their twisted final agony. He didn't want any of his people to forget what sort of killer or killers they were after and why. "Okay," he announced, "let's hear what you've got for me."

The two teams he'd sent door-to-door in the vicinity of L'Ermitage to learn if anyone had heard or seen anything unusual the night of the murders had nothing new to report.

"Not even strangers in the neighborhood?"

The silence in the room was suffocating.

"No one said *anything*?" Mazarelle's displeasure was evident. "Zip?"

Lambert, who had grown up in Taziac, said, "People are frightened."

The inspector gestured to the photos behind him. "I understand. But did you try *every* house nearby?"

"A few of them appeared to be empty."

"Go back. Double-check. Let me know right away if you get anything. In any event, tell me the locations of the empty houses." He glanced around the room. "Now what about the rest of you?"

André Tricot spoke up. He'd come highly recommended by Madame Leclerc, and though Mazarelle understandably hesitated taking him on—anxious to avoid leaks—he felt he'd no choice. She was, after all, the investigating magistrate. As it turned out, Tricot was a good cop, and he'd come up with something. Tricot handed him a plastic bag with two wallets. The brown one belonged to Monsieur Reece. Tricot showed him the New York driver's license with its tiny picture of Reece, guardedly eyeing the camera. Mazarelle recalled the expression. Holding the wallet carefully by the corners and turning it inside out, the inspector went through it.

"Any money? Credit cards?"

"Nothing."

Tricot explained that a farmer who lived on the road to Eymet had called. He'd found his dog playing with it. Tricot had discovered the black wallet, which belonged to Monsieur Phillips, a little farther down the road. He supposed the wallets were thrown from a passing car but had no idea when.

"Also empty?" Mazarelle asked, as he looked through the pockets. Tricot nodded.

"Did you check the ATMs in Eymet?"

Tricot had checked. The one at the BNP branch had been used. He reported that early on the morning following the murders a large sum of cash had been withdrawn on Monsieur Reece's MasterCard as well as Monsieur Phillips's Visa. He handed Mazarelle the duplicate receipts he'd obtained with the times of withdrawal plus exact amounts.

"Well done, Tricot!" The inspector slapped his back approvingly and Tricot, a slim, taciturn man with big, expressive eyes, winced. Mazarelle told him to send the wallets down to PTS in Toulouse at once and see what they could find.

"Okay, what else?"

Bandu had some information for him. He'd spoken to one of his stoolies from Périgueux and gotten the name of a local dealer here they called Rabo.

"We know all about him. Go on."

Bandu said that after a little coaxing he'd admitted Ali Sedak was a regular customer. Recently flashing big bills, according to the junkie.

"Good work." Mazarelle chewed his news over carefully. "Okay," he said, after a few moments. He detailed Bandu and Duboit, who knew the layout of the old water mill where Ali lived, to go out there and find his stash. "Tear the place apart if you have to. The stuff is there somewhere. Get it for me."

"What about a search warrant?" Duboit asked, remembering how difficult Thérèse could be. "She's not going to let us in."

"Forget the search warrant. There's no time for that. Besides, you won't need one. She's not going to make a fuss with her man locked up here."

Bandu, who hated any kind of meeting, was eager to get out of there. "Come on, Doobie. *En route!*"

"But remember, no more 'accidents,'" Mazarelle called after him.

Halfway out the door, Bandu kept going as if he hadn't heard.

Mazarelle grabbed the younger cop by the arm and pulled him back. "Keep an eye on him, Bernard. I don't want her going to the media black-and-blue."

"*D'accord*, boss."

Thérèse recognized one of the two cops out front, looking over their battered VW. He was from the commissariat in Bergerac where they were holding Ali. She wondered why they'd come, feared it was bad news.

"What do you want now?"

"What happened to your car?" Bandu asked.

"Three guys on motorcycles."

"Who were they?"

"How should I know? They wore helmets with visors." She said she'd called the local gendarmerie and reported what happened, and they promised to be right over. "That was the last I heard from them."

Duboit said, "We're here to look around."

"The last time you looked around, you took my father's rifle and said you'd return it. I'm *still* waiting."

What a bitch, Duboit thought. "It's part of our investigation. You'll get it back when we're done with it."

"And what are you looking for now?"

"We've had a report that your—"

"Drugs," Bandu said, cutting him off. "Come on."

"We have no drugs here. What are you talking about?"

Duboit said, "How about the reefer Sedak was smoking the last time I came?"

"You can't do this without a search warrant. I know my rights. I've had enough from you cops. Had it up to here. You're never around when we need you and always show up when we don't. Now get out."

In a low, flat voice, Bandu warned her, "Shut up and sit down."

Thérèse did as she was told.

They started their hunt in the kitchen, yanking open cabinets, checking the shelves, the chipped dishes, looking into the water-stained cardboard boxes under the sink, behind the pipes. Bandu quickly went through the drawers in the refrigerator and, not caring for the putrid smell, slammed the door and muscled it away from the wall to see whether anything was taped to the back. Thérèse, riveted, watched the two cops as if they were wild animals, ignoring the cries of her baby, who had just been awakened. But the crying grew louder, more demanding, and she soon had to feed him.

It took the two of them about twenty minutes to find the hashish, hidden under the wooden stairs outside the back door. Bandu opened the black plastic garbage bag and whistled.

"Look at that, Doobie." He gave his partner a tight-lipped, satisfied smile. "Five keys of 'shish. A nice day's work."

Duboit was as tickled as Bandu with their success. What pissed him off the most was that Thérèse thought she could pull the wool over their eyes. Grabbing the bag, he brought it inside, where she sat on the edge of the unmade bed nursing her baby.

"No drugs, eh? No drugs?" He shook the bag in her face. "What do you call this, truffles?"

"Where did you get that?"

"Under the back stairs, where you hid it."

She said she'd no idea what it was, how it got there.

"Wise up, sweetheart. Right now, I'd say it don't look too good for your boyfriend. But maybe if you cooperate we might go a little easier on him."

"What do you mean?" Thérèse didn't like the way he said it or the way he was staring at her tits. She usually paid no attention to gawkers, amused at the way some men got so turned on watching her nursing that their tongues hung out, but not this time. She put the baby in his carriage and buttoned up.

Bandu saw what was going on and didn't want any part of it. The fool was about to do something dumb. "Come on. Let's get out of here," he said, snatching the 'shish away from him.

"You go ahead. I'll meet you outside."

"Come on, Doobie. Now! You heard what the boss said. No more accidents. Time to go." But the dope wouldn't listen. All he could hear was the blood roaring in his ears.

The young cop pushed her down on the bed. "I'll show you what I mean."

Thérèse screamed at the asshole to get off her. Lashed out with her fingernails, scratched his face. Fighting back furiously, she kicked his legs, his crotch, and managed to push him away. Duboit fell to the floor.

"You bitch!"

Bandu grabbed him before he could get to his feet. "Don't be a jerk, Duboit! I said let's go!" He dragged him to the door.

"Remember," Bandu warned her, "not a word about this to anyone. We can make it nasty for you too."

"You bastards! You planted that bag yourselves, didn't you?"

As soon as they came back to the office, Mazarelle noticed Doobie's face. "What happened to you? The scratches," Mazarelle said, pointing.

Duboit ran his fingertips over his cheek. "Oh that." He laughed and told his boss about crawling under the Arab's bed looking for his stash and running into a broken coil of wire on the bedspring.

"No drugs?"

Stepping forward, Bandu emptied the bricks of hashish onto the inspector's desk and, hearing the clatter as they fell, the members of the task force gathered around.

"It was under the steps at the back of the house."

Mazarelle marveled as he hefted the hashish, amazed at their haul and what it must have cost Ali. It was obvious where he'd gotten the money. No doubt contemplating a new line of work. He congratulated the two men, delighted with what they'd brought him. The next time he took Ali out of the *garde à vue* cell for questioning, he intended to get a confession from him.

"And you were right, boss. We didn't need a search warrant." Duboit gave his partner a sly glance of male bravado and couldn't resist adding, "She cooperated fully."

Bandu wished the young cock would stop strutting all the time and pay attention to business. He told the inspector about what happened to Ali's car and how Thérèse had reported it to the gendarmes in Taziac.

"Did they ever call you about that?" Bandu asked.

Mazarelle shook his head. They'd told him nothing, but he wasn't surprised, only very annoyed. Whoever busted up that car was tampering with evidence. The inspector made up his mind to go out there and look it over before she decided to junk it.

The white Beetle was a total wreck, worse than Bandu had described. The windows were completely smashed and pieces of glass covered the seats, the dashboard, the floor. Its tires slashed, the car rested on its axles. The inspector yanked on the front door a couple of times before he could get it open. The steering wheel looked clean to him. He brushed the glass off the driver's seat, which was worn and badly stained, so it was hard to tell if there was anything worthwhile there. Lifting the rubber floor mat, he shook off the glass, noting a few small, reddish-brown stains that could be promising. Releasing the trunk lock, he went around to the front. The hood was dented, bent out of shape, and when he pulled it up, it echoed like a plangent steel drum. Inside were some tools, some rags, a jack, a spare tire, and a mobile.

Mazarelle gingerly picked up the Nokia by its stubby black antenna. The cell phone was red and blue, the colors he guessed of the hockey team whose name was on the bottom. He felt like a jackass, kicked himself for not having forensics go over Ali's VW as soon as they had identified his bayonet. He slipped the phone into his pocket. As he walked over to radio his men to pick up the VW and take it down to

Toulouse, he felt he was being watched. He quickly said to tell PTS to give it a complete going over, the works. "It's urgent," he reminded them.

He walked across to the stone house and was about to knock when he glanced up. Thérèse was standing at the window with her arms crossed, watching him. He wondered how long she'd been there. It took her a while to unlock the door, and she did so only because the other two weren't with him. Besides, though she'd never admit it, he reminded her of Père Noël. The size of him and his barrel chest, thick bushy eyebrows, his mustache. But he still was a cop, so she kept her distance.

"Okay, what is it now?"

He told her that his men would be coming out to pick up the car. That it could help them find the three bikers who smashed the thing up.

"Take it. It's not doing us any good sitting out there like that in the front yard."

Mazarelle asked what they looked like. Thérèse told him they wore helmets with visors; she couldn't see their faces. What she did see were the black boots, the tattooed birds, flags, skulls, the splashy colors scrawled all over their arms, the cross around the neck of the big guy.

"Oh, one thing more . . ." He carefully pulled out the mobile from his pocket and showed it to her. "Does this belong to your husband?"

"How the hell should I know? It's possible."

"Is he a hockey fan?"

Thérèse drew back, cocked her head, and gave him a look as if he'd asked about her menstrual cycle.

"You know—hockey." He pointed to the name of the team on the Nokia. "Is Ali a Montreal Canadiens fan?"

It was when she folded her arms and told him that she had had enough questions, to go ask her husband, that the inspector saw the black-and-blue marks on her arms. They were fresh, ugly bruises that she didn't have the last time he'd been there.

"Where did you get those?"

"A bonus from one of the men you sent out here this morning. The son of a bitch tried to rape me."

"Bandu?"

"I don't know his name. He didn't leave his card."

"Bandu raped you?"

"I said tried to, but I changed his mind. It was the young one. The one who thinks he's such a smart-ass."

Duboit! He couldn't believe it. Even Duboit couldn't be such a goddamn fool. Mazarelle felt a tsunami surge of anger, followed by a sharp pang of disappointment. But why would she say so if it wasn't true? Though he didn't know what really happened, he knew what he had to do. He reminded her that with a house full of drugs and a husband in jail, she didn't need any more trouble than she already had. Going over to the sleeping baby, Mazarelle pulled out his wallet and dropped a few bills into the carriage.

"A kid can't have too many lollipops," he told her, and quickly left, feeling disgusted with everything—but mostly himself.

The first thing Mazarelle did when he got back to the office was corner Bandu and ask what happened. Bandu, looking uncomfortable, said he'd seen nothing. As for Duboit, he'd be back about three. He had to take his kid to the doctor.

"The older one," Bandu said. "The stutterer."

The boy was going to a speech therapist. In fact, Mazarelle had been the one who suggested it when he heard that the kid was stuttering so badly he was getting into fistfights at school and peeing in bed at home because his classmates were making fun of him. It was good advice. And he had some for the kid's old man too, when he finally showed up with the scratches on his cheek that Mazarelle had been trying hard to forget since talking to Thérèse.

From the expression on his boss's face, Duboit knew he was in for it. Sulking, he followed him out into the empty hallway. But before Doobie could explain, Mazarelle said, "No! Don't tell me anything because I'm not interested in your bullshit."

"But, boss—" he whined.

"You stupid blockhead! Don't you realize she could go to the press with this? I'm not about to let you fuck up my investigation just because you can't keep your zipper closed. How many years have you been a cop?"

Duboit was about to tell him, but Mazarelle had lost all patience. "Never mind. Step out of line again and I'll flush you down the toilet so fast you won't have time to wipe your ass. Understand?"

The crestfallen Duboit—usually never at a loss for words—was dumbstruck.

"Now go get Bandu and bring Ali Sedak into the interrogation room."

Mazarelle thought he'd never feel the same about Duboit again (how could he?) but, as so often happens in life, he was wrong.

There was something pathetic about the Ali Sedak they brought into the interrogation room. No belt, no shoelaces, no flashy gold chain around his neck, and a face drained of color and weary of the around-the-clock electric light. A couple of days alone in the cramped jail cell had taken their toll. As Sedak walked over to sit down in the same chair on which he'd previously sat, Bandu yanked it away and Ali fell hard to the floor. Bandu unlocked one of the handcuffs and, following instructions, hooked him up to the radiator. Just to let him know that this time things would be different. If Ali Sedak was the murderer, the inspector wanted to hear it from his own lips.

Mazarelle put the tape recorder near the edge of the table, closer to the prisoner on the floor, switched it on, and sat down with his cup of coffee. "Now that you've had time to think things over and refresh your memory, monsieur, let's begin again." The sound of Mazarelle's voice didn't always please him in these sorts of situations, but pitching his voice lower than usual he managed to get by with what nature had given him.

The first question he asked was, "Did you steal Reece's wallet and credit cards?"

Ali's answer was an emphatic no.

Taking a sip of coffee, Mazarelle made a face as he wiped his mouth, put down his paper cup, and grunted.

He turned off the recorder and, without getting up, leaned over and slapped the suspect backhanded across the side of his face, a seemingly effortless blow that exploded like a rifle shot. As Ali's head hit the radiator, he cried out in pain.

"Once again." The inspector turned on the recorder. "Did you steal Reece's Visa?"

This time Ali nodded.

"A little louder, *s'il vous plaît*."

"Yes," he mumbled.

Duboit and Bandu exchanged knowing glances. Unlike his boss, Duboit hadn't a shred of doubt Ali was guilty.

"That's better. And what about his MasterCard?"

"I don't remember."

Mazarelle lifted an eyebrow, making it clear that he wasn't satisfied.

"I didn't touch it," Ali insisted. And when asked about Phillips's wallet and Visa he claimed to know nothing about them. "All I took was one credit card and some money. That's all."

"How much money?"

"I don't remember."

"You what?" said the annoyed inspector, his voice ominously controlled.

"Five Curies."

"Twenty-five hundred francs? What did you do with it?"

"I gambled away some at the Café le Riche and bought a few presents with the rest."

"I see." Mazarelle took a sip of his coffee without noticing and asked if Ali had bought any drugs.

"No." His answer leaped out of Ali's mouth, much too fast to be credible.

Trying to get back in his boss's favor, Duboit delivered a powerful penalty kick to the Arab's thigh. "Say, 'No, *monsieur l'inspecteur*,' when the *patron* speaks to you."

"Why are you doing this, *monsieur l'inspecteur*?"

"I will not be taken for a fool. Is that clear? I don't have time for nonsense." But before the suspect had a chance to answer, Mazarelle asked, "Do you know a local dealer by the name of Rabo?"

Ali admitted he knew Rabo but said that he never bought anything from him.

Duboit threw up his hands. "Cut the crap, you horseshit artist. We know you're a user."

"A little pot, that's all." He looked up at the inspector. "You understand, for private, recreational use."

Mazarelle opened the black plastic bag and let him glance inside. "We found this under the back stairs of your house. Tell me about it."

"I never saw that before in my life. I swear it."

"Rabo says you bought it from him."

"He's lying! I'm not a dealer."

"In addition to the hashish, we also found Phillips's mobile in your car, not to mention some bloodstains that may be his too. Do you know how they got there?"

Ali sat on the floor with his head bowed and rocked back and forth as if silently reciting the Koran.

"Talk to me."

"You wouldn't understand."

"Try me. I'm a good listener."

"It's Rabo who planted the hash. He's trying to screw me. I owe him money."

"How much?"

It was three or four thousand francs. Ali said he didn't remember exactly. The inspector thought that was a lot of money and suggested that Ali must be a very good customer.

"Okay, I sometimes do a little dealing on the side. But that shit isn't mine. And as for Phillips's mobile, I know nothing about it."

"That's strange." The inspector found this hard to believe. "You see, we checked and the last two numbers that were dialed on it were calls made to your phone number in the early morning just after the murders."

Sedak's eyes—black wet jewels—opened wide in alarmed confusion. He had the air of a desperate man running for his life.

"I never—never . . ." he stumbled.

"What about the bloodstains?"

Ali felt cornered. "They could be mine," he acknowledged. "When you work with tools you sometimes cut yourself."

Bandu said, "With knives too."

"I didn't murder anybody."

"Yes, that may be so," said the inspector, "but I'm sorry to say that it doesn't look too good for you, Sedak. Just see it from my point of view," he suggested, and proceeded to outline the case against him.

Ali was, as he himself had said, probably the last one to see Phillips alive. And the bayonet he used had been identified as one of the murder weapons, stained with his own blood as well as that of three of the other victims. The blue tape they were bound with was his tape with his fingerprints on it. Furthermore, Ali had also freely admitted stealing money and a credit card from the victims and, most likely, he'd stolen more than one. And why? To buy drugs, a crime for which he already had a well-established history. And then there was the victim's cell phone found in the trunk of his car . . .

"As I say, monsieur, it doesn't look too rosy."

Although badly rattled, Ali was not going to confess something he never did. "You're trying to bury me. Make me your *gogo* because I came here from Algeria and wasn't born in France."

"Don't be an imbecile! Come now, why don't you get these murders off your chest? You'll feel much better, and the procureur will probably go a little easier on you if you do."

"I didn't kill anybody. I know nothing. I'm not a murderer. I'm innocent."

Mazarelle rose out of his seat and loomed darkly over the handcuffed suspect on the floor. "I've lost patience. We'll charge him with four counts of murder, acts of barbarism, drug possession with intent to sell, and theft. Lock him up."

30

THE MEETING IN BOURGES

The gleaming Mercedes-Benz tour bus climbed to the summit of the hill and pulled up alongside the other buses parked perpendicular to the south side of the looming cathedral like piglets suckling on some gigantic sow. The teachers getting off were clearly excited. They had come from Geneva, traveling the pilgrim's road to Santiago de Compostela. Vézelay's Sainte-Madeleine had been interesting, but this was Saint-Étienne, one of the largest and most beautiful Gothic cathedrals in all of France. Their cameras came out almost as soon as they looked up and grasped the splendor, the immensity of the thing. And it was a warm, sunny, marvelous morning for photographs, the cathedral floating in a blue sky with an occasional billowing cloud sailing by overhead.

The neatness of the travelers belied the long distance they'd come. Definitely Swiss. Birkenstock sandals and trim khaki shorts, striped polo shirts, and floppy hats. Though a little taller than most of the men, Reiner fit right in as he put on his sunglasses and followed their guide to the west side of the cathedral. Its five magnificent doorways were framed by two massive asymmetrical towers.

The guide pointed to his left. "That one is called the 'deaf tower' because it has no bells. Perhaps"—clearing his throat—"it really should be called the mute tower." The teachers savored his dry sense of humor. In that way, Reiner realized, they weren't so different from assassins. "And for those of you who enjoy climbing and can still handle three hundred and sixty-five steps, there's the other one, the north tower. In the unlikely event you reach the top, I can promise you a spectacular view."

Reiner was looking forward to it. Carved in the stone arch above the main doorway was an eight-hundred-year-old Last Judgment that the guide called "a powerful vision." Rather than dismiss the sculpture out of hand, he gave it another look. The good confidently waiting for Heaven while the rest dragged off kicking and screaming into the cauldrons of fire and the pits of Hell. A simple cartoon world of rewards and punishments, he thought, trying to wrap his mind around that dusty old shibboleth, but it was hopeless. He hurried to catch up with the rest of his group.

The cathedral interior was enormous. The space majestic with huge columns thicker than elephant legs and chandeliers falling from the ceiling and floating in air. As Reiner expected, the church on Sunday morning was filled with vacationing tourists. A few dozen of them standing around a large cabinet displaying a clock-face and dial beneath it decorated with rams, scorpions, goats, and other zodiacal signs. Suddenly it began to chime—noisily delighting the children. Reiner's wristwatch said 11:23. He was more impressed with the one in Strasbourg that had a cock that crowed on the hour.

Their guide led them down the side aisle past the chapels named after some of the notable families of Bourges who had donated money to the church. He stopped in front of the Jacques Coeur chapel. Its stained glass windows, rich blues and deep ruby reds, cast a wavering light on the faces of the people who were there. None of them looked familiar to Reiner. It was still early. That he didn't spot any undercover cops in the crowd was especially gratifying. Their guide was describing Coeur as a financier, diplomat, and one of the greatest merchants of the Middle Ages. He failed to mention that Jacques Coeur was also a major arms dealer and that Bourges today was a center of the French armaments industry. Though hardly averse to change, Reiner had a soft spot in his heart for tradition.

Only about half their group wanted to climb to the top of the tower. The heavy breathing of the couple ahead of Reiner on the way up sounded as if they might have to be carried down on stretchers. As promised, the view of the city was impressive. Caesar had called Bourges "the finest city in Gaul." To Reiner it looked more like a sleepy provincial town. Reaching into his shoulder bag, he took out his lightweight Zeiss eight by forty binoculars and as he peered through their dustproof, fogproof lenses the view was spectacular indeed. It was only a matter of time before all the others had gone back down, leaving him alone.

Twelve minutes before noon he spotted the two of them walking toward the cathedral. Though still at a distance, they were unmistakable. Thin and fat like Laurel and Hardy. Reiner wondered if they were lovers. In any event, there was nothing funny about these two. He'd never make the mistake of underestimating them. After all, they'd known enough to track him down in Berlin and hire him. It looked as if they'd come alone. Putting away his binoculars at the bottom of his bag, Reiner unwrapped the chamois cloth from his black Ruger P89 and placed the fully loaded fifteen-shot pistol on top where it was easily accessible.

In the almost empty chapel, they recognized him at once. "Ah, it's you. As punctual as ever." Pellerin extended his hand and Reiner took it. But he didn't care for the way Blond held back, his hands out of sight in the pockets of his baggy seersucker jacket. Both of them had mahogany tans.

Pellerin cast a vexed glance about the chapel and said, "I hate to work on Sundays. Let's make this as painless as possible. Then on to lunch. First of all, there's Ali Sedak. Wednesday he'll be formally charged by the investigating magistrate with the four murders in Taziac."

Good news, of course, and rather intriguing. No indictment had been publicly announced anywhere yet. He guessed they had an informer in the procureur's office. Reiner wondered what other connections they had higher up.

"Second, with the murderer formally charged, our problems are simplified. Your money will be deposited in Zurich Wednesday morning."

"Don't disappoint me. I'll be expecting it. And the unfinished business you mentioned?"

"That, monsieur, is where you come in. I said our problems were simplified, not eliminated. Ordinarily this story would now disappear for perhaps a year or so until the trial is held. But the daughter is stirring people up. Every time the Reece woman gives an interview to *France Inter* or *Sud Ouest* or *La Dépêche*, telling them she doesn't think Sedak is guilty, the story comes back like a bad meal."

Hubert Blond, making loud preludial noises, cleared his throat. "And not just in the Arab *banlieues* either. People are saying that if the daughter thinks a snake like Sedak is innocent maybe he is. Even in *Le Figaro*—"

Pellerin broke in, tapping him on the arm, and they waited until two snoopers in front of the chapel had moved on. "So," Pellerin continued, "we need her to go away. Either she goes home voluntarily or, if not, in a box. We'll leave that to you, of course. Frankly, I don't care which, but it has to be done at once."

"No, I'm afraid not. I'm finished with Taziac. I never go back. It's bad luck."

"You created this mess. You should clean it up. Let me assure you that you'll be very well paid for your time."

Reiner couldn't resist. "How well?"

"Name a price."

His was ridiculously high and Reiner knew it, but he'd no desire to take this job. No desire to become the black-haired Barmeyer again. The only way he'd even consider it was for enough money—in addition to what he'd already salted away—to set himself up in the one other business he'd ever been interested in. He watched the two of them exchange glances. Blond, looking dark and worried, kept his hands jammed into his pockets, his mouth shut.

"All right," Pellerin said.

"Half Wednesday along with the other money. The rest within twenty-four hours of my call to tell you that I've taken care of the matter. Agreed?"

"Done. Now let's get out of here before I lose my appetite. Places like this depress me. Besides I'm starved."

All the way to the parking lot Pellerin sang the praises of the Abbaye Saint-Ambroix and its kitchen. On a warm summer day like this, he suggested the cold salmon with fennel confit à l'orange. Simple but succulent, he raved. There was something about the nonstop way he went on that irritated Reiner. And the silence of Pellerin's fat boyfriend made him edgy.

"But when it comes to salmon," Pellerin couldn't resist pointing out, as he unlocked the long black Citroën and climbed in, "how can you touch arctic char freshly plucked out of a chill Quebec lake and brushed with a little honey mustard and a dry white wine simmering over an open fire?" He kissed his fingertips and turned to Hubert, "Right, *mon ami?*"

"Have you two been camping?"

Pellerin smiled and turned on the engine, but Reiner didn't get in. Pellerin rolled down his window.

"You're not coming with us, monsieur?" he asked, astonished.

"I'll be in touch. Toodle-oo!" he called, without looking back.

31

THE HOUSE NEXT DOOR

Mazarelle's men had returned from the neighbors with nothing new to report. As instructed, Lambert had left a list of the locations of the empty houses in the area on his boss's desk. Two of them were old farmhouses for sale—drags on the market—with no takers for years. The third, a large château in the Taziac hills, was rented for the summer to a family coming from Brussels. As for the fourth, it was a vacation house owned by an English family that usually arrived at the beginning of next month.

"Where is it?" Mazarelle asked.

"Now that's what makes it interesting. It's next door to L'Ermitage. But we looked all over the property, and there's no one there yet. Everything's locked up."

Mazarelle agreed with Lambert. The location of the fourth house made it more than a little interesting. Later that day, he went himself to check the place out. Not a bad-looking country house, on the whole, though it didn't seem as if anyone was taking care of the grounds. Downstairs the shutters were closed. As for the car tracks—other than those made by his own men—he'd no definite idea how old they were, but all of them appeared to be tire marks made by the same car. Mazarelle tried the front door, and it was locked. He went in through the back door with the aid of one of the passkeys on his key ring, riffling through them until he found a winner. He switched on the lights. He didn't like doing this kind of thing without a *mandat* when dealing with foreign owners, but under the circumstances . . .

The place was deserted. It didn't look as if anyone had been in there recently. The damp, musty smell in the air was typical of houses that haven't been lived in. Nothing in the sink, nothing on the table, everything spick-and-span. Then his eyes fell on the gun case on the wall as if it were some flea-market treasure. Without the slightest hesitation or difficulty, he selected another of his keys—a small, toothless one this time—and clicked it open. There were two guns inside. Though both were of interest to him as he looked them over—without touching either—it was the shotgun he was especially eager to get a report on. Only PTS could tell him whether or not it was the weapon that had killed Schuyler Phillips. But he'd need the permission of the owner for that. Mazarelle had a feeling that he was definitely on to something here.

A sharp squeaking sound caused the inspector to whirl around. It took him a few seconds to locate exactly where the noise was coming from. Somebody standing outside the house had forced open a shutter and was peering in. He assumed it wasn't one of his own men or he'd have called out his name. By the time Mazarelle got out the back door, hoping to come up from behind whoever it was, he'd fled. Annoyed with himself for letting the intruder get away, the inspector returned to his survey of the interior.

Upstairs, he went quickly through the rest of the house. That too showed no signs of any trespasser. He walked down to the far end of the hall and found the stairs to the attic. There was a door at the top of the landing and, tramping noisily up the narrow staircase, he turned the knob. It was a small gloomy storeroom with a table, some chairs, a stool, a folded cot, and assorted dust-covered cartons of books, bottles, wires, and plugs that made his nose itch. Pale ghostly cobwebs dangled from the ceiling beams. In short . . . nothing.

Not until he was back downstairs did the significance of what he'd just seen dawn on him. Unlike the attic storeroom, the rest of the house was much too clean after having been closed up for months. Someone had been inside, someone he wanted to talk to. Unless whoever it was had been hired to clean up by the owners, get the rooms in order for them before they returned, which of course was possible. Mazarelle would have to find out who this English family was and how to get in touch with them.

On the way to his car, the inspector heard a tractor working in the field behind the house. It wasn't until he got closer that he recognized Chambouvard. The last time he'd seen him was when he was questioning Georgette at their farmhouse across the road and her father suddenly appeared bitching about flics being nosy. Yet he was the one who knew all about the time Ali Sedak left L'Ermitage the night of the murders. A real busybody, Monsieur Chambouvard. What the hell was he doing over here? Could he have been the one snooping at the window just now?

Recalling his previous meeting with the farmer, the inspector was inclined to skimp on the charm even more than he usually did with men. He snapped out his hand like a matador's red flag—confident in himself rather than any uniform—and Chambouvard hit the brakes.

"What is it *now*?" he asked, exasperated. "More questions?"

"What are you doing on this side of the road?"

"Trying to work, if you'd let me."

"This isn't part of your farm too, is it?"

"A *servitude*," Chambouvard explained. "The land belongs to the house, but the hay back here belongs to me. I have the right to cut it early every summer for my animals. And that's the way it's going to stay no matter what foreigner owns the property."

Mazarelle asked the owner's name.

"McAllister." It was obvious that he didn't like the man. "English."

"When was the last time you saw him?"

The farmer glanced sourly down at the inspector from his tractor seat and shrugged.

"Have you seen anyone going in or out of the house recently?"

"That house is none of my business."

Mazarelle suspected Chambouvard knew what was going on in every acre in the neighborhood.

"Where does McAllister live in England?"

"Ask my wife. Maybe she knows. I have no time for nonsense. I'm busy. And now let me get back to my work."

A real pain in the ass. His wife, on the other hand, was glad to see the inspector when he knocked on her door, and she promptly expressed relief that he had the Arab in jail. Madame Chambouvard didn't like that he'd been working so close to her daughter at L'Ermitage. She never trusted the fellow.

"Only a suspect, madame," Mazarelle reminded her, and asked if she knew how he might get in touch with McAllister.

The farmer's wife was happy to oblige. She didn't share her husband's attitude about the Englishman at all. After hunting among her important papers in the bureau drawer, she found what she was looking for. A page torn from a telephone notepad that said Hôtel Gambetta, Bergerac. The name written on it was Neil McAllister with an address and phone number in London.

Mazarelle quickly took the information down. "One thing more," he said, standing at the front door. "Did Georgette ever do any house cleaning for the McAllisters?"

"Oh no! *Jamais de la vie!* Chambouvard wouldn't hear of it."

Returning to his office, Mazarelle placed his call to London. The key question he had for McAllister was whether anyone had been using his house in Taziac. He was sure the Englishman must know all about the murders next door. Who didn't know? The story had been in newspapers all over Europe. Perhaps that was why the family was delaying their return, preferring to wait until the police had their man. They weren't the only ones.

The phone rang a few times and a man's voice answered, but before Mazarelle could tell McAllister what he wanted he was instructed to leave his message after the beep. The message was simple. It was urgent that he call Inspector Paul Mazarelle at the Commissariat de Police in Bergerac, France, as soon as he got home.

32

SEDAK INDICTED

The Hôtel Fleuri was so empty, so peaceful, so quiet that Molly had her first decent night's sleep since arriving in France. She didn't even hear the clanging of the church bell across the square. Her shoulders ached where she'd hit the car when the tattooed son of a bitch pushed her. Otherwise she felt fine. Hungry enough for waffles, bacon, and eggs but glad to settle for the *petit déjeuner* downstairs.

"*Bonjour, mademoiselle.*" The frail teenage girl who'd helped with their bags when they arrived brought her a pitcher of coffee and a small basket of croissants. They were hot, flaky, and delicious with butter and apricot jam. Molly was finishing her breakfast when Monsieur Favier came over, looking smug as a lottery winner. He was actually smiling. As he placed a copy of that morning's *Sud Ouest* in front of her, his stubby index finger tapped the headline that read "Sedak Indicted in Taziac Murders."

"You see, mademoiselle! *Le surineur.* It was the Arab after all."

The lead article on the front page was by Jacques Gaudin, the reporter who had interviewed Molly. In addition to several lesser crimes, the investigating magistrate was charging Ali Sedak with acts of barbarism and all four killings. Gaudin sketched in the details of the crimes and noted that the handyman admitted being the last to see one of the victims alive. Sedak was soon to be moved to the Maison d'Arrêt in Périgueux to await trial.

"I knew it!" trumpeted Favier. "I knew he did it."

All he knew, she thought, was that once they had their murderer, the tourists would be back and his business would return to normal. Getting up, Molly pointed out, "He hasn't been tried yet."

Favier didn't like that.

After breakfast, Molly drove up to Bergerac, eager to speak to Ali Sedak before they put him in prison. She had to park a few blocks away from the commissariat because the entrance was cordoned off. Opposite the building, noisy Front National demonstrators were gathering for a protest rally as reporters and cameramen covered the scene. There were bloodthirsty shouts of "Kill the Arab bastard!" and "Send him home in a box!" One of the signs read "Bring back the guillotine—the only tree that always bears fruit."

It was the nearest thing to a lynch mob Molly had ever seen. The way she felt, they might have been after her. Though she was wearing dark glasses, Molly realized that her picture had been in the papers. She was far from invisible. Without waiting for the heavy truck traffic to stop, Molly raced across the boulevard Chanzy to the Hôtel de Police.

"What's going on?" she asked Mazarelle.

He explained that they were expecting René Arnaud any minute, the local darling of the extreme right. Arnaud couldn't resist an opportunity like this. The FN had planned a big demonstration against the indicted murderer.

Molly said, "I'd like to hear Ali Sedak's side of the story. May I see him?"

Why not? Mazarelle thought. It was worth one last try before their prisoner was taken to Périgueux. Let her talk to him—the daughter of two of the victims, a beautiful, young, sympathetic American woman, eager to hear anything he had to say. It might be just what it would take to make him want to clear his conscience, unburden his heart. Who knows? Perhaps if the stick doesn't work, the carrot will. He gave her half an hour.

Molly was waiting in the interrogation room when Bandu brought in Ali Sedak. They'd removed his handcuffs the night before, and for the first time he'd been able to snatch a few hours sleep. The inspector had told Bandu to leave a couple of cigs and wait outside. Molly eyed his hands, the nails bitten to the quick, the match shaking as he lit up. He sucked in the smoke as if he couldn't get enough, then began to cough violently. She found it almost impossible to believe that this cowardly wife beater, this small, wretched man—his face, after a few days in a windowless cell, as pinched and pale as city snow—had by himself killed her father and mother, let alone all four of them.

No sooner had Molly told him who she was than he swore that he never killed her parents, swore he never killed anyone. But the police wouldn't believe him, nobody would. The inspector had the wrong man. Ali said he'd confessed to nothing, he was innocent. He went on and on in this vein, demanding to be set free, demanding a lawyer, demanding to see his wife.

Molly told him that she'd met his wife. Thérèse had been trying to visit him and would probably be allowed to once they moved him to Périgueux. Molly said that she'd also seen their baby and congratulated him on his son, called him a beautiful child.

Ali's face softened, the color seeped back into his cheeks. "How is he?"

"Fine. He seems fine."

Ali lit his second cigarette with the burning tip of his first. Then a long drag and he began to complain again. They'd refused to let him see his wife, his child, a lawyer, anyone. Ever since they brought him here they'd been mistreating him. Locked in a cinder block coffin with nothing to do, no one to talk to except when they took him out for questioning or brought him a cold sandwich. And how could he sleep in handcuffs on that wooden slab with the light always in his eyes and them watching him all the time? They were torturing him.

"You feel dirty, tired, humiliated," he said hoarsely, his voice cracking. "They won't even let me wash."

How often had Molly found that wife beaters—not unlike alcoholics—were rank sentimentalists, predisposed to slathering themselves with thick gobs of self-pity. She'd more sympathy for the drunks. So she told him there was one thing she didn't understand. How come there was so much evidence against him if he was innocent?

"Coincidences, that's all. What else could it be?"

His question hung in the air like a vaguely unpleasant smell. "Unless . . ." He looked toward the door to make sure it was closed and lowered his voice so that only she could hear. "Unless the flics are trying to frame me."

"Tell me about the night of the murders." As she reached for a hanky from her bag, she turned on her tape recorder.

Ali was so eager to win her over that his story fairly gushed out of him. It was nothing that Molly hadn't heard before. She gave him a skeptical look. "The police say you were the last one to see Schuyler Phillips alive. Is that true?"

"No, no, no, no." Ali's head thrashed back and forth.

"Calm down. I'm listening."

"They're twisting what I said. He was alive when I left."

"Okay, fine. I understand. Then you drove home with your bad back and went right to sleep an hour or so before midnight. Didn't wake up again until the next morning. Is that the way it happened?"

"Yes, yes. I mean no."

Molly moistened her lips with the tip of her tongue. "I'm trying, but you're not making things easy for me."

"The telephone rang in the middle of the night. It woke me, but I didn't get out of bed and, as far as I know, neither did Thérèse. A wrong number. They must have hung up."

"Did the phone ring again a little later?"

"If it did I didn't hear it. Ask Thérèse—maybe she heard something."

"I'll do that."

From outside in the street, shouts and cheers and the martial beat of drums erupted as if a tumbrel had arrived to cart him off.

Ali turned in alarm to his visitor. "What's that?"

Molly guessed that René Arnaud had arrived. "I don't know," she told him, shrugging. She mentioned having seen demonstrators across the street when she drove up.

His face collapsed. Shoulders trembling, Ali began to rock back and forth. "They think I'm the murderer," he cried. "Nobody believes me. Nobody." He banged his head on the table in desperation and might have done himself some real damage if Bandu hadn't rushed in and dragged him away.

The first thing the inspector asked when she came out was, "Did he tell you anything?"

"He says he's innocent."

"And do you believe him?"

Molly hesitated. "Yes, I do."

"Really? Despite the evidence against him and his history of violence?"

"That's right. Because at the time the killer was using his victims' credit cards to withdraw their money from the ATM machines, Ali was at home."

"How do you know that?"

"He said that the phone in his house woke him up. And his wife, who thought he was asleep at the time, independently confirmed the first call at about one a.m. You can probably check it out with the telephone company."

"We have. That still doesn't mean he was there at that time. The two of them could easily have cooked up an alibi."

Molly knew he was right. And the phone calls alone would hardly stand up in court as exculpatory evidence, but she felt certain this wasn't a case of collusion between husband and wife.

"You've got the wrong man, Inspector."

"We'll see."

Much to her annoyance, Mazarelle seemed convinced. "What exactly is *that* supposed to mean?"

"Merely that the calls you speak of were both made on your friend Monsieur Phillips's cell phone, which we found in Ali's car trunk." Molly appeared so stricken by the news that the inspector almost felt sorry for her. "I'm afraid, Mademoiselle Reece, you have too trusting a heart."

It wasn't her heart Molly was worried about but her head. She realized that she was probably right about Ali being innocent, but for the wrong reason. He himself had given her the clue. Her problem was that she'd largely dismissed it as guilty, self-serving bunk. He was being set up by somebody. Oh, maybe not the police, as he claimed, but somebody was out to frame him. It had to be something like that. But Molly wasn't about to tell Mazarelle what she suspected. She had plenty of other reasons to doubt Ali's guilt.

"I just can't believe a guy his size could have handled four people by himself. Even if he killed Schuyler before the other three returned from the restaurant, he still had to tie up my parents and Ann Marie, and then carry them to different rooms in the house. No, I don't think so. He may be a batterer, a druggie, a small-time pusher and thief, but that doesn't make him a quadruple murderer. Not the shaken little man I just saw. Even without heels, I'm taller than he is. The only way he could have killed them is if he had an accomplice."

Though the inspector didn't say so, he too had his doubts. Call it a gut feeling. There was something about this case that smelled bad to him. He also said nothing about the unidentified fingerprints that were found on the tape binding the victims in addition to those belonging to Ali Sedak. And, as always when it came to murder and gut feelings, he reminded himself, the nose knows.

What he did tell her was that the evidence against Ali was strong and mounting. And that they had recently impounded his car. If those were actually bloodstains linked to one or more of the victims he'd seen in it, PTS might well give him something decisive. Anyway, he assured her their investigation was far from closed.

The angry shouts outside grew louder. Mazarelle was becoming increasingly uneasy about the nasty mood of the FN supporters across the street. It could mean trouble. Fortunately they weren't going to move their prisoner to Périgueux for a couple of hours. It was important to him that this transfer be carried out smoothly.

"Where did you park your car?" Mazarelle asked her.

"A few blocks away. Not far. That sounds like quite a crowd outside."

"Would you like me to send along one of my men to help you get past the reporters?"

How considerate, she thought. But she'd no intention of letting him think that she couldn't take care of herself. "No, thanks. They're so busy out there with Arnaud they'll never notice me. Besides"— taking out her dark glasses, she beamed at him as she put them on— "I've got these."

René Arnaud, unlike his leader Jean-Marie LePen, was not a big man, but he was well put together and quite striking with his shaved bullethead. And he was media savvy. He'd brought out an enthusiastic crowd and they applauded wildly, lapping up everything he said. Arnaud spoke bluntly, passionately, and his message was clear.

"I call a spade a spade. They're backward people with a backward religion. Even when they come here legally from North Africa, they don't speak our language and fail to integrate into French society."

Then as the crowd roared its approval Arnaud went on to discuss the evils *les bicots* brought with them from Africa. Bad schools, bad kids, dangerous drugs, SIDA, and rising crime. But most dangerous of all, *beurs* like Ali Sedak—that cold-blooded butcher of four who kept many good Bergeraquois up nights with their loaded shotguns under their beds.

"I promise you, *mes amis*," he assured them, "we'll all be much happier when that piece of shit across the street is put away for good."

Arnaud's speech was followed by delirious applause. Passing by on the edge of the crowd, Molly was fascinated by the scene and the charismatic speaker. She couldn't believe what he was saying. He reminded her of Mussolini with his jutting cowcatcher jaw and racist dogma. She'd made the mistake of stopping to listen when someone spotted her. Soon reporters were crowding around, hemming her in, asking questions. Their cameras clicking like telegraph keys, flashes blazing.

"Look this way, mademoiselle! Over here."

"Sorry," she said, attempting to move away.

"Will you be returning to France for the trial?"

"Mademoiselle Reece," called another reporter, "why are you here? Changed your mind? Do you still think they've got the wrong man behind bars across the street?"

Molly tried to keep calm. "Yes, I do." She hoped that would be the end of it.

"Why is that?"

"I'm sorry," she said, and turned away.

"Why do you think so?" he demanded, louder this time.

"Because Ali Sedak was home and in bed when my parents and their friends were murdered. The police ought to spend their time hunting for the real killer."

There were angry shouts from those in the crowd who heard what she'd said.

Though feeling trapped, Molly wasn't frightened. She just prayed that the reporters, who were standing between her and Arnaud's followers, didn't move.

Deserted by the media, René Arnaud wasn't happy. Informed who she was, he was doubly annoyed. But he hadn't risen in the ranks of the party without knowing how to turn heads and cameras in his direction. Pushing his way into the center of the circle around her, he confronted Molly. Called her a naive young American who thinks Frenchmen need a lesson in *liberté, égalité, fraternité.*

Molly tried to get around him, but each time Arnaud stepped in front of her, blocking her escape. He was a taunting, diabolical cat playing with a mouse.

"Okay," she said, "that's enough."

He laughed at her.

Fed up, Molly cried, "Get out of my way, you fascist!"

Arnaud's face reddened in blotches and he flew into a rage. "I am no fascist," he boomed. Lunging forward, he grabbed her by the collar of her green jacket and held on tight like a pit bull.

"Take your hands off me!"

As Molly tried to free herself from his grasp, Arnaud shook her violently back and forth and the crowd cheered him on. The police who'd been watching came running. Swinging their clubs and pushing back his supporters, they seized him. The crowd howled in anger and, attempting to rescue Arnaud, a shoving match ensued. People began to heave rocks, throw bottles.

A passerby, seeing one of the bottles flying in Molly's direction, lashed out, knocking the bottle aside. In the confusion, he grabbed her by the arm. "You're going to get yourself killed here. Quick! Follow me." She raced after him. Her rescuer seemed to find his way through the back streets as if he knew them all by heart. They were soon blocks away, standing safely below the clock tower in front of Bergerac's own modest but enormously comforting Notre-Dame. Catching her breath, Molly didn't know how to thank him enough.

He pointed to the Café Chat Noir opposite them in the mall. "You look as if you could use a cognac," he suggested, which under the circumstances seemed to her like a damn good idea.

When they were settled at a table with their drinks and she had calmed down, Molly said, "You saved my life. That bottle just missed hitting my head by inches. It was like being in the middle of a full-blown riot." She called it, *"Tout à fait fou."*

He agreed that the scene was bizarre. He'd merely stopped out of curiosity to see what was going on. "Mademoiselle Reece, isn't it?"

Molly glanced up in surprise at her savior and his striking blue eyes, which only seconds before had seemed utterly reliable. "How did you know my name?"

"Oh that." His voice was so calm, so reassuring. "Surely you must realize that your picture has been all over the newspapers, the TV."

"Yes, of course." She'd forgotten and felt a little embarrassed.

"I'm afraid that France hasn't been too kind to you and your family."

"Please don't mind me. I haven't been myself since I arrived."

"Frankly, it's a wonder you're still here," he confessed, and his sympathy was obviously appreciated. *"Quant à moi,* if I were you I'd have gone home by now."

"I've given it a thought."

"Oh by the way," he said, holding out his hand. "Pierre Barmeyer."

They seemed to enjoy each other's company. He told her that he'd just come from Bergerac's Museum of Urban History, which had a little-known collection of prehistoric artifacts considered quite respectable by some experts. He fancied himself an amateur archaeologist. One of the reasons he'd chosen to holiday in the Dordogne was to be near the caves at Les Eyzies, the capital of prehistory. He was actually a vacationing artist renting a house in Taziac, not too far, coincidentally, from L'Ermitage.

"Oh really." Given how small Taziac was, Molly supposed that this wasn't very surprising.

Pierre Barmeyer called it a lovely setting, though the crime had put a pall on his visit. Naturally he felt much better now that they'd caught the murderer.

"If he is the murderer," said Molly.

"You don't think so?"

"Not really. Where did you learn your English?"

Reiner stared at her, wondering what she was driving at. With her bright red hair and lambent green eyes, she was unquestionably a beautiful woman. It was her disconcertingly abrupt style and inquisitive mind that troubled him.

"Why? Is it so bad?" he asked softly, his voice perfectly controlled.

"No, it's really very good of its kind. It's English-English. In a way perhaps too good, too careful. In fact you could be a BBC announcer. But I can hear the German in it."

"You noticed. You don't miss much, do you?" He sat back in his chair and sipped his brandy. "That's because I'm from Alsace. I went to school in Strasbourg."

"I've never been there."

He explained that the Romans called it Argentoratum and that today it was still an important commercial center. Not the most attractive of cities, he frankly admitted, but definitely worth a visit. If she ever went, he offered to show her around.

"It's a deal. That is, if I ever get out of here alive."

"Perhaps I can help."

"You've already saved my life once." Finishing what was left of her brandy and feeling much better, Molly got up. "Now if I can only get back to my car."

He offered to drive her. He was parked just across the street in front of the church. "It's no trouble at all," he insisted.

As Molly got into his small car and fastened the seat belt, she said, "I'm afraid I'm getting to be a burden."

"Yes, but that's all right."

Molly found his honesty disarming and, perversely, liked even better that Pierre Barmeyer was no charmer. But there was something else she felt about this tall, blue-eyed, dark-haired, intense Frenchman that she couldn't put her finger on.

"What's that awful smell?" she asked, catching a whiff of rotten eggs as he turned on the engine.

"This is a Renault," he said, as if that explained everything. "It'll go away once we start to move. It's the catalytic converter." He opened the window as they exited the parking area. "Did you think it was poison gas?"

"Something like that."

The police had dispersed the crowd opposite the commissariat, and all that was left on the street were torn leaflets, broken glass, a few discarded signs. Molly thanked him one last time when they got back to her car, and as she was about to get out he stopped her.

"Yes?"

"What about dinner tomorrow night?"

He looked so grim, she thought, so vulnerable. Was he afraid she'd turn him down? Molly had always felt that in these classic dating situations women had all the power.

"But only if I pay my share. I'm getting a little tired of thanking you."

Reiner felt he could live with that. "Yes, why not?"

He agreed to pick her up at the Hôtel Fleuri tomorrow night at 8 p.m., and as Molly waved and got into her car, Reiner drove off smiling. Amused at the absurdity. Given what he'd been told that morning by his bank in Zurich, Mademoiselle Reece had already paid for far more than her dinner.

The lobby of the Hôtel Fleuri was empty when Molly returned. She hit the silver bell on the front desk, and its thin, sharp, metallic note still hung in the air when Monsieur Favier shuffled hurriedly out from the kitchen, wiping his mouth. His face fell as if he'd been expecting a new guest.

"Oui, mademoiselle?"

Molly asked for her room key and he seemed irritated to be bothered. Perhaps she'd interrupted something. She could hear a TV that was on somewhere inside. The key was connected to a heavy chrome blackjack with a hard rubber tip, nothing you'd want to carry away with you by mistake. She supposed Favier was tired of losing his keys.

"Any messages?"

Without needing to look into the small pigeonholes behind him, he grunted and marched back to the kitchen. Molly raised her eyebrows in annoyance and, hefting her key, walked up the stairs. She wondered if Favier had lost his fondness for American movies.

Molly's first thought on opening her door was that they hadn't cleaned her room yet or she'd entered the wrong one, but the clothes on the floor were unmistakably hers. The bureau drawers were open and everything had been dumped out. Her heart pounding, Molly scoured the small room as if there was actually somewhere in it for someone to hide. Fortunately everything she had of importance was in the bag on her shoulder—her wallet, her tape recorder, her passport, her return plane ticket.

Then she remembered the jewelry. She ran to the suitcase on the floor beside the armoire. Like a dummy, she hadn't locked it. She opened the small zippered compartment inside and there were her parents' familiar rings and watches just where she'd left them. Removing the jewelry, Molly put all of it in her shoulder bag.

Then, one by one, she picked up her clothes, folded them neatly, and tucked them back into the drawers. She felt violated at having someone rummaging through her things, felt almost like crying but angry enough to smash whoever it was. No wonder Favier provided a blackjack in every room. As far as she could tell, however, nothing was missing. If they didn't take the jewelry, what were they after? Molly wondered if someone was trying to frighten her, scare her away, because if so they were doing a good job. And who the hell was it?

She was about to go down to report the break-in when the telephone rang. It was an excited Kevin. She couldn't recall ever being so glad to get a phone call. Kevin wanted to know why he hadn't heard from her.

"I was getting worried about you. Didn't you get my messages?"

"What messages?"

He said he'd called three times and each time left a message with the guy who answered the phone. "What the hell kind of hotel is that you're staying at?"

"I'm beginning to wonder."

"What do you mean?"

"Nothing. It's just that—"

"What's going on there, Molly?"

She told him what she'd found when she came back to her hotel room. "I know I shouldn't have been so upset, but it's been a tough day." She described her meeting with Ali Sedak, who she didn't like and didn't trust, but she felt even more strongly now after seeing him that he wasn't the murderer. Then she told him about the rock-throwing anti-Sedak rally she'd gotten caught up in and René Arnaud, the local FN leader, grabbing and shaking her like a martini.

"The son of a bitch! I wish I'd been there with you."

"Oh Kevin! So do I . . ."

"How can I just drop everything, Molly? We're set to open in two days. The rest of the cast is counting on me."

"I understand."

"I'd feel like such a bastard."

"Of course. Don't mind me. Forget it. This business is taking more out of me than I realized."

"Small wonder. You poor kid. Do you have any idea when you'll be back?"

"Not too much longer, I hope. I don't think I'd last. Miss you, Kev."

She didn't like herself at all trying to play for sympathy. After washing her face, she put on some fresh lipstick and looked herself over in the mirror. "Okay, Molly," she said, "now snap out of it."

Favier was seated at the front desk when she came downstairs.

"Someone broke into my room while I was out."

He was no more alarmed than if she'd asked for another hanger.

"It's not possible, mademoiselle. No one comes into my hotel without my knowing about it. I am always right here."

"You weren't there when I came in."

"Even a camel pees once in a while. So, what are you missing?"

"Nothing, as far as I can tell."

"*Voilà!* Then how do you know someone was in your room?"

"How do I know?" Molly was fuming. "I know because I found the drawers open and my clothes all over the floor. That's how!"

"Perhaps you simply forgot to put them away before you went out."

Molly's eyes went through him like a drill. "*Someone* was in my room."

"Well, maybe in hotels in your country, but in all my years in Taziac there has never been a robbery at the Fleuri. Even one in which noth-ing was missing. You are slandering my hotel, mademoiselle."

"Don't you believe me?"

"Allow me to make a suggestion. If you're not happy here, I suggest tomorrow you find another hotel more to your liking. Okay?"

33

AN INTERIM REPORT

azarelle had come into the commissariat early to use his computer and had just finished his interim report. Tired, he sat back in his desk chair and lit his pipe; the tobacco flared up and glowing shreds of Philosophe showered down on his lap. He brushed them off and, though not especially eager to read what he'd written, reached for the pages in the printer's out tray. Of all the many areas of police work, probably his least favorite was preparing reports. The only cop he ever knew who actually enjoyed writing them was Fabriani the fussbudget, his old boss in Paris, but Fabriani was always a little strange. One of a kind. Someone who, despite the daunting odds against it, still expected the world to stand at attention for him. They had made allowances for each other.

A copy of his report would go to Christine Leclerc and, if the investigating magistrate approved, to the procureur. Though he'd discussed his progress on the case with each of them on the phone and in person, they now insisted on something in writing before proceeding to trial.

"This is what we now know," his report began. "The accused, Ali Sedak, a thirty-three-year-old French citizen, was born in Algeria. As a teenager, he was often in trouble there with the law. His *antécédents judiciares* included robbery, resisting arrest, and drug possession. Arriving in France in 1985, the Sedaks settled in Toulon in the high-crime quarter by the waterfront known as Chicago. His father soon abandoned the family, returning to North Africa. Ali was left behind with his five brothers and sisters and an alcoholic mother who could barely speak French. He grew up on the streets of Toulon, fending for himself. With the exception of two suspended sentences for brawling and drug possession, however, he seems to have kept his nose clean."

After sketching in the background of the accused, Mazarelle outlined the case against him:

Ali Sedak had been working off the books as a handyman at L'Ermitage, which is managed by an English company named Vacation Villas in France that had rented the property to four foreigners for the month of June. On the twenty-fourth, the night of the crime, one of them who was helping Ali with his work—Schuyler Phillips—was killed in a barricaded, hidden room in the barn. The missing murder weapon was most likely a twelve-gauge double-barreled shotgun, based on the number and size of the lead pellets medical examiner Dr. Langlais removed from the body, the nature of the wounds, and two small fiber wads discovered on the floor. A weapon answering to that general description has been found in an adjoining house, and we are currently in the process of locating the English owners in order to gain permission to have it tested.

Phillips's wife and friends were killed soon afterward. The murder weapon used in each of these three crimes was an old World War II bayonet belonging to Sedak, and allegedly used by him in his work. His blood as well as that of his victims was found on it. All three were bound hand and foot with blue tape, the kind Sedak used in his work. Their hands behind their backs, they were each tied in identical fashion—the tape being wound over and under each victim's wrists—and, most likely, by the same person. Though technicians found a number of smeared fingerprints on this tape, only two were clearly identified: one of a right index finger on the tape binding Monsieur Reece and one a right thumbprint on the gag in his wife's mouth. Both prints matched those of the accused.

There were two cigarette butts and a cigar stub on the blood-streaked tile floor in the kitchen, where the cleaning woman Georgette Chambouvard had dropped an ashtray. DNA tests revealed that the cigar had been smoked by Reece. The cigarettes were Marlboro Lights, one of which had been smoked by Madame Phillips and the other by the accused, which would seem to place Ali Sedak in the house on the night of the murders.

In the days leading up to the killings, the accused has admitted that he personally used a large amount of hashish every day, mixing it with tobacco. He also had many gambling debts. It was during this period that Reece reported the theft of his Visa card and 2,500 francs to the police. The Visa was soon recovered at the BNP in Bergerac, where it was seized by the ATM machine after someone had tried and failed several times to enter the correct PIN. When placed in the *garde à vue* cell, Sedak revealed that he'd stolen Reece's credit card.

The morning of the day of the murders, according to the owner of the Café Valon in Taziac, Sedak was there playing pool with Eugène Rabineau. Rabineau—a dealer known locally as Rabo—confirmed this and said that later they went to smoke dope and talk. He said Ali mentioned the rich Americans vacationing at L'Ermitage but nothing more. The dealer told us that he left for Marseilles that afternoon on business and didn't return until the next day. His story is still being checked by my investigators.

Early on the following morning, at 1:24 of the twenty-fifth, 2,000 francs were withdrawn by someone using Monsieur Reece's MasterCard from the Banque Crédit Agricole in Taziac. He was photographed by the ATM surveillance camera wearing a blue bandanna around his head like that worn by Ali Sedak. A half hour later at the BNP branch at Eymet, he used the same card to get 4,300 francs and the Visa of Madame Phillips to withdraw 7,000 francs. That same morning at about the same time two brief phone calls were made on Phillips's mobile to the Sedak house. This mobile was later found in the trunk of Sedak's car. As to the money, it may have been used to buy the five kilos of hashish later seized at his house, though Rabineau emphatically denies having sold it to him.

The inspector then proposed a theory. He suggested that in its origin Sedak's plan was not murder but theft, and drug related:

> If the crimes committed on the evening of the 24th began as robbery, they quickly escalated to murder when Phillips, a big man, put up resistance. After that, apparently the sudden return of his wife and friends sealed their fate.
>
> The principal question is how could one man have murdered all four of these people. A reasonable answer is that he couldn't. The dealer Rabineau, despite his alibi, may well have been involved. The wife of the accused, Thérèse, has been questioned, and there is no doubt that she lied about events surrounding the night of the crime. She has no witnesses to corroborate her story that she didn't go out that evening or the next day because her baby was ill. Although the .22 rifle owned by the Sedaks hadn't recently been fired, PTS examiners found that it does have both her and her husband's fingerprints on it. There is, however, no trace of her presence at L'Ermitage.
>
> On the other hand, is it possible that Sedak could have committed these murders by himself? Perhaps. If he shot one of the victims before the return of the others, he would have been confronting three unsuspecting people. Perhaps they thought their companion had gone somewhere with Sedak. They might well have been sitting at the dining room table, waiting for his return, when Ali appeared. Faced with what they believed was a loaded shotgun, they would have followed his orders to lie facedown on the kitchen floor with their hands behind their backs. He could have taped Monsieur Reece's wrists and ankles first because he posed the greatest threat to him. But after binding only the wrists of both the women, Ali could have gotten Madame Reece to her feet, walked her quickly into her bedroom, pushed her facedown on the bed, and then gagged her and taped her ankles. After that, he could have done the same to Madame Phillips, leading her up the stairs to her bedroom in the tower. With the three of them at his mercy, the rest would have been easy.

Mazarelle signed the report and tossed his pen on the desk. It was okay as far as it went, but there was still too much left to the imagination to satisfy him. Sitting back, he puffed away at his pipe and watched the smoke rings popping out of his mouth like quoits. Oh yes, they probably had enough evidence there to convict. And yet he'd an uncomfortable feeling that something was wrong. Was it the tenacity with which Ali, right from the start, had insisted on his innocence? People who knew him, like Chambouvard and his daughter, agreed that it was possible he stole the credit cards, the money, but not the rest. Even those like Mickey, at the Café Valon, who tagged him a prick didn't believe that he was a monster.

Mazarelle kept thinking of his call yesterday to Toulouse to find out how PTS was doing with Ali's car. He'd been trying to push Didier—the head of operations at PTS—for the results, but he was a hard man to rush. It was what Didier said just before he hung up that troubled the inspector. He'd wondered why in a crime so blood-soaked and violent, his men hadn't found a single bloody handprint or footprint in the kitchen or, for that matter, anywhere in the house. And only two dry prints on the smudged tape, prints as sharp as if they had been carefully planted there.

The ringing of his telephone startled him. Lucille said Mademoiselle Reece was downstairs to see him. Should she send her up? Mazarelle slipped the report into his top drawer and emptied his pipe into the ashtray. Then quickly straightened out the small bowl of daffodils on his desk that Duboit's wife, Babette, had sent him. He wondered how the blockhead had explained the scratches on his cheek to her. Babette was no fool.

The sound of her footsteps on the stairs announced Mademoiselle Reece, who strode into his office as if she had been there a hundred times before. A little angry about something, he guessed, but it did good things for her complexion. Mazarelle had been right about the way a beauty like that lit up a room when she entered it. Her green and yellow scarf a perfect match for her jacket and his daffodils. Before she could say a word, he pulled over a chair and invited her to sit down.

"I've got good news for you," he said.

"I could use some good news."

Mazarelle reported that he'd spoken to the medical examiner. Dr. Langlais would be finished with his tests in a few days. He'd be free to release the bodies of her parents then, and she could take them back with her to the United States.

Molly thanked him. "But right now I need a place to stay in Taziac." She assumed correctly that he'd seen the papers or heard from his men all about her scene with Arnaud yesterday at the demonstration, so she skipped that. She told him what had happened when she got back to her room at the Fleuri.

"I don't know who ransacked it, but I can't stay in that hotel another day."

Mazarelle's face darkened and heavy wrinkles appeared to weigh down his forehead. Mademoiselle Reece seemed to have an uncanny knack for swimming into shark-infested waters. She definitely needed a safe place to stay. He ran the back of his finger over his mustache and thought, Why not? She could be his guest. Why didn't he think of it before? He'd plenty of room in his house, and he'd be able to keep an eye on her at the same time. It made perfect sense. But then again, he reconsidered, an attractive young woman might not understand his motives. Looked at that way, in fact, Mazarelle didn't even trust them himself. Reaching for the phone, he dialed someone he could trust.

"But of course," Louise Charpentier said, when told who it was who needed a roof. She had felt personally outraged about the murders and greatly admired the young woman's pluck when she'd seen her picture in the morning paper and read that she'd called René Arnaud a *facho*. Besides, she didn't think Ali Sedak was the killer either, regardless of the evidence. Racism, pure and simple, she called his indictment. Nevertheless, in the end she trusted her friend Mazarelle to do the right thing. "Bring her right over, *mon ami*."

34

THE ALTAR OF THE BLACK BISON

Everyone in Taziac knew Madame Charpentier. It wasn't that she was loved or respected or even that after more than four decades she still made and sold the best bread in town, which she did. In fact, as an outspoken Communist in conservative Taziac, she was if anything a pain in the ass, but she was Taziac's pain in the ass. Louise Charpentier was as much an institution in the village as its Gothic church or its spring basket festival or Gaston Amiel, its legendary *pétanque* champion.

And everyone knew her story. As a teenager during the war, she became a hero of the Resistance. Working as a courier, she traveled by train carrying secret messages taped to her back. She had many close calls, actually seemed to live a charmed life until her husband returned, wounded and depressed, from captivity, having lost an eye.

Louise Charpentier's hair had been white as flour for as long as anyone in Taziac could remember. Short and brushed straight back off her forehead as if she wanted to see everything and was ready to meet the world head-on. But her face, on the other hand, was remarkably youthful for a woman in her late seventies, who had worked all her life and been through what she had. Work was something Madame Charpentier took great pride in. She was a Communist of the old school, a Communist like Maurice Thorez.

Age had done little to cool the passions of Louise Charpentier, but these days she didn't always have the energy to argue. Although she stood silently to one side behind the counter of her *boulangerie*, leaning on her cane and listening to the chatter of the customers as

Gabrielle filled their orders, it was clear who was in charge. Madame Charpentier was a personage.

Her eyes brightened when the inspector came through the door and she raised her eyebrows when he wrapped her in his arms, kissed her on both cheeks. Complimenting her on the bright blue blouse she was wearing.

"I see you have a new man in your life."

"Make that two," she said drily. "They don't come the way they used to."

Mazarelle rolled his eyes. "I should have known."

"Some detective."

Madame Charpentier greeted Molly warmly, welcomed her to her house and, leaving the inspector to fend for himself, took her upstairs. The smell of the bakery below sweetened the air. The room she showed Molly was next to Gabrielle's. It was small and cluttered with plants and pillows and rocking chair cozy, but it was the mug with a picture of a bearded Che Guevara on the windowsill that won Molly's heart.

When the inspector returned to the commissariat, there was a message for him that Monsieur McAllister had called from London. Finally, Mazarelle thought. He immediately sat down at his desk and dialed the number in London.

McAllister apologized for not getting back to him sooner. He and his family had been away. As Mazarelle had suspected, he knew all about the murders at L'Ermitage and was eager to find out what was so urgent.

"No," McAllister said, he'd given no one permission to use his house in Taziac. "Absolutely not. Why?"

"Your back door was open. We discovered it in the course of our investigation."

"That's strange. I distinctly recall locking all the doors and windows in the house when we left at the end of last summer."

"I see you own some guns."

"Yes, that's right. Two rifles. A Mannlicher and a twelve-gauge shotgun. I do some hunting."

"If it's all right with you, I'd like to have them tested."

"Why?"

Mazarelle heard the alarm in his voice. "Just to be sure. After all, we did find your door open. Merely part of our ongoing investigation, you understand?"

"Couldn't you wait until we return?"

"I have no time for waiting, Monsieur McAllister. Four people have been murdered already."

"Very well," he said grudgingly, feeling that he'd no choice. "You'll find a key to my gun case in the kitchen drawer."

The inspector thanked him for his cooperation.

As soon as he hung up, Mazarelle summoned Duboit to his office. Told him to pick up the guns, wrap them with care, and send them down to PTS for testing. He wanted it done right away. After that, he'd another assignment for him. Just in case they had the wrong man or Ali was part of a team of killers, Mazarelle didn't want to have another dead body on his hands.

"For the next few days until Mademoiselle Reece leaves Taziac, I want you to park outside Madame Charpentier's *boulangerie,* where she's staying, and don't let her out of your sight. Clear?"

"Sure, boss, but why me? Any rookie could handle a job like that. It's so boring just sitting around waiting. Besides, why does she have to be watched anyhow?"

"Bernard . . ." The pause that followed was an abyss into which Bernard chose not to look.

"Okay, okay. I'm going."

The last thing Molly remembered was stretching out on top of the bed to rest for a few seconds. The timid knocking on the door woke her up. It was Gabrielle. There was someone downstairs to see her. Molly had no idea who it might be because only the inspector knew where she was staying, and Gabrielle would have told her if that's who it was. Molly brushed her hair and hurried down the narrow staircase. The bakery was closed and the only ones in the shop were Madame Charpentier and the tall, dark-haired man talking to her. Suddenly he spun around.

"Aha, there you are! You see, I found you."

"Pierre!"

"I hope I'm not too early. You haven't forgotten our appointment?"

"Of course not." In her eagerness to leave the Fleuri, Molly had totally forgotten their dinner date. "But how did you find me here?"

Reiner explained that the manager of the hotel wasn't very helpful, but he'd better luck when he asked the girl in the kitchen. She'd gone to the bakery earlier in the day and her friend who worked there told her about the beautiful American woman staying upstairs, the one whose parents were murdered.

Life in a small town, thought Molly, but Madame Charpentier was not so amused. She felt that Gabrielle had a big mouth for such a young girl.

Molly turned and introduced Pierre Barmeyer to her. Though Molly wasn't particularly eager to go anywhere, she'd promised him and couldn't back down now.

"Just a minute." Madame Charpentier went behind the counter and took a key from the hook on the wall. "Who knows what time you'll be back?" she said, and handed it to Molly. *"Amusez-vous bien."*

It was a crystalline summer evening and Molly loved the smell of the night air once that of the Renault's catalytic converter disappeared. They were driving east toward Les Eyzies. Pierre had made a reservation at a restaurant there for later that evening, but he had something to show her first.

"A surprise," he called it.

She gave him a smile. "A pleasant one, I hope."

"I'll let you be the judge."

Though he didn't have much of a sense of humor, there was this dark, brooding intensity about Pierre that Molly liked. She thought of it as a kind of Wagnerian sexiness. Amused at herself, she settled back to enjoy the ride.

He hadn't been driving long when he realized that someone was following them, but always at a discreet distance and never using his headlights. He said nothing about it to his companion, merely waited till they reached Cadouin and, losing his pursuer there, sped north by the back roads to Les Eyzies and the confluence of the Vézère and the Beune rivers. Then turning off onto a moonlit dirt road, he followed it for about fifteen minutes through fields of poplars and evergreens toward a row of steep cliffs where the road abruptly gave out, and they were swallowed up by darkness and silence.

"Here we are. Come on."

Molly peered through the windshield into the blackness. All she could see were the treetops' inky silhouettes slouching against the sky. Though Pierre seemed to know where he was going, she no longer found that reassuring.

"Where exactly is *here*?" Molly wasn't going anywhere without a good reason.

"La grotte de la Beune. It was discovered only a few years ago and has some truly spectacular prehistoric art. Come on, you'll see. It's my little surprise."

"You mean cave drawings like Lascaux?"

"No comparison," he said dismissively. "Lascaux and the other sites that are open to the public are like Euro Disney compared to this. Come along." He helped her out of the car and turned on his flashlight. "And don't make too much noise. There's a watchman."

Pierre made it sound like a once-in-a-lifetime adventure. Her curiosity piqued, Molly followed him up the steep, narrow path until they came to a wooden barrier with a sign that read Closed to the Public and beyond it a dimly lit shack. Motioning to her, he circled the barrier with Molly close behind.

"Are you sure we can do this?"

"Shhh! Careful."

There were loose rocks underfoot now. As they climbed toward the shadowy arch that was the mouth of the cave, Molly was glad that she hadn't changed for dinner, glad that she was wearing boots and not high heels. Once inside the cave, she immediately felt the chill in the air as they made their way down the passage. Molly put up the collar of the jacket she'd taken. There was no electricity, the only illumination coming from the dim, flickering oil lamps set against the walls. Pale shafts of light licked at the ceiling.

"Where are the drawings?"

As Molly looked up, she lost her balance on the uneven stone floor, and only Pierre's quick reflexes saved her from falling.

"Careful! We're almost there. Only about another fifty meters."

Though he meant to be reassuring, she felt as if she were undergoing a distinctly unpleasant medical procedure. Molly wondered where the narrow, intersecting passages led but didn't ask, fearing that she couldn't keep the alarm out of her voice. Dead ends, she guessed. With every twist and turn of the winding main corridor they seemed to be walking deeper and deeper into nothingness until they entered an enormous shadowy chamber, where the beam of his flashlight was swallowed up by the darkness at the far end. Molly kept looking around, searching, hoping to see something and half afraid of what it might be. All she could think of was bats.

Pierre flashed his light up and moved it slowly across the face of the rock. "Look. Look up there."

The walls were covered with dozens—no, hundreds—of animals. Bulls, bears, reindeer, galloping horses, and magical tusked and antlered beasts the likes of which she'd never seen before and had no names for. And the colors! Reds and yellows and blacks as vibrant and fresh as if they'd been painted only yesterday.

"Oh, Pierre!" She reached for his arm to steady herself. "This is amazing."

"Didn't I tell you? Not fantasyland reproductions but the real thing and seen by only a handful of people. Think of it! Direct to us from forty thousand years ago."

"I should look so good after forty thousand years. But how is it possible after so long? They're in such perfect condition."

"Calcite. The walls happen to be covered with it and, according to what I read, the calcite forms a white, moisture-resistant ground for the paintings. There's also a layer of fine chalk on the ceiling that apparently prevents water from seeping in. You see"—he flashed his light up to the ceiling—"no stalactites."

It didn't surprise her at all that Pierre took his hobby seriously or that he seemed to know what he was talking about. He was even able to explain how the artists could paint so far from the light at the mouth of the cave. Archaeologists had discovered ancient lamps here made from hollowed-out flint in which moss was used as a wick and placed in animal fat or oil. But no human bones. They believe, he told her, that this was a temple devoted to the rites of the hunt. He pointed to the arrows in the reindeer's side. "A prayer for success," he called them.

Entranced, Molly gazed up at the exotic menagerie on the wall and listened to Pierre. He seemed so full of his subject, so completely obsessed by it, she fell under his spell. Flattered that he wanted to share his secret with her and bewitched by the gift.

Ironically, Reiner himself had no particular yearning for the past at all, certainly no wish to be stuck there. If the Magdalenian Age interested him in the least, it was only as a means to an end.

"But there's one animal that they set apart," he told Molly, indicating the direction with his flashlight. "It's the enormous black bison. The largest of these paintings. Archaeologists call it *The Altar of the Black Bison.*"

Molly peered into the shadows. "Where? I don't see it."

"Over there." He raised the beam of his flashlight. "At the far end of the chamber. Let me show you."

"No, don't bother. I think I can see it." She inched forward slowly, her boot soles scraping against the stone, step by step into the blackness, watching her footing, careful not to slip.

"ATTENTION! ATTENTION!" a voice cried out. "What are you doing here?"

Molly, holding her breath, stopped dead in her tracks. Reiner wheeled around to see who it was. The guard angrily shook his flashlight in their faces. "Nobody is allowed in here. Can't you see it's closed? Get out! OUT!" Marching them out of the cave, he demanded to know who they were and what they were doing there. Molly pulled her passport out of her shoulder bag and said, "I'm an American."

"Of course." The sneer in his voice was unmistakable. "And yours?"

Reiner handed over his French *carte d'identité.*

"You at least should know better. This is closed for very good reasons. Now I suggest you both get the hell out of here."

As they walked down the hill to their car, Reiner said, "They're all the same, these *petits fonctionnaires.* Give them a uniform and they think they're Napoleon."

"I suppose he might have been nicer, but we *were* trespassing. Anyhow"—Molly slipped her arm fondly into Pierre's—"I wouldn't have missed those paintings for anything."

Standing by the barrier and keeping his eye on the young couple, the guard waited to make sure that they left. Then he turned and thanked the cop by his side for alerting him. "If you hadn't told me they were in there, she would have been dead. And I would have been out of a job."

Duboit asked, "Who was he?"

"Pierre Barmeyer, according to his ID. From Strasbourg."

Duboit repeated the name "Barmeyer," fixing it in his mind.

"And a damn fool too," the guard said. "Why did he think we have it blocked off like this? They could have both been killed. There's a chasm at the back of that cave that's more than seven hundred meters deep. Slip and fall in there and it'll eat you up without a trace. You'd never be found again."

The Hôtel du Centenaire in Les Eyzies was small, but the *Michelin Guide* called its restaurant excellent, worth a detour. Molly was looking forward to it and was crushed when the maître d'hôtel couldn't find Pierre's reservation.

"But you are in luck," he said, as he glanced over his bookings. "We have a cancellation."

And that evening Molly felt very lucky indeed. Their comfortable table, the soft lights, the delicious food, and waiters who appeared to be genuinely pleased to be serving them. And especially Pierre, who seemed to know that it wasn't necessary to say anything. It was as if she'd been touched by the magic of the cave. Or perhaps it was merely the wine, a seductive bottle of fragrant white from Bergerac.

When their bill came, Molly, as agreed upon, was more than happy to pay her share. She took the check, perfectly willing to cover the whole thing, but Pierre was so genuinely offended that she gave it up, not wanting to hurt his feelings.

Later, though, as they sat in his car in front of Madame Charpentier's bakery, Pierre seemed grumpy. Molly wondered what was bothering him. Usually, with people she knew, she could always tell why the mood of an evening had changed. Not tonight. There was something unpredictable about Pierre. He seemed so guarded, so locked up within himself. Her father would have said that he'd make a great poker player. You had no idea what cards he was holding.

"Anything wrong?" she asked.

"Given the food, I must say I thought that place was too expensive."

Molly indulged him with a smile. "Maybe—but my fish was absolutely exquisite."

"I'm glad you didn't order the pigeon. They cremated the poor thing. Even I could make it better."

"I didn't know you were a cook as well as an artist."

"How could you? You hardly know me."

"That's true. You're full of surprises."

"Yes, I suppose I am." Suddenly leaning over, Pierre took her in his arms and kissed her. He smelled of the cave. Molly started to push him away but then yielded to the pleasure of the moment. His lips tasted of garlic.

"How would you like dinner at my place?" he offered.

"Only if you're as good a cook as you claim."

"Tomorrow night?"

She hesitated. "No, I can't." She gave him her phone number. "Call me on the weekend."

Oh yes, he'd have her! She was worth waiting for. But how much more time could he wait? She'd already mentioned his accent. Not a good sign. If an American noticed it, how much more likely that the French would, given their peculiar sensitivity to their language— the purity of its sound, its diction. Reiner was acutely aware of one thing. The longer he remained in the house where he was staying, the more dangerous it became. No more failures, Reiner swore.

35

LE CYRANO

Molly put down the Sunday paper. She'd been reading an article about two of the lawyers in the murder case—François Astruc, Ali's new defense lawyer, and the investigating magistrate Christine Leclerc. Everything that Molly had heard about Madame Leclerc's thoughtfulness and intelligence she liked. She wondered why she hadn't tried to see her before. Anything to accelerate the inspector's investigation.

Finding her number in the Bergerac telephone book, Molly decided to call her at home. Why not? All she could say was no. But as luck would have it, Christine Leclerc was as curious to see the daughter of the murdered Americans as Molly was to meet the investigating magistrate.

Her house was perched on a terrace overlooking the Dordogne. A lovely view of the river, especially on a hot, sunny day. The white-haired man in the blue smock, who came to the door, smelled of soap. Ushering Molly into the twilight of the living room, he left without a word. She hoped that she'd come to the right house. The shutters were closed and fastened against the heat of the day, the windows behind them opened wide and the lace curtains pushed back to catch any breath of air trickling in. Molly wondered why there were so few air conditioners in this part of France when the country was plainly bristling with nuclear power plants. On a piano inside, she heard someone playing a familiar Scarlatti sonata much better than her mother ever could.

Molly, with a heavy heart, was thinking of her mother when Madame Leclerc appeared in the doorway on the other side of the room. A small woman with a black chignon, dressed younger than her years. In her sparkling white pants and elegantly fitted blue silk jacket with its bright floral pattern, she didn't look much like a judge.

Sitting down beside her visitor on the couch, Madame Leclerc was eager to express her sympathy. She spoke in English, as if to spare her guest any needless pain. Molly considered her English a work in progress. All the same, she did appreciate her kindness in agreeing to see her.

"*Merci beaucoup, madame . . . mais si vous voulez—*"

"English is fine," insisted Madame Leclerc. Her white-haired servant returned, carrying a bottle in a gleaming silver ice bucket. "A cool glass of wine, perhaps?"

Before Molly could say no, he'd poured them both some white Bordeaux. A complex smell of citrus and vanilla. Molly sampled it with pleasure.

"Delicious. But I know how busy you must be these days so let me come to the point immediately. I don't think Ali Sedak murdered my parents."

Madame Leclerc took her news calmly.

"Why is that, my dear?"

"Call it simply professional judgment and based on everything that I've heard thus far. You see, I also work in the area of criminal law."

"Yes, I read about that in the paper."

"As a prosecutor in New York, I've met all sorts of criminals who claimed to be innocent. Some with no more credibility than Klaus Barbie. But in this case I'm inclined to believe the suspect."

"You realize, of course, that he's been indicted and the evidence against him is not unpersuasive."

Her visitor paused, choosing her words carefully. "I think it's possible that he's being victimized."

"A conspiracy?" she asked, studying the pretty young woman and weighing the seriousness of her charge.

Molly explained that she'd spoken to Ali Sedak while he was being held at the local commissariat, and she had taped the interview. Pulling out her recorder, she played excerpts. She didn't believe that this frightened little man was capable of murdering those four people. And certainly not alone. Then she mentioned the phone calls to Ali's house made on Schuyler Phillips's stolen cell phone. They were made at about the same time the killer was using her father's stolen MasterCard to withdraw money from his account. If it had been Ali calling his wife, she said, he wouldn't have immediately hung up. More likely it was someone attempting to throw suspicion on him. Molly concluded Ali was probably telling the truth. "I suspect the caller was trying to frame Ali, make him a *pigeon*."

"Aha!" Leclerc nodded and considered how to begin. From another room, whoever was playing had moved on to a new challenge—a Bach partita, this time—but was finding it heavy going. The music kept starting and stopping.

"As I said before, the evidence against Ali Sedak at this point in our investigation is persuasive. But," she added, "by no means conclusive." And she hoped Mazarelle would soon give her a tighter case against the accused. There were questions still to be answered. Among them whether Ali's dealer, Eugène Rabineau, had played a role in the crime. Did he, despite his denials, actually sell Ali Sedak the five kilos of hashish the police found outside his house? And if Sedak was a dealer, who were his clients?

"Speaking of which . . ." The momentarily distracted speaker sighed as the pianist, clutching at straws, groped repeatedly for the right notes. *Madame le juge* began again. "Rabineau, according to *his* clients, left for Marseilles on business the day of the crime and did not return until the following afternoon. An alibi, yes, but not what I would call airtight."

No, definitely not airtight if junkies were providing Rabineau's only alibi. Molly shared Leclerc's interest in the drug dealer. She was wondering how to find him, when whoever was playing inside brought a fist down thunderously on the keyboard. Within seconds, she heard approaching footsteps and the door at the far end of the living room flew open, daylight flooding in.

The young, curly-headed blond woman was furious. She stood there in her bare feet wearing a tangerine tank top and strawberry panties, a refreshing fruit salad of summer colors. Molly thought she had a cute figure. Her hostess couldn't seem to decide if she wanted to introduce the newcomer. Whether Blondie was her daughter or girlfriend, she was obviously a volcano—an anarchic force in an otherwise peaceful landscape. Molly was reminded of Lola Lola in *The Blue Angel*. Hands on hips, Blondie snapped *"Pardon!"* and slammed the door behind her.

Christine Leclerc winced and smiled. "My protégé," she acknowledged.

Molly didn't laugh at the word, but really! It seemed so old-fashioned.

It was Thérèse who told Molly where she could find Rabo. A bar opposite the Bergerac train station called Le Cyrano in a shabby section of town with racist graffiti scrawled all over the sidewalk, the walls.

Molly drove slowly past the few taxis lined up in front of the station and parked outside Le Cyrano, the big neon sign above its name advertising Amstel. Going inside, she went over to the bar and sat down. The slight breeze from the open windows that looked out onto the street felt good. They were the only windows. The feeble yellow light from the globes on the walls merely heightened the dinginess. There were some people at the tables, but with the weekend train schedule, business was slow. The bartender, a moonfaced dreamer in a red-striped vest, appeared glad to see her.

"Amstel," she ordered.

He poured her a glass, wiped off the bottom, and placed it carefully down in front of her. Molly smiled, a dazzle of perfect teeth.

"You're an American, aren't you?"

"How did you know?"

He shrugged. *"Un certain je ne sais quoi."* He supposed it was the teeth. "From New York?"

"That's right. Ever been to New York?"

"Why would I want to go to New York?"

Molly was eager to tell him but drank her beer instead. If he'd no idea, it wasn't worth the effort.

Molly glanced around the room. As far as she could tell, no Rabo. At least no one who matched Thérèse's description of him. Though she couldn't see the face of the guy with his head down on the table sleeping, he had no rings on his fingers, no ponytail.

"I'm looking for Rabo," she told the bartender.

"Who?"

"Rabo." Had the inspector been pulling her leg?

The bartender had no idea that she'd come to Le Cyrano to score. He was happy to be of service. Told her that Rabo had a delivery to make, but he'd be back any minute. "Have another beer. How do you know Rabo?"

"We met in Marseilles recently." It was certainly worth a gamble. She didn't know what she'd do if Rabo actually showed up. "Promised he'd have something for me the next day, but I couldn't make it."

"Neither could he."

Molly glanced at the barkeep suspiciously. "How do you know that?"

"He came back here the same evening. Missed his connection, I heard."

"You're sure?"

He pointed to an empty table in the corner. "Sitting right there drinking with a couple of *mecs* he picked up on the road. You know, Corsicans? Small, dark eyes and lips that hardly moved when they spoke. All three swollen with secrets."

I'll bet they were, thought Molly, recalling Corsica's legendary reputation as the home of bandits and cutthroats. Could they all have been in it together?

"What time did they leave?"

The bartender didn't like snoopy questions. He snatched up her empty glass and pointed to the door. "Why don't you ask him yourself?"

Molly found it hard to breathe. The guy who'd just come in was talking to the young couple seated next to the front door. He had the dark, scruffy-looking, sour face Ali's wife had described. Molly glanced at his ponytail, his rings.

"Thanks. I'll do that."

"Hey, Rabo," the bartender called out, "a customer here."

Getting up, Molly threw back her shoulders and, taking a deep breath, walked straight toward him, her swaying red hair catching his eye. Turning expectantly, Rabo watched as she strode coolly past him and out the front door.

"Attendez!" he shouted after her.

Molly was sure that her car was being followed. Caught in traffic and creeping along, she became increasingly nervous. It was a dark sedan, black or midnight blue. She couldn't make out who was behind the wheel even when she turned around to look. Was she becoming paranoid? Her eagerness to tell the inspector what she'd learned only made her more jittery.

The cop who took her upstairs wiped his forehead and asked if it was as warm outside as it was in the commissariat. Molly told him that there was a breeze outside. He said in here it felt like a baker's oven. Molly said that it didn't smell like one.

The windows in Mazarelle's office were wide open, but it was still oppressively humid. The air reeking of stale tobacco. The shrill sound of whistling from the football field downstairs scraped his eardrums. Jacket off, Mazarelle sat working at his desk with his collar open, his sleeves rolled up, and the sweat dripping down his back, pasting his shirttail to his thick haunches. The coffee still left in his mug had turned to mud. He looked up as Molly entered and smiled. It wasn't much as smiles go, but it was the best he could do. There was no question he was glad to see her. She was a woman for whom weekends were made. It was just that he still had about a half dozen things to do before he could call it a day. Mazarelle wondered why she'd come.

Molly sat down opposite him and said, "You look a little triste, Inspector."

"Just my mustache."

She laughed, and the fizzy sound of her laughter made him feel ten years younger.

"What brings you here on a Sunday?"

"I have something to tell you."

"Yes?"

"I think Eugène Rabineau may have had more to do with the L'Ermitage murders than Ali Sedak."

Mazarelle heaved a sigh of resignation and accepted the inevitable. He was getting pissed off with her meddling. Though he knew better, he'd hoped that this might have been a social visit.

"Why is that, mademoiselle?"

"I understand that Rabineau claims to have gone to Marseilles and been there the night of the crime, but in fact he returned that same evening with two men."

"How do you know this?"

"They were seen together in a bar opposite the Bergerac train station."

"Le Cyrano?"

"That's right."

"Who were they, these men?"

"I don't know. Friends of his, I suppose. Well?" Molly raised an eyebrow. "Aren't you the least bit surprised that he was here that night?"

"But what makes you so certain that means he was involved in the murders?"

"Why else would he lie about not returning until the following day?"

Mazarelle scratched his mustache and offered her one possible explanation. "He claims that he just didn't want to get involved."

"You mean you *knew* all along that he was back the same day?"

Her lovely green eyes skewered Mazarelle, making him feel even hotter than the room. "No, not all along."

"But you knew."

"Yes, I knew. We've recently been talking to people who were working at Le Cyrano that night. The reason we haven't brought Rabo in is that all of them—the bartender, the waiters—confirm the fact that he was there all night drinking. He left when they closed at one a.m."

Molly's glance went around the office, looking for a way out. "Well," she asked, "what about his two Corsican friends?"

"Now there you may have something. He says they weren't friends.

Claims he didn't know them. Just two guys he picked up on the road named Georges and Po-Po. Had a couple of drinks together and they left the bar about eleven, he said, heading for Bordeaux." Mazarelle raised his large thumb—a scarred, stumpy digit—and moved it back and forth over his shoulder.

"Hitchhiking?"

"Uh-huh. We have an alert out for them. They'll turn up."

Molly got up to leave, feeling a little deflated. "I just thought you should know."

"Look," he said sympathetically, "it's clear to me that you're somebody who's not likely to get lost. But give us a little credit too. We're not all Clouseaus."

"Yes, of course." Molly felt embarrassed. "I didn't mean to . . ."

He shook her hand, thanked her. "I understand you wish to help, mademoiselle. I appreciate that. You mustn't think I'm not grateful. And as for Rabo, don't worry. We haven't eliminated him yet, not by any means. Now"—his voice stiffened and he ran his tongue over his lips—"will you please do me a favor and get off our toes? Quit playing detective."

When she'd gone, Mazarelle sat down, took out his pipe, his tobacco, and started to fill the bowl. Hating how much he'd sounded like her evil stepfather. He noticed she'd left behind a whiff of her perfume. The sort of delicious scent that might easily turn a younger man's head with thoughts. Perhaps he'd ask her out to dinner and, somewhere between the amuse bouche and the Monbazillac, tell her once and for all to stop interfering with police business. Or better yet, he thought, just ask her out to dinner.

PART FOUR

36

MAISON D'ARRÊT, PÉRIGUEUX

The Maison d'Arrêt in Périgueux spread itself out like five splayed fingers of some giant gray beast. Though it was a sun-drenched summer morning with a light breeze that set the tricolor dancing above the Palais de Justice, even spectacular weather could do little to brighten Périgueux's gloomy Piranesian prison.

Mazarelle parked his police car opposite the entrance and got out. He looked tired, rumpled, his eyes red-rimmed, as if he'd been working late and sleeping in his clothes. Which he had been, and probably smoking more than was good for him too. But he was feeling better than he looked. Didier, the chief of the Toulouse PTS team, had finally come through for him. The marks on the floor mat in Ali's VW were, as suspected, bloodstains and the DNA matched that of Mademoiselle Reece's father. Didier said, "My people have been working around the clock for you, *mon vieux*. I hope you appreciate it."

"I owe you one," the inspector acknowledged gratefully. Promising that the next time Didier visited the commissariat there was a very good bottle of Black Label he kept in his office for special occasions and that they were going to have the pleasure of polishing it off together. Mazarelle, however, was griped to learn that the chief had no idea what he was talking about when asked if he'd tested the two guns from the McAllister house.

"Never mind," Mazarelle said, "I'll see that you get them. The twelve-gauge shotgun may have killed Phillips." Duboit, he thought, shaking his head. Why the hell couldn't he surprise me and do what he was told?

As for *madame le juge,* he got what he expected from that party too. "Qualified" approval. She'd sent on his interim report to the procureur who would handle the case in court. Mazarelle didn't need her telephone call to know she'd want a signed confession and Sedak's head on a platter before she'd be satisfied. They always wanted the same thing—more and better evidence. QED. How could he blame her? When you're dealing with people's lives, you don't want to make mistakes and cut off the wrong leg, administer the wrong anesthetic. But he'd found the law a little more complicated than medicine. Even a signed confession wasn't always a guarantee of guilt. Yet he'd almost be happy to settle for that, and now with the proof of Reece's blood in Ali's car he felt he just might get the confession that had eluded him.

The uniformed guard at reception glanced at the inspector's ID, listened to the reason he was there, and told him to wait. Mazarelle wondered why he was getting the fish eye. Putting the phone down, the guard said someone would be there in a moment to fetch him. The prison director wanted to see the inspector.

Mazarelle blew out his cheeks. A bother, he thought. He'd no desire to waste time chitchatting with the top brass. Straightening his old, creased jacket, he was buttoning it up when the director's flunky came to show him the way. Though Mazarelle fully expected to be kept waiting outside the headman's office, cooling his fanny, he was shown right in.

The director came forward, pumped his hand. "A pleasure to meet you, *monsieur l'inspecteur.* Your work on the Taziac murders has been in all the papers."

Mazarelle wondered why the man seemed so nervous. Did he want an autograph? Something was eating at him.

"Of course I know your Commissaire Rivet. He's quite a young man for such an important position."

"Yes, he is young," Mazarelle agreed, his eyelids growing heavier by the second.

"The truth is, I rarely get down to Bergerac. The job here keeps me much too busy. We may not be as large as Rouen or as overcrowded as La Santé but we have our share of fights, rapes, drugs, self-mutilations. Every day we're being sent more and more psychos by the courts, and there are far too few of us to deal with them. I suppose it's the same all over France."

Though the handsome, white-haired director had a sonorous radio announcer's voice, it didn't completely put Mazarelle to sleep. He reminded the director why he was there.

"My appointment this morning to see your prisoner, Ali Sedak, is for ten o'clock."

"Oh yes, the captain of the guards told me about that. I'm afraid I have some bad news for you."

"Bad news?"

"At nine twenty-seven this morning prisoner Sedak was found on the floor of his cell covered in blood and barely conscious. His wrists had been cut."

Though he'd sensed bad news, Mazarelle had no idea how bad it was going to be.

"Cut with what?"

"A double-edged razor was on the floor next to him."

"How did he get a razor? Didn't you have him under suicide watch?"

"*Malheureusement, non.* If we had to put every cuckoo here under twenty-four-hour surveillance, we'd need an additional platoon. Alas, monsieur, we don't have that kind of budget."

Mazarelle demanded, "Where is he now?"

"We, of course, immediately called for an ambulance, and he was taken to Centre Hospitalier in a comatose condition. A few minutes ago I learned that the doctors were working on him in the emergency room, and he seemed to be responding."

Mazarelle headed for the door. "I've got to go."

"Before you do, *monsieur l'inspecteur,* a few seconds more of your time. As I'm sure you're aware, this sort of thing can do no one any good. In such a situation one naturally must be as discreet as possible. It's not good for me, not good for this institution, not good for Périgueux. I'm sure you understand."

"And what if he dies?"

The director paused, as if the thought had never occurred to him. "Oh, I don't think so."

Mazarelle was amazed. All those snow-white hairs and nothing in his head. Mazarelle limped hurriedly out the prison gate to his car. As he sped, siren blaring, toward the hospital, he thought that if worse came to worst, he still had a chance for a deathbed confession.

The waiting area outside the emergency room was crowded, people talking in whispers. A nurse called out someone's name, and a well-dressed woman in her fifties got up, holding a blood-soaked handkerchief to her nose, and followed her. At the front desk the inspector was told he could go inside.

A tall, bearded doctor with a stethoscope around his neck was talking intently to a heavyset, middle-aged man holding a worn leather briefcase. Mazarelle identified himself and asked about Ali Sedak.

The doctor pointed to the gendarme filling out forms at the desk.

"Dead. He never regained consciousness. Maybe if we'd gotten him here a little sooner, perhaps then . . ." Someone was calling him. Not knowing what else to add, the doctor apologized and walked briskly away.

"A tragedy," said the man with the briefcase.

He introduced himself as François Astruc. Mazarelle had seen a picture in the paper of the militant, high-profile defense lawyer from Toulon. With the financial help of Ali's sisters, Thérèse had managed to hire him for her husband, but now it was all for nothing.

Astruc said, "I know that since he was put in prison, his morale had plummeted. But we were preparing for trial and I personally believe, though you may not, that we had a good chance of success. Even that didn't cheer him up. So sad . . ." The lawyer shrugged. "If only I hadn't been late this morning for our appointment, he'd have been found sooner and this wouldn't have happened."

"What time was he expecting you?"

"Nine. I was held up by a telephone call and didn't get to the prison until twenty minutes later. When the guard and I found him on the floor of his cell with his wrists slashed, he'd already lost a lot of blood but was still breathing. What a shame! To have been driven to take his own life."

"You believed he was innocent?"

"Of course I believed he was innocent! What kind of question is that? Innocent and despairing of justice. The first time I met him he said, 'I wouldn't be in prison if France didn't have two kinds of citizens—those born here and second-class ones like me.' Why else would he have killed himself?"

"In my experience," the inspector offered, "it's the guilty ones who kill themselves."

"Your experience and mine differ, monsieur," Astruc replied coldly. "The outrage of Ali Sedak's death lies entirely with the prison authorities and people like you, Inspector, who had a responsibility to safeguard my client's life and failed."

On Mazarelle's list of least favorite people, defense lawyers like Astruc ranked right up there just below murderers, pederast priests, and *pégriots* who stole from blind men's cups. Why, he asked himself, why do I waste my time?

There was a public phone near the entrance and, checking his address book, he dialed the procureur's direct line. When he told d'Aumont who was calling, the procureur seemed pleased. As Mazarelle hoped, he hadn't heard yet. Mazarelle certainly didn't want him to learn the news of Sedak's death from TV reports. He promptly explained where he was and why.

D'Aumont was furious. It was inconceivable to him that the director hadn't arranged to have the new prisoner watched around the clock.

"The man is an imbecile! The only reason he got the job was because his father was once mayor of Périgueux. That plus the fact that he has a good tailor. But thanks to you, Inspector, Sedak would have been found guilty no matter what. The evidence against him was overwhelming."

Mazarelle told him of PTS's discovery of Reece's blood on the floor mat in Ali's car.

"*Voilà!* An open-and-shut case. Outstanding, Inspector!"

Mazarelle was annoyed with himself for feeling as pleased as he did about the procureur's bureaucratic flattery, which he knew was largely hot air. Though he thought they had a case, it was hardly open-and-shut. For example, the shoes Ali was wearing the night of the murders. According to the lab report, they didn't have any blood on them. Not a trace. How could that be if he was in the kitchen at L'Ermitage, where the white tile floor was awash in Reece's blood? Unless, of course, those weren't the shoes he was wearing. As for Ali's suicide, Mazarelle certainly didn't see it as a clear message from the land of the dead of either guilt or innocence. Nothing more than a simple miscalculation. A clever manipulator's desperate attempt to win sympathy as the wrongly accused, while being saved by his lawyer's timely arrival. Unfortunately for Ali, Astruc's telephone rang as he was leaving and he answered it.

37

LOOSE ENDS

Bandu, who was talking on the phone, glanced up as the inspector—hangdog and prickly—lumbered into the task force meeting room, looking exhausted. He headed for the coffee machine like an old steam engine climbing a steep grade, the smoke from his pipe streaming behind him. Bandu suspected a migraine. Putting his hand over the receiver, he said, "I hope you don't mind my saying so, chief, but you look like shit."

"Nobody's perfect."

"Anything wrong?"

"Yeah." The inspector sipped his black coffee. "Where's everybody?"

Bandu told his caller, "I'll get back to you."

Their task force had been cut in half following the indictment of Sedak. Bandu was the only one there now. He reported that Vignon was screening the last of their tapes from the digital face-recognition system he'd set up in the mall and the others hadn't come in yet.

"What's the matter?"

"Ali Sedak is dead."

Bandu winced. "How did it happen?"

"Suicide." Mazarelle didn't want to talk about it. "I'll be upstairs if you need me."

The first thing he did when he got into his office was take four aspirins and hope they'd do the trick. Since leaving the hospital, he'd lost his appetite and, despite having had nothing to eat, he felt as if he'd put on a ton. Mostly dead weight. It wasn't that he saw Ali's suicide as a tremendous loss to society—one criminal less. The loss was the loose ends left behind. Mazarelle honestly believed that he'd been within a hairbreadth of learning the truth about what had happened. He comforted himself with the thought that if Ali was the murderer, he probably didn't do it alone, which meant there were eyewitnesses still alive who knew what happened that night.

Without knocking, Duboit breezed in, smiling like a kid at a carnival. "I just heard the news. Exactly what you were afraid he might do. Sort of like a confession, isn't it, boss? Well, good riddance. One less to worry about."

"You don't like Arabs very much, do you Bernard?"

"Me? I love Arabs, but in Algeria, Libya, Morocco. Not here in France. Anyhow"—folding his arms with satisfaction—"I guess that wraps things up for us."

"What gives you that idea? Don't be a blockhead. We're not finished yet. Besides, what about the two guns I asked you to send to Didier for testing?"

Duboit groaned.

"That was *important*, Bernard!"

"Sorry, boss. I'll take care of it right away. I have a lot on my mind lately."

"Never mind. I'll do it myself. All I want you to do is keep an eye on Mademoiselle Reece till she goes home."

"Awwrrrr . . . Do I have to, boss?"

"Unless you'd prefer filling potholes or stocking supermarket shelves."

Duboit whined. "I hate sitting around in a car, twiddling my thumbs."

"Try jerking off. Frankly I don't care what you do, just stay with her."

"All right. If I have to, I'll do it."

"That's better."

"I mean she's not a bad-looking woman. But it's no fun seeing her screwing around with her new French boyfriend. Those Americans don't mourn very long, do they?"

"What new boyfriend?" the inspector asked. "Who?"

"Never saw him before. He's from Strasbourg."

"How do you know that?"

"Because I'm a cop."

Mazarelle felt his headache getting worse.

"Okay, okay." Duboit could see that his boss wasn't in a playful mood. He told him how he'd followed the two of them from Madame Charpentier's *boulangerie* to Les Eyzies and la grotte de la Beune and how he'd alerted the guard, who examined their papers and then kicked them out.

"That cave," Duboit reminded him, "isn't open to the public."

"Then what were they doing there?"

"Fucking around, I suppose. Maybe they were old friends. It sure looked that way to me. By the way, his name is Pierre Barmeyer."

"Do what I told you, Bernard. Just get back there and don't let her out of your sight. Okay?"

"You mean you really don't think the case is over yet?"

"The only one it's over for is Ali Sedak. Goddamn it, watch her, Bernard!"

Mazarelle knocked the ashes from his pipe into his wastebasket. Why couldn't Bernard just do what he was told and stop being a pain in the ass? The last thing he wanted was to have another foreigner butchered in his neighborhood. Especially a young, pretty one who seemed to attract a great deal of attention wherever she went, not all of it welcome. Who was Pierre Barmeyer from Strasbourg and how did they become such good friends so quickly? Mazarelle realized he was behaving more like a jealous husband than a detective. But he'd always been something of a brooder.

On nothing more than a hunch, he picked up the phone and dialed Daniel Couterau, an inspector he knew at the Commissariat de Police in Strasbourg. He asked him for whatever they had on a Pierre Barmeyer.

"Tell me, Paul, how come you only call me when you want something?"

"Because I don't want to waste your time."

"Very funny. You still have that brut sense of humor. That's nice."

"What about my Pierre Barmeyer?"

"Is he from Strasbourg?"

"I think so."

"Approximate age?"

"Say somewhere between twenty and fifty."

Couterau laughed. "That's a lifetime."

"Yeah, I know."

"Anything else you can tell me? An address? Profession? Military service? Disabilities?"

"Sorry."

"You're not making this easy for me, Paul."

"I know."

"I'll see what I can do. But don't hold your breath."

"Please, Daniel, as *soon* as you can. This is important."

No sooner had Mazarelle hung up than his phone rang. At first he thought that Couterau was calling him back, but it was a low voice that he didn't recognize. Dwight Bennett was on the line from Paris. He was worried about Molly Reece. He'd tried to reach her at the Hôtel Fleuri, but the manager told him that she'd checked out and left no forwarding address.

"I was wondering if you might know where she is. Has she gone back to the United States?"

"Mademoiselle Reece is fine," Mazarelle said, and hoped it was true. "She's staying with a friend of mine who runs the bakery in Taziac." He gave him Madame Charpentier's telephone number.

Bennett thanked him. "That's a relief. Oh, by the way, I saw you got an indictment against Ali Sedak. When does the trial begin?"

Mazarelle sighed. "There'll be no trial. Ali Sedak committed suicide this morning."

Bennett was stunned. "I'm sorry to hear that, Inspector. Did you think he was guilty of killing all four of them himself?"

"That was for a jury to say. It's too bad that now we'll never know their decision."

As Dwight dialed the number Mazarelle had given him, he thought of Ali Sedak. Poor son of a bitch.

"Dwight! How did you manage to find me here?"

Hearing her voice on the phone, Bennett felt better. He asked why she'd left the hotel.

"I needed a change."

Her breezy tone made him suspicious. "Did anything happen?"

Molly, not wanting to go into detail about her Arnaud episode, said simply, "Someone broke into my room there."

"You're joking!"

"No big deal. I thought it best to get out, that's all."

"I'm glad you did. Will you be leaving Taziac soon?"

"Soon. But there's nothing to worry about. I'm staying with the inspector's friend Madame Charpentier. She's great." Molly glanced at the white lace curtains in her room, the Che Guevara mug on the windowsill. "It's really quite cozy here. I'm perfectly fine."

"Did you hear about Ali Sedak?"

There was something dark hiding in his voice. "Why? What do you mean?"

"He's dead. Mazarelle told me that he committed suicide this morning. Cut his wrists."

"How awful! Even a bastard who treated his wife like a punching bag didn't deserve to die like that." All Molly could think of was how pale and frightened he seemed when she saw him at the commissariat, and those pathetic fingernails of his bitten to stumps.

She said, "I hope the police aren't planning to bury the case with his body. Did Mazarelle say anything to you about that?"

"He said there was a lot of evidence against him, but now that he's dead we'll never know."

"That's exactly what I'm afraid of."

"Leave it to the inspector, Molly. I know him. Trust me, he doesn't give up easily. Okay?"

She didn't say anything at first. Then finally she said, "Okay."

He didn't believe her, but he'd said what he could.

Bennett opened his office door and told Barney that he wasn't taking any more calls, didn't want to be disturbed. The recent, surprising news from Taziac had to be sifted, sorted, and added to the file. Dwight Bennett's Paris embassy post was a magnet. Sensitive data from all over France and abroad passed across his desk. Business developments, money laundering, political shifts, technological breakthroughs, espionage, terrorism, drugs. A series of dots to be put together. Recognizing relationships and their significance was what he was paid for. Normally Dwight was good at it. In this instance, however, he'd been having trouble finding a clear pattern. Time to rethink. Regardless of Ali Sedak's suicide, there didn't seem to be any place for him in the picture.

Leaning down, he unlocked his bottom drawer and quickly found what he wanted—a large folder with the bland commercial title Franco-German Exports. He ran his eyes over the ELINT transcript that had been forwarded to him a month ago from their station in Berlin. It was stamped Top Secret—one of dozens collected via bugs from rooms at the new Hotel Adlon. Like the old Adlon, the new one was still interesting to the Company. A place where people of importance stayed and international business deals were made, though probably not many like the one recorded here.

A murder had been commissioned. Someone in France—probably a foreigner—was to meet with an accident, which Dwight took for a dusty old underworld euphemism, before the end of June. But who? Where? The speakers were cautious, but inadvertently they'd dropped a few tiny clues. For instance, the Quai d'Orsay. How was the Foreign Ministry involved? And Simone. Was that Simone Nortier—the minister's deputy? The man they wanted for the job was an "Ossi." Curious, yes, though not terribly suggestive. Perhaps the target was German.

More helpful to him were their references to foods typical of the region where the murder was to take place. On that basis, Bennett had narrowed it down to two or three locations. Since then, the only even remotely relevant crime that had occurred was in Taziac, in the Dordogne. But why four people? And as for the killer, Ali Sedak was no more a professional hit man than he was an Ossi. Besides, Pellerin called him "Herr Reiner." Bennett found the contradictions frustrating. The intriguing connections, however, were another matter.

Clipped to the typed transcript was the photograph that McCarty had returned after checking the bugs at the rue de Berri. Bennett had discovered it among the pictures he'd requested from Berlin. They'd all been taken by their surveillance camera across from the main entrance of the Adlon on the day of the meeting between the hit man and his employers. Bennett had assumed that the killer would be in one of them. Another face in the crowd but a face that might be familiar to him. What he hadn't expected were the two French agents coming out the door of the hotel whom he recognized instantly. Émile Pellerin and Hubert Blond.

Although Bennett had heard his old friends had retired from the Direction Générale de la Sécurité Extérieure, he knew—even before he'd received confirmation of it—that their Adlon room number would turn out to be 501, the number stamped on the transcript. One doesn't completely give up a life in the secret service any more than a career in crime. They were a team, Pellerin and Blond, and a good one too. At the end of the eighties, Bennett had worked with them to crack a drug case they called the Southern Triangle—an international gang transporting heroin from Karachi to Marseilles to Savannah, Georgia, the drugs hidden aboard giant container ships. But in 1990, when relations between the Company and DGSE cooled, he lost track of them.

Much later Bennett learned that Pellerin, who'd been attached to the French embassy in Washington, had been charged by the State Department with "activities incompatible with his diplomatic status" and booted out of the country. Once again, he'd been teamed up with his pal. This time it was industrial espionage—an operation known by Americans in the trade as a Tinker to Evers to Chance. Blond, working in Silicon Valley, was stealing high-speed computer chips and sending them to Pellerin in Washington, who passed them along to Paris via diplomatic pouch. It wasn't anything that the Chinese or the Russians or the Israelis or, for that matter, the Americans weren't doing, but the French had the bad luck to be caught at it. *Tant pis.* Undoubtedly it sped their retirement. Or semiretirement if this current operation was sanctioned, which he couldn't be sure of, given its highly unusual nature.

Dwight wondered if they were merely trying to fatten their retirement pensions by going into business for themselves. As he recalled, the two of them had expensive tastes. Perhaps they'd been hired by some wealthy private party to subcontract a crime. If so, Molly's father was certainly a possible target. But he knew of no hint of any friction between him and his partner or that the Reece-Campbell Gallery was anything but solid gold.

Bennett thought it possible that in some fashion Pellerin and

Blond might still be working for the French government. Which might explain the reference to the Quai d'Orsay. What he remembered about both of them was that they were graduates of the prestigious École Nationale d'Administration and gay. With their elite education and personal relationship they always seemed to feel like outsiders in the DGSE, where most senior positions were reserved for ex-soldiers, ex-cops. A rogue operation, however, would suit them well—especially if economic espionage were involved. In that case, Schuyler Phillips would have been the most likely target.

Though Bennett had a strong sense that there was a web linking the Hotel Adlon to the quadruple killings in Taziac, he couldn't fathom how the murder of Phillips and the three others could be, as Pellerin said, "worth every centime to our friends." Who were these generous friends? And then, of course, there was the little problem of the identity of the killer. Who was this Herr Reiner?

38

THE HOUSE NEXT DOOR

leeping, which was once second nature to Mazarelle, had become a lost art, and the death of Ali Sedak hadn't made it any easier. Not to mention how much he'd been drinking lately. He was glad he still had a major murder case to unravel or he might be seriously depressed. The inspector pulled out his passkey and went in through the McAllisters' back door, turned on the lights, and glanced around. Everything looked just the way it had the last time he'd been there. Yet he couldn't help feeling something was out of place, and as he tried to pin down what it was, he heard someone upstairs. Motionless, Mazarelle listened hard, but the footsteps had ceased. Had he imagined them? Lately he was more and more jumpy. He searched for his pipe but must have left it in his office.

Then he heard the sound of the car pulling up outside. It was Lambert, who had made good time and brought everything he'd asked for. Mazarelle hurried into the kitchen with Lambert in tow and, after irritably rummaging through a couple of drawers, found the key that McAllister had mentioned.

"Come on." Mazarelle limped quickly into the living room and opened the gun case.

"Nice smell," said Lambert, placing the rolls of canvas, wrapping paper, and tape he was carrying down on the floor.

"Cedar," the inspector said. "That's odd."

"How so?"

"That's usually used for hope chests, not guns."

They both slipped on their latex gloves. Mazarelle took out the double-barreled shotgun first, cracked it open to make sure it was unloaded, then looked it over from butt to barrel, and sniffed the muzzle.

"Has it been fired recently?"

"It's been fired, but I've no idea how recently. Could have been ten years, ten months, or only ten hours ago. More important is whether it's the gun that murdered Schuyler Phillips. For that, we'll have to wait to hear what they say in Toulouse after they run ballistics and we find out if we have a match. As for me, I'm feeling lucky, so take it." He handed him the gun. "Wrap it up carefully, and guard it with your life."

The other gun—a Mannlicher-Carcano—was also unloaded. To Mazarelle, who was no small arms expert, it appeared to be in good shape, as if it hadn't been used very often.

But even if it had never been fired, which was highly unlikely, this one in the hands of an accomplice who left prints still might have played a part in the murders.

Lambert packed up the rifle and laid it down gently beside the other one on the table. The inspector's plan was for Lambert to take his car and express the guns down to PTS, where Lambert was to *personally* hand them to Didier for testing. And if Mazarelle didn't get the test results by the next day, he swore he'd come down there himself to get them.

"Not to worry. I'll tell him, boss. But first," he asked, looking around, "where's the toilet?"

"Try upstairs. And step on it. Meanwhile give me the keys to your car and I'll load up the trunk."

By the time the impatient Mazarelle had locked the guns in the police car's trunk and checked out the garage, which was empty except for what looked to him like fresh tire tracks, he'd expected Lambert to be ready to go. What the hell was keeping him? Was he shitting his brains out? There was no sign of him when he went back inside the house. Mazarelle, pulling himself along the banister, went up the stairs two at a time in search of his missing squad member. The hallway was deserted.

"Come on, Lambert!" he trumpeted. "Move your ass and let's go." Mazarelle had heard strange tales about constipated people sitting on a crapper for as long as half an hour who had fainted dead away, suffered heart attacks. He went down the hall peering into the empty rooms and banging his fists on the closed doors.

"A minute, boss. I'm coming."

There was a loud rushing of water followed by Lambert stepping out from behind a door with a newspaper in his hands. He waved it in Mazarelle's face.

"Did you ever see this article? It's a piece on the Taziac murders, our task force, Sedak's suicide, and all about you and the big murder cases you handled in Paris and how you tracked Sedak down. It makes a good story."

The inspector snatched the copy of *Sud Ouest* out of his hands. There was a large photograph of L'Ermitage on the front page. His eyes dashed nonstop over the article's opening paragraph, but that was enough.

"Where did you get this?" He returned the paper.

"It was over there on the stool."

"Did you happen to notice that it was dated yesterday? That's when I read it in the commissariat. Whoever left it here was in this house— probably sitting exactly where you were just now. And might still be in here for all we know." The full impact of his realization galvanized Mazarelle into action. "There's a room upstairs. Make sure it's empty. I want you to check all the hiding places up there no matter how small, even mouseholes, and leave nothing to chance. After that, see if you can get into the attic. I'll take care of the rest of the house. Hurry, Lambert, but watch yourself."

Mazarelle sped through the rooms, flew down the halls like a heat-seeking missile. There were no surprises. "How about you?" he asked, when his man returned.

"Nothing." Lambert brushed the cobwebs off his jacket with the newspaper he was holding as he came downstairs. "By the way, did I show you this?" He flipped the pages until he found where the article he'd been reading was continued. Holding it up in front of his boss, he poked his face playfully through the hole. "Somebody removed part of the ending."

The inspector turned the page around and felt a chill go through his bones. There had been something printed there that had been ripped from the page. "It was a picture of me," he recalled.

"One of your many fans, no doubt." Lambert was enjoying his boss's discomfort.

"No. No fan."

The edgy Mazarelle's lips barely parted as he dismissed the idea, his angular jaw tense. Holding the paper up by its corners, he examined the jagged hole in the page. The eye of the house seemed to be watching every move he made. It gave him one of the most peculiar feelings that he'd ever had. It felt as if suddenly, after a long and difficult hunt, he himself had become the hunted.

39

A HIGH-RISK GAME

Reiner's love of the game had brought him back to the rue Blanche. He hadn't been to the Café Valon since his meeting there with Ali Sedak, but Javert remembered. Even though the Valon was crowded, Javert found him almost as soon as he sat down at a small table in the rear of the noisy, smoke-filled café. The dog sniffed the newcomer's shoes, his cuffs.

An elderly customer at the next table who'd noticed the two of them said, "You make friends easily. Javert doesn't like everybody who comes in here."

"Yeah." He didn't deny it. "I'm okay with animals. It's people I'm lousy with."

That seemed to muzzle the nosy old fart. Reiner patted the mutt's head, and the contented animal wagged his tail and trotted off. Everything should be so easy, Reiner thought. His dinner with the American woman was set for the next night, and he was looking forward to their last meal together, an end, finally, to this *gottverdammt* job. Then good-bye Molly, *adieu* Taziac. Meanwhile he'd only time to kill—too much time. But with a glass of *rouge* and a cig, he felt right at home.

Reiner studied the TV screen high up at the far end of the bar. Amused that despite the Barcelona sportscaster's description of the weather for the big game as sunny, the thick cigarette smoke in the café made the Spanish city appear surrealistically foggy, even sinister. How he would have enjoyed sitting in the stands at the Camp Nou stadium, happily wedged in with the more than ninety thousand fans already there. Reiner saw himself decked out in his red Bayern München cap, cheering wildly and having the time of his life.

Reporters were calling the Champions League final that year between England and Germany the highest-risk football match in a decade. On the Barcelona streets, five thousand *policía* were deployed to crack down on hooliganism. On the pitch, the umpire too had no patience for troublemakers. When a Manchester United thug collided violently with a Bayern forward within the box, the ump's whistle instantly shrieked—a prelude to a German free kick. Reiner nodded his approval.

The English players formed their defensive wall in front of their goal. Reiner leaned forward, his eyes locked on the screen, as Bayern's star midfielder Mario Basler positioned the ball. To have the superb Basler on his own dream team some day, Reiner would gladly empty out every penny in his piggy banks.

From twenty-five yards out, Basler approached the ball, planted his left foot, and rocketed the ball spinning into the air. It looked to Reiner as if it was going straight at one of the English players—his folded hands cupped protectively over the family jewels—but the ball curled round the base of the human wall and, faking out the keeper, buried itself into the bottom of the far corner of the goal. The Bayern supporters leaped to their feet, waving their arms, out of their minds, shouting gleefully.

Reiner lifted his wineglass—a silent toast to the brilliant precision of Mario Basler and his exquisite kick. Truly a thing of beauty. The football seemed to have eyes. Only six minutes into the game and the German team was already up 1–0. Though not a betting man, Reiner was sorry not to have bet on this one. Catching the widow's eye, he ordered another glass of *rouge*.

After Basler's early lightning bolt, the game was furiously contested by the two powerhouses. Back and forth, the action seesawed across the field punctuated by heart-stopping spikes of adrenaline. The English eleven, a scrappy team that fought hard, had been damn lucky. But the confident, alert Germans stopped them at every turn, deflecting their passes, smothering their shots, and counterattacking brilliantly. Reiner was sure that any minute they'd score again. Some time later, however, when Inspector Mazarelle came through the front door and asked a sweating Mickey V for the score as he hurried past with a clinking tray full of empty beer bottles, nothing had changed.

"Still one–zip, Bayern," the owner replied. He put down the empties behind the bar.

The inspector glanced at the crowd. "You're busting at the seams today."

Since Mazarelle began working all hours on the L'Ermitage murders, he'd been dropping by late most evenings for a nightcap or a bite to eat, but even at night he'd never seen the Valon so busy. Usually it wasn't a bad place for a quiet drink. Mickey was okay, the food passable, and when you were dealing with death all day it was nice to be surrounded by a little life. Best of all, after a few drinks, it was only a short walk down the narrow, gravel-covered back alley to his front door.

"It's a big game," was all the owner said, hurrying back for more empties, but that was enough. They were both football fans. The inspector went over to the bar. It was then he noticed Thérèse standing behind it staring at him.

"I didn't expect to see you working again so soon," he said.

"We have to live. You don't work, you don't eat."

"Where's the baby?"

"With a friend. What are you drinking?"

"Give me a cognac."

"Anything to eat with it?"

He glanced at the lunch specials listed on the chalkboard. "How are your sausages and lentils today?"

"Same as usual. Nothing to crow about. You want it or not?"

"With mustard."

He could tell she still blamed him for her husband's death even after he'd explained what happened. Rather than send somebody else, he'd gone to the old mill himself to tell her. He felt he owed her that. If Ali didn't deserve to die—if he'd simply run out of luck—and she had a legitimate gripe, it was one he could live with. She didn't believe him when he said it was suicide. Demanded to know what her husband's last words were. For some reason, Mazarelle hadn't expected that she actually loved the creep. There's no telling what people set their yearning hearts on, tossing them away like empty cans. Recalling her drawn, frightened face, he would have liked to reply, "Your name." Or to have told her that Ali confessed to the killings, and see if she'd spill the beans. In fact, he just told her the truth.

Thérèse returned with the cognac and suggested he find a seat somewhere if he could. She'd bring him the sausages when they were ready.

"With mustard," he reminded her, and handed her a bill.

"Forget it. Mickey says it's on the house."

"Okay, you keep it."

As Mazarelle made his way to the rear of the café, he noted that as usual most of the people there were locals. He waved back to some of the blue overalls from the scrap metal shop up the block who congratulated him. "You see, Inspector," their boss shouted, "business in the village is picking up already, thanks to you." Mazarelle wanted to straighten him out then and there, but decided another time. Spotting an empty chair with a leather jacket on it at a nearby table, he limped over, asked the guy with the long hair if it was taken. Glued to the game, the stranger ignored him. At the next table, an old guy who knew the inspector by sight—a mountain of a man with a mustache—timidly eyed what was going on. Hoping for fireworks.

"Mind some company?" Mazarelle asked again.

"Company?" The stranger, looking irritated, peered up at Mazarelle.

Most summers there were tourists around Taziac, but not many newcomers wandered off the beaten track and found their way to the Café Valon—especially this summer. The inspector wondered who he was. Positive he'd never seen him before. But what was odd to Mazarelle, though it might have been his imagination, was that the stranger seemed to recognize him.

"I love company," the stranger decided. "Sit down, sit down."

Reiner couldn't believe what he'd just done. Rather than fleeing danger, he seemed perversely eager to court it these days, even revel in it, testing himself in the crucible of risk. He was amazed at how he'd changed since coming to France. Hardly recognized himself anymore. A sure sign that he never should have returned.

Mazarelle picked up the leather jacket, which had a strong, musty smell that was not unfamiliar to him. "This yours?" he asked, sitting down.

Reiner grabbed his jacket and tossed it over the back of his chair. "Did that guy over there call you inspector? You a flic?"

"I've been called worse."

"Inspector *Mazarelle*?"

"How did you know?"

"I saw your face in the newspaper. You take a nice picture."

"Good sleuthing. You should be in my business. What's your name?"

Reiner smiled. The flic had absolutely no idea who he was. He was really enjoying himself. The situation was priceless—sitting side by side with the man assigned to track him down. He had this wild urge to tempt fate a bit more. Why stop when you're having fun? Live a little. "You're the guy who captured the L'Ermitage murderer, aren't you?" Raising his glass with a nice flourish, he said, "*Chapeau*, Inspector."

"Thanks, but nobody's caught him yet."

Reiner turned from the game and stared at the police officer. His voice when it came had lost its twinkle. "What's that supposed to mean? I read in the paper that you'd caught him."

"Sorry to disappoint you."

Reiner shrugged. "These days you can't trust anybody."

"You're right about that." Why didn't he want to give him his name? Mazarelle had the creepy feeling that this guy was laughing at him. He wondered if Ali's death had him looking over his shoulder now, hearing footsteps. Mickey V's dog, tail wagging, trotted over to Mazarelle. The inspector grabbed him and gave Javert his usual affectionate two-fisted pat that was more like a firm Swedish massage.

"No wonder he likes you," said Reiner. "He's a flic too. How come you became a cop?"

Mazarelle considered his question and chuckled. "Not trusting people, for one thing. Another, I suppose, is my father was a fire chief. I figured I'd try something different. What about *your* father?"

"A nonentity." Reiner dismissed the subject with a wave of his hand. He had little desire to pursue it.

The inspector refused to let him off the hook. "I'm interested," he insisted. "What did he do?"

"Not much. He was injured in the army. Couldn't find a job when he came home, so mostly he just hung around. A dull life neatly rounded off by a boring death. Except for his stay in the military, the only risk he ever took was getting up in the morning."

Mickey V came over, put down the steaming special, and, like magic, produced a jar of mustard from under his apron. "Thérèse says this is yours."

Mazarelle sniffed. "Smells good."

"Are you coming in for dinner this evening?" the owner asked. "The chef's special tonight is duck confit, one of your favorites."

"I'll be in. But late."

"I'll save you some." He picked up their empty glasses and asked the inspector, "Another round of drinks?"

It was useless to try to be heard above the noise. Noting that his tablemate was absorbed in the action on the screen, Mazarelle nodded—another round for both of them. The café had become a battlefield of booing, cheering, stomping feet. Only a few minutes before the half and the English had just been awarded a free kick. Number 7 would take it. As he brushed his long, blond hair out of his eyes, the boos grew louder, the cheering more desperate. The Valon fans appeared frozen in a World War II time warp—split between rabid Pétainist Vichyites and Free French Gaullists. Mazarelle had to laugh at the old guy at the next table pumping his cane like a baton as he led those cheering the Brits' kicker.

Reiner scowled at the Anglophiles and the decrepit old bone bag making a fool of himself.

The inspector said, "Number seven. That's Beckham, isn't it?"

"That's him. Too pretty for my taste."

Mazarelle announced having read somewhere that he was one of the highest-paid players in Europe.

"One hundred and forty thousand a week." The stranger knew everything about him, had apparently read all the football fanzines. "And that doesn't include what he gets from Adidas and Pepsi for endorsements. Do you realize that's more than Arnold Schwarzenegger makes?"

"I guess he's worth it."

Reiner stared at him as if he were certifiable. "You're joking."

"We'll see," the inspector said, as Beckham stepped up and blasted the ball. Had it gone straight, instead of way wide of the Germans' right goalpost, it would have tied the score. The inspector winced. An admirer of the French star Zinedine Zidane, he philosophically observed, "He's no Zizou."

Reiner needed another drink. The owner seemed to have forgotten all about them. He tried to get Thérèse's attention for a refill, but she was busy. It was the half now.

"Not a bad first half," the inspector said.

"At least the first six minutes." The stranger appeared annoyed by the thirty-nine that followed, unable to fathom why Bayern wasn't way ahead by now. He waved in the direction of Thérèse, who was taking other orders. "What are you drinking, cognac? This round is on me."

Mazarelle was on his feet. "My treat," he called on his way to the bar. "The next is yours."

Reiner saw no reason to argue about it. He'd been watching the excited old fool at the adjoining table, who throughout the half had been scurrying back and forth to the crapper. This time as he tried to get up he lost his cane. Reiner handed it back to him.

The old man seemed surprised. "It's not easy getting old," he said, as he stood up.

There was a momentary look of contempt on Reiner's face. "What's the big trick? All you have to do is hang around long enough."

The old man enjoyed the joke. He had a shrill, grating laugh, more like a wheeze than a laugh. Reiner hated it, and Reiner wasn't joking. He flicked his foot and the old man lost his cane. He went sprawling, banging his head hard on the cement floor. His friends rushed to his aid and, lifting his wafer-thin, crumpled body, hurried him out the door. Reiner watched them go. No one had seemed to notice his footwork.

When the inspector returned, the stranger was watching the young couple on TV driving through Barcelona, their child strapped safely in his seat in the back. All three of them smiling from ear to ear. A car commercial.

"Still here?" the inspector asked, laughing as he put down their drinks. "I thought you might have left."

The stranger was not amused. "Of course I'm still here. The only way you'll get me out of here before this game is over is to arrest me and drag me away."

Mazarelle grinned. "Speaking of which, what happened to the old boy they just carried out?"

Reiner shrugged. "He must have fallen. At his age and that thin it doesn't take much. The slightest breeze."

"What's that up there? A new Mercedes?" The inspector sipped his cognac.

"The new S class model."

The inspector was impressed. "A good-looking car." The black sedan gleamed like something in a jeweler's window.

"In a way almost too good," Reiner said softly, thinking that if things had worked out differently with Phillips's rented Mercedes, he would no longer be in France. No, no, he told himself, that way lies madness.

Puzzled, the inspector asked, "What do you mean 'too good'?"

"All the standard safety devices they put in nowadays. Air bag, supplemental restraint systems, seat belt pretensioners, brake assist, traction control, electronic stability control."

"What the hell's wrong with that?"

On the spur of the moment the only thing Reiner could think of was "Too expensive."

Mazarelle noticed the players drifting back from their locker rooms for the second half and inquired how Bayern had scored their goal. The stranger brightened and described Basler's remarkable free kick but, feeling that he'd failed to do it justice, became annoyed with himself. He snatched up the inspector's small paper napkin and asked for a pencil.

"Will this do?" Mazarelle gave him his pen.

Reiner swiftly sketched in the goal, the defensive wall of players, the position of the two stick figures he labeled Basler and Schmeichel. Then with a neat dotted line he tracked the triumphal curving path of the ball past the goalie into the net.

"You see?" He pushed his drawing across the table.

"Impressive."

"Exactly." The stranger leaned back, arms folded in satisfaction, and balanced himself precariously on the spindly rear legs of his wooden chair.

Mazarelle took out his pipe. He filled it with Philosophe and methodically tamped down the tobacco. "What did you say your name was? I don't think I've ever seen you in Taziac." Though said in passing while he busied himself hunting in his pockets for matches, it was not exactly random chitchat at this point.

"Funny, I was thinking the same about you." Reiner felt that in knowing his man the advantage was all his. That was what made the little cat and mouse game he was playing with the inspector so extraordinary.

"Have you been in here before?" Reiner asked.

"Oh, a few times," the inspector said casually. "Do you live around here?"

"I'm on vacation."

"Taziac is a good place for a vacation. Especially if you like peace and quiet. That is"—the inspector lit up and sent a stream of gray smoke across the table—"until recently." The two men exchanged wary glances.

Reiner, seeing the players take the field, announced, "Here we go," and brought his chair legs down with a crash. The second half was about to begin.

Bayern got off to a quick start. The Germans seemed the fresher of the two teams and more determined than ever to break away from their English defenders. Again and again they challenged United's goalie, but each time he scooped the ball up and put it back into play. Reiner groaned. He was becoming more and more frustrated. Throwing his head back, exasperated, his eyes searched the café's pressed tin ceiling for divine intervention. The football gods had turned a deaf ear to Bayern's dejected fans. With time running out, perhaps they wouldn't need another score to win.

There was almost no regulation time left on the clock when Manchester's Teddy Sheringham took what had to be his team's last chance. It was a corner kick—a high, driving one and curving at an impossible angle. Reiner watched the normally dependable Kahn move toward the approaching ball. Leaping across the mouth of the goal, the fully extended German goalie reached for it but, eluding his outstretched fingertips, the ball somehow slipped into the net. Sheringham threw up his arms, exultant. Shouting and pounding him on the back, his English teammates celebrated the equalizer and the red-and-white-clad United fans in Barcelona danced deliriously in the stands.

Reiner was disgusted. How lucky could they get? Bayern had the match under control for nearly ninety minutes and with only seconds left let it get away from them. He'd never seen such sloppiness, such utter stupidity in his life. Now they'd have to go into overtime. Though he tried not to look back at Bayern's missed opportunities, the furious Reiner felt like a steaming volcano inside. He pounded his fist on the tabletop. Startled, the inspector jumped back, bumping into the table, knocking over his chair—their wineglasses and his empty plate fell to the floor. People at nearby tables turned to see what had happened. Thérèse hurried over with a broom and swept up the broken glass.

The stranger's outburst had surprised the inspector. Though his mind knew better, his body had been trained to react instantly in such situations, as if the man's anger had been directed at him. Taking out a handkerchief, Mazarelle wiped off the wet sleeve of his jacket. "Sorry," Reiner said, as coolly as if nothing had happened, but he knew by the look on the inspector's face that he'd made a mistake.

In that fleeting moment Mazarelle had a thought. It was nothing more than a hunch about this excitable stranger with the musty leather jacket that he'd been sitting next to for more than an hour now, this unknown visitor who refused to tell him his name. Whoever he was, this guy might well turn out to be trouble. He definitely wanted to know more about him. When the game was over he'd tail him, find out where in Taziac he was staying. Until then, he intended to keep as calm as he could, enjoy the end of the game, and not let this weirdo out of his sight.

Three minutes was all that was left. Injury time. The already keyed-up crowd in the café grew increasingly restless watching the game as the seconds ticked by. With only a few ticks left on the clock and the score still tied 1–1, United was awarded another corner kick.

It was up to Beckham now. Even Reiner, who thought him overrated, considered the Englishman a threat. His fans believed that at his best, in a tight game such as this one, he could make all the difference. They watched Beckham, forgetting their drinks, as the side of his foot met the face of the ball and sent it gracefully arcing to Sheringham, who flicked it to Solskjaer—dubbed by his teammates the "baby-faced assassin"—who slammed it home. The perfect trigonometry of a championship.

On TV the overwrought announcer screamed "GOAL! GOAL! GOAL! GOAL! GOAL!" Bayern Münich players were all down on the turf rolling around in agony. They couldn't believe what had just happened. The café erupted. Manchester United fans were on their feet, cheering, dancing, leaping up and down. Ole Solskjaer's splendid right-footed blow had been a stab in the heart of the Bayern rooters. They were disconsolate. Asked his reaction, one of the German players said, "I don't have words to describe such a sickening moment."

Mazarelle, who'd been enjoying the interviews with the players, turned to see how his tablemate was taking what had happened, but he was gone. Vanished. The inspector rushed to the front door. Shoving people aside like bowling pins, he plowed through the noisy crowd. Almost lost among the many cars parked in front of the café was a black Yamaha with a gleaming chrome exhaust. A second before the motorcycle's engine roared into life, he spotted the stranger's leather jacket as he sped off down the narrow rue Blanche.

Mazarelle was determined not to let this guy get away. If he'd nothing to hide, why was he behaving as if he did?

Siren wailing, the inspector's car raced down the hill after him, sped around the church in the main square, flew past the town hall, and went barreling out of town in hot pursuit. His quarry was heading north toward Bergerac on D14. Mazarelle turned up the volume of his siren, but the stranger was riding a rocket. He'd no intention of stopping. Switching on his radio, the inspector put in a call to the commissariat and Bandu answered, a dependable rock when Mazarelle most needed one. He quickly described the situation and instructed him to set up a roadblock at the intersection with N21. That done, he stomped on his accelerator and began to pass cruising cars as if they were telephone poles. Mazarelle was almost on top of the Yamaha when the motorcycle began to slow down. Pulling up behind it, he got out, troubled that he didn't have a gun with him.

"Why didn't you stop?"

"I thought you were after somebody else."

"Let's see your license."

The biker unzipped his jacket and went through his inside pockets as if he expected to find what he was looking for. "I must have left it at home."

Bristling, Mazarelle ordered him to take off his helmet. It was impossible to see his face through the tinted visor.

"Why?"

"You want me to take it off for you?"

The biker removed his helmet, astonishing the inspector. The guy he'd been chasing had done a Houdini. Here was a beard, a face he'd never seen before, not to mention a thick chain around his neck with an Iron Cross. He remembered Thérèse's description of one of the bikers who'd demolished Ali's car. Perhaps it was the furious chase that made him lose his cool, perhaps simply frustration at having lost his man.

"Who are you?" Mazarelle grabbed the big guy, dragged him off his chopper.

"Let me go."

"You're one of the three assholes who smashed up Sedak's VW, aren't you?"

The biker wasn't expecting to be fingered for that old prank. Lunging at his accuser, he pushed him away. Surprised by his sudden move, the off-balance inspector crumpled to the ground. He felt a shooting pain and grabbed for his twisted ankle. The roar of the fleeing motorcycle soon dopplered into the distance. Mazarelle sat there in silence on the shoulder of the road rubbing his aching ankle in a Job-like trance, but he'd no doubt he was to blame for being such a jerk. The police car's radio crackled alive. Pulling himself to his feet, Mazarelle answered. It was Bandu.

"I've got him."

"*Formidable!*" he shouted. "Well done, Bandu! I want you to book him for destroying evidence, obstructing justice, harassment, and resisting arrest. You can also throw in twisting my ankle with intent."

"Are you coming into the commissariat?"

"Later. I've got something important to do first."

The Café Valon was almost deserted and there were only a handful of customers inside when Mazarelle entered. As he went over to where he'd been sitting, he was noticeably favoring his good leg. How lucky can you get? he thought. He still had a good one left.

The inspector bent down and searched in the dim light underneath the table and chairs, running his hand over the scuffed and grimy floor. Nothing. His fingers came up damp, smelling of stale wine. Then he remembered that Thérèse had swept up the mess and asked her where she'd dumped it.

"In the bin with the other trash. Where do you think?"

The bin was under the bar. It took Mazarelle a while to go through it without shredding his hands on broken glass. Eventually he found what he was looking for and, trying not to smudge any prints on the napkin, carefully pocketed it. His pen, though, was gone. Probably swiped. Not the worst thing that might have happened to him when dealing with a killer.

Mickey V was busy at the rear, folding the extra chairs and stacking them up. In the warm café, his shirt collar was open wide at the neck, sweat stains under his arms. It wasn't every day he worked this hard for his money. Mazarelle asked if he'd ever before seen the guy he'd been sitting with.

"You mean the long-haired guy? Yeah, he's been in here."

"Know who he is?"

He'd no idea. "Some hippie. Ask Thérèse. He was playing pool with her husband. Maybe she knows."

But she didn't. Ali had mentioned the stranger's name, but Thérèse had forgotten it. "Maybe Borman or Baumgartner. Something foreign like that. All I know is he was looking for a job."

"What kind of job?"

"Who remembers? Maybe construction. Stonemason. I've got to go." She called to Valon. "I'll be back in an hour, Mick."

"Wait a minute," Mazarelle yelled after her. "Could it have been Barmeyer?"

"Maybe. But like I said: Who remembers?"

The inspector on his way out left instructions with Valon to call him immediately if the stranger came back. "Don't forget! It's important." He squeezed the owner's arm to be sure he had his full attention. "Okay?"

Mickey struggled to loosen his grip. "Okay, okay!"

From the road, Mazarelle called the commissariat and asked to speak to Tricot. He told him he'd be there in about twenty minutes. He wanted him to leave right away for Toulouse with a piece of evidence to be scanned for prints and returned afterward. See if any of the prints matched those on the shotgun Lambert was bringing Didier. Tricot said he was ready to go. Mazarelle had been pleasantly surprised by André Tricot. He'd proven to be a valuable addition to their squad. Perhaps the inspector had become a little *too* suspicious lately even of his own men.

Then there was the matter of finding whoever the long-haired stranger was. He had to be tracked down. Though Mazarelle had his doubts about him being a laborer or stonemason, that possibility had to be explored. He'd get Bandu and Thibaud to question the Taziac supervisors handling the historic restoration of the village— see if anyone who'd recently been hired matched his description.

While clutching the steering wheel with one hand, Mazarelle leaned down and massaged his aching shank, which felt as if something might be broken. Probably nothing more than a sprain. And last but not least before going home to wrap his ankle in a cold compress, he wanted to pay a visit to the commissariat. Make sure their Nazi prisoner was resting comfortably before throwing the book at him.

40

THE BOX TO BAIT THE TRAP

einer couldn't believe his eyes when he returned to his hideout and found the gun case in the living room empty. He'd thought that his biggest loss that day was a football game. The two rifles were nowhere in the house. If he'd any luck, they might have been stolen. A larky visit from their carousing French neighbors perhaps, or the local teenage scum scrounging for knickknacks to pawn. But given how cleanly the guns had been taken—no signs of break-in—both were highly improbable. More likely, and much more dangerous, was that Mazarelle and his flics had been there.

When Reiner returned to Taziac, he thought his one problem was the Reece woman. He'd believed that his handyman scenario had worked perfectly—that Mazarelle was content with Ali Sedak as lone perpetrator of the L'Ermitage murders. Yet, along with attending to the Reece woman, almost out of a mix of habit and caution, he'd also been watching the inspector, tracking his movements. A useless time filler, Reiner thought, while he waited to finish the other job. But he now realized that he'd been too easily swayed by the newspaper accounts of Mazarelle's great success. Then to learn—from the inspector himself—that Mazarelle was apparently not satisfied! Reiner supposed that, like the stubborn American woman, Mazarelle would probably never quit his hunt for the killer.

Well then, he'd simply have to take care of both of them. Reiner welcomed the opportunity. Felt energized by the risk he was taking in staying on in this house. And by the pressure of time. He guessed it'd take no more than a day or two before analysis of the guns would help the flics discover that their murder case had spread next door. Soon they'd be back in force and swarming. He knew he could meet the challenge, but he couldn't afford to waste a minute.

Tonight it would be Mazarelle's turn. Tomorrow the orphan. He'd do both in his own way, with care—after all, he was an artist, not a butcher. So what if everything he did wasn't a masterpiece? How many Sistine Chapel ceilings did Michelangelo paint or how many *Guernicas* Picasso? He already had some exciting ideas percolating. In no time he'd have a custom-made plan set up for each of them. But both plans would have to be foolproof this time. No fuckups like the failed cave fiasco or the Phillips job—he still couldn't believe what happened there and how he'd lost control. In the current circumstances, he'd have no second chances.

It wasn't often that he had such a worthy adversary as the inspector. Though there was no money in his removal, which of course was an ugly blemish in any plan, Reiner was already anticipating the thrill of the challenge. He'd begin with what he'd been given. Late that night Mazarelle would be going for dinner at the Café Valon. Stuffing himself with duck confit, that well-known favorite of his. Plus a bottle of wine, to add to the several cognacs he'd had earlier in the day. Which would mean a full stomach, a slow step, and a pickled brain on his way home. So far so good!

Okay. So he'd be walking back alone, perhaps humming some American ditty to himself. The inspector, he'd read, loved American music. And as usual at that late hour, he'd take the shortcut down the gravel-covered alley to his house on the Place Mestraillat. Reiner had watched him take this route before. There were no streetlights in the narrow alley, no signs of life from the three, empty medieval buildings—one dating back to the fourteenth century—under reconstruction. The only light came from the rear of the few houses that were occupied. Based upon the way the weather had changed that late afternoon—the wind kicking up the dust and storm clouds gathering, filling the sky with enormous dark towers—it promised to be a moonless night. Perfect for what he had in mind.

But first he'd need a large cardboard box. It didn't take him long to find just the ticket under the kitchen sink. He pulled out a brown corrugated box, the name Le Creuset printed all over it and designed to hold a large Dutch oven. Reiner emptied out the sponges, oven cleaner, floor wax, paper towels, rubber gloves, and jumbo plastic garbage bags. He lifted the empty box. The size looked right—big enough to hold a small pit bull or a medium-size cocker spaniel. After some minor adjustments, he thought, it should work beautifully.

Then, soon as it got dark, he'd leave to set the stage and wait for his leading actor to step from the wings. And after he'd said his piddling farewell lines, it'd be *"Auf Wiedersehen, cher monsieur l'inspecteur!"*

41

HOUSE OF WOODEN HEADS

s soon as he'd given Bandu and Thibaud their marching orders with a description of the stranger in the Café Valon, sent Tricot off to Toulouse with the napkin for Didier, and, last but not least, taken care of the garbage in the *garde à vue* cell, Mazarelle left for home to attend to his ankle. The weather on the way turned gloomy, overcast, humid; and Taziac, when he arrived, felt like it was wearing a heavy, damp woolen overcoat. Though they needed rain, he wasn't looking forward to it. City people rarely do. He took the boring mail out of his box, unlocked the front door, and lumbered in—tossing the bills and advertisements onto the kitchen table. Pouring himself a glass of whiskey, he dropped into his big, comfortable red chair. The pressure on his ankle was causing him grief.

The whiskey helped. He was about to see what else might help when he realized that this was one of the rare times when he sat down in his chair that Michou didn't suddenly swagger into the room and leap onto his lap. When he left the house, she'd no desire to go anywhere. He shuffled into the kitchen and saw that her bowl was empty. Taking out one of her special treats from the cabinet, he keyed open a small can of sardines and emptied it into her bowl. She couldn't resist that. Ordinarily he'd even share one or two of the rich, oily sardines with Michou—a gesture of camaraderie he didn't always feel—but the pain in his ankle seemed to have affected his appetite. He wondered how she'd gotten out of the house. The one thing he knew for sure was that she'd be back.

Upstairs, taking off his clothes, he sat naked on the edge of the bathtub and turned on the water. The cold felt good. The injured ankle, on the other hand, felt lousy when he touched it. Though swollen, it was luckily not yet a grapefruit, and the cold would keep the swelling down, the pain manageable. If it didn't get any worse, he'd survive.

As he sat there cooled by the water rushing into the tub, he went over what it was that troubled him about the unpredictable stranger at the Café Valon. For one thing, why did the fellow tell him he was in Taziac on vacation but tell Ali, according to his wife, that he was here looking for a job? Why would someone lie about a thing like that? And why did he refuse to give his name? Or say he was a stonemason when his hands were as free of calluses as a baby's backside? Curious, sure, but none of these were exactly capital offenses. Likewise, no crime that he was a German football fan, or his little angry outburst when München began to screw up. Yet the intensity of his gaze as he watched the last agonizing life-or-death minutes of the game was unusual. Oddly enough, it was almost the same way he stared at the halftime Mercedes-Benz commercial and its vaunted safety features. Which reminded the inspector of what happened when Reece took his friend's Mercedes and nearly lost his life. An accident Phillips himself might otherwise have been the victim of when not only the car's brakes but also its air bags failed to work—and most astonishing of all, both at the same time.

All of which, he supposed, added up to nothing more than a nexus of possibilities. In short, the inspector didn't care for the smell of him. And speaking of smells—he turned off the rushing bathwater— what about that leather jacket of his with its stale, musty odor, as if he might have been staying in a house that had been closed up for months, a house similar to the McAllisters'? Now maybe if you had a name to go with it, Mazarelle, you'd really have something. He was getting closer but still no cigar.

Mazarelle wrung out the wet washcloth, tied it around his ankle, and deciding to forgo dinner and forget aspirins, he prescribed himself another glass of whiskey and a bed.

The sound in the dark that pried open his eyes was the kitchen cuckoo clock. His wristwatch swore it was ten o'clock. Though he hadn't slept as long as he'd wanted to, the few hours had done him a world of good, along with what had once been a cold compress. He untied it. Feeling hungry, he padded into the kitchen, opened the refrigerator. Though enjoying the cold air on his bare thighs, he wasn't impressed with what he saw. Michou's sardines were still untouched in the bowl on the floor, but that hungry he wasn't. Then he remembered Mickey's duck confit surrounded by its caramelized onions and orange glaze waiting for him at the Valon. He threw on his clothes and limped out the door.

No question, Mazarelle concluded after daubing up the last of his dinner's exquisite gravy-soaked morsels, he was glad he'd changed his mind. It would have been worth even a much longer and more uncomfortable trek. A Lucullan feast to end a trying day. The duck as rich as Midas and meltingly tender, the local cèpes plucked fresh from their bosky depths and ennobled by the bird's savory fat and garlic. The entire meal glorified by a heady, opulent, but not ostentatious bottle of Saint-Émilion that seemed to remove any hint of pain from his left leg.

At the door, he heartily shook hands with Mickey, relaying his compliments to Giorgio the chef, and with that the inspector walked off into the night, feeling buoyant, at one with the universe. Not only pleasantly light-headed but light on his feet as well. The alley on the way home was a black pool of silence with only occasional splashes of light. The air still warm, heavy, but no moon, no stars, no rain, no pain. With Mazarelle humming a jazz version of "La Vie en Rose," à la the great Louis. But not so loud that he failed to hear the giggling up ahead, even though he could see no one there. The tires on the gravel creeping up on him from behind he'd missed completely. Then came the angry, jangling bell sounding its alarm.

Mazarelle whirled around to see what all the noise was about. But before he realized what it was, the bicycle that was almost upon him swerved wildly, skidded, and raced on by. "Idiot!" Mazarelle shouted after him. "Put on your light."

He stood rooted to the spot, watching the bike's flickering red taillight flipping the bird at him as it disappeared down the alley. "Damn fool," he said, relieved and chuckling to himself.

At the rear of the house across the way, a light suddenly went on in an upstairs window and a woman looked out to see what the noise was all about. The inspector walked on, but before the light went out he saw the couple in the alley with their arms around each other, the face of the laughing young woman gleaming.

"That you, Gaby?"

"Inspector Mazarelle!" She sounded surprised, but she had seen him coming—weaving drunkenly in their direction. "That guy on the bicycle was certainly in a big hurry. He didn't hit you, did he?"

"Imbecile. Completely batty. Thinks he can see in the dark. What are you doing out at this hour anyhow?"

"Félix and I were just coming back from seeing some friends. You remember Félix, don't you, Inspector?"

He nodded at her thin, sullen pal with the gold earring shimmering in the shadows. She had pointed him out, hanging around the bakery, when Mazarelle had asked about boyfriends. But she insisted he wasn't. Just a friend, *not* a boyfriend. "He's too serious for me," she'd said. "The only thing funny about him is his name."

Just like her mother, he thought. Not particularly smart about men and always looking to be amused. That's what fascinated the youthful Martine about Mazarelle, she later admitted, after she'd found him. He used to think he'd found her. A young, beautiful woman who'd fallen in love with the stories he'd told her about the bizarre, psychotic minds he'd encountered, the adrenaline rush of solving crimes, the dangers of the life he'd led. What she was really looking for, he discovered, was an abortion. She'd soon change her mind about that too—along with so many other things in their relationship.

The inspector asked, "Don't you have school tomorrow?"

"School!" She laughed. "There's no school. It's the summer. My vacation."

"You're right. And this summer you're working in the bakery. Don't you have to get up early to help Louise?"

"I'm an early riser."

"Don't talk nonsense. You're a growing girl. You need your sleep. At least eight hours every night, according to the doctors. Sleep, they say, heals all wounds and comforts the afflicted."

"You hear that?" Gaby grabbed Félix's arm and yanked. "Bedtime," she told him, giggling.

Just like her mother, he thought, as he walked away. He hadn't gone very far when he heard a cat crying. But it wasn't just any cat, it was Michou. He was sure of it. And she wasn't simply unhappy. He knew her unhappy sound, the same bawling one she made after climbing a tree and discovering she couldn't get down. This time she was scared-out-of-her-wits terrified. In fact the closer he moved to its source, the more horrific her wailing became. It sounded as if someone were torturing her.

"Don't worry, Michou! I hear you. Hold on!"

The animal's awful howls seemed to be coming from the house of the wooden heads, a fourteenth-century stone structure destined for renovation. Time had reduced it to a roofless frame. Its walls were still standing (some provisionally supported by thick beams), as was the front doorway with its three carved wooden heads over the lintel—the foreheads squished, the mouths grimly turned down. Once inside the doorway, Mazarelle was surprised that even without a roof the interior was darker than the alley outside. He stopped to get his bearings. The howls filled every inch of the blackness with torment. Groping in his pocket, the inspector pulled out his Swiss Army knife, a compact model appropriately called the Midnight Manager. He flipped on its bright LED, hurrying toward the rear wall and the explosively shaking cardboard box on the ground.

"Coming, Michou! I'm coming!"

As he got nearer, he could see that the box had been wrapped like a mummy from end to end in tape. Was this some awful prank cooked up by a demented neighborhood kid to amuse himself? Nothing was going to get out of that box alive. Mazarelle tore into the tape—turning it into harmless plastic fringe—then ripped off the box top and out leaped one very frightened cat. The inspector grabbed Michou before she could get away and attempted to calm her down. It was a slow process, but he thought he was making progress when, without warning, he began to sneeze violently and dropped his light. As he bent to pick it up, Michou bolted.

"*Merde!*" cried the inspector.

The heavy beam narrowly missed his head as the timber brace crashed to the ground. At first, he wasn't sure what it was. Then came the second brace, and the creaking of the wall of stones grew louder, the way the roar of an avalanche rolls over you before the mountain does. Mazarelle yelled for help and started to move in the opposite direction as if he imagined he might somehow outrun it, but he didn't have a chance.

Gabrielle and Félix hadn't gone very far and, having found another dark corner, weren't planning to, when they heard the tumultuous noise and the inspector's shouts. Amazed at what must have happened, they ran back at once to see how they could help. Félix noticed a white light leaking out from under one of the piles of stones and said, "Come on!"

The two young people were a good team as they furiously lifted the large stones in a desperate effort to free Inspector Mazarelle. Despite their frantic energy, youth, and intensity, it took them a while to get to the bottom of the pile. When they reached it, the white light was still on but there was no sign of the inspector. Gabrielle, her face sweaty, flashed the light at another pile looking for a sign and spotted a shoe sticking out. "Look," she cried, "it's his shoe."

"Are you sure it's his?"

"Of course it's his. Look how big it is."

Félix peered inside and whistled. They were big shoes to fill. Size 50, extra wide.

Gaby thought it was just as well his foot wasn't in it. She told Félix to keep digging. She was going to call the police and get some help. As she hurried away, she failed to see the bicycle's flickering red taillight swallowed up in the distance.

42

THE BILL COMES DUE

Reiner was up and about before the first gravel truck of the day. His last day in France, and the sun peeping out over the dew-drenched fields. It promised to be another hot, humid one, but cloudless blue and brushed with fair-weather, salmon-pink, Day-Glo streaks. And for him, a busy day. First, the phone call to Paris, where he had news for his employers. Their bill had come due.

Locally at that hour, there'd been no traffic to speak of on the road out of town. The Total station at the crossroads hadn't even opened yet. Leaning his bicycle against the glass telephone booth, he checked the tires. Rubber taut on the rims and leak-free, treads still as good as new. Perfect. This bike belonged to the Missus, and its tires held their air the way a Japanese pearl diver holds her breath. Dialing Pellerin's number in Paris, he deposited the long-distance toll.

The ringing telephone reached out for anyone on the premises—turning Blond over on their mattress and burying him under his pillow. It woke up a cranky Pellerin, annoyed to have been pulled out of bed so early. "A minute," he whispered, when he realized who it was. Why, he wondered glancing at the clock, was he calling at this hour? Dragging himself and the phone into the living room, he closed the door behind him.

"What's wrong?"

"Nothing's wrong. I've finished the job."

"You mean—?"

"All taken care of. You have five hours to make the last half of your payment. I'm expecting it in Zurich today by high noon. Don't fail me."

"No problem." Pellerin promised, "The money will be there."

Until confirmed one way or the other when he spoke to Spada in Numbered Accounts, Reiner wasn't holding his breath. More convinced now than when he began that the retired French agents couldn't be trusted. Assuming they'd do one of two things: pay him the money they owed him or rat him out. But even if they never paid him in full, he'd already made a killing. (This weakness for puns, where did it come from? France, as he'd already suspected, was having an unwholesome influence on him.)

Regardless of what they did, however, they'd suffer the same consequences for delaying his departure. Reiner intended to dispatch them as permanently as he had the inspector under the medieval stone wall. As for the American woman, she was on the menu for later that evening. Pierre Barmeyer carefully covering his tracks in France as if he were never there. He was genuinely looking forward to showing Molly Reece how good a cook he was, proud of his skill. A crooked smile spread across his face in anticipation of his pleasure. He savored the thought of her visit. The secret of his omelette aux champignons was, of course, the mushrooms.

43

MAZARELLE CHECKS OUT

That morning Rivet had received the call almost as soon as he arrived at the commissariat. Captain Béchoux, the head of the Taziac gendarmerie, had bad news for him. Late the night before, Inspector Mazarelle had been the victim of a terrible accident in Taziac. He appeared to be seriously injured. His men immediately called for an ambulance from the Centre Hospitalier de Bergerac, where the comatose inspector was taken.

"I'm at the hospital now," Béchoux said. "I'll wait until you arrive. I suggest you hurry."

"I'm on my way." Dropping everything, Commissaire Rivet, accompanied by Bandu, rushed to Mazarelle's bedside. By the time they arrived, the captain had been called away. He left behind one of his men, Gendarme Leduc, to stand guard outside the patient's room and obtain a statement from him when he regained consciousness.

If he ever does, Leduc thought, when he and the two new arrivals viewed Mazarelle's motionless body. Leduc explained that one of the teenagers who'd found the inspector knew him well. She'd done housekeeping work for his terminally ill wife before she died and now worked part-time for him. She and her boyfriend had found the inspector under a collapsed wall inside one of the oldest buildings in town. They had no idea what he'd been doing there. She thought he'd been drinking.

The commissaire sized up the situation at once. Taking Leduc aside, he explained that it was important to prevent reporters from learning what had happened to Inspector Mazarelle. He wanted to keep the news out of the media to avoid any sensationalism that might interfere with the inspector's recovery. Though he didn't say it, he also wasn't eager to have the uniforms taking credit in the press for rescuing one of his own men. And with that, Rivet thanked the gendarme, dismissed him, and placed Bandu in charge of Mazarelle's security while in the hospital.

Bandu also wanted to keep what had happened to his boss as quiet as possible, but for a different reason. He didn't believe that the stone wall collapsing on him was an accident—a wall that had been reliably standing for hundreds of years. And if it wasn't an accident, it was a crime and perhaps linked to the Taziac murders. If so, when whoever was responsible discovered that his victim was still alive, he might return to finish the job. Bandu had been on all sorts of murder cases before, but never one in which the inspector in charge became the target. The ruthless villainy of it made his blood boil. Bandu stood guard at the door, protective, gimlet-eyed, his arms laced forbiddingly across his chest, barring intruders.

"I'm his doctor," insisted the white-coated Roland Pascal, attempting to get by him. He pointed to the ID card draped around his neck. Bandu saw little resemblance between the man and his photo, but the sleeves and shoulders of his lab coat fit him to a T. Bandu waved him in.

Dr. Pascal checked the patient's pulse, temperature, breathing, and wasn't alarmed about his still being unconscious. He'd given the inspector a strong sedative. "He'll be awake shortly," he told Rivet. "I want to keep him in the hospital another twenty-four hours for observation, but based on my examination and X-rays, I'd say the inspector is in surprisingly good shape. In short, a very lucky man. Except for his obvious cuts and bruises, he's gotten off almost scot-free."

Some doctor! Mazarelle concluded. Where did they get this clown? Stretched out on the bed, he was a mass of aches and pains and this joker was patting himself on the back. Mazarelle had no desire to open his eyes and argue with the expert, but maybe he'd do better with a couple of aspirins. He felt like crap.

A peevish Bandu at the door could be heard saying, "How should I know? Ask his doctor. He's in there now."

Heads turned as Madame Leclerc, the diminutive investigating judge, strode into the room. Chic as always in a tailored black suit and a striking green, white, and tangerine scarf with a Matisse pattern. She'd just called Toulouse about another case and Didier had gotten on the line. He'd been trying earlier to reach the inspector at the commissariat and learned about his accident.

"Naturally I came right over as soon as I heard," she told the commissaire. "How is he?"

Before Rivet could reply, Mazarelle began restlessly to move, to mutter, to open his eyes and blink at the light. Rivet asked him, "Can you tell us what happened?" Mazarelle rose up on his elbows and looked around the white hospital room, startled by all the people staring at him, trying to make sense of it and recall how he'd gotten there. It was like a bad dream.

Brushing Rivet aside, Madame Leclerc inquired almost tenderly, "How do you feel, Inspector?"

Hearing the judge's voice, Mazarelle closed his eyes—unwilling to deal with her—and fell back on his mattress. She told him she was relieved to see him awake and looking much better than she feared from what Didier had told her. She said, "He'd been trying to reach you about the guns you sent him for analysis. Didier said you were right. The shotgun was the weapon used to murder Monsieur Phillips."

Opening his eyes, Mazarelle licked his lips, his tongue a fur ball. "Any fingerprints?" he whispered, his voice crusty like dried paint.

"No fingerprints. Didier said he found none at all. Why didn't you tell me about this?" she demanded angrily, recalling how ticked off she'd been when she heard. "I had no idea what you were doing. I told you to keep me informed. If Ali Sedak wasn't the murderer, then who is?"

Mazarelle lifted his head and stared at her. "Goddamn it!" he shouted, eyes blazing. "That's what I'm trying to find out."

The doctor was not happy with Madame Leclerc. "You've upset my patient," he said, his lips barely moving. "I think that's quite enough for now. I'm afraid you'll all have to go."

Madame le juge glared at him. "But I'm not finished."

"*Au contraire,*" snapped the doctor, taking her by the arm.

As they started to leave, Mazarelle opened his mouth to say something but let his head fall back on his pillow. He gazed at the ceiling. "If you're looking for black-and-white answers," he mumbled, "you're going to be disappointed."

Madame Leclerc glanced at the commissaire to see if he'd heard what Mazarelle said. Rivet tapped his forehead and suggested soothingly, "Let him sleep."

Not long after they'd all left, Bandu went to the men's room at the far end of the hall and, returning, thought he'd heard the inspector's telephone ringing. He ran back, but before he could get there the ringing stopped. Shrugging, he took up his silent vigil at the door and, pulling over a chair, soon nodded off.

The call was from Duboit. He'd heard what had happened to the boss and wanted to know how he was.

Mazarelle mumbled something that he didn't understand, and Duboit said, "Speak louder, chief. I can't hear you. How you feeling?"

The patient felt his headache getting worse. "I've been better."

Duboit wanted to know if there was anything he could do to help.

Mazarelle appreciated the offer, because Bernard, whatever his shortcomings, was not an ass-kisser.

"Thanks, but your job is Mademoiselle Reece. Are you keeping an eye on her, Bernard?"

"That's *all* I've been doing. Babette barely recognizes me anymore."

"I'll get someone to back you up when I'm out of here. Meanwhile, stay with her, Bernard. There's a killer still on the loose who'll stop at nothing."

Bandu, who'd been daydreaming, thought he heard Mazarelle moving around in his room and, when he went inside to look, was astonished to find him out of bed and getting dressed.

"What the hell are you doing, chief?"

"Going back to work. Come on."

"The doctor said you can't get out of—"

"Stuff it! Don't waste my time on nonsense. This was no accident. We're dealing with attempted murder here. I want you and Lambert to get down to Taziac right now and cordon off the crime scene at the house of the wooden heads. But first drop me off at the commis-sariat. Let's go."

As he brushed past an astonished nurse in the hallway, who tried to stop him, the inspector wondered if his men would find Michou's dead body crushed under a pile of stones or if, by some miracle, she still had one of her nine lives left.

44

TREASURES OF PÉRIGORD

Reiner had used only two of the six rooms on the second floor of the house, but he'd been in all of them. So he cleaned them all up as well as the hall, where he found a few more pieces of the mug he'd busted. Then he closed all the doors, except the bathroom's. Less to do after dinner. He didn't want to have to waste too much time removing all trace of his stay before leaving. The downstairs would be a postprandial job.

Outside, Reiner gathered a jar full of wildflowers—yellow daisies, red clover—and filled it with water. Women liked that sort of thing. For a tablecloth he used the white sheet draped over the couch. Not exactly perfection, but it would do. What counted most was the food. He was amused at how eager he was to show Molly that even with the simplest of dishes he really was a good cook. He was looking forward to their final romantic tête-à-tête. A shame it would have to be their last—a great-looking woman like that who kissed with her eyes wide open and held you as if she meant it—but she knew too much about him. Unfortunately he couldn't afford to leave her behind.

In Bergerac, opposite the church of Notre-Dame, Reiner found the small gift shop near the café where they'd had a drink. One of those stores full of interesting jars and tins of Earl Grey tea from London, biscottinos from Milan, and wonderful French mustards, jams, jellies, nuts, and pâtés wrapped in yellow cellophane and rib- bons. He bought a large gift-wrapped box called Trésors de Périgord containing white truffles, foie gras, pruneaux d'Agen, plus a bottle of Monbazillac and one of Cahors. A sort of going-away present. Despite the outrageous price, it was perfect. On the way to his car, he spotted a rack of newspapers in front of a stationery store and bought a copy of *Sud Ouest* and *La Depêche*. There was no mention yet of the dead inspector, not even of an accident in Taziac. Strange, he thought, but he was confident it was merely a matter of time.

Back in Taziac, he left his present on the kitchen table and skipped out the back door toting a wicker basket on his arm. "To market to market to buy a fat pig." All in all, Reiner was feeling rather pleased with himself. There was nothing quite like fresh-picked mushrooms to make a memorable dish, and he'd been impressed by the variety of those he'd seen in the woods behind the house.

Reiner mused on the mushroom hunts of his youth in Germany and how sly mushrooms could be, camouflaged like animals almost to invisibility and then, as soon as the danger passed, popping suddenly into view. He kept his eye on the ground as he moved slowly through the trees, brushing aside the sun-splashed gnats hovering in his way while refocusing on the shadows where his mushroom prey huddled together at the base of an oak tree. Their soft cap a wonderful orange, the foot white. He knelt down and taking out the hunting knife he'd bought in Bourges as a souvenir—a popular French model with a carved handle—he cut into the thick white flesh and, sniffing its characteristic walnut odor, took a bite. Delicious! The magnificent *Amanita caesarea,* celebrated raw or cooked since antiquity. It would be a meal she'd remember as long as she lived. His bizarre laughter echoing through the trees sent the looping swallows skying.

He collected a half dozen of these fragrant beauties and seven medium-size cèpes with their tawny brown suede crowns. His little basket was filling up with gustatory gems. The rest of the hunt promised to be more difficult, but he was pleasantly surprised to come upon a couple of earth-speckled grayish-yellow cousins of the cèpe—the sun-worshipping satanas, the nasty black sheep of the boletus family. Rarely fatal, but always sure to produce a very bad stomachache.

The *Amanita phalloides* was another matter altogether. Reiner found the prize of the hunt in a remote clump of beech trees. Its slim white foot stepping delicately out of the ground gave no hint of how lethal it was. *Vorsicht! Der Knollenblätterpilz.* The world's most dangerous mushroom. Its beautiful greenish-yellow cap shaped like an umbrella could reduce a strapping muscular brute to skin and bones by quick unpleasant stages of diarrhea, uncontrollable convulsions, and hepatic coma. It was an awful way to die but the amanitas, like all families, have a dark side. This was the yin and yang of the mushroom world. Humming softly to himself, Reiner snipped off the five death caps and added them to his tasty mycological sampler.

At the house, he put aside the choice ones he wanted for dinner and then unwrapped his present and, adding the two santanas and four of the deadly phalloides, he repacked it. He hadn't at all liked the way the two French smart-asses did business. Bad-mouthing him for what happened in Taziac and then trying to stiff him on the bill. When it came to accidents, Reiner's amour propre was involved as well as the fact that he'd a reputation to protect. As an irresistible grace note, he tied a neat white card to the package on which he'd written *"Félicitations et bon appétit."*

On the drive to Bordeaux, he checked his watch and pulled off the road to call Zurich. Monsieur Spada said he'd look. He soon returned with the news that there had been no deposits that day to his account. Not that it would have made any difference in his plans for Pellerin and his fat friend. In the end, Reiner had gotten not much better than he expected from those two, and a good deal worse. His patience with them had run out.

At the central post office in Bordeaux, he checked the Paris phonebooks and was furious to discover that Pellerin was not listed. How could he have been so stupid? Momentarily tripped up, a seething Reiner raced through the white pages, searching for him under the name of his boyfriend Blond, which he eventually tracked down. They were both living cozily on the fashionable rue de Berri in the eighth arrondissement. Apparently someone was paying them quite well to do his bidding. Back in Reiner's car, he picked up the gift box and wrote in the address. Then puzzling over the return address—for a minute even considering leaving it blank—he had a brilliant idea. Since they both had once worked for the government, he put down an address he knew they couldn't resist.

The Mérignac Airport was to the west of the city. Following the heavy truck traffic and signs that said *frêt,* he found the office of the DHL courier service. It was crowded inside and hot, hot, hot, but one more customer with sunglasses was scarcely noticeable. So much the better, he thought. When it was his turn, Reiner asked the young man with the bandaged hand for one of their large red-and-white shipping boxes, pasted on the label he'd prepared, and slipped his gift box inside. Although many paid with credit cards, he paid cash.

"Merci, monsieur," said the sweating clerk, promising him that it would be delivered in Paris the next day.

"Avant midi?"

"Oui, oui." Heaving the box onto the large pile behind him, the clerk turned to his next customer. *"Madame?"*

Reiner scowled. Fortunately, his little present was packed in two strong boxes, which was a comforting thought. Otherwise, it might end up squashed like Mazarelle. As he drove across the Garonne east of the city, he noticed a French warship docked on the quay below. A destroyer. Even motionless it was a streak of gray, sleek as a shark, and like a shark a perfect killing machine. *Zerstören.* The German word for destroyer popped into his head—so much better than the French or English. Not simply to demolish but to do so utterly, reducing an enemy to infinitesimal bits, dregs, dust. *Zerstören.* The word alone gave him a mouthful of pleasure. On his best days lately he'd felt he too had that same sort of terrible Nietzschean power, a gift not given to many. Reiner smiled at the thought.

45

PELLERIN'S PLAN

Pellerin, in a white terry cloth bathrobe, was seated at the kitchen table of their rue de Berri apartment reading *Le Figaro* and drinking the strong, eye-opening Colombian coffee that he loved when he heard the loud throat-clearing preludial rumble behind him. Glancing over his shoulder, he felt his spirits sink. His barefoot friend stood there, holding his head in pain—his stomach, hanging over the tight band of his white boxer shorts, shaking. They'd hoped that retirement from the service and going into business for themselves would put an end to these awful headaches of his.

"*Ça va,* Hubert?"

"I've been better, *merci.* Just one of my migraines. Right now I feel like bloody *pisse.*"

Pellerin patted him on the backside. "It'll pass," he commiserated. "They always do. Sit down and have some coffee."

"Who was that?" Blond fell heavily into the chair opposite and, eyes closed, rubbed his forehead with his fingertips. As Pellerin poured him a cup, he reported that they'd just received an early morning wake-up call from Klaus Reiner.

"And?"

"Good news. He tells me our problem is solved."

Blond glanced up. "Dead?"

"I don't know and don't care. As long as she's out of the way, and this time it was done more discreetly than the last. He says he wants the rest of his money."

"Are you going to pay him?"

"Of course not. Don't be foolish. Especially now that we know the shipment from Chad has arrived in Tianjin."

"What are you going to do?"

"Just what we said. Get rid of him."

"Yes, but how?"

"Look at this."

Pellerin folded his paper in half and placed it in front of his friend. It was a small story on the third page. The German serial killer, Dieter Koenig, had been spotted yesterday at the French border near Mulhouse. Still on the loose, Koenig, who had escaped from prison in Stuttgart, where he'd been serving a life sentence and had been on the run for seven months, was the subject of an intense police manhunt. He'd made headlines in the German press while Pellerin and Blond were in Berlin. Two elderly married couples living in the same house in Karlsruhe had been tied up and brutally slain, and Koenig was the prime suspect.

"Yes . . . So what?"

"Look at the picture, Hubert! Look at him. The long straight hair, the athletic build, the intense gaze. And the age somewhere between thirty and forty. Think, Hubert, think! Who does he remind you of?"

"Please, I'm in no mood for games. What are you driving at?"

"Don't you see? All we have to do is tell German Interpol that Dieter Koenig has been seen in the vicinity of Taziac and traveling in France under an alias. Then they immediately alert French Interpol headquarters in Lyons, reporting the sighting of Koenig and his role in the Karlsruhe murders. When Lyons puts out its alarm for the escapee, the message is: 'Armed and dangerous, use extreme caution.' *Et bien*, Hubert, you know very well how our local hair-trigger gendarmes operate—shoot first, get drunk after. And that, *cher ami*, will be that."

Hubert, his head resting on his fist, had been listening in rapt attention to Pellerin's plan, and his orbicular face beamed as if a black, all-consuming storm cloud had lifted. As his friend got up to make his call, Blond watched him go, admiration filling his eyes to overflowing like tears. Perhaps now they might actually be able to afford the *résidence secondaire* they had only dreamed of.

46

BACK TO THE WALL

When Bandu dropped him off at the commissariat, Mazarelle rushed upstairs to his office without saying hello to anyone. His men in the squad room—not to mention Rivet—might get the wrong idea about his bare feet. Besides, he'd no time or desire to explain. He tiptoed past the commissaire's open door and, slipping into his own office, quietly closed his door. From the bottom drawer of his desk, he yanked out an old pair of beat-up loafers—two large black gunboats—that he kept there for torrential rains and other emergencies. No socks, but Mazarelle never aspired to sartorial perfection. He was no peacock.

The inspector felt better with shoes on. The next thing he did was call PTS in Toulouse. Didier couldn't believe that Mazarelle was out of the hospital. He'd heard that he was almost at death's door. "What a constitution!" he cried good-humoredly, marveling at the man.

Mazarelle had no time for his bullshit. He asked if it was true that the twelve-gauge shotgun he sent down was the one that killed Phillips.

"*Absolument, mon vieux!* No question."

"And no fingerprints at all?"

"That's what's unusual. Someone—whoever fired it, most likely—wiped the weapon totally clean. I checked it myself."

"And the Mannlicher-Carcano?"

"Also clean as a whistle. Somebody didn't want to leave any tracks behind."

"Thanks." As Mazarelle put down the receiver, he was thinking over what he'd just been told. The twelve-gauge shotgun was definitely the murder weapon but with no prints, no trace of the shooter, it wouldn't be easy to link the murderer to it.

The inspector then called the Taziac gendarmerie and asked to speak to Captain Béchoux. When Béchoux heard who it was and that he was in his office, he was incredulous. He'd known that the Bergerac doctors at the Centre Hospitalier were good but had no idea they could work miracles. Béchoux said, "I went over early this morning to see the wall. That was a terrible accident you were in. What were you doing there at that hour of the night?"

"I'm not exactly sure."

"My men who called for the ambulance gave me a very gloomy report. You were lucky those two kids found you when they did. They saved your life."

"What two kids?"

When the captain told him who they were, Mazarelle began gradually to piece together in detail the series of events from the previous evening after he'd left the Café Valon. So, he told himself, there you are, Mazo. You and your snap judgments. Maybe she's not such a scatterbrained kid after all. In fact, maybe the only one *dans la lune* is the gaga inspector.

Mazarelle dialed Louise at her bakery, and Gabrielle picked up. She was thrilled to hear his voice sounding very much alive and that he was out of the hospital. "Hold on," she said. "I'll go get my aunt."

"No, don't bother." Mazarelle explained that he was calling to thank Gabrielle and her friend Félix, said it was the least he could do. They'd saved his life. He was grateful. "Yes, *very*," he told her.

Perhaps it was his serious (almost contrite) tone, which was so unlike his usual bantering style in their chats, that made her feel so uncomfortable, almost embarrassed. Gabrielle couldn't believe that after what he'd been through the inspector had called just to thank them. Before hanging up, she said, "I found your Swiss Army knife with the flashlight. Don't worry. I'll keep it safe for you. Okay?"

Mazarelle left the office early that afternoon and drove back to Taziac to visit the crime scene while there was still light enough to see. But first he dropped in at the Café Valon for a quick glass of *rouge*, some goat cheese, and a few questions. The wine and cheese were no problem for Mickey. But when it came to providing any new information about the long-haired stranger, he'd nothing to offer. The guy hadn't been in, but Mickey hadn't forgotten. The black-and-blue marks on his upper arm were a reminder. The inspector told him that was why they were there.

Mazarelle found it curious that one day the fellow seemed to be everywhere, and the next he'd fallen off the face of the earth. His men had turned up not a trace of anyone fitting his description working as a stonemason at any of the medieval restoration sites in Taziac. But when the inspector approached the house of wooden heads and saw the pile of stones and rubble from the collapsed wall that had very nearly taken his life, as well as the fluttering yellow tape that Bandu and Lambert had strung up around the crime scene, he'd the same uncanny feeling of being hunted that he sensed in the McAllister house. Oh no, this was no accident.

Lambert reported that Bandu had returned to the commissariat. Their analysis was that one of the wooden braces holding up the rear wall must have shifted or been somehow dislodged, and once the wall began collapsing inward the other beam followed. As to what caused it, they'd no idea. The inspector listened patiently to his account and said nothing. The only unusual items among the heavy stones at the crime scene was a large shoe, which Mazarelle promptly claimed as his own, and a crushed corrugated box.

The inspector took the badly mangled box with its shreds of clinging tape and studied it closely. Though he couldn't be sure, he believed that this was the box in which Michou had been held captive. Printed on the outside of the box was Le Creuset. The sight of it made his flesh creep. Strangely enough, he'd seen that name on a box in a house he'd been in not long ago. But where? He felt certain there'd been no Dutch oven in it, but if he could recall where he'd seen the box, maybe he'd have some idea how Michou got inside. If he could only remember where.

"You didn't happen to find a dead cat, did you?"

"Here at the crime scene?"

The inspector nodded.

The dour Lambert glanced nervously at the heap of stones. "No," he said. "No fatalities of any kind. Though there did seem to be some stones with bloodstains."

Mazarelle's fingers shot up to the bandaged stitches on his forehead. "The blood was probably mine," he acknowledged. He hoped so anyway. He'd hate to have lost that cat.

Before leaving he told Lambert to take photographs of the crime scene and call it a day. He was going back to the commissariat. He walked down the alley to the Place Mestraillat. He'd parked his car in front of his house, next to the old stone pump. What caught his eye wasn't the car but the cement step beside the pump. Children loved to jump off that step when Michou wasn't stretched out on top of it soaking up the last sunbeams of the day. Which was exactly what she was doing now as she waited to get into the house for something to eat.

Mazarelle grabbed her, hoisted her up for a hug, overjoyed to find the smug, grossly overweight animal none the worse for wear. He stroked her belly. Pressing her to his face, the two of them danced cheek to cheek. Michou whined, making it clear that she was far more interested in eating than dancing.

"Okay, okay. Hold on!" He pushed his key into the lock, threw open the door. Actually more than a little surprised with how pleased he was to have her back again and discover that he wasn't sneezing.

Though early evening, it was almost as light as late afternoon and hot, despite the breeze, when Reiner arrived to pick up Molly. Madame Charpentier's bakery was still open. Through the front window he could see the old bag jabbering with a customer about to leave, while behind the counter the cute young blondie was busy straightening out the *pâtisserie* in the showcase. He held the door open for the woman with the packages. She smiled and dubbed him *très gentil*. Inside it wasn't too uncomfortable—there was a fan turning quietly in the corner—and the lip-smacking smell of yeast, cinnamon, and raisins overwhelmed his taste buds. Reiner was getting hungry.

The minute Madame Charpentier saw him, she told Gabrielle to call Mademoiselle Reece. When Molly came down, she had on the one all-purpose dinner dress she'd brought with her, a short black shift with spaghetti straps, and black sandals, plus her gold teardrop earrings. Gabrielle thought she looked chic. Molly asked him if he'd heard the news about Ali Sedak's suicide and told him the little she knew. Reiner showed no emotion. He listened like a judge, without comment, but he didn't miss a word.

Louise Charpentier made no secret of her feelings. She thought it awful the way they treated immigrants in France, grossly unfair how difficult it was for Arabs to get papers, to get work, to get a break, disgusting how they were always the first to be suspected when a crime was committed and the last to be treated like human beings rather than dirt.

Perhaps it was his silence that caused her to ask, "What do *you* think, Monsieur Barmeyer?"

"I think . . ." Reiner said, choosing like Iago not to wear his heart on his sleeve, "I'd like one of your best baguettes for dinner."

"They're all the same," she snapped, a sour expression on her face. Louise Charpentier didn't care for either smoothies or trimmers.

"The best bread I've ever tasted," Molly offered, trying not to offend Pierre as Gabrielle handed him a fragrant baguette that was still crisp from the oven and took his money.

Molly knew Louise could sometimes be impatient, even blunt, but wondered why in this instance she seemed so put out. Lifting the key from the hook behind the counter, Molly said, "I shouldn't be too late. I'm going to Pierre's place near L'Ermitage." At the door, which he held open for her, she stopped and turned, sensing that something was troubling her new friend. It was clear that the two women, so different in age, temperament, and background, genuinely liked each other. Molly called to her, "He's doing the cooking tonight, Louise. I hope he's as good as he thinks he is. Wish me luck."

Before returning to the commissariat, Mazarelle, with no time for a nap, had a shot of whiskey. Then he swapped the old rain-stiffened loafers he'd been wearing for a comfortable pair of running shoes he used when taking his 120 kilos out for a stroll. Not that his ankle was still bothering him, because by now he'd almost forgotten about it. But the rest of his physical parts—especially his aching back and stitched-up face—had known happier days. And the accumulated heat in his office didn't improve his condition one jot. Taking his pipe from the ashtray, he lit up by plunging a match into the tobacco left in its half-filled bowl and burning his index finger.

"*Merde!*" He threw down his pipe and was sucking his finger when the telephone rang.

"Yes?" he barked angrily.

"That you, Paul?"

Recognizing his friend Couterau's voice, Mazarelle forgot the pain in his finger.

"Did you find anything, Daniel?"

"Maybe. We made a sweep of our files and came up with a single Pierre Barmeyer. He might be the guy you're looking for. A thirty-six-year-old teacher in a Strasbourg *lycée*. Could that be the one?"

"A teacher? Do you know if he's away on vacation now?"

"Yes, he's away. Permanently. Pierre Barmeyer died last year in a rock climbing accident in Switzerland."

"You're sure?"

"Gstaad. Next time I hope you'll give me a live one. Now can I go home?"

"Thanks, Daniel. I owe you one."

Whoever this Barmeyer was, Mazarelle feared he was bad news. Using an assumed identity—and having authentic papers to prove it. He was either hiding something he'd done or, worse yet as far as the inspector was concerned, something he was about to do. The thought that the mysterious Pierre Barmeyer and the stranger he met at the Café Valon who'd played pool with Ali might be the same person made his eyes smart—like in a scrum when you're blindsided and get a fist in the face. Some freak blow out of the blue. Mazarelle had to warn Molly at once, put her on guard without scaring her out of her wits. He prayed that he hadn't waited too long to insist that she go back home.

Louise Charpentier answered the phone. Molly had left with Pierre Barmeyer about a half hour ago. Asked if she knew where they went, Louise said they were going to his place for dinner.

"And where's that?"

Louise wasn't sure. She recalled Molly saying that he was staying at a house not far from L'Ermitage.

Mazarelle felt a bone stuck in his throat.

"Anything wrong?"

"No, no. Ask her to call me at home when she gets back."

"I'll probably be sleeping, but I'll leave a note."

"*Merci bien,* Louise."

Whatever his real name, Pierre Barmeyer was his man. He was using the McAllister house as his hideout. How was it possible that Mazarelle had been in there and not found him? How could he have forgotten that it was there in the kitchen he'd seen the Le Creuset box? How had he not recognized that it was the musty smell of the McAllister house that he sniffed on the stranger's leather jacket in the Café Valon? No wonder that house seemed to be stalking him, that stranger in the café, eyeing him with amusement. Goddamn it, they were! Shoving himself away from his desk, Mazarelle thundered down the stairs and rushed into the shadowy office of his task force, which at that hour was empty.

The only lights came from the three spectrally glowing computers that Roger Vignon had set up in the middle of the room. One ran CHARDON (Comportements Homicides; Analyse et Recherche sur les Données Opérationnelles Nationales), their special software for identifying perps by finding similarities in criminal operations. Another used ANACRIM (Analyse Criminelle), the first-rate national gendarmerie system for hunting serial killers. The inspector had managed to wheedle it out of the tin soldiers at the start when he and his men, suspecting that the murders at L'Ermitage might not have been committed by locals, were still following a two-track investigation. And the third, a police computer, contained *le réseau Rubis,* the Ruby Network.

Mazarelle flipped on the overhead fluorescents, sat down at the police radio, and tried to reach Duboit, but there was no answer. "Come on, Bernard, where the hell are you?" Wherever he was, Mazarelle assumed that he was tight on Barmeyer's tail and keeping a close watch on Molly. He hoped to hell that he hadn't fallen asleep or gone into a café for *un petit verre.* Then he remembered Duboit's mobile and dialed that number—also with no success. In a last-ditch effort to reach him, the inspector left a call on his beeper, which Bernard sometimes wore on his belt, but Mazarelle wasn't too hopeful.

Tired of wondering whether to stay put and keep trying to reach Duboit or go after him, the inspector went to see if there was any coffee left that was drinkable when the ringing began. Since leaving Paris, he hadn't heard that sound often. It was one you didn't forget or confuse with a phone call. There were no routine messages on the Ruby Network. They all were important, but some were ringing and urgent, and a few were very urgent—the screen pulsating with flashing lights and sound. This one from Interpol headquarters in Lyons was *très, très urgent:* Dieter Koenig, escaped German serial killer, rumored sighted near Taziac. Koenig believed to be armed and dangerous. Proceed with *extreme* caution. Photograph follows . . .

Mazarelle had no time to wait for pictures. He hurried back upstairs and yanked open the bottom drawer of his desk. His silver .38 Special was dusty, which made it seem only a little heavier than it was. Wiping it off on his sleeve, he cracked the revolver open and spun the empty cylinder. It looked okay. He tore open the box of bullets, took six, and loaded them into the cylinder. Grabbing a handful, he dumped them into his jacket pocket and stuffed the gun into his waistband. On the desk, Martine, smiling mischievously at her husband the famous homicide detective, watched him go.

47

THE OWLS IN THE CUPOLA

einer pulled off the road at the gravel pit. "I missed the turnoff," he explained. Backing his Renault around, he waited for the car that had been following them to pass.

Molly was annoyed. "Why doesn't he put on his lights?"

Reiner suspected it was the same car that had been following them on the way to Les Eyzies.

When they drove back, she wasn't surprised that he'd missed his turnoff. It was completely unmarked and, even though still twilight, it was impossible to see any house from the road below. The narrow dirt road zigzagged dizzyingly to the top of the hill, where the dark, secluded, three-story house was set back in a sea of high grass like a crouching animal. As soon as he shut off the engine and they got out, Molly could hear the crickets, smell the lavender. A large sprawling country house, but it didn't seem as if anyone was paying much attention to it.

Reiner opened the front door and fumbled for the light switch.

"This is great," she said. It was surprisingly cool inside, comfortable, but sort of musty like a wine cellar.

"It'll do. It's fine for a short stay."

"Mind if I open a window?"

"Unfortunately there are no screens. If you like, later we can shut off the lights and open the windows."

The furniture was minimal, but there were two fireplaces and the space was roomy enough even for an artist. Besides, how much furniture does one person need? Molly often thought that she could do with fewer chairs, tables, and boring junk in order to make more room for her books.

"How about something to drink?" he offered.

"Lovely."

Molly was admiring the wildflowers and candles on the dining room table when she heard the shot from the kitchen. Before she'd time to find out what had happened, Pierre was back with two wine-glasses and a bottle of champagne. He poured them each a glass.

"*Amor y pesetas*"—lifting his glass in a toast—"*y tiempo para gastarlas.*"

"I'll drink to that—whatever it is."

The bubbly white was cold, crisp, silky-smooth, and delicious. The gold label said Louis Roederer, Brut Premier.

"Hmm, not bad!"

"Good?"

She laughed as he refilled her glass. Molly was losing some of the edginess that she'd felt on seeing him again. There was something unpredictable about Pierre that she found intriguing, but it made her a little nervous. She asked what had been in the empty case on the wall.

"Guns, I suppose," he replied after a pause, suggesting whatever it was he couldn't care less.

Molly pointed her glass at the framed reproduction over the fire-place. "What about Turner? Does he interest you?"

Reiner sipped his wine and reserved comment.

"I once studied that painting in a course on nineteenth-century British art."

"There is no nineteenth-century British art."

How typically French, Molly thought. And he wasn't joking either because he didn't joke. Pierre had a casual way of making sweeping categorical statements that took her breath away. She asked him: What about Blake, Constable, George Stubbs?

He brushed them away like gnats.

"What about Angelica Kauffmann?" she demanded heatedly, burying the sudden thought that Kauffmann might have been born in Germany or Switzerland, but this was no time for full disclosure.

"Never heard of her."

"Well, you should have. She's not bad. But then you don't even seem to care for Turner."

"That's right. Why should I? I don't do seascapes and don't like them."

"What sort of art *do* you do?"

He looked at her as if surprised by her question, though Molly felt he was pleased that she'd asked.

"I do faces."

"That sounds interesting." Not having glimpsed any sign of his paints or canvases, she was genuinely curious. "I'd love to see your work, Pierre. Do you have anything that you've done here?"

"Have you forgotten? This is my vacation," he reminded her, refilling her glass.

The third glass of champagne tasted even better than the first two. Molly walked over to the fireplace. "Do you know what it's called?"

He glanced up at the small tilted ship with no sails, its masts like twigs, in a storm-tossed, white-capped, churning sea.

"I have no idea."

"The Slave Ship."

She told him that Turner had read an article about a slave ship on which an epidemic had broken out and the captain, who was insured against the loss of slaves at sea, but not by disease, dumped his human cargo over the side. Molly found the cruel things that people did to one another in this life almost beyond belief. "Isn't that awful?"

"No, not really. The captain was a businessman. A smart, practical shipowner with an investment to protect. Not some idealistic Pollyanna. He wasn't out there in the middle of the screaming ocean risking his ass for nothing. It makes perfect sense to me."

Molly set her glass carefully on the mantelpiece. Placing her hands on her hips, she glanced down and shook her head in wonder, not knowing what to make of him.

"You're kidding. You've just got to be kidding."

Reiner could resist her no longer. The tight black dress, the red hair, the bright mocking eyes. He reached out, put his arm around her waist.

"What's the matter? You're shivering."

"It's cooler in here than I thought." She looked up. "What was *that*?"

He'd heard it too. A loud, crashing sound outside, as if a large tree limb had fallen close to the house. Jumping up, Reiner went over to the dirt-streaked window and looked out.

"Probably a deer. They're all over this place in the early evening. Hunting for food, I imagine."

"Which reminds me," Molly said, giving him an easy champagne smile, "what's for dinner? I've worked up an appetite."

"Good. Come on."

Dinner, he promised, would be a revelation. Simple, delectable, and a meal that she would never forget. The main course a local favorite, omelette aux cèpes, which he could throw together in no time. The secret, he revealed, was in the mushrooms. Admiring them as he took each one from the basket and cleaned it, deftly cutting the heads from the stems and slicing them into thin strips. Then when the oil in the pan was hot, he tossed in the mushrooms and, as soon as they took on a light golden hue, lowered the flame and covered the pan. Molly was impressed. It was obvious that he knew exactly what he was doing.

"Now they have to cook very slowly for a while. That's another secret. Would you like a salad?"

"Okay, but let me help. I'm to salads what Verdi is to opera."

He handed her the endives, the grater, the Roquefort. "It's all yours. I'm going out to get some wood for the fireplace. Like some music?"

He turned on the radio, revving up the volume so that the pulsing rock beat filled every corner of the kitchen.

"Je t'aime, je t'aime, je t'aime,
Oh! Ma tendre blessure—"

As Reiner slipped out of the house, the back door closed on Johnny Hallyday, muting the old heartthrob's yearning, lovesick voice. The light from the kitchen windows spilled onto the woodpile in the backyard. Reiner had thought there was an ax nearby, but all he could find was a heavy shovel. When he lifted it up, an army of ants underneath the blade—hundreds of them—went scurrying for their lives in all directions.

Hidden in the tall grass at the front of the house, Duboit rubbed his leg where he'd injured it tripping over the fallen tree limb. It was scraped but not bleeding—at least not very much. The music from inside the house sounded like they were having a good time. One of Johnny's golden oldies from the seventies. He hadn't heard it in years. Why the hell was he here anyhow watching her getting it on with lover boy when the case was over? The only one who didn't seem to know it was the *patron*. Duboit wondered what the real reason was that he was so interested in this young woman. Maybe he had the hots for her himself. His boss liked them young and tender. When they looked like that, how could you blame him?

These days the *patron* had him working more hours than even the uniforms had to put in. His kids had begged him to take them fishing on the river this weekend, and the best he could do for them was a maybe. Of course Babette didn't like it either. If not for Monsieur Mustache—the old hard-ass—he'd be home in bed with her right now, getting his balls rubbed.

The very thought of his adoring *chouchoute* sent flutters of delight rippling over his hairy back, his aching thighs, and he was thinking of getting the hell out of there when Reiner came up from behind and smashed him over the head with the shovel, a crushing blow. Duboit rolled over onto his stomach, his legs thrashing about in the grass as he tried helplessly to get up, the toes of his shoes stitching the ground. Reiner hit him again and again in rapid succession, and only ceased hitting him when his arms grew weary and he noticed that the meddler had stopped moving.

Rummaging through his pockets, Reiner quickly found his identification. A cop, just as he thought. He grabbed the stiff's legs and dragged him back to the woodpile, where he was less likely to be seen, and then hid the bloody shovel under some bushes. Nobody was paying Reiner for this one. It was simply another freebie to cover his ass, but he'd no intention of making a habit of it. Reiner had to admit that there was a certain pleasure in this kind of killing—the rather crude, intimate physicality of it was so different from the cool, calculated, somewhat distant way he'd usually handled these matters before coming here. He hoped that it wasn't becoming addictive. You start to give away what you've been selling and it's hard for customers to tell the difference between a successful businessman and a psychopath.

Mazarelle spotted Bernard's car parked on the shoulder of the road a short distance beyond the turnoff to L'Ermitage. He pulled up behind it and got out. The car was empty. On the backseat he found Bernard's mobile and put in a hurried call to Bandu. He didn't like talking to an answering machine but briefly described where he was, told Bandu to come as soon as he got his message and bring along as many of their men as he could get hold of at that hour. The guy they were after was the German serial killer Dieter Koenig. He was armed and dangerous. *Very!* Watch your step, he warned him, and clicked off. The inspector felt about as confident that Bandu would get his message as if he'd thrown it into the sea in a bottle.

Mazarelle limped up the steep dirt road as quickly as he could, trying to keep down the noise of his heavy breathing. The roar in his ears sounded like the steady pulse of a pile driver repeating the name Koenig, Koenig. It was Dieter Koenig who was the Café Valon stranger, Koenig the killer who'd gone next door to murder Mademoiselle Reece's parents and their friends. And now she was inside there alone with a homicidal maniac. Where the hell was Bernard, who was supposed to be on duty protecting her?

At the top of the hill, he noticed lights coming from within the house. A few shutters at the back were open now. He made his way cautiously to the rear of the house and could see Molly moving about in the lit kitchen and hear the music. Sensing something behind him, he wheeled around. Was that someone in back of the woodpile watching him?

"Bernard?" he called in a smoker's whisper. "Bernard?"

Keeping away from the light, Mazarelle rushed across, hoping to find out from the young cop what was going on inside. But it wasn't Bernard at all. Only what was left of him. The poor bastard stared up at his boss accusingly through sightless eyes, his head, his face covered with blood. The inspector searched frantically to find a pulse in his neck, but there was nothing.

"Bernard!" His voice trembled—a choked, aching, broken staccato sound. He took Doobie in his arms. Wiping the ants, the blood from his face, he closed Duboit's eyes and brushed the wet, bloody hair from his forehead.

"Bernard!" he gasped. Poor Doobie had had no idea what he'd been up against. Mazarelle blamed himself for that. If only he'd been able to reach him in time.

Reiner came back with an armful of logs and soon had a fire going. Turning off the radio, he complimented Molly as she put the finishing touches on her work, sprinkling the two salads with a flurry of dried parsley. She mentioned that he needed a new calendar. There was a problem with the one he had hanging behind the door advertising the local branch of Crédit Agricole—its safe deposit boxes and ATM machine open twenty-four hours a day.

Reiner seemed puzzled.

"It's last year's."

"Hmm . . . You're right. Blame the rental company." First it was the missing guns and now this. She was, he thought, a little too observant for her own good. He lifted the cover on the pan. "They look almost ready."

"They smell wonderful." There was a loud scratching noise coming from upstairs. It was the third time that she'd heard it. "What *is* that?"

"Owls."

"Really?"

"They have a nest up on the roof in the cupola. If you like I'll show it to you after dinner."

"Yes, I'd like to see that. Incidentally, in addition to your owls, do you happen to have a bathroom?"

"On the first floor. Turn right at the top of the stairs. But don't be long. We're getting close."

As she went up the stairs, she paused at the high landing and looked down. The angle was like a Hitchcock scene, she thought, watching Pierre expertly cracking each egg and, parting the shell with one hand, dropping its sunburst yolk and viscous white into a blue bowl. He was so intent on what he was doing it might have been brain surgery. She enjoyed the serious look on his face, even though it was only eggs.

Molly put on the bathroom light and shut the door. The old-fashioned bathroom had a tub with clawed feet, a toilet with a water tank on the wall that depended on gravity to work, and toilet paper that required a case-hardened backside. It felt to her like sandpaper. There was no soap anywhere, nothing in the medicine chest except a bent bobby pin.

Before going back downstairs, she walked over to the window at the end of the hallway. The big house next door was dark, but seeing its pointed tower outlined against the early evening sky, Molly suddenly realized that it had to be L'Ermitage. And so very close! Her legs shook and she leaned against the wall, trying to catch her breath. She hadn't fully grasped how near Pierre had been to her parents on that terrifying night. She walked back down the long, empty hallway and for the first time noticed that all the doors were closed. It had the feeling of an off-season hotel but to Molly's alcohol-drenched imagination it might have been Bluebeard's castle. If asked what was behind each door, would Pierre call them private places not to be violated by others? Anxiously, she opened the nearest door—half expecting a bloody torture chamber or the bodies of his murdered wives—and turned on the light.

Much to her astonishment, it was almost bare. She tried the next room. There was hardly anything in that one either. Both of them spartan rooms with uncovered mattresses and pillows, but it was obvious that Pierre was using the second one because his sunglasses and shoulder bag were on the bureau. Molly opened the top drawer. It was empty. In fact all the drawers were empty. Not knowing what to make of it, she hesitated for a second and then—like any Eve or Pandora—opened his bag.

There was a black shirt, a parka, some papers, a black baseball cap with a sapphire-blue griffin on the front, and something heavy and bulky wrapped in a chamois cloth. Opening it, she found his black Ruger. Alarmed, Molly hurriedly wrapped up the gun and put it back. Next to it was Pierre's French passport. The unsmiling picture made him look older but it was the directness of his gaze that was unmistakably Pierre. The bag also held three more passports from Germany, Spain, and Poland. Though the names were all different— Klaus Reiner, Max Kämpe, and Zbigniew Wilozinski—the pictures, except for the hair and Wilozinski's beard, were all, astonishingly, Pierre.

Molly knew in an instant that she was in over her head. Trapped and defenseless in this isolated house with an armed and possibly dangerous man who was no vacationing artist from Alsace. Who was this Pierre Barmeyer? Whatever reason he might have for owning a gun, what innocent explanation could there possibly be for all these forged passports? Why hadn't she been smart enough to come here in her own car? And why didn't she have a usable cell phone with her instead of a useless tape recorder? Quickly she threw the passports back in his bag, closed it, and turned to see Pierre standing in the doorway.

"So there you are. What are you doing in here?"

How long had he been there? Molly felt as if all the champagne in her blood had turned to water.

"Didn't you hear me calling you?"

"Is dinner ready?" Switching off the light, she closed the door, slipped past him, and, eager to go downstairs, headed for the staircase. "I'm starved."

"Hold on—as long as I'm up here, let me show you the nest."

"Now?" She'd be damned if she would. The thought of crawling around on the roof in the dark with Pierre Barmeyer, or whatever his name was, no longer seemed quite so appealing to Molly.

"What about dinner?"

"It can wait. I turned off the flame on the mushrooms."

Reiner had everything ready, the eggs beaten to a froth, the mushrooms golden brown—half of them covered in the pan and half mixed with minced garlic and placed on two plates, but just one had the pulverized death cap buried beneath the cèpes. Only the guest of honor was missing and, lo and behold, where should he find her but upstairs, snooping into his personal things. He felt angry enough to entertain a more hands-on exit for mademoiselle.

"Come on. This way," he said, urging her toward a doorway at the other end of the hall. He held open the door for her. "It'll only take a minute. I think you'll like it. Go on up," he invited, turning on the upstairs light.

Molly eyed the narrow, steep staircase that appeared to lead to an attic. There was a landing at the top of the stairs and a large window. With Pierre behind her, how could she back out now? Molly started up the creaky steps. At the landing, Pierre pushed past her and threw the window wide open.

"Look at that, Molly."

The window gave onto a breathtaking view, overlooking the low-pitched, red-tile roof that extended across the entire house. To Molly the roof seemed almost as long as a tennis court.

"Here," Pierre said, taking her arm. "Just step out onto the roof. I'll help you."

"You go. I'll watch."

He appeared to be annoyed at her change of heart.

"No." Molly shook her head emphatically. "I don't think so."

"I thought you wanted to see the baby owls. Isn't that what you said?"

Molly glanced out the window and hesitated. That was what she'd said, all right, and what he'd promised to show her. The fact that he'd left his gun downstairs was a definite plus. Perhaps there was a perfectly reasonable explanation for the different passports and gun in his bag. And, after all, he had saved her life. But there was no way she was going to go out on that roof with him. She'd lost her taste for ornithology.

"Why don't you show me from here?" It seemed to Molly a sensible alternative.

Reiner swept her up in his arms.

"Hey! Hold on! What the hell are you doing?"

"Don't worry. Here we go."

She felt she was flying. Effortlessly, he lifted her through the window and stepped out onto the roof, putting her down on the tiles.

The sun had set an hour or two earlier, but the tiles still felt warm under her hands. It was such a clear night that far in the distance she could see the moonlit bell tower of the church in Taziac. Standing up, Molly found herself under a theatrical ceiling of lights, a spectacular star-filled sky that seemed close enough to touch. In spite of herself, Molly was awed by the spectacle.

"Careful," Pierre cautioned her. "We wouldn't want any accidents up here."

Molly wondered if she was doing him an injustice. Not too far from her, midway on the roof, was the cupola just as he had said—a trifle weather-beaten perhaps with a dented copper roof and some missing and broken panes of glass.

"I don't see any owls."

"You will. Walk straight ahead. But watch your step. And don't look down. I'll be right behind you."

"No, please, Pierre—" Molly's one thought now was somehow to keep him at a distance. "Just stay where you are. You make me nervous. Let me go by myself."

"If that's what you want. Sure, go ahead."

The light spilling out from the window helped her see where she was going. Walking carefully, Molly concentrated on the cupola ahead and instinctively did her best to avoid the white stains on the roof tiles the closer she got. She thought she could hear scratching sounds as she approached. With Pierre at a distance, Molly felt steady, more confident.

Then, in the blink of an eye, he was behind her, his breath on her neck. Without warning, he shoved her violently. Molly shrieked, lunged for the cupola. Grabbing hold of it, she gritted her teeth and held on for dear life.

"What the hell are you doing?" she screamed. "You nearly pushed me off the roof."

"Sorry. I tripped. An accident. Here, let me help you."

"*Don't* touch me!" Molly knew that it wasn't an accident. There were no owls up here. Owls hoot and she'd heard nothing but scratching noises. Rather than throwing her into a panic, she was strangely calm. Or both simultaneously. And most of all furious at his betrayal. Molly quickly put the pieces together—the passports, the gun, the proximity to the murder scene. But why? What had she or her family or their friends ever done to him? And *who* was he?

"Keep away from me."

Pierre drew closer. "Don't be foolish. I'm only trying—"

"Stop, monsieur!" ordered the inspector. "One more step and it will be your last."

Mazarelle, his powerful chest heaving from his charge up the stairs, stood framed by the open window, his .38 gleaming in the moonlight, its muzzle fixed on his drinking companion from the Café Valon. Without any hesitation, he vaulted through the window and hit the tiles full force, the loose bullets in his pocket clicking like castanets. Until landing on the roof, he'd forgotten about his ankle. The rush of adrenaline quickly eased his pain. He knew full well what sort of bastard he was up against after seeing what he'd done to Bernard. Unlike Ali Sedak, a petty crook who lacked the warped, feverish imagination to operate on such a murderous scale, Koenig was a maniac who lived in a sick dream where there were no limits.

Mazarelle shouted, "Stay where you are!" Tightening his grip on his gun, he raced toward the cupola.

"What's this all about? Put that gun away."

"Shut up!" Mazarelle had been looking forward to this confrontation with the L'Ermitage murderer, but not on a rooftop, not in the dark. What the hell was keeping Bandu and the others? "Get your hands up where I can see them."

"My hands *are* up. What's wrong with your eyes?"

"Higher," he ordered fiercely.

"Who are you?"

"You know damn well who I am. The only way you'll get away from me this time, Monsieur Koenig, is if you can fly."

"Koenig?" Reiner stared at him incredulously. "My name is Pierre Barmeyer. You're making a serious mistake. I've never seen you before in my life. Are you mad?"

The inspector was becoming increasingly infuriated. This son of a bitch was laughing at him. Not only was he a multiple killer, but he didn't feel a pinprick of guilt.

What could you expect from a madman? Turning toward Molly, he called, "Are you safe there, mademoiselle?"

"I'm okay."

"Good. Just don't let go."

"The window," cried Molly. "He's trying to escape through the house."

"Hold it," Mazarelle shouted, raising his revolver. "Not another inch!"

The fleeing German, who already had one foot through the open window and was about to pull himself in, glanced back and sneered at the inspector. "I've had it with you, *du verdammter Arschficker.*" Throwing back his head, Reiner laughed hysterically, a piercing, bone-chilling challenge to Mazarelle.

Without missing a beat, the inspector squeezed off a single round. A crack shot, he aimed for the back of the German's thigh. He wanted his man alive.

"Missed!" whooped Reiner, a full-throated cry of triumph, and laughed again. "Not even a flesh wound!" But losing his hold, he suddenly fell backward onto the roof and began to slide toward the gutter. Followed by a gleaming trail of blood on the red tiles. On the edge of the roof, he teetered like a broken weather vane. Lunging toward him, Mazarelle caught the German by one leg and held him, dangling in space. Reiner's furious howls blended with the swelling sound of approaching sirens from the police cars racing up the hill. Finally, Mazarelle thought, the cavalry to the rescue.

"Inspector!" Molly cried. Brushed by the outstretched, beating wings of a large owl returning to its nest, she'd lost her terrified grip on the cupola, slipped on the white droppings and gray pellets left by the birds. Unable to stop herself, Molly began to tumble. Mazarelle saw her coming, her luminous red hair streaking across the night sky like the flaming tail of a comet. He had no choice. Letting go of the German, he caught Molly and held on tight, felt her wildly beating heart. Or was it his own? What he hadn't expected was the loud, hysterical laughter that fell through the darkness and ended as neatly as a snipped thread.

When Reiner hit the flagstone walkway three stories below there was no cry, no earsplitting crash. His body struck with a dull thud, the sound a bag of cement makes when it's thrown from the back of a truck.

"*Ça va, inspecteur?*" someone called out from below.

It was Bandu. Mazarelle could hear the concern in his voice. Could almost see it in his face and that of the other members of his squad looking up at him, the flashing blue lights on top of the two police cars illuminating the eerie nocturnal scene.

"We'll be down in a minute," the inspector called. "Did you find Bernard's body?"

"Doobie? Is Doobie dead, chief?" Bandu's voice disappeared into the night air as quickly as if he could hardly ask, much less bear to hear the answer.

"It's behind the woodpile."

"Poor guy! Okay, chief. I'll take care of him."

"What about the *salaud*?"

"Don't worry." Stepping back to show his prize, Bandu revealed the body of the German crumpled at his feet. "*Il est foutu, patron. Kaput!*"

PART FIVE

48

MAZARELLE MAKES A CALL

emeteries didn't bring out the best in Mazarelle. Reminding him of Martine's funeral and how unseasonably hot it had been, the small group of mourners who showed up, and the foul smell of manure from the nearby farms. Never before had he felt so lonely. As for Bernard's good-bye, there was quite a crowd. Besides Babette, their two boys, the family, and friends, everybody from the commissariat who could be spared was at the graveside. Rivet, of course, came resplendent in his commissaire's dress-blue uniform, looking stiff and solemn as a headstone. Afterward, as Mazarelle went out the cemetery gate, the raw, rusty screech it made was exactly the way he felt on that gray, lifeless day.

Back at the commissariat, and even after several shots of Black Label, the inspector remained haunted by the unshakable gloom of the cemetery. He tried his favorite brier pipe, lit up an overflowing bowl of Philosophe. His heavy breathing into his pipe stem sent a fountain of angry sparks shooting crazily through the air. Of course Mazarelle was angry, so mad it smelled as if his mustache was ablaze. Glancing down, he saw that it was the wastebasket burning. He jumped up; emptied the crumpled, smoldering papers on the floor; and in a cool, businesslike way began stomping out the glowing embers.

Gnawed at by unanswered questions, he was unable to concentrate on anything very well. The thought of the last time he'd seen Bernard turned his stomach. Doobie's head so badly mangled that the mortuary director had urged Babette to keep the lid closed on his coffin during the service. And coffins reminded Mazarelle of one more piece of unfinished business.

Picking up the receiver, he dialed Paris. Elizabeth Barnes, Dwight Bennett's secretary, told the inspector that he was on another line. Could he call the inspector back?

Mazarelle said he'd hold.

In less than a minute, Bennett was on the phone.

"*Chapeau, inspecteur!*" he congratulated Mazarelle. He'd read in the Paris papers all about his deadly rooftop encounter and how the inspector had saved Molly Reece's life. "Well done. Speaking for my embassy, I can't tell you how grateful we are for what you did. You're quite a hero."

Mazarelle hesitated, clearly uncomfortable with his bullshit. "I just do my job."

"This Koenig seems to have been as bad as they come."

"Bad, yes. A homicidal maniac, according to Interpol. But whoever that was up on the roof," Mazarelle went on, "he wasn't Dieter Koenig. It turns out that Koenig was just arrested a few days ago by German police officers at the central train station in Mannheim. In the entire time he'd eluded recapture, Koenig claims never to have left Germany."

"Then who—?"

"I wish I knew. What I'm sure of," the inspector added, "is that he was the same cutthroat who murdered all four vacationers at L'Ermitage, and the same one who later killed one of my own men by beating him to death. We sent the German authorities everything we had. Prints, photos, DNA, and the four passports he was carrying."

"Four!"

"That's right. One German, one French, one Polish, one Spanish. All of them with the same face but different names. And they've told us that the murderer couldn't have been any of them."

"You're certain about the German?"

"Positive. The German passport was stolen. Klaus Reiner was a journeyman football player for the East German Hansa Rostock club in the eighties. He's still very much alive."

Bennett cleared his throat. "The truth is Reiner was the name we knew him by."

"You knew about him?"

"We had information suggesting that these murders might be the work of a paid assassin hired by two former French DGSE agents—Émile Pellerin and Hubert Blond. *They* called him Klaus Reiner. It seemed as if his assignment was to eliminate an American vacationing in Taziac. Murder was Reiner's business. I'm not sure, but my guess is that the target was Schuyler Phillips—"

"How do you know that?" Mazarelle interrupted.

"The usual way. I get paid to know things like that."

"Goddamn it!" Mazarelle exploded. "If you knew all that, why the hell didn't you tell me?"

Bennett hesitated. "I'd only have been speculating."

The inspector's patience even on good days was not without limits, and this was not one of his better days. He hated to be stonewalled.

"Don't you realize that it might have helped us?"

"Perhaps . . . But I wasn't free then—"

"And now?"

Though Bennett bobbed and weaved, Mazarelle finally managed to drag out of him a story that was both strange and disturbing. The inspector wondered where he got his information. Did the CIA have an illegal tap on the retired agents' home telephone? But when he tried to get more details, Bennett cut him short.

"I'm busy, Mazarelle. How about telling me why you called?"

The inspector didn't care for the snotty tone any more than the far-fetched tale he'd just heard. He realized he'd get no more from Dwight Bennett. "I thought you might be interested in knowing that the bodies of Mademoiselle Reece's parents are now being released from our custody, and she's planning to leave tomorrow. I've arranged for two hearses and a motorcycle escort to take them from Bergerac to the Bordeaux airport. I'm sure she could use your help in getting back to Paris and then at Charles de Gaulle. Is that possible?"

"Absolutely," he cried. "I'll take care of everything. Tell her not to worry. I'll be down on the first plane tomorrow morning."

Though relieved for Molly's sake, Mazarelle had to admit to being less than thrilled.

49

LEAVING TAZIAC

Gabrielle was busy with customers when the inspector entered the *boulangerie,* but not too busy to give him a smile that—along with the wonderful smell of Louise's fresh-baked bread perfuming the air—brightened his melancholy mood. She said to go right up. Mademoiselle Reece was expecting him.

Molly was in her room, packing. Bennett had called to tell her he was arriving the next day and would help her through French customs. She thanked the inspector for asking him to come. Said she could use Bennett's experience with the details and was glad to have it. The black T-shirt she wore made her face appear paler, thinner, tired, her green eyes larger and even more striking than he remembered. Mazarelle, who knew how much she'd been through, was touched by her vulnerability. Her reference to customs reminded Mazarelle of news he had about her father's partner, Sean Campbell.

"Sean!" Molly was surprised the inspector remembered.

Apparently he'd been stopped at Charles de Gaulle Airport while attempting to leave France with a small Cubist painting in his luggage—Braque's portrait of Gertrude Stein.

"Your Monsieur Campbell made the unfortunate mistake of trying to take part of France's cultural patrimony out of the country without an export license, and the airport customs agents discovered it. Probably his worst nightmare."

Molly shook her head sadly. Her father had trusted Sean. She had been much less sympathetic. When she'd heard that Sean was in France, she'd even wondered if he wasn't somehow involved in what happened. There'd been so many twists and turns to the investigation. She'd been startled by the newspaper story of the background of the serial killer named Koenig from whom Mazarelle had saved her. Molly had never heard of Koenig before then. She'd tried to come to terms with that idea, but then she'd spoken to Bennett.

Turning to Mazarelle, Molly said, "Bennett just told me that the reporters had it all wrong. His real name was neither Pierre Barmeyer nor Koenig. Is that a fact?"

Mazarelle stroked his mustache. "Yes, that's true. As you saw from the passports he carried, the man who tried to kill you used several different names, several nationalities. But regardless of his real name, you and your family have nothing more to fear from him."

"I hope you're right, Inspector. The awful truth is there's not much of my family left to kill." Though she spoke in anger, it was impossible for him to miss the deep sadness in her voice.

Like the writing of reports, Mazarelle hated this part of the job. It was always hard for him to come up with the right words to say and the right way to say them. In these situations, he tended either to say too much or nothing at all.

"I see," began Mazarelle softly, and stopped. "I'm sorry."

She nodded without looking at him. Then suddenly glancing up, a worried look on her face, Molly asked, "What makes you so certain you've seen the last of him? Did you bury the body?"

Mazarelle seemed almost relieved to answer her question. "German Interpol wanted it in connection with their ongoing investigations. After that, he'll be cremated."

"Did you find out his real name?"

"No, I didn't. On the other hand, he looked German, spoke French with a German accent, was a die-hard German football fan who operated out of East Berlin and probably was German. But whatever name he was born with and whatever sort of artist he might have been, I have no doubt he was the Taziac murderer."

Lowering the top of her suitcase on the chenille bedspread, Molly sat down on the edge of the bed opposite the inspector, who had claimed the rocking chair.

"I owe you a great debt, Inspector," said Molly, her eyes glistening. "I want you to know how grateful I feel that you found my parents' murderer, and more than grateful to you for saving my life. But whoever the hell he was, why was he trying to kill me? I don't understand any of it. Was he totally mad, or was there something else involved?"

"I wish I could explain everything to you, mademoiselle, but some of it is still a mystery to me. If Dwight Bennett is to be believed—and I'm not at all sure about that—the murderer was a paid assassin whose target was Schuyler Phillips. According to Bennett, your parents and Phillips's wife were, in his words, 'collateral damage.' Even Ali Sedak and my man Duboit seemed to fall into that category."

"Collateral damage! That's my parents he's talking about. What a depressingly grotesque idea . . ."

Mazarelle took a deep breath, and his whole body seemed to sigh in resignation at the sadness of things. He too found it overwhelmingly depressing, if true, that all the other Taziac deaths might have been merely gratuitous. An *ad valorem* death tax added to the cost of doing business. Mazarelle supposed that all CIA agents were trained to think in that cold-blooded way. Such jargon wasn't called *la langue de bois* for nothing.

"But, Inspector, if Bennett is right, who was behind this and why did they want to do away with Phillips?"

"Bennett claims that it could have been a 'back-channel operation' originating somewhere in the stratosphere of Matignon or the Quai d'Orsay. Someone at or near the top casually letting it be known that it would be nice if something were done. Little more than that. A vague wish, a scarcely audible aside to ensure plausible deniability, and all the messy little details left to others."

Molly shivered. She didn't want to believe it, but she could imagine it. The seemingly innocuous "If only . . ." The subordinates who took the hint. The hired gun who carried it out. The hideous results. And most monstrous of all was the power of those who could set such forces in motion and believe they could get away with murder scot-free.

"Does any of that make sense to you, Inspector?"

"To me, mademoiselle, it sounds far-fetched. On the other hand, I don't think Bennett was being open with me. Perhaps with you—an American—he'll be more forthcoming. Ask him tomorrow. You'll have time on the plane to Paris. And bon voyage home."

As they were about to part, they hugged each other and Mazarelle was impressed that in spite of all she'd been through, she was still a very strong young woman.

"You know, *ma chère* Molly, you're not the only one. I'm leaving Taziac too."

She was obviously surprised.

"Yes, I've made up my mind to go back to Paris."

"Now?"

"No, no. A few days. I've some business here to take care of first. My report. They don't let you get away quite so easily in the *police nationale*. Fortunately," he added, his tone adobe dry, "it's not every day that you shoot somebody."

Molly smiled in sympathy. "Are you planning to retire?"

It was a serious question and the inspector had given it serious thought. "I've considered retiring, but what would I do? Play *pétanque*? Work on my tan? Homicide is my life." Glancing down and contemplating his worn shoes, his stained and wrinkled pants, he read the braille of his scarred forehead with his fingertips and said wistfully, "Such as it is. Besides"—he winked at her—"I'm much too young to retire, *n'est-ce pas*?"

On his way back to the commissariat, Mazarelle munched on the *myrtille* tart he'd picked up on the way out. He was glad Molly was finally going home. Above all, he was glad she was going home in one piece.

50

PARIS: RUE DE BERRI

ite, Hubert! *Vite!* Come in here. Hurry! He's just landed."

On the edge of the white brocade couch in the living room, Émile Pellerin leaned forward and watched the giant Airbus roll into view and stop before the red carpet. The door in the side of the plane popped open and out strode President Chirac, who, despite the long trip, looked fresher that Botticelli's Venus, his hair sleeked back and gleaming. Waving and smiling at the official reception committee awaiting him, he descended the portable stairs.

Hubert rushed in and, seeing what his friend was watching on the television screen, sank down heavily on the couch beside him.

"He looks glad to be there," noted Hubert.

"Of course he's glad. Look at that."

At the bottom of the stairs waiting for him with open arms was the president of China, Jiang Zemin. The two leaders—one tall and the other short, bespectacled, moon-faced—awkwardly embraced each other with broad smiles as the band struck up the French national anthem. After Jiang had welcomed him warmly, Chirac spoke of France's strong and inviolable ties to China. Then side by side, they inspected the rows of Chinese military honor guards standing straight as spears, their white gloves holding glistening, bayonet-tipped rifles, the white braid on their uniforms looped through the epaulettes on their left shoulders.

"After the *bombardement*, it's hard to believe that he's actually there," said Blond.

Pellerin nodded. It *was* hard to believe that the Chinese had forgotten the NATO bombs that turned their Belgrade embassy into splinters. But the plan he and Hubert devised had worked perfectly. The large wooden crates from Tornade, stenciled High-Speed Train Wheels and addressed to the Société de Chemin de Fer du Tchad, had stopped in Africa only long enough to be recrated and redirected. Shipped from Chad to Tianjin, the new advanced NATO trainer, the T-9AX, had arrived in time and changed everything.

The Chinese must have been astonished that Chirac could get them such an unexpected gift. Without it, they'd need years to develop the avionics themselves. Émile loved the irony. If NATO's bombing had, in effect, ruined Chirac's plans for trade talks with China, then, as fortune would have it, the NATO trainer had succeeded in unrolling the red carpet for him.

The CNN reporter announced that in about an hour Mr. Jiang, along with more than one hundred important Chinese Communist Party members, would host a formal banquet in the Great Hall in honor of the occasion, a grand affair for the visiting French trade delegation, which included twenty-one CEOs of leading French corporations such as Total Fina, Airbus, Thomson, and Michelin.

"Can you imagine what that will be like?" Pellerin wondered aloud. "The toasts, the applause. The ten or twelve courses, each more mouth-watering than the one before—succulent chiu yim squid or perhaps king prawns for appetizers followed by winter melon soup and then Lake Tungting striped bass supreme, plus soft 'celebration' noodles, and paper-thin, double-crisp celestial roasted duck. Then topping it all off—sweet almond pudding with sliced dates for dessert. And enough exquisite teas and wines to float a cruise ship. Oh lovely!" he gushed, hugging his friend.

"Look." Blond brushed him aside. Among the crowd of dignitaries, he'd spotted their friend Simone Nortier, the foreign minister's deputy. "There's Simone with her minister."

Tomorrow, according to the voice of the offscreen CNN reporter, the two leaders would go behind closed doors for one-on-one talks on trade and human rights issues, and the French president was expected to extend an invitation to President Jiang to visit France next spring.

Blond said, "She seems to be having a good time."

"She deserves it. She's earned this trip. If it hadn't been for Simone suggesting us to her boss, he wouldn't be there either."

Blond thought that was a good point. "Of course," he added, "we deserve some of the credit too. After all, we were the ones who found Reiner for her."

"Simone hasn't forgotten. But do you remember what she called him when she phoned to tell us their trip to Beijing was on?"

Blond tried to recall but couldn't.

"A mixed blessing," said Pellerin. "So we don't want to claim too much under the circumstances. We wouldn't want to be too pushy."

Blond's slow smile of recognition was met by Pellerin's wink of approval. "The one thing I hope she does remember," Blond said, "is to bring us back some fortune cookies." The two friends were laughing and congratulating each other on Simone's good luck when the doorbell rang.

Pellerin unlocked the dead bolt, opened the door a crack. Their visitor was a complete surprise, though not an unwelcome one. It was merely that it had been so long since they'd last seen him—more than eight, perhaps almost nine years since the Southern Triangle. He threw open the door and drew their visitor in, delighted, pumping his hand.

"Look who's here, Hubert. It's Bennett. Dwight Bennett. Where have you been keeping yourself, *mon ami*? Let me look at you. It's been ages. And still as young and handsome as ever."

Blond came forward and stiffly shook Bennett's hand. Actually, he liked the American. It was his friend Émile, the flirt, he didn't care for at the moment.

Bennett glanced at the two suitcases in front of the hallway closet. "Going somewhere?"

Pellerin seemed not to have noticed the suitcases were there. "I see we still haven't put them away. A wonderful vacation! We went camping in the New World."

"Canada?"

Blond turned to his friend and asked, "How did he know that?"

"The baggage tags, Hubert."

Pellerin had once estimated that there were as many as eighty

American agents in France, with thirty of them clandestines. More agents—after 1991 and the Soviet breakup—than from any other country. And the youthful-looking Bennett was probably the most important of the lot.

Émile Pellerin took their visitor's arm. "Our Dwight is as quick as ever, I see. Come along," he said, leading him like royalty into the living room, which was high-ceilinged and white with marble-topped tables. Bennett would have liked a large, spacious apartment just like theirs, but on the other side of the Seine. As they chatted, the retired agent described the joys of fishing for arctic char in the chill, teeming waters north of Montreal.

"I envy you two. Especially those great tans."

"You think so?"

Pellerin went over to the gilt-framed mirror on the wall. Lifting his chin, he ran his fingers over his neck, his face, and smiled at the color of his skin. "I'm afraid mine is already beginning to fade."

Bennett turned to Pellerin's beefy friend. "It's good to see you again, Hubert."

"What can I get you to drink?"

"It's a little too early for me."

"Nonsense," Pellerin said, going over and turning off the television set. "Especially today when there's reason to celebrate."

"Reason?"

"It's not every day we have a visit from our old friend."

Blond glided silently in his sandals over the waxed parquet, and a cold bottle of Rosette from Monbazillac materialized on the coffee table. Bennett sipped the wine but it was much too sweet for him. This was, after all, a business call. But before he could get down to business, his friends invited him to stay for lunch.

"Believe me, you won't regret it. Let me show you." Pellerin went inside to the kitchen and returned with a large shipping box he placed on the table. It was addressed to Hubert from Élysée Palace.

"I see you two still have friends in high places."

Blond grinned with pleasure.

Nesting inside the large box was another, smaller one, like a *matrioshka,* and printed on the lid was *Trésors de Périgord.* Opening it, Pellerin disclosed a trove of mushrooms, truffles, and other gourmet delicacies from the Dordogne region. He held up one of the grayish-brown mushrooms, sniffed its bosky aroma, and declared it *"parfait!"* For lunch Hubert was going to make them cèpes à la péri-gourdine, and Pellerin, sphinxlike, having discovered among the cèpes a few choice amanitas—known to connoisseurs everywhere as "the queen of mushrooms"—promised their visitor nothing less than a culinary revelation.

Bennett was curious about the enclosed card. "What are the congratulations for?" he asked Blond.

Hubert couldn't seem to remember. He glanced helplessly at Émile.

"Stop joking, you big ox. That's what we've been saving your mushrooms for. It's Hubert's birthday. An old schoolboy friend of ours from ENA never forgets a birthday."

Bennett suggested, "That's probably why he now works at Élysée."

Pellerin raised his glass. "To dear Hubert. *Joyeux anniversaire*, dear heart."

"Another year. No wonder I didn't remember."

It wasn't until their American visitor was standing at the window and Pellerin was pointing out to him the tiny swatch of the Boulevard Haussmann in the distance that Bennett mentioned their recent stay at the Hotel Adlon in Berlin.

"But how did you know we were there?" Pellerin asked.

"Word gets around."

"We love to travel. It's one of the joys of retirement."

Bennett assumed that they'd been doing a lot of traveling that summer. He knew that it was when they'd returned to their rue de Berri apartment that Pellerin had made his call to German Interpol.

"I was told you were in Berlin on business."

"Didn't you hear what he said?" Blond demanded. "We're retired now."

"Well almost," his friend corrected him, "but not quite." Pellerin went over to the elegant small desk near the window and handed Bennett one of their new cards. It read P&B CONSULTING. There was a phone number.

"Ah, I see. What exactly do you do?"

"A little of this, a little of that. No heavy lifting. Hardly anything too strenuous anymore. And there's nothing like being your own boss. Right, Hubert?"

Bennett wasn't interested in their routine. Especially after Molly's persistent questions on the flight back to Paris. Questions about the assassin and who had hired him and why, questions to which he was certain they held the answers. And he wasn't inclined to beat around the bush. "So then, who is this Klaus Reiner?"

Blond looked as if he'd been zapped by lightning.

"Klaus Reiner?" Pellerin repeated the name as if he'd never heard it before. "I've no idea. Perhaps you can tell us what this is all about."

Bennett fully expected Pellerin's response and knew that he'd have to wing it. He didn't need to mention the passport found in Taziac with the *Ossi*'s name. He was happy, rather, to refresh their memory about Suite 501 at the Hotel Adlon in Berlin. Their meeting and hiring of a man called Klaus Reiner. His job: to kill the American CEO of the multinational corporation Tornade, Schuyler Phillips, vacationing with friends in the French village of Taziac in the Dordogne.

"But as to why you wanted Phillips dead, I can only guess."

"Please do!" Pellerin smiled at him encouragingly. Unlike Blond, he appeared to be enjoying himself.

"I'd say it had something to do with a shipment from Chad to Tianjin."

"A shipment? What sort of shipment?"

Despite his suspicions, Bennett had to admit, "I'm not sure."

Pellerin threw up his hands. "*Alors!* There you are. You Americans! It must be your movies. Not only are you the hyperpower, but you have the hyperimagination as well. Even after two hundred years you're still a nation of wild dreamers." He put his arm around Bennett. "Perhaps that's why I'm so fond of you, Dwight."

"I'm afraid you've got the wrong party. I don't think of myself as terribly wild at all," Bennett said drily.

"Oh but you are, you are. Oh yes," he assured him. "Though it's a part you hide and not many see."

Blond saw nothing even remotely *Peau-Rouge* about the well-cooked American. On the other hand, he undoubtedly knew more than was good for him.

"In any event," said Pellerin, "we'll have some good laughs about your shipment over lunch."

"Sorry. I'd love to stay, but I can't. Happy birthday, Hubert!"

Staring at each other, the two of them listened to their visitor walk across the hallway and enter the open elevator cage. As the metal gate closed and the creaky, old-fashioned elevator slowly descended, it seemed to suck all the air out of their lungs.

51

MAZARELLE RETURNS

iven how long it had taken for Mazarelle to settle down in Taziac, he was surprised how little time it took him to leave. He wasn't even sure when he dialed Paris that he still had a job there, but his old boss at the commissariat in the *quatrième* had asked him to come home. Fabriani had been following the case of the murdered foreigners in the media and was impressed by the way Mazarelle had dispatched the Taziac killer. And now that his wife had passed away, the commissaire asked, was there really any reason for him to remain in the provinces?

Mazarelle, a little more cynical than he once was, assumed that a call had been placed from the Ministère de l'Intérieur, a request made, some arms twisted. *Voilà!* The way of the world. So he'd left the house and all the furniture with Louise to sell. The money to be kept in trust for Gabrielle. A smart young girl like that would find a good use for it.

Other than Michou, some personal photographs, his treasured collection of jazz CDs, Mazarelle had taken few possessions with him. He wanted a fresh start. The apartment he rented was near the Place de la Bastille. Not very large, but how much space did he and Michou require? He aimed to keep his new life as simple and uncluttered as a Brancusi.

Best of all, his apartment was close enough to the commissariat so that he could walk there. That was all the exercise he needed at his age. Strolling down the fashionable rue Saint-Antoine on his way to work, he could watch all the chic, beautiful, cool-eyed women in the world go by. The sounds of traffic nonstop, the smell of chestnut trees in the air.

Sitting at his old, beat-up wooden desk and scanning a copy of *Le Figaro,* the window behind him open to the morning stir of Paris, Mazarelle felt as if he'd never left. He'd forgotten how smooth, how fragrant the coffee here was. Not at all like the bitter stuff they used to cook up in their Bergerac squad room. As he turned the pages of the newspaper, a small article below the fold caught his eye, some names that he wasn't likely to forget. Émile Pellerin and Hubert Blond. The two former DGSE agents who, Bennett had told him, had hired the Taziac murderer. He'd filed them away on his mental Rolodex. So what were they up to now?

Le Figaro said they were dead. Accidental victims of food poisoning. Two days ago they'd been found in their apartment on the rue de Berri and rushed by ambulance to the Hôtel-Dieu. The inspector was familiar with the hospital's emergency casualty center, one of the best in Paris. Tearing the article out of the paper, he pocketed it for safekeeping. That was an accident he wanted to know more about.

After repeated telephone calls, he finally reached the doctor in charge of the emergency center.

"Yes, late last night. Food poisoning," said the doctor, confirming the cause of their deaths. "Most probably toxic mushrooms."

Mazarelle was skeptical. "Isn't that strange? I mean Parisians don't eat mushrooms and die anymore."

"Apparently some do," the doctor insisted. "Strange would be if they were both killed by lightning. Or killed by a shark while swimming in the Seine. But toxic mushrooms can make a person quite sick, and there are some phalloides that kill people. I understand even experienced mushroom hunters—gourmets, as well—may mistake deadly members of that family for edible ones."

"Did you send blood samples to the central laboratory of the Paris police?"

"Why should we?" he bristled. "There was no official request. Nothing irregular. Let me assure you, Inspector, this was an accident."

As soon as the doctor had gotten off the phone, Mazarelle spoke to the head nurse and obtained the rue de Berri address of the two men. He left at once, hoping to arrive at their apartment before anything had been touched. It was not far from the Champs Élysée, a well-tended, late-nineteenth-century art nouveau building with narrow curving balconies. He pushed open the heavy wrought iron and glass front door.

The concierge's loge appeared to be empty, but he knocked anyway.

"Yes?" A gray head popped out from behind a screen. An alert woman in a blue cardigan looked him up and down. It was plain she didn't approve of anyone quite so large. "How can I help you?"

A typical cranky Parisian concierge. What she really meant was I'm busy. So make it snappy. Mazarelle showed her his police ID, explaining that he wanted the key to the Pellerin and Blond apartment.

"You too?" She told him they were upstairs now cleaning it out.

The inspector didn't care for the news. "Who?"

"Government agents. From the Quai d'Orsay with a court order. They've been taking out boxes of stuff for the past hour. Said they were almost finished. I told them I wanted a receipt for every single thing they take."

"Okay, okay! What apartment?"

"Fourth floor."

Mazarelle ran into the lobby and repeatedly jabbed the elevator button. The dangling cables remained motionless, the elevator stalled somewhere in the building's upper regions. Tired of waiting, he thundered up the crimson-carpeted staircase that circled the open elevator shaft, and by the time he reached the third floor his legs were as tight as banjo strings. Slowing to catch his breath, he thought he heard the elevator going down and, turning, saw the top of the descending car. He hurried to the fourth floor and rang the bell, pounded on the door. It was unlocked.

Mazarelle called but no one answered. He rushed into the apartment and out onto the balcony. Leaning over the wrought-iron railing, he spotted three men in raincoats running to the black Citroën parked not far from the front door. All three carried boxes. Mazarelle's booming voice filled the narrow street, but they didn't even glance up out of curiosity, unwilling to show their faces. The inspector went back inside to see what they'd left behind.

It was a large, fancy, bourgeois apartment with marble-topped tables and gilt-framed mirrors. Pellerin and Blond seemed to have been doing well for themselves. Whatever those three guys had taken it wasn't the furniture. Mazarelle found what was probably missing behind the door marked P&B CONSULTING. Except for a few meaningless scraps of paper left on the floor and some unattached wires, the room was empty. The trio had descended like driver ants and cleaned out everything in their path. Mazarelle imagined the room had once been full of computers, printers, disks, copiers, correspondence, file cabinets, travel records, appointment calendars, checkbooks, address books, reference books, maps. Who knew what else?

He walked into the kitchen. It was a mess. The stink of soured milk turned his stomach. Dirty dishes and pots in the sink; piles of old newspapers, magazines, and advertisements on the floor. He went through the bags and boxes in the corner, but they were empty. He picked up a large but otherwise ordinary shipping box beneath the others. The colorful gift box inside was what interested him. Though he'd seen many just like it in gift shops all over the Dordogne promising irresistible *Trésors de Périgord* with pictures of the local gourmet delicacies they contained, this one was empty. But what it did have was an unsigned white card on which was written *"Félicitations et bon appétit."*

Unable to bear the smell any longer, Mazarelle grabbed the two boxes and carried them into the living room, his backside sinking like a medicine ball into the white pneumatic pillow on the brocade couch. He searched for his pipe, which still had some tobacco in it, and lit up. A small welcome-back gift of Philosophe from his friend Monsieur Small.

Mazarelle picked up the white card and studied it. Reaching into his back pocket, he pulled out his wallet. Ever since his long-haired drinking buddy at the Café Valon had made his sketch of the Munich team's goal, Mazarelle had been carrying the folded paper napkin around with him like a lucky charm. Which it might yet prove to be. There were striking similarities in the handwriting. The letters on both the card and the napkin bending italically as if in a high wind, the *c* in *"Félicitations"* as glum and closed mouth as in the name Schmeichel, the *a* in *appétit* crookback like that in Basler.

Mazarelle felt a shock of recognition. He was certain that this message had been written by the Taziac murderer. If the card in fact accompanied a gift of deadly mushrooms, then its ironic good wishes reeked of the German's sense of humor. The inspector needed no further evidence. He knew without a doubt that the food poisoning of Pellerin and Blond was no accident. It was murder. Even more extraordinary, the two former French agents would seem to have been killed by a dead man. Was it *une flèche du Parthe,* a final stab at payback? And from beyond the grave? If so, add two more bodies to the German's hit list.

Pulling himself up, the inspector went over to the window, sat down by the telephone at the small desk. He knew he'd made a remarkable discovery. He had to tell someone about what really happened to Pellerin and Blond. Perhaps their former boss at the DGSE. But the three men hadn't come from the DGSE. The concierge said the Quai d'Orsay had sent them, the Ministère des Affaires Étrangères. What did they want here? If he called the ministry now, he knew they'd tell him nothing. And, besides, how could he claim murder when even the head doctor at the emergency center of the Hôtel-Dieu called their deaths accidental? Though he doubted there was anything to be done, perhaps his commissaire would have some advice.

Picking up the receiver, he began to dial the commissariat, when he realized he was holding a dead phone. He slammed it down. Someone had already disconnected the telephone line. Possibly the same someone who was interested enough to clean out their office.

Mazarelle dropped the gift card into the breast pocket of his jacket, scanned the apartment, and opened the door. As he waited for the elevator, he thought back to his talk with Molly at the bakery. Recalling her telling him that Barmeyer had promised her a meal she would never forget—a mushroom omelet. She was lucky to get out of that house alive.

Downstairs the concierge stopped him at the front door.

"Where's my key?"

"You never gave it to me. The apartment was open," he said, and let the door slam behind him.

Outside in the street, the sky had clouded over and it was beginning to drizzle. In a few long strides he crossed the narrow rue de Ponthieu and ducked into the arcade, taking a shortcut to the Champs Élysée. At the end closest to Ponthieu—a shoe store, a bookshop, a *bureau de change*—it was a little worn with age, having seen better days. At the far end, the one closer to the great boulevard, were the fashionable boutiques. Mazarelle paused in front of the bookshop to glance at the tall racks of postcards. The popular Paris tourist attractions on one rack, on the other the leading stars of French cinema with a sprinkling of such international icons as Charlot, Garbo, Bogart, and Shirley Temple.

He'd just picked out a card—one of Louise's favorites, Jean Gabin—to send her a few words, when he caught a head-spinning whiff of cheap exotic perfume. Staring up at him, a short, bony young woman wearing spike-heeled boots and a denim skirt the size of a doily. She pointed to the top of the rack, her lashes fluttering, and said, "I need help."

Mazarelle held up the picture of Alain Delon. "This one?"

She pointed to the card next to it.

"This?" He held up Depardieu and she smiled. It was then that he felt a hand sliding across his bottom and stealthily slipping into his back pocket. His wallet twitched, came alive, gliding up and away as if it had wings. Snatching it out of the air, Mazarelle noted the hand attached to the wallet was hers.

"Let me go, you bastard! You're crushing my fingers." She had a voice like a foghorn, stopping people in their tracks.

The inspector glanced around to see if she was part of a team. Fabriani had warned them about gangs of pickpockets roving like bedbugs all over the city. Attacking tourists, especially Japanese tourists, whom they considered easy marks. Did she think he was a Japanese tourist? Mazarelle found that hilarious.

"You'd better try another line of work," he advised her. "I'm a cop."

Irate, she shouted, "Are you some sort of plainclothes flic faggot?" The bystanders were having a good time.

"Don't push me, *chérie*. Just beat it before I decide to take you in. Now fuck off! With your luck you'd do better selling crutches."

She fled, scurrying away while she still had the chance.

When the inspector came out the other side of the arcade, the lights were on up and down the Champs Élysée. Despite the drizzle and open umbrellas, the boulevard was crowded with window-shoppers. Traffic was a nightmare. Though he suspected that back in the apartment Michou was already sitting on her favorite windowsill, her nose pressed up against the cool glass, watching for him, she was going to have to wait a little longer for dinner. Caught in the current of the crowd, he passed Franklin Roosevelt and walked on toward Clemenceau. Enjoying the fresh air, the smell of the drizzle. He wanted to stay outside just a little longer before going down into the Métro.

As he walked, Mazarelle mulled over the case of the late Pellerin and Blond, their shadowy doings. Their official visitors today seemed to confirm that the two of them were engaged in some illicit political scheme. Probably freelancing for a client who needed deniability. As a form of risk management, Pellerin and Blond would necessarily have kept their distance from anything French. He supposed that was why they went to Germany for their killer. But who was their client? And why did that client want Phillips dead? These were the questions that haunted him. The unfinished business he'd brought with him from Taziac. Murders outsourced to private contractors could be shrouded in multiple layers of obscurity. Impenetrable by normal police work. Difficult, maybe impossible to resolve. But Mazarelle was an optimist. Eventually drowned corpses rose to the surface. The inspector hoped he'd be there to get the answers, that one day he'd discover who green-lighted the Taziac murders. The real name of Klaus Reiner.

Coincidentally it was then he heard it, the loud, hysterical laughter that he'd never forget. Like the wild, thrilling soprano saxophone of Sidney Bechet. Amid the blaring horns, the barking dogs, the piercing sound seemed to come from a rowdy group of young people on the other side of the avenue. A sudden knife-edged gust of wind swirled around and through him, chilling his bones, and the rain began to come down in sheets. Mazarelle turned up the collar on his jacket. What he needed was a raincoat, a glass of whiskey, a dry pair of socks. He wasn't very far now from the Clemenceau station. Clenching his empty pipe in his teeth and stuffing his hands in his pockets, the inspector—head down and buffeted by the rain—limped hurriedly along the boulevard. Pulse normal, lungs clear, heartbeat a steady clip-clop.

ACKNOWLEDGMENTS

This book is a work of fiction, and all of the characters in it are fictions or, if in any way similar to actual individuals with familiar names, are treated as fictions. Though the picturesque village of Taziac is imaginary, it resembles many found in southwestern France in the vicinity of the Dordogne River. Several events, such as the U.N. bombing of the Chinese embassy in Belgrade, actually did occur, as did the memorable UEFA Champions League Final soccer game in Barcelona between Manchester United and Bayern Münich—the bombing in early May 1999 and the game later that month. I've taken the liberty of setting the game in July of the same year. Unhappily for my ardent German fan, Klaus Reiner, the score remained exactly the same in art as in life—Manchester United 2, Bayern Münich 1. Georges Braque's small cubist portrait of Gertrude Stein exists, as far as I know, exclusively in this novel.

My thanks to all of the following for their help with the manuscript, which I greatly appreciate: Cal Bedient, Georges and Anne Borchardt, Jerome Charyn, Arnaud Desjardins, Ronit Feldman, Rob Goldberg, Michael Lopez, Nancy Marmer, members of the Gendarmerie d'Issigeac, Jörg-Michael Schwarz, Cork Smith, and Nan Talese.

Printed in the United States
by Baker & Taylor Publisher Services